THE MAKERS

Book 1 in the *Sree Kaano* trilogy

Christa Yelich-Koth

COPYRIGHT

This book is a work of fiction. All characters and events portrayed in this book are either products of the author's imagination or are used fictitiously.

No AI was used in the creation of this story, either internally or cover art.

THE MAKERS

www.CYKauthor.com

ISBN Hardcover: 978-1-958105-15-3

Published by CYK Publishing
Wisconsin, USA

Cover art: CC Covers

Look for other books by Christa Yelich-Koth
www.CYKauthor.com

The Detective Trann series

SPIDER'S TRUTH (Book 1)
SPIDER'S RING (Book 2)
SPIDER'S QUEEN (Book 3)
SPIDER'S RIFT (Book 4)
SPIDER'S LIE (Book 5)

The Land of Iyah trilogy
(YA fantasy)

THE JADE CASTLE (Book 1)
THE JADE ARCH (Book 2)
THE JADE THRONE (Book 3)

Eomix Galaxy Novels
(Sci-fi/fantasy)

ILLUSION (Book 1 of 2)
IDENTITY (Book 2 of 2)
COILED VENGEANCE

THE MAKERS (Book 1 in the *Sree Kaano* trilogy)
THE BINDERS (Book 2 in the *Sree Kaano* trilogy)

Graphic Novels/Comics
(Sci-fi)

10th Anniversary Collector's Edition Omnibus of HOLLOW and HOLLOW'S PRISM series

Special Thanks

Sandra Yelich: Thank you for pushing me to show more of this world, even when I didn't know what it looked like! My stories wouldn't be as full and vibrant without your input.

Conrad Teves: For your wonderful cover art. You truly make my designs come to life.

Thomas Koth: For beta reading on such a short timetable and providing much needed feedback and support.

To you, the reader: THANK YOU for continuing to read my stories and to ask for more.

THE 17 RULES OF ASSIGNMENT

1. The Re'Ris were created by the Makers to eliminate the weak.

2. Only the Makers determine the Targets of Assignments.

3. Assignments must be given top priority in the life of a Re'Ris

4. A Re'Ris may never refuse an Assignment.

5. Emotional detachment is necessary to succeed in an Assignment.

6. A Re'Ris must attend Lessons during their childhood and recite the Oath to the Rules and the Oath to the Makers. These Lessons are written by the Makers and taught by Superiors. Any changes in the Lessons will result in the immediate Targeting of that Superior.

7. A Re'Ris child may apply for their First Assignment at age 15, the Age of Progression. If the child does not apply by the age of 16, they are considered "Expired" and will automatically be sent to work for the Labor Force.

8. Only after the successful completion of an Assignment will a Re'Ris Cross Over to become an assassin and receive all the benefits awarded to that status level.

9. Any attempt to leave the planet before an individual has Crossed Over without a legal guardian will result in said individual becoming a Laborer with no option of assassin once they reach the Age of Progression.

10. Children under the Age of Progression will never be Targeted.

11. A Re'Ris may request knowledge if they are a Target and can defend themselves if they are. If they are successful in eliminating the assassin, they are upgraded in status and absorb all the future Assignments given to that assassin.

12. A Re'Ris who fails an Assignment is demoted in status to Laborer and may only live under that title and its responsibilities.

13. If a Target dies by natural or indirect means, the assassin is neither rewarded nor penalized.

14. If an assassin is killed while on Assignment, by any means other than by their Target defending themselves, the Target's name will be returned to Central Processing for a new assassin.

15. A Re'Ris may never seek revenge if a Target or an assassin is killed.

16. A Re'Ris must immediately report to authorities in Central Processing if they are aware of any individual not following the Rules.

17. Upon judgement by the Makers, failure to abide by any of these Rules will result in the individual(s) being demoted to Laborer, becoming a Target, or being arrested.

Chapter 1

Oh, Makers.

Oh, Makers she's dead.

I can't believe it. My sister is dead.

Faan is dead.

I should be happy. Why am I not happy? What's wrong with me?

Sree dropped the datapad he'd been reading onto the bed, which showed upon it the news about his sister's Passing On. Quick steps took him across the bedroom and back as thoughts continued to whirl inside his mind.

The letter, sent by some off-worlder named Torrak, explained what had occurred. That Faan assisted in taking down the remnants of the Aleet Army, and that Sree's family should know she'd proved the Aleet Army had been behind his parents' deaths. Their demise had not been a transportation orb accident like his government claimed.

Sree's mind struggled to take it all in.

Faan was dead.

She'd been right all along.

Their Mother and Father had been murdered, not eliminated.

And before she left to prove this, Sree belittled her about her theory.

Sinking down next to the bed, Sree placed his face in his hands, pressing his fingertips into his temples. *What under the Stars am I supposed to do now?* he thought. *I'm fifteen standard years old. My parents are dead and now my sister is dead. I'm going to be stuck living with my Mother's Mother...*

...until I complete my First Assignment.

Sree's spiraling notions of grief and confusion at the deaths of his family members paused as a wave of nausea rippled through his body when he thought of his First Assignment. He swallowed down a mouthful of acidic vomit and felt a sense of calm return.

Then he gagged.

The contents he upheaved missed the basket he grabbed. Retching motions shuddered through him, tightening his chest, pulling at his stomach, which was now completely empty, and yet he couldn't stop. His body seemed to want to expunge the horror he felt, not only for the loss of his sister, but for the fact he now existed on his own.

Eventually the movements subsided and Sree sat there, gasping for breath, tears moist on his face. A breeze from the cracked-open window soothed his clammy skin.

Sree went to get a rag to wipe up the remaining mess on the floor. Before he returned, he gripped the sink in the washroom for support while he peered at his image in the reflector unit—dark gray skin like his Mother's, shimmering with iridescence, short white hair, one eye slightly bloodshot from a broken blood vessel that had ruptured during his retching—all of which disturbed him and he quickly turned away. Though he still felt unsteady, he forced himself to wet the rag and returned to his bedroom to clean the thick, teal carpet.

While he scrubbed, he thought about his present situation. His Mother's Mother would come upstairs soon, and she would probably want to talk to him about the datapad. Sree didn't ever get deliveries and he knew his Mother's Mother would have an interest in its contents.

Pausing in his cleaning, he wondered what he would say. That the government she trusted in told their family a lie over a decade ago? That the last words Sree said to his sister had been hurtful? That the only remaining active member of the Kaano family, a family who were admired and revered by the entire planet, was an embarrassing teenager who felt too afraid to complete his First Assignment and hadn't Crossed Over yet, even though he'd been eligible to apply almost a year ago?

Tears that could no longer be blinked away spilled from his eyes. He hadn't cried since the age of seven, when he'd been thrown from the transportation orb during the accident, when his Mother and Father hadn't responded to his yelps of pain.

It wasn't an accident. Murder. Say it. They were murdered. Faan knew it all along. Even though it meant their deaths fell outside of the Rules.

A new notion prickled his mind. The Rules of Assignment. He hated them. He'd *always* hated them. But what could he do? They'd been set out by the Makers of his world to guide his species, the Re'Ris, along the "right" path.

Words formed in his mind, almost on their own, as the Oath to the Rules recited itself. It had been ingrained in him as it had every other child on his world, spoken with devotion during educational classes from the Superiors.

"I pledge to uphold the Rules of Assignment as were handed down by the Makers. I pledge to learn these Rules and follow them for the rest of my life. I will honor and obey the Lessons as instructed by my Superiors, whose knowledge has gone into the

interpretation of the Rules."

Everyone followed the Rules, no matter what. The idea that his Mother and Father could have been killed outside the Rules had been beyond preposterous. It felt...unnatural. Yet Faan still decided to prove their deaths happened some way other than by assassination, and Sree had done nothing but nag her about it.

And why did you really *do it?* he thought. *Why did you treat her that way? Because you thought she might stay if she realized her mission was useless. Because you didn't want to be left alone with only Mother's Mother. Because you didn't want to be by yourself for your First Assignment—the first time you have to assassinate someone...*

Because you are a coward.

The thoughts left a stale taste in his mouth, like something black and sickly. He knew he should want to complete his First Assignment. Everyone else seemed to. But something inside him couldn't fathom the idea of taking someone's life.

Why not? His whole family had done it. They'd all prized themselves on their assassination skills. Even the capital city of the world where they lived, Cand, had erected a statue of his sister, who'd excelled above every other assassin record on the planet.

Yet, try as he might, he never felt comfortable with the concept.

And now Faan is gone. The only person left who possibly could have helped me through my First Assignment, helped me understand what's wrong *with me for not wanting to take a life.*

Sree's memories drifted back to the last time he'd seen Faan, before she'd left on her quest to find their Mother's and Father's murderer. Faan had been practicing her skin-shifting abilities...

"And what am *I* supposed to do while you're gone?" Sree crossed his arms and glared at his older sister. He stood in the family room of his family's split-level house. Decorated in blues and greens, the room contained a glass-paneled ceiling housing hundreds of pinpoint golden lights, emitting a soft glow over everything. Sree always felt most comfortable here, with the tall, reddish-orange vines outside climbing the corners of the windowed wall, their edges curling against the panes of thick glass. Sweeping dark green curtains were parted by gossamer strips of satiny blue. The furniture, plush and expensive, completed the look, its swirled pattern of indigo and emerald a compliment to the dark blue carpeting with its spring green lattice pattern. Their Mother's Mother was very well financed, having been a successful assassin who'd lived long enough to retire, and several years ago offered to redecorate their home in a more luxurious manner.

Sree didn't like this room because of its wealthy attributes. He enjoyed it because it represented the space where he and his Mother and Father had spent the most time together.

Before they'd been in a transportation orb accident nine years ago and Passed On.

Faan kept her face neutral at his whiny comment about her leaving. "You will continue with your Lessons and be good. I won't be gone for very long." She resumed her workout against the only blank wall in the house, the one connected to the family's pattern-changer. She closed her eyes as she continued talking. "And Mother's Mother will be with you, too."

Sree didn't register her words right away as he became distracted by his sister's training. Recognized as possibly the most accomplished skin-shifter on their planet, even Central Authority had granted Faan special permission the year before their parents' Passing On to start her First Assignment at the age of 13, two years sooner than usual.

Sree watched in awe as the pattern on the wall changed, stripes or leaves or mist, and his sister blended in with each background perfectly even with her eyes closed. She often said she could feel the wavelengths of light and match them, without needing to see them. Sree had never been able to do that. He wasn't sure anyone else on their planet could do that, either.

Every member of the Re'Ris species had the ability to change their skin color, normally ranging from light to dark gray, to match their surroundings by light reflection and skin pigment alteration. The layered chromatophores would enlarge and shrink to change color, while the melanin in their skin determined the lightness/darkness of the skin tone.

Each Re'Ris child became trained at an early age to control these changes. This ability, embedded into their genetics, was something the Makers added to the Re'Ris when they genetically engineered the species. Faan proved to be exceptionally good at controlling her color-change and rapidly excelled in her classes and her career. She exemplified the ideal citizen on their world, and many considered her to be Re'Ris perfection.

Sree didn't really care about any of that. She was just his sister. And since he never really felt comfortable with the idea of eliminating Targets, he often avoided family stories or conversations about it. But he did love to watch her practice. He wasn't nearly as talented as her—camouflaging drained a Re'Ris after a short time, and he often found it difficult to fight off that fatigue—but she never seemed fazed by it. She'd even learned how to go weeks without sleeping to keep up with a Target who may have gotten a strong lead.

"Are you listening or are you staring at me?" Faan's voice cut through Sree's admiration.

"Listening," Sree lied with a scowl. He forced himself to remember what she'd said. "I don't need Mother's Mother to stay with me. I'm old enough to watch myself until you get back."

"Old enough?" Faan scoffed. "You *should* be old enough. But you've been fifteen for a while now and you haven't even *applied* for your First Assignment yet, much less completed it."

Sree's face flushed with embarrassment, and he felt relieved his sister's eyes were still closed. A Re'Ris could apply for the

First Assignment anytime between the ages of 15 and 16 standard years old. Sree had been stalling, but he couldn't tell his 'perfect' sister such. "That shouldn't matter for something like this. It's not fair! I'm above the Age of Progression. Staying home by myself should be fine. It's not like I'm going to leave the planet or something. I don't need Mother's Mother here." Sree didn't want to say why, but he didn't like spending time with his elderly relative. All her stories revolved around Assignments—hers, her Passed On husband's, her children's. It made Sree uncomfortable to hear the graphic details.

Faan's ice blue eyes opened and she sighed, turning off the pattern-changer. "Yes, you're no longer considered a 'child' once you turn fifteen. But you know more status is placed on those who've finished their First Assignments and Crossed Over. If you simply paid attention and did the work, it would already be completed. It's just because you're too—"

"Emotional," Sree finished for her, digging a toe into the soft carpet. "You always say that."

"Well, it's true. 'Emotional detachment is necessary to successfully complete an Assignment,'" she recited.

"Fifth Rule of Assignment. Stars, sis, you don't have to quote the Rules at me." Sree slumped into one of the cushy chairs and stared sulkily out of the room's window. He watched their planet's red sun set and the street's additional heat and light sensors increase as day slipped into night. Their sun, now aged and not the bright yellow it had been in the stories of long ago, didn't burn as hot as during its juvenile stage of life. Cand adapted, adding heat lamps to most streets and buildings, but Sree heard some poorer areas of the planet didn't have them. Those people, mostly factory and business Laborers, used alternate heat sources—some of which even came from the black market. Unfortunately, many unapproved warming lamps had been known to explode after prolonged use. He felt glad his family weren't Laborers.

"Why can't I just come with you?" Sree asked. "I could work on my Lessons. And what better teacher could I have to learn about Assignments than you?"

"What reason would you like?" Faan sat down in the chair across from him and ticked off the excuses on each finger. "You're too young? It will be too dangerous? I'm not allowed to teach you Lessons because I'm not a Superior? Or how about you're not allowed off-planet without parental consent until you've Crossed Over?"

"Oh, that last one's no problem. We'll just reconstruct Mother's and Father's ashes and ask them if I can go," Sree said with a sneer.

Faan's eyes narrowed in anger. "Sree—"

Sree cut her off. "You know what I mean. I'm just so frustrated! Ever since Mother's and Father's accident..."

"Murder," Faan mumbled.

"...I haven't had any freedom!" Sree continued, ignoring his sister's comment. He didn't put any stock into her insane theory that they'd been murdered instead of killed in a transportation orb collision. He'd been with them when the crash happened. All his memories revolved around the front end of the orb exploding, shards of glass stinging his face and arms, and being thrown from the vehicle, screaming for help that never came.

Faan put her hand on Sree's knee, which brought him out of his morbid memories. "I know it's been hard for you since they Passed On. And I know I haven't been a very good replacement, seeing as how I am on Assignments so often. But if you'd finish your First Assignment, then you would have all the freedom you want."

"Spoken like a true patriot!" Sree snapped, pulling away from his sister's reach.

Faan stood, placing her hands on her hips. "Sree, you need to get past these childish temper tantrums and do what you are meant to do. Our species was created, designed, and bred to be perfect assassins. It is our purpose in life to complete Assignments the Makers have chosen for us and in doing so fulfill our own destinies, become whole, and keep our names. The balance of our society depends on the wisdom of the Makers to choose those Re'Ris who must Pass On and in our faith that those choices are right and just."

Heat rose inside his chest. He felt so tired of hearing that rhetoric spewed in his face over and over again. "Surprise, surprise. The Oath to the Makers, completely verbatim, straight from the Lessons. You don't even know if what you just said is true."

"Careful, Sree," Faan warned quietly. "Someone could hear you."

With a lick of his lips and a quick glance out the partially opened window he said, with a lowered voice now, "I didn't say anything treasonous."

"But you're skirting that boundary line pretty close."

"Look who's talking," Sree countered. He reached over and closed the window as night finally settled. A large moscat, an insect with ruby-colored wings, which sparkled as if covered in tiny stars, fluttered outside the window, interested in coming into the lighted room. "You preach the Seventeen Rules of Assignment as if there is no other way to live and yet you defy them by going off in search of Mother's and Father's *alleged* murderers."

Faan's already pale skin whitened further. "I haven't gone against any of the Rules!"

"What about Rule Fifteen? It says you can't seek revenge if a Target... or, umm..."

"...or the assassin is killed," Faan finished. Before Sree could speak, Faan continued. "But Mother and Father weren't on an Assignment. I checked."

Sree ignored this bit of evidence. He would rather his sister stay home than worry about the validity of her theory. "How about...umm...Rule Twelve?"

"A Re'Ris who fails an Assignment is demoted in status to Laborer and may only live under that title and its responsibilities? That hardly applies here."

He shook his head, searching his brain for the correct number. "No. I meant Three."

Faan hesitated. "Assignments must be given top priority in the life of a Re'Ris."

Sree smiled smugly. "Aren't you on Assignment right now? Isn't pursuing these 'mythical' murderers keeping you from your *precious* work?"

"My Assignments are *my* business."

"Not according to Rule Sixteen. It's my duty to report if a Re'Ris is not following an Assignment."

The skin around Faan's eyes tightened. "You wouldn't dare..."

Sree sighed. "No, sis. I'm supposed to tell on you, but *I* wouldn't. The problem is, *you* would."

Faan tucked her short platinum blonde hair behind her ears. "I would never turn you in. You are my family. We are one."

Sree dismissed their traditional family motto. "Yes, you would. You follow the Rules blindly. They define your whole life. They dictate what you do, when you do it, and who you are. Face it Faan, you're twenty-three years of age, you have no friends on-planet, no relationship with a mated partner, no life! You never question any of it. You don't even think about who you're killing. All you do are Assignments!"

"Why shouldn't I?" Faan countered. "I'm great at what I do. I have better control of my skin-shifting than anyone else, I have never been detected on an Assignment, and...and... nobody wants to hang around with the best assassin on the planet." Faan slid into an oversized, navy-blue sweatshirt, but Sree noted the color fluctuations on her cheeks at this admission, indicating her embarrassment. She quickly composed herself and switched into anger. "And since when did you become so wise about life that you can tell me how poorly I live mine? You haven't even completed your First Assignment."

"And once again, that's what it all comes down to, isn't it!" Sree yelled, throwing up his arms. "How could I *possibly* know about life if I haven't taken one yet?"

Faan ignored his sarcasm and pulled on a pair of black gloves. "Exactly. You can't understand life unless you've experienced death."

"I've experienced death," Sree said. His voice shook with rage. "I was there when Mother and Father were killed while you were gone on Assignment. Or have you forgotten? I'm perfectly capable of understanding death because I watched the life leave their eyes."

The sting of Sree's words became obvious in Faan's contorted facial reaction, but her response came out in measured tones. "Mother's Mother will be here soon. I will be on the planet Juha. My Target fled there when she learned she was targeted. Luckily, Juha is also where I have a contact who may have information about Mother's and Father's murders, so I will be able to take care of my Assignment *and* find out about Mother's and Father's killer. I told you, I'm not breaking any Rules. I will let you know what I discover."

"You don't even care."

His sister got to the door and paused at his dismissive comment. She spoke softly, her ice blue eyes cast downward. "I know I haven't been around much since Mother and Father were killed. I know it's been tough for you, that you struggle with the concept of being a Re'Ris and what that means." Her gaze met his, her voice nearly a whisper. "Do you think I *like* dealing out death? I've been off-planet. Other species live in harmony with each other and intentional death is a crime. To them, what we do, what we *are*, is considered immoral and evil." Faan opened the door to leave. "I can't help it if I've been genetically created to be the perfect killing machine. But I'll tell you something I've never told anyone. I would have risked the consequences of not fulfilling my Assignment the day Mother and Father died if I could have been there. Because maybe I could have saved them. Anything to keep from losing them. Anything to spare you what you saw, what you're going through now."

Surprise hit him. He never thought he'd hear her say something like that. She'd always been so cold, so distant. The perfect assassin. She constantly chastised him for his own emotional state. To know she would have broken the Rules to change that day...

"Sis..." he began.

"Sometimes I wish things could be different," she continued. "Sometimes I wish we weren't meant to be assassins. But the laws were created by the Makers and are all-binding." Faan smiled at her younger brother and her tone returned to normal. "Be good for Mother's Mother. I'll contact you soon. You are my family, we are one."

With their motto recited, Sree watched his sister leave their home.

Bringing his thoughts once again to his current surroundings, Sree saw and hated the greenish curtains that blew in the light breeze, the digital artwork that he'd collected during his childhood covering the deep blue walls. Everything in his bedroom reminded him of a time he'd been so naïve, so ungrateful, taking those around him for granted.

That fight had been the last time he'd seen his sister.

Now she'd Passed On.

Gone. Forever.

And Sree was all alone.

CHAPTER 2

Vuun didn't know what to do. She'd tried everything she could to get her Daughter's Son to leave his room. She knew the death of his sister had been a blow, but how long could Sree stay isolated? The boy needed to come out sometime. It wasn't as if he'd been responsible for Faan's outcome. Her death should be celebrated, as per their species' customs. Why did this family insist on mourning those who have Passed On?

With a clasping of her fingers, she crossed the kitchen, her arthritic hands a constant reminder of her age. Most Re'Ris didn't live as long as Vuun. On a planet of assassins, it could be a tough world to survive. Her age stood as a symbol of holiness to some of their species. She'd been so successful as an assassin that she had *actually* reached retirement. In doing so, she earned the right to live out the rest of her years without being targeted.

But this family...She'd never met such stubborn individuals, especially for being so successful on their world. Why did they rebel against everything? The Makers knew what was good for the Re'Ris. Why would someone ever question that?

As leaders of a political party who fought against the tyrannical Aleet Army invasion, Vuun's Daughter and her Male Mate had been noble citizens of Re'Ris. Their children should have been proud of their accomplishments when they'd died in that orb accident.

But Faan still pursued the matter with zeal, convinced someone killed her Mother and Father, not accidentally, but on purpose, outside of the Rules. Could you imagine? *Murder?* How disgusting. No one on this planet would stoop so low as to inflict murder on another Re'Ris.

Vuun shuffled into the next room, where she'd been staying since Faan's Passing On, and retrieved a small box, sliding her painful fingers over the cover. Her originally dark grey skin now appeared nearly translucent. She could barely skin-shift anymore. Once an acclaimed assassin, she often felt useless now. Thankfully she could still help her Daughter's Son ready himself for his First Assignment.

Her fingertips paused on the top of the box, the etching of her Male Mate's name carved with care on its surface.

So much had changed in her life. On this world.

Vuun's rambling thoughts continued.

Why had Faan pursued the idea of murder? Yes, she'd read the letter from the off-worlder explaining Faan's death. So what if her Mother's and Father's Passings On hadn't been an accident? Did it matter if Aleet Army members ended up being responsible for having them killed? That army didn't need to follow the Rules. Informing other Re'Ris of how they died wouldn't do anything for the Kaano name, so none of it mattered.

And why did Sree still grieve? Faan was dead. Her death had been celebrated for over three standard days on their planet. Faan denoted an icon for other Re'Ris to strive toward. Why tarnish her name with sorrow?

Of course, Vuun conceded, that kind of legacy was hard to

live up to. Not to mention the grand assassination records of Sree's Mother and Father, but really! The boy had taken to sulking. Sulking! It reflected poorly on a Re'Ris to act in such a way. And he really couldn't afford to let his emotions cloud his judgment right now. Not when his First Assignment deadline hung so close...

Gently, she slipped the box into her pocket. Vuun let out a huff, pulled her shawl tighter around her shoulders, and shambled into the food prep area. She hated how cold the nights had been lately. She really had to speak to the maintenance staff about increasing the heat lamps. But they had at least left her a plate of red sauced *kuats,* a sticky fruit which had nearly reached the end of its season. Though she enjoyed preparing meals, she hated shopping for the food, and loved that the staff would often bring in samples of their own wares.

Focus, she told her wandering mind. *First things first.* With a determined exhale, she slowly hobbled up the stairs to the second floor, balancing the plate in her good hand, as she passed the digital photos of her beloved Daughter and Male Mate. They'd made it a tradition to add a digital representation of their physical selves each year. While ascending, the photos became pictures of them with first one then their second offspring, until that shifted again, and the final one, which had been taken the previous sun turn, only showed herself, Faan, and Sree.

Now, with Fann gone, the next photo would only be of herself and the boy.

She shook her head, scolding herself for her nearly sorrow-filled thoughts. Families change all the time. That's the way of life and death. He may have experienced several abrupt changes which were unexpected, but regardless, he needed to start his First Assignment.

He's running out of time...

Chapter 3

Sree heard a hesitant knock at his bedroom door. He ignored it at first, then lowered the datapad in his hands at the voice on the other side.

"Sree? Dearest?"

A knot of anxiety formed in his gut. He really didn't feel like talking with her right now. "What do you want, Mother's Mother?"

"I brought you something to eat if you're hungry."

A pause. His tight stomach disagreed with her offer. "Not really."

Silence for a few moments. "Well, I'll just leave it outside your door in case you change your mind. I'll be downstairs if you need anything."

Sree listened as the pattering of footsteps moved away.

With a huge sigh, he flopped backwards onto his bed, staring up into the swirls of yellow and jade covering his ceiling. He knew his Mother's Mother meant well, but to Sree it just felt like she...hovered. As if her presence could make him get over whatever bothered him so he could get on with his life.

Which meant completing his First Assignment.

Unfortunately for Sree, his First Assignment *was* the problem. The pain over Faan's death still ate away at him, like a hole that nipped on the edges of his insides, but the fact remained that Faan's death had already happened, and his First Assignment had not.

Sree never told anyone his secret, not his family, nor his classmates, but he didn't *want* to be an assassin. Faan may have glimmered a bit of insight as to his reluctance, but he'd never specifically said such words out loud.

He didn't really know *why* he didn't want to be one. It wasn't as if he thought killing was wrong—he understood the need to remove those in society who no longer served a function and killing provided an efficient way to do that—but it just didn't *feel* right to him.

At first, he thought others must think this way as well, but when he cautiously inquired about the subject with his classmates at Lessons, they all spoke of nerves or pressure, not the desire to *not* be an assassin.

So, he'd kept it all tucked away inside him, living in denial, until he'd hit his 15th birth year—the Age of Progression when a child is legally considered an adult—and the moment a Re'Ris can apply for their First Assignment. Then, all his revulsions and anxieties about killing someone hit him full force. Since applicants were given a full year to apply, he'd continued suppressing his feelings, and ignoring the deadline, as long as possible. But only two standard days remained until his next birth year.

Which meant only two standard days left to register.

The main issue to him felt like he didn't have the choice *not* to kill someone, unless he didn't mind working in the Labor Force for the rest of his life.

Which, according to his Mother's Mother description, would end up being maybe 10 years, tops, before he ended up useless and became Targets. For someone who is designed to kill, becoming a Laborer couldn't be a satisfying life.

Sree shuddered at the thought. He'd heard tales about the things Laborers had to do. They were responsible for keeping the cities running by doing the worst, most disgusting, most tedious jobs there were: things like waste management, animal keeping, and farming. Yes, they also could be doctors and officers and work for the government, but that required years of training and education, and both sounded awful to Sree. But the worst sounding position was that of an office worker.

Ugh., What a horrible way to live, shut up in a room for twelve hours a day doing nothing but crafting letters, checking figures, and shuffling through datapads of information.

Sree knew that on the planet of Re'Ris, you toiled in the Labor Force if you didn't maintain your assassin status. At that point, an individual received a number to be known by instead of their name. It made sense in the order of their world: if you weren't an assassin, you weren't allowed to be yourself anymore. You became a title and a number: Laborer 123 or whatever. Nobody on the planet kept their own names except assassins. Laborer, Central Authority, Superior, even Head Superiors. Those terms *became* the person's identity.

The notion of losing himself terrified Sree.

Sree knew he wouldn't make it if he ended up doing labor. His family had always been well-off and he'd never done any of that kind of menial work in his life.

But could he kill to stay away from it?

Running away wouldn't work—they'd just send someone after him. Even leaving the planet wouldn't matter. Re'Ris *were* allowed to travel off-world to find their Targets, but if he Crossed Over and left and never checked back in for his next Target, eventually he'd be considered a rogue individual and an assassin would be sent to apprehend him.

Sree reluctantly got up off the bed, opened the door, retrieved the plateful of food from the floor, and brought it back into his room. Flickers of deep red light from the setting sun crossed his room on occasion as the wind blew harder against the curtains. He absentmindedly chewed bits of the dinner, his stomach reminding him that he'd hardly eaten all day, but his mind kept focusing on everything else other than digesting nutrients.

He couldn't run.

He didn't want to kill.

And he'd never survive as a Laborer.

But what else could he do?

Chapter 4

"At least he's getting out of the house," Vuun said into the audiolink. Though she usually preferred to visually chat through the vidlink, Vuun hadn't dressed yet for the day and didn't want her friend to see her in such a disheveled state. "And it's about time, too. It's been days since he heard about Faan's death."

She paused as her friend spoke, stirring the contents of the pot in front of her. Cooked food at home represented a rarity for many families on Re'Ris, as heat sources were an expensive commodity, and most meals were prepared at cafeterias or larger assembly lines for the masses. Sometimes assassins hired Laborers to cook food in their own homes. With their family's excellent assassination record, beginning with Vuun and her late Male Mate's beginnings, they'd wanted for nothing, financially. They could afford anything they sought, and more. But Vuun always found a sense of calm when she prepared food, so she often did so of her own accord.

The job of assassin, since it embodied the design of what a

Re'Ris should ideally be, was considered one's existence. If you fulfilled it properly, the government afforded you various luxuries, depending on the Target, the timeframe, the difficulty, etc. Most assassins lived a privileged life, with things like food, lodgings, and monetary credits offered as rewards for your kills. The longer you remained an assassin, the more you accrued. If you retired, like she had, you could live on your savings comfortably for years. But once you died, those savings vanished, not passed down, so they only mattered while you lived.

Though, and she didn't want to even admit this to herself, without her Daughter's and Male Mate's income since their deaths, her financial situation wasn't quite as luxurious as it had once been. And now with Faan gone...there would be even less advantages she could afford. She hadn't expected to take care of the young man by herself. It represented another reason she really wanted Sree to fulfill his First Assignment—the two of them could use the extra compensation.

"I don't know why he's waiting," Vuun continued to her friend, examining a spoonful of the runny substance. It still needed to thicken. Maybe she'd missed a step? She knew she should have had one of the helpers assist her, but she used to know this recipe by heart, and pride held her at bay from asking. Besides, she'd cut the Laborers' time in half to help ease the financial change.

Returning to the conversation she said, "Sree goes to Central Processing mostly. Probably doing research on previous Assignments. I've helped him out with tips and tricks that I've learned over the years...oh you know, things like 'stake out Central Processing in case your Target still goes there to check on their status,' or 'get familiar with their home so you can practice your skin-shifting,' things like that. Nothing I'm not *allowed* to tell him. Just general things, you know, and hints like what's frowned upon in the assassin world such as poisons and incendiary devices, things we all learn at some point. I felt it only fair to fill in where his Mother and Father would have... Well, either way, at least he's out of the house."

Another pause as her friend made some passive aggressive statement.

Vuun clucked her tongue. "Yes, he's still eligible for his First Assignment. Although he is cutting it *quite* close. His sixteenth year of birth is in two days. I told his Mother years ago to watch out for him, that he seemed nervous about the event, even at such a young age...no I'm not speaking ill of the dead...I'm just saying what I told her..."

Vuun waited through her friend's lecture, stirring the pot's contents, still not satisfied. Now she wished she had a Laborer here. She felt fairly certain she'd forgotten a key ingredient. Something purple, she suspected, based on the current color.

"Anyway," Vuun went on, cutting into her friend's rant, "I think Sree is finally ready to Cross Over. Poor dear, with the pressure on him to perform well, it's no wonder he waited so long.... I *know* I've said before that he should've done it months ago, but I'm just saying that I understand why he may have waited. I mean, with my Daughter and her Male Mate and their accomplishments during their lives, not just with Assignments, but also their political careers, and then my Daughter's Daughter being a genetic marvel and succeeding so highly in her Assignments, and to have all *three* of them die for such a noble cause as standing up against... yes I *know* it's history now, but for an impressionable youth such as Sree, to live up to that...well I'm just *saying...*"

CHAPTER 5

Sree *had* been spending a lot of time at Central Processing, but not for the reasons his Mother's Mother thought.

Sometimes I wish things could be different.

Sometimes I wish we weren't meant to be assassins.

But the laws were created by the Makers and are all-binding.

You are my family, we are one.

His sister's last words chanted through his head like a twisted mantra. He'd lain in bed for hours the morning he'd received the datapad with the news of her death, hoping, *praying* that he'd figure out a way to make those first two statements be true. But he realized sitting around wasn't going to solve anything. Time would slip by whether he left his room or not and only one place he could think of might have information to help him.

Central Processing.

A location Sree usually avoided. It embodied everything he hated about his world, with its large metallic structure, its cold, uninviting coloring, and its rows upon rows of seemingly sky-scraping, windowless walls, which blocked out the planet's large red sun.

And now here he was, inside, waiting in line to sort through data files. He wasn't really sure what he could discover with only one day left before his 16th day of birth. All he knew was if he didn't find something, he'd receive the seal of "EXPIRED" on his account and would be placed into the Labor Force.

All around him other citizens waited in massive lines, most likely all of them Laborers, since assassins usually had private access to the CrossLattice system. Their eyes looked blank, their feet slow. He imagined if the dead could be brought back to life, Laborers would embody their appearance and mannerisms.

Sree kept his head down. Even though he knew no one could tell just by looking at him about his plight, his anxiety convinced him otherwise. He felt sure one of them would point him out, calling him a traitor for attempting to find a way out of his First Assignment. These individuals may not be happy, but at least they'd all *tried* to become assassins. All he could see around him were faithful Re'Ris, dutifully following the Rules in a building he hated so much. How much more would they hate him for trying to skirt the very system that would put him here, too?

While waiting, Sree thought about that very system, and the building he currently stood in. Central Processing, considered the center of the city of Cand, held the offices of the Superiors, special Re'Ris who had been chosen to teach the Lessons to Re'Ris children concerning the Rules set down by the Makers. Viewed as the central hub of processing, determining, or allocating Assignments for each Re'Ris to follow, Central Processing also held the main governmental system of Cand, comprised of a top group of individuals called Head Superiors. They earned their high place in society through a special selection process to continue leading the people on their planet by example and make sure each city on the planet flourished under the Rules.

Many citizens also came here, like the ones around him, to check their assassin status, whether they had been promoted and given a Target, had become a Target, or were still considered a neutral citizen. These standings could be checked from home, but if a citizen didn't have a vidlink connection from their own house, which was out of reach financially for many, they could come here instead at no cost. The Makers wanted everyone to have a fair chance to defend themselves.

Which, for Sree, also meant that by coming here in person he could check things anonymously, since he wouldn't be uplinking to the CrossLattice system from a terminal in his home which could identify him. He didn't want anyone to know about his investigation concerning a loophole to get him out of his plight.

The terminals were packed, as usual, but Sree eventually found an open workstation on which to begin his search. His skin shimmered with dread.

Only one day left.

He needed something, *anything* that would clear him from having to complete his First Assignment but wouldn't result in him becoming a Laborer. His fears had increased ten-fold over the past week as the deadline crept closer. Today they seemed to have doubled yet again.

Sree now knew, in his gut, that it wasn't just because he feared killing someone. He really believed there had to be something else to give his life meaning.

Faan once told him that since other planets criminalized killing, with a few exceptions, they looked down on Re'Ris. No one on Sree's planet could comprehend how assassinating those who were no longer useful in a community, while also sharpening and honing the skills of the assassin, could be a negative thing. It helped curb overpopulation, maximize limited resources, and minimize epidemics. There also hadn't been a war on Re'Ris in thousands of years, whereas on other worlds, Sree had heard about the most horrible things individuals would do to each other for claims on land or material possessions. Imagine murdering someone because you are jealous of their status? Or something as trivial as jewelry or their mode of transportation?

Not to mention the resources wasted on those who no longer served the community. Sree heard stories of individuals who got sick and infected others, killing thousands. He didn't understand: why not isolate them? And if their illness would result in death anyway, why not remove them before they infected others? Faan spoke of free will which allowed individuals to basically kill others because they didn't want to follow safety procedures. Shaking his head, Sree often changed the conversation at that point, unable to grasp the selfish nature that existed elsewhere.

On his world, basics were provided for everyone. Lodgings, food, medical assistance, even transportation. Of course, those who succeeded in their assassinations earned perks, as well they should, for their expertise. Though they may be envied, no one was ever attacked or killed because of these extra bonuses. On other worlds, individuals feared being attacked in their own homes, in their vehicles, even while walking down the street. Their very own community members slept on the streets, begging for food and help, while those around them walked by without a second glance. Currency or power became their status symbols, gave them inflated egos, and pitted them against their own neighbors. It made very little sense to Sree.

But even if the Rules made more logical sense to him than the guidelines on other worlds, being an assassin never felt right to Sree, no matter what he learned in his Lessons about the Makers' will or what his classmates and family told him.

So, since he'd heard the news about his sister, he spent every free hour he could at Central Processing, scouring those same Rules and Lessons, looking for any way out he could find even as time slid by, bringing him closer to his deadline, no matter how much he wished it wouldn't.

Chapter 6

The day before Sree's 16th day of birth arrived.

The final day he could apply for his First Assignment.

He'd lost.

Sree's feet moved him mechanically down the seemingly endless corridor inside Central Processing to one of the rooms allocated by the Administrations Office for Assignment specifics. Earlier, he'd waited in the lobby, a digital number assigned to him, surrounded by dozens of others whose facial expressions ranged from eager to anxious. Sree felt a complete sense of disconnect.

Why couldn't he be normal? Excited, like Faan had been? Or even just nervous about performing the task? Not this rising dread lodged deep in his gut that for some reason told him this wasn't *right.*

But time didn't care. Logic laughed. And eventually he heard his number called.

The corridor, painted in flat greys and blues, dragged out in front of him, as if tempting him with each breath he took to flee. One young woman burst out of the numbered room directly to his left. He jumped, then noticed the flushed look of accomplishment on her face.

Why can't I feel that way?

Sree shook his head. At this point, it didn't matter. He could resist all he wanted, but maybe once he applied he'd feel better? After all, his species had been designed for this—the perfect hunters. Instinct would take over. Genetics would prevail. Or so he told himself.

Fully in denial, Sree entered the room he'd been called to.

"Don't dawdle," the man behind the desk said. "Come in, come in."

Sree examined the tiny off-white room, lit by harsh artificial lighting, filled with nothing but a desk, a vidlink communications system, several datapads, and the Laborer. The Laborer wore the sage green standard uniform of an office worker. His skin appeared as an even darker gray than Sree's, but had an odd yellow tinge to it. Strangely, to Sree's eyes, the Laborer's skin hardly appeared iridescent at all, a key feature to help with skin-shifting.

Maybe that's why he's a Laborer? Sree wondered. *Maybe he wasn't good at color-changing or couldn't do it at all and so failed as an assassin?* But then why hadn't this man's Target been the victor instead? Technically there wasn't any Rule or Lesson that said you *had* to be able to skin-shift well to be an assassin. Sree couldn't imagine a successful assassination without it, though.

Maybe the man had missed the deadline to apply? Then, he'd automatically become a Laborer. Or maybe he'd run out of time trying to catch his Target?

Why is the reason this man is a Laborer important to you? Sree admonished himself. *Who cares why he failed? Focus!*

The Laborer glanced up from his vidlink system as Sree approached.

"Welcome to the Applications Department at Central Processing. I am Laborer 63-992. How may I be of assistance today?"

A lump formed in Sree's throat. "I'm here to apply for my First Assignment."

The Laborer gave a weak smile and then spoke as if he'd recited these words a thousand times. Sree assumed he probably had. "Congratulations on taking the first step to fulfill your purpose as a Re'Ris. The Makers are proud and stand behind you in your efforts. I am the Laborer who will assist you. All I need is some personal information and we can get started." Laborer 63-992 shuffled through some datapads and began scrolling through a list of questions. "Here we go. Name please."

"Sree Kaano," he muttered. His mouth felt dry. He still couldn't believe this was actually happening.

Laborer 63-992 stopped inserting information and his eyes widened before he peered at Sree, as if seeing him for the first time. "Kaano? As in, a *Kaano*? You're Faan's brother, aren't you?" he asked in a hushed tone.

A pang of grief struck him at his sister's name. "Uh...yeah."

The Laborer's face genuinely lit up. "It's an honor, Sree Kaano, to be processing your First Assignment application. Your sister was a hero to me...well, to all of us, actually. A loss to our world, but pleasant blessings that she has Passed On."

Sree squirmed in his chair. "That's great," he muttered.

The Laborer continued, oblivious to Sree's discomfort with the subject. "Oh yes, Faan Kaano, a hero indeed. She is what every Laborer wishes they could have been. I, myself, often dreamed of having her skin-shifting abilities and having the whole city recognize my brilliance..." Laborer 63-992 trailed off, his eyes glazing over. He stared slightly over Sree's shoulder as if looking into his daydream.

Sree cleared his throat and the Laborer snapped back to attention.

"Let's move on to the next query, shall we?" Laborer 63-992 smiled once more, but again it appeared fake to Sree, as if the man were going through the motions while his mind remained lost inside his fantasy.

A slew of standardized questions came next, from date of birth confirmation to anything that might prevent him from fulfilling his First Assignment in the allotted time.

Sree hesitated at this last question. His mind raced. He'd done everything he could, scoured digital file after digital file in Central Processing on the regulations surrounding Assignments to find an excuse to get him out of having to kill someone, but to no avail.

Faking sickness only lasted until you got better, and if you didn't, you were considered weak and placed in the Labor Force. Same thing with an injury or loss of limb. Same for mental illness. Same for family emergencies. Same for loss of property or anything that would deter you from being able to successfully complete the Assignment.

Everything led him to the same conclusion of, "Fix it soon or it's off to the Labor Force. NO EXCEPTIONS."

He'd even thought about trying to modify the system so as to switch his name with someone else's, like his Mother's Mother, who reached retirement because she'd filled her Target Lifetime Quota, but he had no idea how to do that. Not to mention the fact that his Mother's Mother would then start getting Assignments again. Unfortunately, even if he *were* a technological genius, it wouldn't matter. Only the Makers could make changes to the system.

The words came slowly, like they had to be pulled from his mouth. "There is no reason why I can't perform my First Assignment."

"Excellent," the Laborer continued. "You'll receive your First Assignment tomorrow, through a package delivery system, at the location you've listed as your residence. If something happens and you are unable to perform within the prearranged timeframe, there is contact information for you to use." He paused, his glassy stare now clear. "Do you have any other questions?"

Sree swallowed. *Yes,* he thought. *Can I just not do this?*

Instead, he said, "No. Not that I can think of."

"Wonderful." A few more taps on the datapad. "You're all set! It was an absolute pleasure to meet the last standing non-retired individual of the house of Kaano. I'm sure you'll do great things on our world and I know myself and everyone else very much looks forward to what your future holds!"

Sree sat there, mouth slightly open, his gut clenched so tightly he wondered if he'd be able to stand up.

"Mm," he finally managed, non-committal.

The Laborer waited a few beats. "You're...you're free to leave now."

Shock overtook him. The entire process had ended. It was done.

Tomorrow he'd receive his First Assignment.

"Right," he murmured. With a swift and awkward movement he stood, nearly knocking over the chair.

"You can close the door on your way out," Laborer 63-992 said, returning his attention to the datapad on the desk.

Sree gave a nod, turned, and exited.

The corridor, endless on his way in, seemed too short now, as if hurtling him forward through time. Moments of life slithered away, speeding towards tomorrow.

With leaden feet that seemingly had a mind of their own, Sree left Central Processing, hardly noticing the increase in hustle and bustle as the day progressed and more Laborers began their shifts. Turning directly left, he headed towards a transportation orb station. Three covered holes in the ground, which contained three individual transportation orbs, sat in front of him. Swiping his monetary card at the nearby kiosk, one of the holes opened, and a sleek, gray, oval-shaped transport popped out of the ground. His card granted him access to any type of orb, but he only ever used those like the ones in front of him, made for a single person.

Sree hadn't thought about the benefits of success in his family, especially financially, in quite some time. Consistently his way of life included access to many perks and bonuses as compared to others. The public transit system being one of them.

Most Re'Ris, as Laborers, had to slog their way around town inside their own tiny box-like one-person vehicles, called tixas, dealing with long lines of traffic, unreliable wait times at checkpoints, and the constant fear of running out of credits. Not to mention traffic could often be a route that assassins might use to eliminate a Target, so consistent routes to work were often frowned upon, which led to more clogged traffic and varying times arriving to work. Leaving well in advance for a shift often happened on a daily basis. A magnetic grid allowed these tixas to only travel to certain areas, from designated parking lot to designated parking lot, and though you could choose your route from the allotted options, traffic jams still occurred often.

Some services, like Emergency Recue Facilities and Central Authority, had modified tixas that held up to six individuals and could navigate outside of the magnetic roads, but Sree hadn't had much interaction with them.

City transit was available to any individual, though it was a paid mode of transportation, and came in three levels of orbs: single, group, and multiple. Regulated by the CrossLattice system, the oval-shaped orbs raced underground, quickly and efficiently bringing citizens to their desired locations.

Because of his family's financial status, Sree carried a single orb transportation card. He used to travel with his family in a group orb, whose access points occurred at more central locations around the city, but he often listened to the music offered in the compartment instead of engaging in conversation. He'd never been on a multiple orb, which held up to fifty individuals at a time. These access points were fewer and further between, with their entrances a level beneath the topsoil, accessible by a set of stairs or ramps. Sree didn't like the idea of not entering topside, waiting on an underground platform at a specified time with dozens of others for his transportation to arrive.

Now, stepping into the single orb, Sree regretted the time spent alone. He never traveled if he could help it, never went anywhere with friends because he didn't have any. And now, with most of his family having Passed On, no one remained to spend time with.

I'll spend the rest of my life alone, he thought as the vehicle whisked him towards his home.

Emptiness overwhelmed him. He thought the grief after his sister's Passing On had been hard. But this feeling? Somehow it felt worse.

He'd end up letting his whole family down by not completing his First Assignment and he couldn't even tell them sorry when he did.

With a shuddering exhale, Sree determined at that point he'd make his family proud. He'd show the world he could be worthy of the Kaano family name. He'd become an incredible assassin and through that accomplishment, he'd feel connected to his family again.

As his orb reached its destination and he exited, he walked the remaining steps home, his gaze lost amongst the turned off heat-lamp-filled street, his mind lighter, focused on the task at hand.

But try as he might to mentally push himself forward, his stomach still remained unyielding in its anxiety-laden tightness.

Chapter 7

Sree found himself surrounded. Multi-color-changing entities covered any possible escape. They shimmered in and out of view, each of them carrying various weapons, angled towards him.

They crept forward, closing in on him, speaking in one voice the words of the Oath of the Rules Sree had grown up reciting in his Lessons:

"I pledge to uphold the Rules of Assignment as were handed down by the Makers.

"I pledge to learn these Rules and follow them for the rest of my life.

"I will honor and obey the Lessons as instructed by my Superiors, whose knowledge has gone into the interpretation of the Rules."

Sree tried to speak, to beg them not to make him a Target, to promise he'd complete his First Assignment.

But he could tell they didn't believe him.

They knew the truth.

He was different. Damaged.

And no longer useful to the world.

Now, just another Target.

Knock. Knock. Knock.

Sree's eyes flashed open, his heart racing as the remnants of the dream still lingered in his mind. He wiped his dry lips with a shaky hand.

"Come in," he gurgled as the chanting images faded away. The comfort from his own bed calmed him. The feeling quickly switched into a sense of dread as he realized what waited for him today.

His First Assignment.

No time remained.

He shuddered, remembering the day before. The whole situation had been so...unsettling. The Laborer taking Sree's information, all the while not *quite* in the same reality as Sree, then his idolization of Sree's family, and finally setting up Sree's First Assignment.

For today.

With his insides as hard as a rock and his chest feeling constricted with dismay, Sree watched as his Mother's Mother, draped in a flowy aqua gown that she usually saved for special events, stepped through his bedroom doorway, a tray of food in her hand.

"Hello, dear," she told him, setting the tray down gently next to his bed. "I thought you might be hungry, what with a long day ahead of you to search out your first Target, so I baked you your favorite: chopped pleen!"

Sree looked at the dish and fought the urge to throw up. It *usually* ranked as his favorite dish, but on this day, the choice of pleen, which looked uncharacteristically like a pile of bloody innards, was the last thing he wanted.

"It looks great," he lied.

Vuun grinned. "Well, as soon as you're done eating you should come downstairs. I have another surprise for you!"

"Can't wait," he lied again.

Vuun left and Sree swallowed hard as he looked once more at the plate of food. With a shiver, he picked it up and shoved it under his bed.

It wasn't as if he planned to return home anyway.

The determination he felt to "make his family proud" after exiting the transit orb the previous evening immediately evaporated upon arriving home. When he entered the living room, he discovered some sort of...shrine?... created by his Mother's Mother to honor his Mother, Father, and sister, Faan. A datapad scrolled through successful mission after successful mission, using the color-changer to display these images on the wall next to their portraits, which she'd taken from the stairway and arranged on the mantle. Near tears, she then wrapped Sree up in a hug, so excited for him to begin his First Assignment the next day.

The pressure to follow in their footsteps intensified and he retreated to his room as soon as possible, turned off the lights, and pulled the covers over his head as if still a small child.

He couldn't do it.

He couldn't be them.

He would fail immediately and bring shame to himself and his family name.

So that night, after the futile attempts to find a loophole, the expectational burden of family honor from his Mother's Mother, and the heaviness in his belly, Sree prayed to the Makers he would find another way out.

The irony of praying to those who'd created him to be an assassin in the first place didn't escape him and he spiraled even harder into his despair.

This morning, facing his Mother's Mother's famous pleen, he knew only one option lay before him. An option that would never work, but what other choice did he have?

He'd have to go on the run. Eventually they'd send someone after him for desertion, and he'd become a Target. But right now, he couldn't think of anything else except getting as far away as possible until he figured out something else.

But run where?

The question merited some thought. Where *could* he run? He didn't have any living relatives besides his Mother's Mother. Besides, relatives would be the primary location an assassin would look for him, if an individual's own family didn't turn them in to Central Processing for dereliction of duty. He didn't really have any monetary credits of his own to stay at a hotel, since he only ever used his family's money, nor could he remain any longer at the hotel they assigned him after his temporary one-week pass expired, which was the time limit given to each First Assignment.

As far as leaving the planet altogether, he didn't have any transportation to do so. He couldn't buy a ship, for both monetary and non-guardian consent reasons. Even if he stowed away on someone else's craft, where would he go? He didn't have any skills or credits, he didn't have a Universal language translator, and he didn't know any other languages. He hadn't realized how completely sheltered his life had been, solely revolving around Lessons and his family's accomplishments.

The only other option would be to join the Labor Force willingly. Once assignment of the initial Target occurred, the assassin could volunteer for the Labor Force, if done so within the first day and no attempt at assassination had been made. Basically, you couldn't change your mind if you failed at eliminating a Target; you had to decide you already *were* a failure and coward right away.

After all the horror stories he'd heard about the Labor Force, he truly believed he'd bring more shame to himself and his family if he opted for that route. Better to be a deserter once and forgotten than demoted in status and shame his family name forever.

So, before the fleeing would actually occur, he had one last hope, that something in the Target package itself would offer him that desperately searched-for excuse to stall his First Assignment. Maybe a problem with the logistics or a fact about the Target or their location or some kind of difficult arrangement that would give him time to figure out an alternate plan.

At the same time, terror flooded him at the possibility that nothing could save him now.

Which explained why when the package arrived bright and early that brisk morning, Sree promptly hid it under his pillow and lay fitfully in bed until he managed to drift off to sleep once more.

Currently, it lay unopened, still hidden from sight.

"Sree!" he heard Vuun call from downstairs. "Are you coming?"

Sree couldn't avoid it any longer. His Mother's Mother would probably want to capture digital images of him holding up his first datapad or something like that. He grabbed the Target Package from under his pillow and tore open the top.

But he couldn't force himself to look inside. An anxiety stronger than anything else he'd ever felt gripped him. He didn't want to see his Target's face. Didn't want to know their name.

Well, at least this looks *like I looked at it,* he rationalized to himself. Heading to the door, he grabbed his packed bag on the way. He still managed to retain enough sense to take some necessities with him if he decided to go on the run.

When he reached the bottom of the stairs, he found his Mother's Mother waiting for him in the kitchen, a smile lighting up her entire face, holding a beautifully carved metal box.

"Open it," she told him, handing it over.

Sree placed the wrapped datapad on the counter and shifted the pack on his shoulder. Taking the box gingerly in his hands, he lifted the cover, his eyes widening at the teal velvet-lined box's contents.

"I hope you like them," Vuun gushed. "They were your Mother's Father's."

Two intricately woven pieces of metal lay in the box, shining under the kitchen lights. The metal gleamed with iridescent shades of blue and green, the colors of their family crest.

Wrades.

Sree's breath caught in his throat. He remembered seeing the body jewelry on the mantle when he'd been a child. They'd always held a place of honor in his home. Not even his parents or sister had been allowed to wear them. The pieces themselves were worn as bracelets, wrapping twice around the arm, both above and below the wrist bone.

"They are incredible," Sree said, unable to hide the awe in his voice. Picking up one of the pieces he slid it over his hand, the metal cool against his skin. He thought it would feel inorganic, like any type of normal metal would, but he knew their history—they'd been through a process called "pressing," where the metal became folded over itself so many times it felt smooth to the touch, like a second skin.

Vuun smiled fondly at the bracelets. "Your Mother's Father wanted to give them to you for your First Assignment, but he Passed On when you were very young. I told him I would keep them for you until you were ready."

Sree's skin began to prickle, but not from the chilly metal. "He specifically wanted you to wait until my First Assignment?"

"Of course, dear. They are weapons, you know. They're designed so that you can easily access the release nodule yourself." Vuun reached over to one wrist and pressed the spot where the metal met together. In a flash, the lower part of the bracelet whipped around his wrist and extended over his middle knuckle, creating a solid piece of metal, like a blade. The tip had been sharpened to an exquisite point.

"You see," Vuun continued, "you simply make a fist and then wherever you strike, the blade pierces first. The same folding process used to soften the metal against your skin was performed on the edges of the blade as well. When retracted, it lays completely harmless on your wrist. But it'll slice a branch off a lotha tree clean in half with minimal pressure."

The image of what this would do to someone's arm or neck flashed vividly through Sree's mind. Pushing down the sense of bile that wanted to rise into his throat, Sree wrapped the blade around his wrist, and it effortlessly molded back into place. "I'm sure they're very effective," he said with a forced smile.

"I'm sure your Mother's Father would be happy to know that you'd killed your first Target using his wrades, just like he did. He designed them himself, you know." Vuun slid the other wrade over Sree's left wrist and then dabbed at her eyes. "Now you hurry along, dear, and good luck. I will check in with Central Processing to read your progress so I'll know when you've finished your Assignment and be coming home for dinner. No rush, of course. Take the days you need."

Sree had briefly forgotten that for each First Assignment the assassin was given a standard week to complete the successful assassination of their Target and that he needed to check in with Central Processing as soon as he finished. If completion didn't happen within that week, the assassin needed to report the reason why. Extra time could be allowed if there were some sort of extenuating circumstances, like the Target fled off-planet, but many times Central Processing would send a different assassin if they felt your reason didn't have enough merit. Depending on the decision of Central Processing, you would either be targeted yourself or become the newest member of the Labor Force.

"Right," Sree answered. A lump formed in his throat. He reached out and gave her a brief hug. "Thanks for everything."

Vuun waved away the gratitude. "I will see you soon, dear. I can't wait to hear all about what happens!"

Sree stopped in the doorway, hesitating to leave the home he'd felt so safe in—not wanting to believe he would never return.

He suddenly found it difficult to swallow.

"You are my family," he told her, "we are one."

Vuun shooed him out the door. "No need to be so formal dear. I will see you soon enough."

Sree watched as she closed the door on him.

"Goodbye," he whispered.

Chapter 8

Dollops of gray and black clouds passed above, blotting out most of the sun except at their edges, which were limned in red from the sunlight behind them. The air seemed full of tension, as if the city were waiting for the clouds to burst in their pregnancy. Blue electricity crackled around the tips of the lightning towers, created to draw in the planet's unusually high amounts of electrical energy which occurred during their storms. Large, grated drains covered the middle of each intersection, shuttling the rainwater underneath the city and onward, hundreds of kilometers to the nearest standing bodies of water. Without the elaborate drainage systems, the capital would be flooded within days, as the hardpan soil didn't allow for adequate drainage.

Sree currently stood under the awning of a local restaurant in a darkened corner next to the Central Processing building in downtown Cand, twirling the Target Package around in his hands, while trying to figure out a plan of action. It had been a full day since he'd left home and four days remained of the standard 6-day week for him to find a way out of this mess.

His plan to "run" had proved embarrassingly fruitless almost immediately. Endurance and physical strength were not his strong suits. He hadn't even made it a quarter of the way to the nearest town, Bria, when he'd twisted his ankle. It had puffed up to an alarming size, and Sree then hobbled back to Cand to find a local pharmacy carrying something to help with the pain and swelling. Unable to continue traveling, he then realized he needed to locate a place to sleep for the night. Desperate, he opened the Target Package enough to obtain the information detailing where they'd stationed him for his lodgings. The rest of the evening found him in his designated hotel room, nursing the injury and feeling like a fool.

The following morning, hunger eventually drove him to the restaurant next door, since he'd already eaten everything he purchased the previous day, and he devoured two meals off the menu. The food and water he'd brought in his pack to last him throughout his "running away" scenario now seemed ridiculous in its small measure.

He felt like an even bigger idiot.

Now, he just stood outside underneath the awning, staring at the accumulating clouds.

I can't run.

I can't escape.

I can't volunteer to go into the Labor Force.

I can't become targeted and killed.

And I can't kill someone.

Sree snorted. He hadn't left himself with anything he *could* do.

Only one option remained. He knew he had to look at the Target, if only to try to find some kind of loophole with the kill, but his willpower seemed lost behind his cowardice.

The first huge plops of rain splashed onto the street. Portable protectors buzzed around many of the citizens to keep the rain off, while a few who'd been caught unawares picked up their pace and covered their heads as they moved. In his haste to leave, Sree neglected to bring one of those with him, even though he knew how often it rained.

He couldn't even get that right.

With a huge sigh, he fully peeled open the parcel, his chest tight with anxiety. Peeking inside, he saw the datapad. Once removed and turned on, it revealed a picture of a middle-aged Re'Ris with dark hair, pale iridescent skin, and light violet eyes. His smile appeared gentle.

What could possibly make you a Target?

Sree tapped a few areas and read the man's name and address listed on it:

Wiin Niino
Building XET
Cand

Sree closed his eyes in disappointment. He'd been hoping the Target would live in another city, so Sree would have more time. But instead, the man lived in Cand, Sree's current location. And by the looks of his building letter code...

"No," Sree murmured under his breath. "It can't be..."

Building XET sat across the street from the restaurant.

Right in front of him lived his Target.

Anxiety twisted his guts. Sree glanced down at the picture once again. The man continued to softly smile.

What am I going to do?

Lightning bolted brightly in front of him.

Make a decision, he thought. If he couldn't make himself go after the Target yet, he could at least take a step towards doing something. *At least get off the street.*

The Cand Hotel, where he'd been assigned to stay for his First Assignment, loomed over him.

Right next to the restaurant.

If nothing else, he still had four days left before his deadline. Four days to find the courage to do what he'd been designed to do. There were rumors about tips or tricks for your First Assignment—do you go after the Target immediately, do recon, get to know their routine, etc.? Even his Mother's Mother had given him pointers when she could. Everyone in school gossiped about these tactics, convinced they knew exactly what they'd do when their First Assignment came up.

It had always been strange, though, when a fellow classmate wouldn't return from their First Assignment. At some point, the school would announce the names of the successful candidates. No mention occurred afterwards of those who'd failed and began their life in the Labor Force.

Since you could begin your First Assignment at age 15, and Sree had chosen not to, he'd naturally gravitated towards younger peers who were less concerned with their First Assignment, though the topics of their conversations eventually always came around to the same two things: how exciting it would be to kill someone and how amazed they were at Sree's family line.

Both topics made Sree fairly uncomfortable.

Because of this, he found himself retreating further from these discussions over the past year, eventually isolating himself and becoming an outcast. Especially because he quickly became the oldest one at his school. Most didn't wait very long past the Age of Progression to apply. And Lessons ended when you turned 16 anyway, so as he approached that milestone, his peers disappeared one by one.

Something he hadn't taken into account when he'd figured out how alone he'd be without friends.

There could still be a way out of this, he told himself. *You may not have to kill your Target.* The words circled in his head over and over again and he desperately clung to them, believing the more he thought them, the more likely they would come true.

As he walked through the doors to the hotel, he wondered about his classmates. What would they think when his name didn't float over the speakers at school as a success story? How much shameful gossip would be spread about him, ruining his family name when they learned of the disgraceful avoidance of his genetic line?

Guilt ate at his insides. How could he not go through with this Assignment after everything his family had accomplished? They'd devoted themselves to protecting their planet, their culture. And he planned to destroy all they'd worked for.

Stop being so dramatic, he scolded himself. *You aren't that important. Your family's name will be fine, no matter how much you mess things up. Their accomplishments won't have changed just because you can't live up to them.*

The words sounded hollow, even to himself. He knew their reputation would indeed be tarnished. It was only logical. But at this point, he realized he'd thrown out logic ages ago.

Besides, he finished thinking as he headed towards his hotel room, still desperate, *maybe you can somehow still eliminate the Target? Do what you're meant to do, meant to be.*

His insides clenched even tighter at the thought.

Chapter 9

Panaan held tight to her Mother's hand as she tried her hardest to keep up. Paranoia seemed to have infested every inch of her Mother's mind and had only gotten worse over the past few months. At nearly 15 standard years of age, Panaan understood the aspects of their world, that there were Targets who needed to be eliminated, and that lately her Mother feared becoming this more than anything else.

She supposed it could be because Panaan's Father had been targeted and eliminated when she'd been three. She hardly even remembered him anymore. Her life and her memories over time consisted pretty much of just she and her Mother.

But her Mother had been struggling at her Laborer's job the past couple of months. She'd come home each night, more tired than ever, complaining about extra hours and harder tasks. Recently, several coworkers stopped showing up for their shifts. One a week. After the fourth incident, her Mother looked into it—they'd all become Targets and been subsequently eliminated.

"I knew it!" her Mother said at the time, practically hissing the words. "They are targeting my coworkers. It's just a matter of time before I'm next!"

Panaan, who'd been styling her own silvery locks, accidentally knocked her elbow against the doorframe at the outburst and rolled her eyes. "Mother, that's not how the Makers choose Targets. You know this. It's not personal. I'm sure your coworkers did something to become Targets." Rubbing her throbbing elbow, she internally cursed their small lodgings. They'd had to downsize after her Father's Passing On and the one bedroom for the two of them started to feel more and more cramped the older she'd gotten.

"That's what I used to think. Your Father, he tried to tell me otherwise. He said he was special, a threat, and those in charge knew it. He'd disappear for days at a time, claiming he needed to do research about himself, about the Makers, but I just thought... stupidly I worried he'd found another romantic interest besides myself." Her Mother shook her head, spittle at the corner of her mouth. "But I was wrong. Don't you see? He'd become a threat and someone at the top is using their power to eliminate threats. And you don't understand, Daughter. My coworkers and I, we saw things. Things at work. Things we weren't supposed to..."

When Panaan pressed her for more information, her Mother wouldn't divulge anything else about the statement, saying only she didn't want her Daughter to know information that might make her a Target as well.

Panaan reassured her, dismissing the "Target" theory. "Just do your job and you'll be fine."

But her Mother couldn't seem to calm down about it.

Even worse, she wouldn't let Panaan out of her sight.

So, they'd walk, together, the seven blocks to Central Processing every morning before Lessons, hand in hand, even at Panaan's age, to check if her Mother was a Target or not.

Two days ago, her Mother's worst fear was confirmed.

She'd become a Target.

Panaan almost found this to be a blessing in disguise. Now, they could prepare for an attack, and, if successful, her Mother may even become an assassin! Targets could defend themselves, and if they won against an assassination attempt, they were awarded all the status and accolades of their assassin. Panaan often let herself get caught up in imagining their new life—other Re'Ris no longer looking down on them and being free to move to a more upscale location, currency in their pockets to burn.

But today, her Mother came home early from work, forehead wrinkled, lips tight. She hadn't said a word, just pulled Panaan from their apartment. They'd traveled well over a mile to an area they didn't usually go, away from her school and her Mother's work at Central Processing

"Mother," Panaan called out with what breath she had left. "Can you slow down? What's going on?"

Her Mother's answer came via a tighter grip on her Daughter's hand and a more forceful tug forward.

They turned the last corner of their street and hurried down the next street. Across the way sat the Cand Hotel. They'd gone in a huge, weaving circle to end up just a few blocks south of Central Processing, when they usually approached the building every day from the north. Her Mother must have wanted to change their route so they wouldn't be found by an assassin so easily.

Panaan always loved to look at the buildings around Central Processing as they walked; she rarely made it to this section of the city but enjoyed the architecture here just as much. The structures were all different. Some were rectangular and made of stone, full of rows upon rows of windows that looked like neat little teeth. Others were short and fat, with rounded black roofs, like little capped fungi. She'd often stare at the closed curtains to some of the buildings, making up stories about the Re'Ris inside and their living situations. If in the hotel, perhaps they were on vacation, trying to get away from their boring Laborer positions—although she didn't really know if Laborers were *allowed* vacations. She and her Mother certainly had never been on one. Or maybe these mystery Re'Ris were entertaining interplanetary visitors in their homes—here to see their beautiful planet's capital or to start a new business.

But they'd never come from this direction before and the Cand Hotel surpassed anything she'd seen so far. It appeared tall and slender, with glistening tinted windows for walls instead of the flat dull metal utilized by Central Processing.

To her surprise, her Mother dragged her towards the hotel instead of continuing on to Central Processing.

Excited by the change, Panaan wondered if her Mother planned to fight back against her assassin. She knew *technically* she wasn't supposed to help, but no Rule stated that a bystander couldn't be a distraction. Once inside, however, her focus shifted to the glory of the internal design of the building.

First, the ceiling stretched high above her head, as if the first and second floors didn't exist. At the top were jeweled lights of different shapes and sizes, looking like an intricate constellation. Second, intricately woven cloth braids of multi-toned gold and white hung from the ceiling, crisscrossing in some areas. The lights glinted off the glittery gold and shed sparkles across the ceiling and upper walls. And lastly, everything shone and gleamed, polished to perfection, so that in multiple moments she could see reflections of herself and her Mother in the countertops, tiled floors, and mirrored walls. She'd never experienced anything so extravagant in her life and had *no* clue as to why she and her Mother were in a place like this.

Having gawked enough, Pannan then noticed a young man moving through the lobby, his eyes full of pain, his face pensive and tense.

For a moment, the sight of him made her sad, but then, as she and her Mother headed to the elevator, her attention shifted away from him and into excitement at seeing the lavish room they'd acquired.

Chapter 10

Wiin Niino's eyes raced beneath their lids as the dream flashed through his sleeping mind.

Sweat from his body dripped everywhere.

Why was he sweating? He shouldn't be nervous. He'd done this over a dozen times already.

Maybe because of the heat?

After all, he currently sat cramped inside a cabinet, waiting.

But it wasn't hot. In fact, he felt quite comfortable—his back pressing gently against a stack of clothing, his head resting on the inside of the cool metallic door, his eye peering through the crack between the door and its frame. He didn't even need to use energy to skin-shift since his Target wouldn't be able to see him in this hiding spot.

Then why? He was soaked *with the stuff. It slickened his hands and face. It slid in rivulets down his shirt and along his spine.*

What's wrong with me? *he thought.* I'm doing what I'm supposed to. I'm here to kill my Target. Nothing is out of place. Nothing is different.

And yet his breathing came in shallow wheezes and his skin itched. His head pounded while his jaw clenched.

Then, movement.

His breath caught in his throat. His Target had returned home. She dumped a stack of datapads on the table and pulled her hair off her face and neck, securing it into a sloppy up-do. With a sigh, she pulled out a chair and began sorting through the mess.

A Superior? *he wondered. Although she looked very young to be teaching. Perhaps she was new and she'd taught the wrong Lesson? Is that why she'd been targeted for assassination?*

What does it matter? *he scolded himself.* It doesn't matter what she's done. You've never cared before.

She picked up one of the datapads and leaned against her chair. Absently twirling a piece of loose hair, she began to wordlessly read the screen.

Wiin wondered what she was reading. A Lesson? An Assignment? An essay from a student?

Stop this! Stop seeing her as an individual. Just get rid of her!

But he couldn't stop. He couldn't make his brain quiet. Thoughts kept racing through his head about her identity and what made her so weak that she had to be permanently removed from the Re'Ris species.

It's not your job to figure that out. She has already been judged. Just do it!

He burst forth through the cabinet door. Her eyes widened and she shrieked. The datapad slipped from her hands and clattered to the floor.

He'd already reached her by that point, hands locked around her throat, cutting off the scream, cutting off her air.

She got in one kick.

Air whooshed out of him and his grip slackened for a moment. He heard her gasp.

"Kill me," she said, her voice hoarse from the strangulation, "but others will discover Central Processing's lie—!"

His hands tightened before she'd finished the last word. She struggled for a few moments, but after that, no fight remained. Her iridescent skin blued, her eyes bulged.

She went limp.

He let go. Her body crumpled to the floor.

Her final words stuck in Wiin's mind. What had she been talking about? What did she mean? Sounded something like Central Processing's lies?

It doesn't matter, *he reminded himself.* She's dead. You did your job. She's...

And then he heard it. The soft yet unmistakable sound of air being drawn into someone's body.

She was breathing.

She wasn't dead.

KILL HER!

He fled.

Scrambling out of her home, he sprinted down the street. He ran for blocks, not stopping until a leg muscle seized up and he fell to the ground.

Oh Makers, *he thought.* I left her alive. I left her ALIVE!

Wiin's eyelids flew open. His skin, which had been color-changing during the intensity of the dream, settled into its natural dark, shimmery gray. The dream faded, but the memory remained. Three years ago, he'd left his Target alive. To this day, he still didn't know why.

He stretched out his long fingers, feeling over the metal-edged book in his lap. He'd fallen asleep reading again.

Most Re'Ris's didn't even know non-digital books still existed, relying on datapads and computer terminals to provide them with reading and writing materials. But Wiin had gained possession of several antiques, and his small residential unit contained stacks of metal books, plant fiber tomes, and cloth scrolls. He'd often wonder about their varying sizes, some not much larger than his palm, others wider and taller than his torso. The inks and etchings on many of them were faded and worn, but their beauty, their feel, and most of all their scent felt almost like an intoxicant to Wiin. He would sometimes sit for hours, breathing in the stale odors, while feeling his life's stressors melt away.

If anyone in Cand, or anywhere else on the planet for that matter, looked inside Wiin's unit, they would have come to one of two conclusions: either believe him to be insane or realize exactly what he possessed and immediately call Central Authority.

These items were unlike anything else on this world. Originally located inside Central Processing, the collection he now stored took him months to acquire, and still more existed. He wondered how many individuals even knew of their presence, but it seemed, so far at least, they did not know of their absence.

However, if everything went to plan, their absence would not remain secret for long...

Wiin shifted the book off his lap, walked through the space in his apartment to a window, and peered out into the evening.

The boy sat in the restaurant across the street, still not ready to confront his Target, using up as much of the remaining three days as possible to avoid his destiny.

Wiin pitied him but steeled his resolve.

This is the only way...

It was almost time.

Wiin thought he'd be nervous, knowing what would occur soon, but a contented calm flowed over him. He felt ready.

He only hoped Sree would be ready, too.

Chapter 11

Sree couldn't seem to leave the restaurant today. Not because he still felt hungry, he just didn't know where else to go. So, he either paced in his hotel room or sat here.

Two days had already passed. He'd never known time to slip by so stealthily.

He spent the bulk of the previous day researching his Target, Wiin Kiino, with the hopes of discovering a way out. Or something that might make it okay to eliminate him. Sree realized he didn't have any idea what made an individual a Target in the first place. Did the Makers have criteria? A checklist which showed the balance of useful versus useless, and when the scales tipped too far to one side, you became a Target?

If any information existed about Wiin, Sree couldn't find it. Or didn't have access to it. Besides an address, the only other information he'd found told him that Wiin worked at Central Processing.

But that seemed odd. Sree frowned. There *had* to be

something else about the man's background. Basic knowledge about an individual was public. Work span. Schooling. Relatives.

But in Wiin's case...nothing.

How could this be? How could someone exist, but have such a limited record?

So today, Sree sat in the restaurant, not really tasting the food he ate or paying attention to the digital ads splayed on the beige-toned walls. The atmosphere felt a bit on the cheap side, with glowing multi-colored lights in the four corners and a twinkle-booth in the center for anyone celebrating a birthday, anniversary, or completing their First Assignment. He'd never been to a place like this before because his family either had their food prepared and delivered for them, or his Mother's Mother made it. The rare occasions they went out to eat were at much more upscale venues, with private rooms and personalized menus.

Instead of leaving the restaurant, Sree stared at building XET across the street, where Wiin lived, next door to the Cand Hotel.

The ironic coincidence was not lost upon Sree. Of all the places on Re'Ris, his Target lived within seconds of walking distance from the hotel he'd been designated to stay in for his First Assignment.

He couldn't have asked for an easier kill.

Why couldn't there have been anything *less easy about this?* Sree thought, his gaze half hollow with despair. *Even where he works would make this kill easy. I could just wait in hiding, skin-shifted, until he showed up for his job at Central Processing. No one would care if I eliminated him in broad daylight outside the building in front of everyone else. And my Mother's Mother told me it's the easiest way to secure a kill—if the Target doesn't know they are a Target, they may still go to work.*

Many Targets had been killed that way over the years. Apparently, it became a running joke among assassins to secure a kill in this manner and was often scoffed at as an amateur move. His Mother's Mother would sometimes tell him about her elite circle of friends, some retired, some still active, and their accomplishments. The hierarchy of how "good" your assassinations were never appealed to Sree, but his Mother's Mother would spend hours on the vidlinks gossiping with them about it.

Sree's stare across the street hardened as the sun began to set in the sky. Since normal shift hours had ended, he doubted his Target remained at work. He wondered if the man had gone home already, currently standing behind one of the darkened windows in the apartment building across the way. Did he already know he'd been targeted? Had he fled? Set a trap for Sree? Or could he still be oblivious to his fate?

Sree assumed that since Wiin worked at Central Processing, he probably knew he'd been targeted. Workers there had the easiest access to such information, what with the multitude of CrossLattice terminals at their disposal. So, Sree didn't want to just walk up to the man's door. A trap seemed to be the most likely outcome.

The server cleared the half-eaten meal from the table. "Anything wrong with the food?" she asked, her voice chipper.

"No."

Oblivious to Sree's plight, the busy server nodded at two new customers who entered the establishment and said to Sree out of the side of her mouth, "Let me know if you need anything else," before walking away.

"Hm," Sree said, non-committal. He didn't mind her leaving him alone. The less attention he brought to himself, the better.

Peering around the restaurant, he wondered how many of these individuals were Laborers versus being assassins? How many were currently Targets? Or on Assignment? What were the ratios? Sree had never taken the time to ask his family these sorts of questions.

Faan once spoke to him about her off-world travels, and how

her identity as an assassin needed to be kept secret.

"Why?" Sree asked when he'd been very young and just learning.

"Because others don't understand our world, our ways. The Makers, in their infinite wisdom, choose those who no longer serve a purpose." She'd scowled at Sree's incredulous expression. "They aren't monsters. That's why they allow Targets to learn their status and give them a chance to redeem themselves by killing their assassin first." She'd smiled. "On some worlds, citizens kill each other over petty reasons, like food or money. They start wars because of deities or land. And they have entire authority organizations to punish those who do. It's so... uncivilized."

"We have Central Authority," he countered.

"True, but how many Re'Ris actually get arrested? You'd have to really mess up, and our Rules are pretty simple. Besides, I'd rather be a Target than in a jail cell. Or exist as a Laborer."

That had been his family's mentality as long as he could remember, instilling the worst dread inside him about being anything except an assasssin. Until their Mother and Father died. Then, everything changed about Faan...

She became obsessed with the idea of their parents being murdered, instead of dying in an accident.

No one believed her.

And then she'd died proving her theory to be correct.

The news story surrounding her findings about their Mother and Father still remained unpublished. Sree wondered why, but his Mother's Mother said that murder hadn't happened for generations, and she felt certain no one wanted to report on it. Even if orchestrated by off-worlders, what good would it do to bring a stain to his Mother's and Father's names? To be murdered? Like animals?

But Sree now knew the truth. It hadn't been an accident. And he hated that Faan died to prove this while no one else knew.

Thoughts of his family still rolling around in his mind, Sree noticed a mother and her daughter across the street. He'd seen them the day before. The daughter appeared to be close to his age, maybe a little younger.

Had she completed her First Assignment yet? Did her mother feel pride and now wanted to bring her daughter to a victory lunch to celebrate? Were his own Mother and Father watching from beyond, and instead of being honored by his actions, were shaking their heads at his cowardice?

Sree's guts roiled inside him and he turned his view away from the two across the street. With quick movements, he headed towards the restroom to splash water on his face and calm himself down from his racing thoughts.

Chapter 12

On the third day at the Cand Hotel, Panaan saw the young man from the lobby sitting in the restaurant across the street. While she and her Mother walked each day in seemingly endless circles, Panaan had nothing to do but look around. She'd tried to make relevant conversation, but her Mother wouldn't respond to any pertinent questions.

She noticed the young man the very next day as they left the hotel. He did nothing but stare, never moving. He didn't even seem to breathe. Though she liked to imagine stories for others, she found it difficult to think of one for him. He seemed so strange. So...removed.

A mention of him to her Mother when she saw him there again resulted in a brush off, a distracted "that's nice, dear" as they kept moving. The hotel had a strict policy—no food inside—so they needed to leave each day to eat. The nearby restaurant, where the young man sat, promised higher bill prices than they could afford, so they walked a few blocks to a nearby market and bought already prepared processed food which could be eaten straight from the container.

Even though they'd only been eating this way a couple of days, Panaan already tired of the food. They were by no means rich, but her Mother saved up and bought a portable heating unit, a single, to cook on at home. Every so often they could skip going to the massive cafeterias which offered the cheapest meals, and instead ate something specially prepared from her own recipes.

Today, Panaan secretly wished for any other food, including the cafeteria meals, which at least were hot. Eating cold, processed food didn't suit Panaan and she complained about it that morning.

"We need to save money. And we need our strength," was her Mother's curt reply.

Strength for what? Panaan hoped there would have been some sort of defense plan in place against the assassin that would find her Mother, but it seemed as though her Mother's only goal revolved around avoiding the situation by simply not going home, merely attempting to survive past the time limit for the assassin to complete their mission.

But in Panaan's mind, there lay the problem. You never knew how much time an assassin received to complete their mission. First Assignments were given 6 days, or a standard week, but future Assignments were given the amount of time deemed necessary by the Makers, depending on difficulty of the task, location of the Target, etc. Her Mother's assassin may be coming from the other side of the planet and have months to complete their task. This would prevent them from staying indefinitely at the pricey hotel. Not to mention her Mother couldn't keep calling in sick at work before someone came to check on her status.

But any attempt on Panaan's part to suggest a different strategy fell on deaf ears.

As she and her Mother left the Cand Hotel this current morning, their third day since her Mother learned she'd been targeted, Panaan's breath caught in her throat. The young man was there again in the restaurant! So still, unmoving, unblinking it seemed. His face a paler gray than his usual dark coloring, his lips slightly slack, his eyes glazed over.

Maybe he was dead.

"Mother!" she cried out. "The man in the restaurant is still there. This is the third day!"

As if finally hearing her daughter, Panaan's Mother jerked her head in the direction of the young man.

"Oh Makers!" she cried out. "Oh, please no. I haven't done anything wrong!"

Fear clenched at Panaan's chest. *Wait,* she thought, *could that mean Mother thinks this young man is...the assassin?*

Shifting her gaze from her Mother's terrified face, a gasp escaped Panaan's lips.

The young man no longer sat by the window. He'd disappeared.

A yank on her arm as her Mother pulled her away from the street and towards an alley.

"Ow!" Panaan cried out. But then she saw it. A flicker. A shimmer. Against the alley wall.

"RUN!" her Mother yelled.

But following the command wouldn't make a difference. Panaan wasn't a Target. Nothing would happen to her. And she couldn't even help her Mother defend herself.

"I promise, I won't tell anyone what I saw!" her Mother pleaded to the seemingly empty alleyway.

Then the shimmer materialized between herself and her Mother, blocking her vision, the hooded individual facing away from Panaan. The figure stood just a little taller than herself. Thin, agile.

With quick movements, the assassin struck.

A gurgle from the opposite side of the killer.

From her Mother.

Immediately after, the figure vanished, color-changing to match the grayish-brick surroundings, as if they'd never been there.

Her Mother lay in the alleyway, her eyes wide open in terror and shock, a long piece of metal sticking out of her neck.

Panaan screamed. She couldn't help it. She knew, intellectually, this might be a possibility, but now, seeing that it actually happened...

Frantic, she raced to her Mother, feeling for a pulse she knew wouldn't be there.

"Mother..." she managed, her voice strangled. "I'm sorry...you warned me...I thought..."

Tears blurred her vision. But they weren't out of sadness.

They were out of anger.

Panaan glared across the street to the vacant spot in the restaurant where the young man had been sitting.

She remembered everything about his face.

He'd done this to her Mother.

He'd taken away the only person who mattered to her.

He was just doing his job, she tried to reason with herself.

But Panaan couldn't shake what her Mother told her—about her coworkers disappearing. About a plot against them. Against her Mother.

Thoughts began to churn in her mind, lashing out at her sanity, propelling her into a state of frenzied compulsion.

This wasn't right.

Things were not what they were supposed to be.

Her thoughts focused into a pinpoint of blame, rage, and grief.

The young man from the restaurant must be involved in the conspiracy.

CHAPTER 13

"Are you all right?"

Sree glanced up at the server who'd spoken, his hands clenched to stop them from shaking. He'd just returned from the restroom, feeling a bit calmer, but still on edge. A small datapad showing his bill sat in front of him, but he hadn't picked it up yet.

"I'm fine," Sree lied.

"Don't tell me it was your meal," the server said, eyeing him warily.

"No," he managed, making the payment. "I haven't been feeling well. I'm going to head out."

"Okay, but I'd use the rear entrance. A Disposal Team is across the street right now."

It took a moment for Sree to register what the comment meant. A specific division of the Labor Force was assigned to remove and dispose of the bodies of assassinated Targets. Every building, every home, every street corner had a system in place if someone found a body or saw an assassination: press a button, call the Disposal Team.

Which means someone across the street had just been eliminated.

Sree's head shifted against his will, moving his eyeline towards the situation outside, compelled to look at the situation. Sure enough, the team currently lifted a body for removal. The young woman he'd seen earlier with her Mother sat on the ground, staring at the activity, seemingly in shock.

The restaurant bustled around him. Business as usual.

No one cared that someone just died across the street.

And why should they? Targets were eliminated all the time. You couldn't live on a planet full of assassins and not be comfortable with seeing someone killed on a regular basis.

The server nodded towards the rear entrance. "That way," she said again. She peered at his face for a moment, her brows pulling together. "Feel better," she added.

Keeping his head low, Sree exited, avoiding the final clean-up of the scene as he crossed behind the emergency vehicle, and headed toward his hotel room. Once inside, he took a seat on the squishy bed, facing the window. Clear skies mocked him with their sense of serenity. Clenching his jaw, he forced his hands together, willing them to quit trembling.

It wasn't as if he'd never witnessed a death before. In fact, the first assassination he remembered seeing had been performed by his sister when he'd been 10 and she'd been 16. They'd gone on an outing, just the two of them, so she could teach him about flying their family's personal starcraft. Faan often used it to follow Targets off-world.

Sree recalled having been very excited. He rarely got to spend time alone with Faan and, even though she strictly went along with everything concerning The Makers, the Rules, and her patriotic duties, she also loved teaching him new things. His favorite part about time with her though? She would often treat him to one of his favorite desserts: fillapops.

Sree could even picture the bright blue frozen treat, similar to the color of the flowers in the front yard of their house, when suddenly they'd taken a detour from their usual route home.

"Why are we going this way?" Sree had asked.

Faan bent down to his height and pointed at someone outside a nearby diner. "See that man, there?" she asked.

Sree nodded, locating the tall, lean individual, who currently whistled a tune while he worked.

"He is no longer a productive member of society. The Makers have decided he is no longer of value. So, he's now..." she said, waiting for him to finish her sentence.

Sree scrunched his forehead. "A Target?"

Faan treated him with one of her rare smiles. "Exactly."

He beamed at her.

"Now," she said, with a wink. "Watch." Before his eyes, she seemed to shimmer out of existence, using their genetic skills to match her surroundings.

Doing his best to track her, which involved him squinting and assuming the slight curve of a figure in the light must be her, he stared down the alley at the man, who tinkered with the digital sign hanging in front of his shop.

A strange gurgling noise issued from his mouth. He clasped a hand around his throat, which began to bleed, before collapsing to the ground.

Within moments, Faan returned in full sight next to Sree.

"And what do we do now?" she asked, her voice the same tone, even though she'd just killed someone.

"We find an orange button!" he answered. They located the button to call a Disposal Team. Faan even allowed him to press it.

He'd been so happy, so proud to be a part of Faan's seemingly incredible life.

However, and Sree had never told a soul, but when they'd walked away, he'd peered behind him at the body, now laying in an ungraceful heap on the street corner.

And a cold sweat broke out across his skin.

Any excitement he'd had moments before because of answering his sister's question correctly dissipated faster than his fillapop could melt under a heat lamp.

He'd brushed it off, convinced his feelings towards assassinations would change over time.

So far, they hadn't. And now, sitting in the hotel room, recalling the woman's body being carried away in the alleyway, hearing the cry of anguish from her daughter's mouth...Sree knew he'd never feel all right about it.

And yet here he was.

Waiting to perform his own First Assignment.

To end someone else's life.

Unable to push aside such unhelpful repetitious thoughts, Sree lay on his bed staring at the hotel's ceiling, his mind centered around Wiin Niino's upcoming death. But not by his own hand.

Perhaps Wiin would walk out of his apartment building and get hit by a moving tixa.

Or fall out of his window to his death.

Or be burned up when his building got struck by an atmospheric electrical discharge that set the place on fire.

Anything that would make it so Sree wouldn't have to kill him.

But Sree hadn't even seen Wiin leave the building in the last three days.

Maybe he died in his sleep? Or slipped and fell and broke his neck? Or...

Sree rebuked himself. How could he sit here and hope somebody would die?

Besides, he should *want* to kill the Target, not hope that Wiin would be accidentally killed so that he wouldn't have to go through with the assassination. He wasn't supposed to be hiding away in some hotel room, praying for a man to be dead.

And yet he couldn't help wishing it. Maybe then he could just *say* he'd killed Wiin. And Sree would still be able to Cross Over and then get off this planet and run...

"It doesn't matter," he said out loud. "He's not going to be dead. He's probably resting comfortably watching vidlink programs and thinking, 'Life is so great right now.' And then I get to burst in and slice a hole in his body and watch him die."

Sree rolled over, stuffing the yellow-wrapped pillow underneath the side of his face. *You're being an idiot! Just do this one thing and then you can Cross Over and not embarrass your family and get off this stupid rock and...*

And what? Even if he left the planet, he'd still receive Assignments. He wouldn't be able to stop killing until his own Target Lifetime Quota became filled, and with his family background, he assumed the Makers would want him in the assassin business for the rest of his life.

Listen to me, still thinking about Assignments as if there is something wrong with them. Get over this! The Makers knew that evolution could only develop correctly if the weak were expunged. And the only way to do that is to determine who is weak and have them removed from society so that others can flourish.

"But what makes someone weak?" he muttered, once again circling the same still unanswered subject. "What are the determining factors the Makers look for? Is it that they are doing poorly as Laborers? Is it that they have committed crimes against other citizens? Is it that they look strange or act weird or think about things that Re'Ris aren't supposed to think about?"

Sree's gaze drifted toward the image of Wiin splayed across the datapad, which lay on the nightstand next to the bed. *Take him,* he thought, continuing the rant in his head. *This man looks nice and happy and sweet and gentle. What could possibly have made him so terrible that he no longer deserves to live? Is he a coercer? A thief? A bad dresser? Why have I never wondered what makes someone useless before?*

Panic threatened to overwhelm him as such thoughts continued to mount, churning out of his control to silence them. *How can the Makers just* know *he is supposed to die? And why do they think I'm the one to do it? Is he an easy kill? Or a challenge given to me because of my family name?*

Anxiety made its move and a flash of heat surged throughout his body. He wiped away a thin film of cold perspiration from his upper lip, noticing his hand had changed color against his will from the stress. An internal dialogue fought inside his head.

You have no choice. You are out of time. You have to kill him.

I CAN'T.

You have to. You don't want to die. You can't run. And you musn't let your family down, not after everything they've been through. You have to do this.

I CAN'T. I CAN'T!

Go. Now. Don't think about it. Just walk out of the room. Walk across to his building. His apartment. Kick open the door. And do it.

I CAN'T MURDER HIM.

It's not murder. He's supposed to die. It's ordained.

LEAVE ME ALONE.

How can I? I'm you.

Sree's feet moved. He didn't ask them to. He didn't *want* them to. But they moved anyway.

They left his hotel room, transported him across the street, and into Building XET.

Programmed. That's what it felt like. Something had programmed him to continue towards his Target. Fear? Instinct? He didn't know.

Wiin's floor.

Wiin's unit's hallway.

Wiin's door.

In some delusional corner of his brain, which held no semblance of common sense or rationality, Sree truly believed that in the time it took him to leave his hotel room, walk across the street, and make it to Wiin's apartment, he would have discovered a way out of this whole mess.

Unfortunately, no change in circumstances or brilliant plan had popped into his head.

Sree stood there, invisible to the naked eye. The door appeared ordinary—metal, with an etched carving of the apartment number. The hallway looked like any other hallway, with pops of light and woven lines of brown and beige along the walls. Dark brown carpet barely flattened underneath his feet, the knap already worn down from the thousands of steps of residents and visitors before him.

Sweat glazed his palms. He frantically wiped them against his pants as he stared at the only physical thing standing between him and killing.

This is insane. What am I even doing here? I don't want to assassinate this man. I can't *assassinate this man! But if he knows I'm here to kill him, he's going to kill me. What am I going to do?* He couldn't seem to let go of the repeating thoughts and they spiked his anxiety even higher.

So, he simply stood there, staring at the door—his right hand twitching occasionally as if tempted to grab the handle while the toes in his feet gripped the insides of his shoes as if preparing to run. Torn between attacking and fleeing, he couldn't do either.

In that moment, he pictured Wiin opening the door, smiling, wondering about Sree's visit.

And while picturing that image, Sree absolutely knew he couldn't kill that man.

He chose to be a Laborer instead.

All the shame and embarrassment it would cause his family didn't matter. The pain and drudgery he'd learned about Laborer's lives would now be his own because he'd never eliminate Wiin.

Resigned, Sree let out a deep exhale, and even though he'd doomed himself to a terrible existence, he knew he wouldn't continue with the Assignment and began to turn away.

Faster than he thought possible, the door swung open, revealing black space behind it.

Sree's skin-shift vanished at the shock. He did no more than gasp before a hand reached through the dark doorway, grabbed him, and yanked him inside.

Chapter 14

Blackness appeared in front of him when he opened his eyes. Sree could hear his own heartbeat. It pounded so loudly that he knew whoever else occupied the room must be able to hear it, too. Yet no one commented on its frantic beating.

The rest of his surroundings offered nothing but complete silence. Struggling to get control of his body's desire to replace adrenaline with anxiety, Sree forced himself to slow his breathing and lower his heartrate. He'd trained with his sister to do this. He could hear her reminding him not to panic.

He was simply inside the unit of the man he needed to kill and couldn't see or hear anything.

No. No need to panic whatsoever.

Except...at least he wasn't dead.

Did Wiin plan on toying with him first? To what end? Assassinations were usually done in the quickest way possible. They weren't malicious or hatred-fed. They were Assignments to be carried out, no different than cleaning up your room or watering the plants.

Except Sree only knew what he'd been taught in Lessons. What his family believed and relayed to him. He'd never truly been out in the world to experience firsthand what others thought or did. Perhaps others felt differently about their kills...

Just before his emotions paralyzed him, Sree heard a noise—a soft hiss followed by a tiny burst of light. Moments later a flame flickered to life a couple meters away from him and a soft glow filled the room. Sree blinked repeatedly and took in his surroundings.

The room appeared quite large, with wide, curtained windows. The bedroom and a lounging area were combined in the main space. A small kitchen nook nestled on one end while a partially opened door revealed a washroom opposite.

The sparse furniture all looked supremely comfortable—not the fashionable décor his Mother had decorated their first house with, which looked beautiful but felt uncomfortable to use, or the expensive and plush items of their second home picked out by his Mother's Mother, where the rooms seemed to go on for miles and were balanced perfectly with their furniture and decorations, like impartial showrooms. No, this place felt relaxing, minus the sense of dread that hovered in the air.

However, even though there weren't a lot of pieces of furniture, other objects and items filled the space instead, which gave it a sense of coziness and safety that one could only find in a place full with things that were loved by the occupant.

Studying further, Sree didn't see any sort of pattern to the objects for decoration. They filled the apartment in a seemingly random order, placed on top of shelving units or leaning against the baseboards. Large urns, technological gadgets he couldn't identify, medical equipment...

What is *all this stuff?*

Before he could contemplate further, Sree realized what many of the things were.

Books. Dozens of books.

Real books.

A different feeling flooded him: awe.

Sree had heard about books. Everyone had. In school, a student would be taught about tomes that once housed vital information. Examples from other worlds were sometimes passed around in class, to show how fragile and useless they were, their pages ripped or stained or even illegible due to moisture. Over the years, digital means proved more trustworthy to the Re'Ris—information couldn't be deleted permanently by a fire or a thief; backup files would prevent that. And since the Makers controlled everything, no one could splice or change the information without their consent, so it remained accurate over the centuries. To maintain this constancy, tangible sources of information were eventually removed from society.

A few pieces still existed in museums or at some universities, where Laborers had access to material that might be pertinent to their jobs, or a student could head over for a history field trip, but Sree had never been privy to these excursions; they'd been optional and he'd never felt the urge to attend. Because of this, he'd never actually *seen* a book in real life.

Sweeping his gaze across the room, Sree saw some books, most of them larger than the width of his body, sitting precariously on the shelves along the walls. The rest were scattered around the room: on the floor, on short tables, on cushioned chairs. Some lay open, and he noted their construction consisted of varying materials, with tattered pages faded and yellowed, or metal edges rusty and chipped, and even plant-based sheets curled and frayed.

Suddenly, a man appeared in front of him.

Sree's realization of his predicament returned full force, and he shifted his attention to the man sitting next to the light, its flame flickering inside a twisted glass bulb. The contraption looked ancient and extremely hazardous. No one used fire as a light source anymore. Electric heat sources were much safer. One slip and that small flame could wipe out the entire contents of the room, not to mention the rest of the building as well.

Terror flooded him once again. Could this man be a psychopath?

Sree finally found his voice. "Are you Wiin Niino?" The words came out guttural and automatic. He didn't even know why he'd asked. Sree already recognized him from his picture. Right now, he only cared what this man planned to do with him.

One corner of Wiin's mouth raised into a half smile. "Yes, Sree. I am your Target, Wiin Niino." He paused, the smile still lingering. "Are you going to finish your First Assignment and kill me?"

Shock hit Sree. "How do you know who I am? You're not supposed to know who your assassin is, only that you've been targeted.

"Answer my question and I will answer yours. Are you going to kill me?"

Sree feared responding. This wasn't how things should go. His Target simply striking up a conversation with him? Could it be a ploy to stall for time? A trap to gain information about him, or his family? The Kaano family name had success and wealth attached to it. Could this be...for ransom? Blackmail?

"You're my Target," Sree muttered.

"That's correct. I've been assigned to you for elimination." The man's dark gray skin fluctuated a bit, shimmering as if a weak wind rippled across his body.

Could it be that this man had failed as an assassin because his color-changing ability didn't work anymore? Is that why he wanted to stall? To convince Sree not to finish the deed, spare his remaining years?

Wiin asked once more, "Are you going to kill me?"

Sree hadn't been prepared for anything like this regarding an Assignment. Faan never told him a Target would want to speak with him. To what purpose? None of this made sense.

Thoughts filtered through Sree's head faster than he could process them, but none of them gave him any more insight into the situation. Oddly enough, though, he didn't feel threatened.

He should. Everything about this scene screamed "wrong." And yet...

Sree took a deep breath. Words fell from his lips without his consent. "I...I don't *want* to kill you," he said. He regretted them instantly, feeling like a pathetic weakling.

"But you are my assassin. I am your Target. *Want* is irrelevant."

More thoughts. More questions. Did this represent a normal type of First Assignment? A way to be evaluated? To see if an individual has what it takes, no matter the situation?

But how did the man *know* Sree's identity? That was impossible! Only the Makers knew the assassins when they assigned them to their Targets. And yet this man did. He'd probably known for days. He could have gone to Sree's house and killed him first. He could have checked around at local hotels and found out Sree stayed right across the street.

Instead, here they sat. Wiin let Sree find him. He'd let him come all the way to his apartment. Even though Sree'd been skin-shifted, Wiin still opened the door, somehow knowing he stood there, and pulled Sree inside to begin a conversation.

None of this made any sense.

Shaking his head, Sree demanded, "What's going on?"

Wiin's smile widened. "Not until you answer my question."

Sree didn't like this game anymore. The wrades on his wrists seemed to itch with their desire to complete the Assignment. And Sree was starting to not like this man.

Remaining firm, Sree said, "I'm not saying anything else until I know what's going on."

Wiin's face hardened. Apparently he didn't like that Sree wouldn't play along. "It shouldn't matter to you. You should have killed me already. What's stopping you?"

"I..." Anger surged up inside him. He thought about all the pressures in his life, pushing him this way and that to act a certain way, be a certain way. He thought about how much he didn't want to be here at all, what it took to even *get* himself to come here. "Look, I don't know what your problem is, but I can be whatever kind of assassin I want to be. It's my choice to decide when to kill you. It could be one second from now or the last moment before my time is up. As to if I will or not, I haven't decided yet."

"Well, I can't tell you what's going on if you're going to kill me."

Sree'd been trapped in a game like this before by his sister and wouldn't fall for it. "Uh-uh. You said if I answered your question, you would answer mine. You didn't say I had to answer with a 'yes' or 'no' response. I told you I haven't decided. That's an answer."

Wiin tilted his head, the amused smile returning to the corner of his mouth. "True. And clever. Very clever. That's good. You'll need to be clever." He crossed his legs. "You do realize that by *not* killing me you are signing your own death warrant."

Sree tensed and rose from the chair, prepared to flee. "Are you going to kill *me*?"

Wiin fully grinned. "I don't have to. Someone will be sent to eliminate you for failing your Assignment. You're too well known to keep you alive as a Laborer. But it wouldn't make much sense for me to bring you here if I was simply going to do it myself."

Confusion creased his brow. At first he wondered why he wouldn't become a Laborer. But then Wiin's other words trickled into understanding. "*Bring* me...? What do you mean? You're *my* Target. I found *you*."

Wiin paused, then spoke, his tone self-reflective. "I am taking a huge risk. And I believe you are who I need to help me, but..."

Confusion turned into bewilderment. "Huh?"

A sigh. Wiin then gestured for Sree to have a seat once more. "I've come too far, may as well go through with it. It'll be out of my hands soon enough and if it's not you, it's no one."

Still having no clue as to what Wiin's words meant, Sree found comfort in the only thing he could: he'd been offered a seat instead of the tip of a blade at his neck.

Sree sat once again on the plush chair across from Wiin, the only piece of furniture not currently covered by a book or strewn pages.

After a forceful inhale through his nose, Wiin began. "I arranged for you to be my assassin."

Stunned by the statement, Sree nearly slid off the edge of the chair. He eyed his captor. *The Makers choose Targets. Period.* "That isn't possible. You're not...only the Makers—"

Wiin cut him off. "Normally, that's true, but also no, obviously," he said, motioning towards his appearance, "I'm not one of the Makers."

Notions began to click together inside Sree's mind, but they only led to more questions. "If that's the case, how could you have any say in deciding assassins or their Targets?"

Wiin poured himself a drink from a long glass tube filled with honey-colored liquid. It smelled a touch floral, with some sort of earthy tone underneath. He offered some to Sree who declined, still leery about the whole situation.

"I work for Central Processing," Wiin explained, taking a sip from his drink.

A different feeling flooded through Sree. This man was a Laborer. But...he didn't seem worn down or beaten. His eyes remained vibrant, his skin a dark yellowish gray.

"But I need to start earlier," Wiin went on, "from before I was transferred there. Three years ago, I was given an Assignment. Nothing out of the ordinary, but when I arrived to kill my Target, I couldn't do it."

Sree's eyes widened. The man's statement represented grounds for treason. But he also hadn't killed someone, similar to how Sree didn't want to now. Intrigued, he asked, "Why not?"

A momentary look of wistfulness crossed Wiin's face as he took another sip of the thick liquid. "This is my favorite drink, you know. Extremely expensive. Imported. From a planet you've probably never heard of. But the Guardian who raised me brought it home one day after an off-world Assignment. Had my first taste around your age. Have wanted more ever since. Fitting, timing-wise, that I finally could afford to buy a bottle last week ..."

Sree shook his head, not understanding the randomness of this man's words. Could he be senile? Who cared about a drink? He'd just told Sree he hadn't killed his Target.

With a clearing of his throat, Sree re-encouraged Wiin to continue. "You were saying, about your Target? Why you didn't kill them...?"

Wiin smacked his lips after a longer drink. "I don't really know. I had killed before. Many times. And like I said, there was nothing remarkable about this Target or the circumstances for the kill, but I just couldn't do it. It didn't seem to make *sense* to me anymore. I kept wondering about her, about who she was, what she'd done to become a Target in the first place. It was as if...something in my brain changed, clicked over into a different thought pattern. But to this day, I don't know why."

"So, you didn't try to kill her?"

"Oh, I did. Strangulation. A preferred method for me, actually. I liked that it wasn't sloppy. No mess. Little to no screaming. I never liked the screaming."

Sree gulped. The wrades on his wrists seemed to twitch. Would they be *his* preferred method of eliminating his Targets?

Wiin's eyes cleared, as if pulling himself from his own thoughts. "I thought I'd killed her, but her breathing began again. And I ran."

"You...you ran?" Sree said, in disbelief.

"Yes. I fled the scene. I knew the first attempt on her life had been pure muscle memory. But knowing I'd have to try again...I couldn't do it. So, I left her there."

"Is she...is she still alive?"

Wiin shrugged. "I didn't check on her afterwards. Call it cowardice, but I didn't want to know if she'd died or if a new assassin finished the job. Because a part of me hoped she lived, and that felt too treasonous to admit."

A chill of relatability shivered through Sree. He felt like this man could be him, as though Sree would've reacted the same way. "So that's how you became a Laborer. You were demoted for not having finished your Assignment."

Wiin gave a soft smile. "They don't send experienced assassins to the Labor Force."

Sree frowned. "They don't? But Rule Twelve says—"

"I know what it says," he interrupted. "Do you think the Rules are followed all the time? Do you believe they would let someone like me go about my life as a Target, given another chance to become an assassin, after a failure that made no sense? No. Assassins that fail, especially later on in their careers, become Targets."

Sree shook his head. "That...that can't be true. The Laborers...where else do they come from?"

"Anyone who wouldn't make a good assassin from the start. Those who are unhealthy. Those who can't color-change well. Those who are unable to manage assassin tasks physically or mentally or emotionally. Anyone who can't plan an assassination. Etcetera. Almost all Laborers are chosen before they even start their First Assignment. That's why there are so many of them."

Sree now wondered about all the Laborers who existed on the planet. He never thought too much about them, but did they really outnumber assassins? If Re'Ris were designed to be assassins, why were there more Laborers? And to be sent off as

Laborers before they'd even attempted to become an assassin? That couldn't be true. "How could they possibly be chosen before they even do their First Assignment?"

A long sip and a sigh of contentment before Wiin responded. "They are weeded out in school. The Lessons help with that. Superior's notes are taken into account. Those who would make bad assassins are determined almost immediately. They are given 'fake' First Assignments with planted Targets, who help them to fail, so they can become Laborers. It's a way to 'maintain' the Rules to the outside world without seeming to break them."

Sree's head swirled with conflicting thoughts. This man just finished casually telling him that everything he'd been taught wasn't true. That most Laborers were chosen before they even got their First Assignments. That failed assassins *never* became Laborers at all, just became targeted themselves.

Fascinated, Sree thought about this. First of all, society deemed it inconceivable that the Rules were wrong. And yet... why would Wiin tell him lies? What could be the point of risking his life to make fake claims?

Second, if this were all true, he could see why the Makers wouldn't tell the Re'Ris that they would become Targets if they failed at an Assignment after being a successful assassin. It would change everything. Assassins endured plenty of stress just to complete their Assignment. The Makers *wanted* the assassins to be successful. But maybe it became obvious those who'd failed had proven too disgruntled once they became Laborers? So, the Makers decided to remove them from society instead?

Whatever the reason, Wiin still existed. Alive and well. After three years. How could that be possible if he hadn't completed his Assignment? "If what you say is true, why didn't you become a Target?"

"I cheated the system. Made sure I was 'demoted' to the Labor Force."

"So... if you're my Target now, does that mean you failed at your job at Central Processing? That you're no longer useful as a Laborer so you're a Target again?"

Wiin got up, made his way to one of the stacks of books, and ran his hand over each of their spines, as if searching for a specific title while he continued talking. "Actually, I fit in quite well at Central Processing. I didn't mind it. Preferred it, actually, to being an assassin. Horror stories are told of the walking dead who hate their daily lives, but it's not really like that. I enjoyed what I did. And I felt more comfortable as a Laborer than I ever did as an assassin."

Floored, Sree couldn't believe what he heard. He'd always been told Laborer jobs were grueling, demanding, and life-stealing. Could their lives be better than he thought?

Wiin continued. "But I knew they wouldn't let me stay there, not forever. They'd find me out eventually. Because I began poking around in areas I shouldn't." Pausing as he rested his fingers on a specific book, he concluded his story. "Ultimately the idea of being an assassin froze me to my core. I became *obsessed* with the notion that killing was wrong. Like you, I wanted to find something that proved it, and since I had access to all the archives at Central Processing, I thought I might have a better chance than most."

Sree shook his head. "What do you mean *all* the archives? Everyone has access to the archives."

Wiin gave him a soft smile. "Again, that is what they would like you to believe."

"Who are 'they?'"

"They are the ones who are in charge."

"You mean the Makers?"

"No. The Makers are a completely separate group. I will get to them soon enough. I mean the Head Superiors. I told you, Sree. I made *myself* a Target. *Your* Target. On purpose." Wiin set down his empty drink to pick up the book he'd chosen.

Sree's head spun. What could Wiin possibly mean? The

Makers were the only ones who were in charge, had been for...well since the creation of the Re'Ris species. Head Superiors existed to make sure the cities on the planet were *following* the Rules. They didn't *make* them.

Sree frowned, realizing now that Wiin must be part of some sort of conspiracy theory group. His sister had once warned him about folks like this, but he hadn't really cared at the time. She'd said they not only saw shadows that didn't exist, they created them so they felt justified in their notions.

Except...except no one had believed Faan when she said their Mother and Father had been murdered, not assassinated. And she'd been right...

Wiin picked up the book he wanted, wider than his torso, and awkwardly lifted it. Made of plant fiber, its binding appeared broken, its pages torn. With delicate movements, he transferred it over to the small table next to the chair Sree sat on. "As I was saying, I had access to *all* the archives, digital and otherwise, at Central Processing, including the very books you see in this room."

Sree sat up straight in his chair, a different sort of tension shooting through his body. "You mean you *stole* these books?"

Wiin nodded, oblivious to the fact that Sree appeared horrified by the crime. "Yes, Sree, I did. And once I'm dead, you will be the only one who will know what these pages contain. It is my hope that after knowing, you will be driven to find out what else is still hidden."

Sree's focus narrowed, fixating on a single word in what Wiin just said. "Wait a minute. What do you mean, once you're *dead*?"

Wiin blinked. "Well, you'll have to kill me, of course. I know you don't want to, which is why you're an excellent candidate to continue on with my mission, but it's the way it must be."

Blood drained from Sree's face. He stood up quickly, overturning a stack of books next to him. They banged into each other in the small space, particularly loud to Sree's ears. Babbling words burst from his mouth as he moved away from Wiin. "You...you don't know anything about me. I can do what I want when I want and I'll kill you if I want and...and you can't tell me when to ...or...what, do you want to die? Did you fix the system so that I'd kill you because you want to commit suicide? That's insanity! You're insane!"

"Sree, sit down."

"No!" he screeched, his voice shrill with panic. "I don't *want* to sit down. I don't even want to be here. You're crazy! And I'm going to tell the Central Authority about what you've done and then they will take you away and then..."

"...and then you won't have to kill me." Wiin finished for him. "Even now, even after all I've told you, all you care about is *not* having to kill me. You are still looking for a way out, aren't you? Except that there *is* no way out. Even if you succeed, even if you don't kill me and they for some un-Maker-ish reason allow you to stay alive, do you think they won't give you another Assignment? How are you going to get out of that situation? And the next? And the next?"

"I don't...I don't feel..." The room began to sway and the flame dimmed in and out. It became too much. He couldn't do it. He couldn't handle it.

"Sree?" he heard Wiin call out.

"I just..." Sree's eyes rolled upwards and he fell, crashing into the table next to him, knocking its contents to the floor. His head hit the plush carpet and a moment later he slipped into unconsciousness.

Chapter 15

Panaan sat at a desk, surrounded by several dozen others, all of which were empty of occupants. The white domed room echoed with the taps of her toes against the floor, but she didn't notice. She'd just finished the final class of her formal education because tomorrow was her birthday and she could apply for her First Assignment. Even though an individual could have up to a year after they turned 15, Panaan wanted to do it right away. But she couldn't seem to leave the room.

She'd been sitting for hours.

All her classmates had left for the day. They would return tomorrow, as usual, only ending their education when they applied for their First Assignment.

But she didn't want to go home. Her Mother wouldn't be there.

Because she was dead.

There'd been some outward expressions of sympathy from her friends, but Panaan could see past the pity in their eyes to...disgust. Panaan now held the status of an orphan of two eliminated Targets. The shame of that outweighed any feelings of compassion.

Obviously, they thought her Mother, and possibly her Father, had been some sort of drains on society, since they'd been targeted. That's what being a Target was all about, after all.

Panaan knew the truth, at least about her Mother. And yet, a doubt fluttered in her mind. Could there have been something her Mother did wrong that warranted becoming targeted?

The paranoid rants of her Mother—how her coworkers were becoming Targets—lodged inside Panaan's mind. She couldn't get the words to stop replaying over and over again within her brain.

Panaan knew the Rules quite well. She'd been studying for months, eager to make a name for herself, to help raise her family's status. Not that they wanted for anything—they were provided with food and housing and necessities by the government, as was customary for every individual—but Panaan wanted to give her Mother more. Now it wouldn't matter.

Shaking away the wishful thinking, Panaan's skin shimmered with mixed emotions beneath the harsh fluorescent ceiling lights. She may not have been first in her class, but she reached the top five for color-changing ability. She mostly struggled with textures of backgrounds, something that only the best could achieve well, but she did excel in maintaining her skin shift for extended periods of time. She still felt confident, though, that she'd be good enough on her First Assignment.

Focus on that. Complete your First Assignment. It's the only thing left you can do to make your Mother proud. And to prove to everyone your family isn't a failure.

But another thought wouldn't go away either. She'd become fixated on the image of the young man who'd sat in the restaurant.

Tapping her feet against the floor once more, Panaan thought about the Rules. Rule #15 specifically stated that a

Re'Ris could not seek revenge against either an assassin or a Target, if the Target defended themself, for the elimination of the other.

But Panaan imagined walking up to the young man from the restaurant. She wouldn't even need to skin-shift. He wouldn't recognize her. Why would he? He only would've cared about her Mother's identity for his Assignment. So, she could stroll up to him and kill him for what he'd taken from her.

Panaan shook away this notion. To murder someone? It didn't feel like her. It was unbecoming of a Re'Ris to think that way at all.

And yet...

Could there be a way to get away with it? Accidents still happened, even on a world of assassins and Targets.

Perhaps create a scenario where he could die and she wouldn't be blamed?

Her nearly 15-year-old-mind hated the blackness of the idea.

But her heart...the one which loved her Mother more than anything else, which felt soothed after her Father had been targeted years ago, it only understood that the young man was wrong to have taken her Mother away.

That means the Makers are wrong, too, you know. If they chose your Mother and Father to be Targets and you think it's wrong, then they must be wrong as well.

Panaan dismissed the conjecture, not prepared to think such blasphemy even inside her own mind.

One step at a time.

Go to Central Processing.

Get her First Assignment.

Eliminate her Target and Cross Over.

Become an assassin.

And then make a plan to find that young man.

Chapter 16

Sree groaned. He stared at the back of his eyelids for a while before opening his eyes. The soft glow of a subdued light filled his vision. He lay on a comfortable plush chair, a blanket strewn across him. The flame-lit lamp sat on the small table beside him, illuminating the space.

"Hello," he heard a voice say. Looking up, he saw Wiin standing over him. "Good to see you awake."

Sree shoved the blanket off himself, embarrassed that he'd lost consciousness. "How long was I out?"

"Not too long." Wiin offered something to drink. "Feeling better?"

Noting his parched mouth, Sree accepted the refreshment this time. The liquid felt cool and restorative, sliding gel-like down his throat. "I guess so. I'm still a little lightheaded."

The two of them were quiet for several moments, allowing Sree's mind to recall their previous conversation.

Somehow this man had made it possible to choose Sree as his

assassin.

He'd stolen all these books from the center of the most heavily guarded city on the planet.

And he expected Sree to continue with his Assignment and kill him.

All this information made his mind feel as if it had been somehow bent, twisted in a way he'd never thought possible. The drink may have quenched his thirst, but a different sort of dryness aggravated his throat.

"I'm not going to kill you," Sree blurted out, continuing his firm denial.

Wiin let out a soft sigh. "It's my hope that after you hear what I have to say, you will realize it's the best thing to do."

Sree shook his head, denying any possibility that he'd ever kill someone. He'd finally come to that conclusion outside the doorway that he'd rather carry the shame of becoming a Laborer.

But this man claimed Sree couldn't be a Laborer even if he wanted to. He'd become a Target no matter what.

One step at a time. Regrouping his thoughts, he replied with a steadier tone, "You told me you'd assigned yourself as my Target. That you brought me here. Since you aren't a Maker, how is that possible?"

Wiin held up a hand. "We're getting off course. I'll answer you, but we can't start with that question. Not until I explain a few other things first." He paused, his forehead creased. "Are you positive you want to keep listening to what I have to say? It'll change everything for you, and once I tell you, you can't un-hear it. It'll be with you for the rest of your life, whether you decide to embrace being an assassin, go on the run, or...or whatever you choose. On top of that, you can't talk to anyone about what I tell you. You'll have to lie. To *everyone.* Family, friends, officials. You can't risk it, even if you love them, even if you trust them, even if you're threatened. They won't understand." He took a last slug from his bottle of honey-colored liquid and rolled the bottle between his hands for a few moments. "But I think...I think it'll be worth it. I pray to the Makers that it is. It could change everything, for you, for the planet. And maybe, *maybe,* you won't have to ever kill again. That's the best offer I can make. The rest is your choice."

Sree squirmed in his seat. All the "maybes" meant nothing if this man expected Sree to kill him after he finished speaking, so Sree didn't really want to hear anything more. At some point Wiin would stop talking and he would expect death. Sree's only other option would be to leave, now, before anything else happened.

And then what? he thought. *It will still go on record that I didn't finish my First Assignment. According to Wiin, I'll then become a Target.*

One other choice didn't really help either, but at least it felt in his control.

Stall. Until a better opportunity presented itself.

Sree knew the likelihood of changing this situation would be infinitesimally small, but right now he had zero other viable possibilities, so stalling had to be better.

Plus, he found himself curious as to what else Wiin might say.

Sree steeled himself for whatever came next and said, "Go ahead."

A weight seemed to lift from Wiin's shoulders, and he relaxed into his chair. "Before I begin, there is one thing you must know. It will go against everything you've ever been told, but if you don't believe it, you won't believe anything else I say."

Feeling as though he'd already heard plenty of things he didn't think he'd ever hear, or believe, he shrugged. "Okay... what?"

Wiin leaned forward. "The Rules of Assignment are a lie."

Through an uncomfortable grimace, Sree said, "I know. You said the Rules aren't always followed."

"That's not what I mean. I mean the Rules, as you know them, aren't true. They aren't the real Rules the Makers originally created for us. What we've been taught are a lie."

Sree felt surprised that Wiin hadn't been struck down dead by an electrical discharge for uttering such blasphemy. Unable to help himself, he began to clench and unclench his fists. He'd not been prepared for such a statement. A Re'Ris's whole world, their very existence, became challenged by that declaration. Sree couldn't listen to this. He *shouldn't* listen to this. Rationalizing, he thought it must be nonsense, spouted by a radical, bent on taking over the government. That must mean his original assessment of this man had been correct—a conspiracy theorist who got pleasure from spreading gossip to get attention.

But the man across from him didn't seem insane. Instead, he appeared calm and rational. Merely having a discussion. The situation didn't even feel as though Wiin wanted to convince Sree of anything, more like...he simply spoke the truth and Sree just didn't agree with it yet.

Wiin scooted to the edge of his chair. "I understand what you are feeling. I was just as conflicted as you are. It felt just as...wrong...when I discovered the truth. But the Rules *are* a lie. Or at least they've been changed to fit what our present government needs them to be. And I have started to accumulate proof." Wiin stood, grabbed a different book from the shelf, and placed it on the nearby table, stacking it precariously on top of the first one he'd grabbed, the one he didn't get the chance to open because Sree had passed out.

Sree's tense moment subsided, but it didn't help the confusion in his head. He felt like he was coming apart at the seams. His heart pounded, his body ached, and his thoughts were a jumbled conflict between all that he'd learned throughout his life and these incongruous ideas. During these brief instants, Sree once again felt highly tempted to run out the door and never look back, this time because he feared what else Wiin might utter.

But a tiny rebellious spot in him almost *hoped* Wiin spoke the truth.

If the Rules *were* a lie, then he wouldn't feel so bad about not wanting to follow them. Maybe everybody felt like him, and they instinctively knew the Rules were wrong, but no one would dare say anything.

Not without proof.

Which Wiin claimed to have.

A flash of his sister entered Sree's mind, how she'd seemed different after their Mother and Father died. Could this be how she'd felt when she learned the truth about their deaths? Sick to her stomach but also glad to know the certainty of the reality she believed?

Wiin opened the top book and increased the lamp's flame to shed more light on its pages. He gestured for Sree to come and look. Sree stood and craned his neck.

"There are two secret areas at Central Processing," Wiin began as he slowly paged through the book, its fragile nature apparent in the worn pages. Sree watched the movements curiously. This one, like the one beneath, appeared to be made of plant fiber. Sections nearest the inner spine still appeared whitish, but moving towards the edges, yellowing and browning had occurred during its aging.

Wiin continued, "I gave them names, the Stasis Room and the Archive Room. In the second one, I discovered the books and artifacts you see here. I spent months acquiring them, one at a time, secretly stealing them from the Archive Room, not daring to return for weeks or months, just in case someone caught on. I took those nearest the door, darting in and out, smuggling them back up to my apartment. Once here, I studied them. Many of them contain clues that led me to believe the Rules as we know them are false."

Sree noticed the book contained graphs and charts, though Wiin appeared to be looking for something specific as he continued to turn the pages.

"But how can that be?" Sree asked, recalling the words he'd learned in his Lessons. "The Makers wrote the Rules when they created our species to give us direction and meaning to our lives and to weed out the weak from the strong. The Makers then give us Assignments, choosing the weak and assigning them as Targets so that our species may grow stronger, giving us the perfect evolutionary path to become the perfect species."

Wiin paused and cocked an eyebrow. "My boy, have you ever seen a Maker? Have you ever known *anyone* who has seen a Maker?"

Searching his mind, Sree came up empty. "No...but..."

"But nothing. The Makers no longer exist. They are extinct. By my calculations, they have been gone for about twelve thousand years."

Sree's denial came instantaneously. "Just cuz I've never seen them doesn't mean they don't exist. They could be alive somewhere, in a place where we can't access them."

Wiin tapped his fingertip on the edge of the book. "You are very perceptive, which is why I don't base my statement on theory alone. Again, I have proof."

Sree felt his resolve weaken. Desperate for this to be the truth, he forced himself to look at all angles, not wanting to believe this theory unless he could be sure. Could everything Sree had ever known be truly a lie? And did that somehow mean he wasn't wrong to not want to kill? "But what about the Assignments? They are still given to us. If the Makers are...extinct, then who is choosing the Targets?"

"That one I'm not exactly sure about, proof-wise. I have my theories, but regardless, I know the system has been corrupted."

"That can't be possible."

"If I could corrupt the system to bring you here, is it really so inconceivable that someone else already has?"

The three implausible thoughts battered around inside

Sree's mind.

The Makers were gone.

Someone else controlled Targets.

The Rules were a lie.

It felt as if Wiin had told him that breathing air was a myth—that it didn't actually matter if you inhaled and exhaled. That if you stood still and did nothing, you wouldn't die.

The last of his strength faded and Sree felt his legs buckle underneath him. Abruptly, he sat. He wondered how much shock a body could take in a day. Taking slow breaths in and out, Sree got himself under control. But it remained a thin control that threatened to shatter at any moment.

Something inside him prevented the panic attack. That same small spot, desperate and eager, wanted Wiin to prove what he'd found.

And though Sree's brain wanted to deny everything he'd just heard, his heart longed for everything to be true.

Sree sucked in a deep breath. "Show me what you've found."

CHAPTER 17

"Why wouldn't I be worried?" Vuun spat into the audiolink to her friend. "My Daughter's Son's timeframe for his First Assignment ended yesterday and he hasn't reported in and there has been no mention of his death." Vuun currently sat on the nearest recliner, her leg lifted because she'd overdone pacing around the kitchen with worry the past few hours and the arthritis in her hip screamed at her to stop. Where could Sree be? She couldn't lose him. She just couldn't. Death may be natural on this planet, but she didn't want to be alone, the only other remaining family member gone forever.

Vuun paused, listening to her friend.

"Of course I know that if he doesn't report in it means they will demote him to Laborer," Vuun continued. "I'm not senile!"

She waited as her friend spoke, forcing herself to calm down. The last thing she needed would be to have her circle of friends gossiping about her lack of emotional control.

"You can say all you want, but I don't believe he failed. I

know something else must have happened. He's from *my* family. *We* don't fail. Perhaps he's injured and can't get to a medical facility. Or maybe he's being held captive by his Target...oh I *know* that's absurd, but I can't discount the possibility..."

Vuun grimaced at her friend's response.

"No, I won't do anything foolish. I know the Rules. This Assignment is his responsibility. It's just that he's the only kin I have left...sometimes I just wish the Rules never existed!... Oh no, don't report me. You *know* I didn't mean that!"

* * *

Panaan never considered she'd spend her 15th day of birth waiting to get her First Assignment.

Not that she hadn't been excited about becoming an assassin. But she and her Mother had made some amazing plans for the day itself—a tour of Central Processing's musical archives, a trip to Altaamina Lake, where tiny whirlpools of magenta-tipped waves swirled into eddies before shooting up into the air like mini geysers, and then finishing it all off with a meal at her favorite restaurant—The Lotha Tree. It served the best desserts, and her mouth began to water just thinking about it.

But Panaan could no longer do any of those things with her Mother.

The Laborer in front of her rambled on, his chair squeaking each time he leaned forward during his prattle, until he finally handed Panaan a datapad personally instead of sending it as a package to her home.

"Since your situation concerning your Mother is a touch... unique...and those lodgings will be reassigned within a standard week to another Laborer, any deliveries for you will be diverted here until alternate housing is found for you. I believe because you have accommodations given to you for your First Assignment during the standard week timeframe, you don't have anything permanent set up yet, though you are welcome to stay in your Mother's home if you finish your First Assignment early until its ownership is reallocated. Up through that point, you'll receive this and any future Assignment information directly from me."

Pointing to the datapad, he continued. "Everything you need to know is here, including your funds and of course, your Target. If you do not complete your First Assignment in the allotted timeframe for any other reason besides major illness, for which the Assignment will be postponed, a physical accident that renders you unable to continue on, for which a hearing will be held to determine your future eligibility as an assassin, or death, either by accident or at the hands of your Target, you will be demoted to the Labor Force."

Panaan just sat there, her thoughts still remembering the feel of Altaamina Lake's waves on the edges of her toes as her Mother laughed in the sunlight.

The Laborer, an older gentleman with nearly white-gray skin, finished his obviously memorized monologue, then let out a sigh. "Kids these days," he mumbled, "they used to at least flinch when I mentioned demotion. Desensitized–all of them."

The Laborer's words cut through her daydream and Panaan couldn't help but smile. Her Mother used to complain about the same type of thing regarding younger generations. Then the smile turned into an internal pain so deep at the thought that her Mother will never say anything like that to her again that she gasped.

"Are you all right?" the Laborer asked, a frown touching his lips.

Keep it together, Panaan thought, forcing the grin once more onto her face. "I'm fine. Just...can't believe this is actually happening."

The old man's eyes softened. "I know it's scary, especially without any other family by your side, but you can do this. And I promise, if you can't, being a Laborer isn't that bad, either." He puffed out his chest. "I'm actually the oldest Laborer in the capital! Just do your best, but if you're not cut out for the assassin route, I'll make sure to keep an eye out for you and see that you're looked after as a Laborer." He nodded at the door. "Good luck."

Two hours later, squatting over her incapacitated Target, Panaan realized the Laborer had been saying those words to comfort her. To comfort someone who he believed to be a normal 15-year-old.

She imagined the young man's face from the restaurant as she currently squeezed her Target's throat.

But I'm not normal.

The body stilled and lay at her feet. It could have merely been sleeping.

I'm an orphan.

Her Target was dead, though she'd not cared at all, because she'd imagined this elimination being that of the young man. In her heart, she wanted to do the unthinkable.

And soon, I'll be a murderer.

Chapter 18

It was the morning after Sree's final day to finish his First Assignment and report in.

Sree, however, had forgotten all about the timetable. Instead, he'd been in Wiin's living unit doing nothing but discussing information and sifting through the dozens of books, artifacts, and datapads. After fatigue finally won over curiosity, he'd nodded off for a few hours in one of the comfy chairs, a massive metal-etched tome splayed open on his lap. Wiin had let him sleep, but the wafts of a freshly-made breakfast woke Sree. It took several moments to get his bearings before he took the plate of food held out by Wiin and devoured the entire contents.

"Thanks," he said between mouthfuls, not realizing how hungry he'd been.

"Brain power uses up a lot of energy. And you read almost the entire night."

"I couldn't stop. There is so much information here," Sree said.

Wiin had shown Sree the clues he'd discovered while he'd infiltrated files at Central Processing. He'd found several deleted references revolving around genetic modifications and related experiments involving chromatophores, mentions of requests for Rules' translations, and one year's census of the Makers, which showed an obscenely high death toll, after which the census-taking stopped.

From these clues, Wiin had theorized that there must be something else to the story of how and why the Re'Ris had been created. So, he'd dug further into the databases, looking for whatever he could that would explain these missing pieces.

And that's when he'd stumbled upon it: a chamber inside Central Processing's main building, a room he called the Stasis Room, which contained preserved non-Re'Ris remains..

Sree simply sat, completely enraptured by the man's findings.

"The bodies looked a lot like our species," Wiin told Sree the night before, "but there were some significant physical differences. Their height, for example, was much shorter than our own, and their skin had a darker yellowish tinge to the grayness. Their eyes were larger and their fingers were long and curved. They looked like this..." At that moment, Wiin opened up one of the texts and Sree found himself gazing at a copy of a picture that hung in the Great Hall of Cand—an artist's rendition of the Makers dated several hundred years before Sree had been born and the only drawing of them displayed for public access. Etched into the rounded border around the figures were words written in the Makers' language, which Sree didn't understand. The picture depicted the Makers standing above a mass of Re'Ris, their long, curved fingers outstretched over the group, as if offering them something, their skin mottled with dark yellowish-gray.

"I've always loved this picture," Wiin had said. "I always felt connected to it. And the words around the archway: 'Creators and Created, both Saviors,'" he translated. "It spoke to me..."

The portrayals of the Makers were eerily similar to Wiin's description of the bodies he'd seen in the Stasis Room.

"You think you found the Makers?" Sree asked, awed.

Wiin nodded. "Yes." He closed the art book and reached for a small datapad which had slipped sideways on a shelf between two other books. He turned it on and a small screen hummed to life. On it were two genetic sequences.

"What am I looking at?" Sree asked, not comprehending the information.

"I took a sample from one of the bodies," Wiin answered, "and compared its genetic sequence with a sample of my own." Wiin paused. "It is almost an exact match. The sequence differs by about point zero zero one percent."

"What does that mean, exactly?" Sree asked.

"We are the same species," Wiin concluded. "We *are* the Makers."

That astonishing piece of information had come during the night and even though he read through other books and information, the thought lingered and weaved through his thoughts until he'd fallen asleep. How could the Makers be the same as the Re'Ris? Comprehension eluded him. The Makers had *created* the Re'Ris. They *couldn't* be the same species.

Could they?

He'd stared for a long time at the genetic sequence match. The fact that he hadn't been very surprised when told Wiin *stole* the genetic material from what he assumed to be an actual Maker made Sree realize the depth of his investment in the situation. Law-breaking hadn't seemed to register on Sree's mental radar what with all the new information he'd recently acquired. Actually, Sree didn't know if a law for something like this even existed. Or if that type of theft would've crossed anyone's minds to have a law about.

Sree wondered if the Makers' reverence made them, as a species, seem less real than everyday Re'Ris. He'd always pictured them living in the upper floors of Central Processing and...and what? Did they eat and sleep like he did? Did they bathe and use the washroom like every other Re'Ris? Were they born? Did they die and decompose? Imaginings of something more always filled his mind—beings that were elevated above the pettiness of everyday life, above the mundane, above the physical needs of a normal body.

He'd heard stories from his sister of intangible deities that other species prayed to, sacrificed to, in order to change their lives, their fates. Sree always found that strange, wondering how someone could worship something they didn't even know truly existed. The Re'Ris *knew* the Makers existed. Or, at least, according to Wiin, they *did* exist at some point, although not anymore.

So, the idea of stealing genetic material from their deceased remains cast such a large shadow over the realm of reality that Sree had no idea how to process it on a legal or criminal level.

Instead, all he could absorb revolved around the unfathomable idea that the Re'Ris and the Makers were one and the same.

If that is the case, then why don't the Makers look exactly like us? Why did they call us a different species name if we are the same? And how else are we different?

While Sree thought, Wiin glanced at the time reader on his wall, shook his head, and hurriedly moved around the room. He grabbed a tiny bottle from the kitchen nook, downing it in one gulp. Sree noticed the grimace on the man's face as he swallowed the contents, but remained too preoccupied by his thoughts about the previous several hours, trying to find something, *anything* that would explain Wiin's genetic results and answer the questions that tumbled through his head, to wonder what Wiin just drank.

But there was nothing. No new answers. No resolutions made themselves known.

Frustrated, Sree hefted the book off his lap and onto the

nearby table.

"There's nothing else here," he said, defeated. "It's just the same clues you've already told me about. There is a reference to a large death toll in a census one year and then after that the census stops. Talk about an illness from which the Makers suffered, but no follow-up on it. There is mention of genetic modifications and experiments, but no charts or reports about the actual tests. And then the requests for a copy of the translated Rules, but there are no originals in the Makers' language, not that I could read it anyway. This is so aggravating!" Sree pressed his fingertips against his pulsing temples, trying to ease their pain.

"But what if there *are* other texts and reports?" Wiin asked, tossing the vial into a nearby waste receptacle. "There are more texts and books and artifacts in the Archives Room. There must be additional proof in those. Why else keep them all together, hidden away?"

"You mean the hard-to-get-to rooms you mentioned hidden away at Central Processing." Sree said it as a statement rather than a question. "The rooms you can't even get into anymore because you don't work there because you made yourself a Target."

Wiin hastily chose three books, a couple of artifacts, and the container that held the genetic sample results. Stacking them on top of each other on the table next to Sree, he then picked up a strange container with a spray nozzle attached to it.

Sree finally noticed the man's odd behavior and stopped his complaints. "Wiin, what are you doing?"

With a no-nonsense tone, he replied, "I miscalculated. I didn't realize yesterday was your last day to eliminate. I thought we would have the rest of today to keep discussing things. I've kept you too long, which will complicate matters."

The gravity of the situation hit Sree. "Oh, stars," he swore, glancing at his own timereader. "I'm over my time limit? I was supposed to report in hours ago!"

"I'm sorry. I should have paid closer attention. Yes, our time is up. All that's left is to burn my living unit and everything in it except the few items that you'll need for evidence. I thought we'd have time to transport all of them to your place, but..." He shook his head and then tapped the stack of items. "These are the most important pieces of proof—they show the Makers suffered from an illness and are most likely extinct, that they made us out of themselves, and there are translated versions of the Rules." Turning, he began to spray the shelves and furniture behind him.

"Wait, wait, wait." Sree stood up and grabbed Wiin's arm. "Are you insane? You're going to burn all these other texts? How can you do that? We need all the proof we can get!"

Wiin shook himself from Sree's grip. "We don't have any time. It's bad enough that we've taken this long, but you are only a few hours over your limit. Any longer, they won't *care* about your reason. They'll think you failed anyway. They will kill you."

Sree ran his fingers through his hair, wracking his brain for a way out. "You said you fixed it. The system. Just do it again! Give us more time or reset it or whatever."

"You don't understand. It's already in the system. I can't change it once it's been set in motion. The inconsistencies won't make sense, and Targets are tracked very carefully at Central Processing. Besides, I'd been planning this for weeks. I knew I wouldn't survive. Only you weren't who I'd planned to bring into all of this to help."

"I wasn't?" Sree said, frowning.

"No. I had planned to make Faan Kaano my assassin. To expose her to all of this and get her to assist me. But she died."

Sree felt his stomach tighten at his sister's name. Grief he shouldn't feel, according to their customs, still clung to him, but anger superseded that. "Sorry her dying messed up your plan," he said, his tone full of irritation and sarcasm.

Wiin's face crumpled. "That may have changed things, but her death affected me as a Re'Ris, not because of my plan. I, like many others, was saddened to hear of the loss. As much as we were supposed to rejoice in her Passing On, we wept."

Sree blinked several times, surprised.

"Oh yes," Wiin said with a nod, placing one more book on the stack, though it balanced awkwardly and looked as if it may fall over at any moment, "we grieved. We cried, we yelled, we pounded our fists in anger at the loss."

"But...but grief isn't... I mean, we aren't supposed to...".

"I know. According to the Lessons, we are supposed to rejoice when a fellow Re'Ris Passes On. We are told that it is a beautiful experience one goes through where their energy is once again reunited with the Makers. But it never felt right to me. And after my findings, I can't be satisfied with this tradition anymore. Especially if the Makers no longer exist."

Sree couldn't believe someone else felt grief like he did. But then, he shook his head. "It's a good thing you didn't have her be your assassin. She was too dedicated to her work and the Rules. She would never have listened to you."

A pause. "Perhaps before your Mother and Father were murdered this would have been true. But that act changed her somehow. She wasn't the same assassin she'd been before. And citizens noticed. Not in the way I did, because I thought she could also be an asset, but she made them think differently by how she presented herself. Though she tried to hide it, her own grief and determination showed through. As for me, without someone like her to support me, I knew no one would listen to my theories, no matter how much proof I found. I'm a nobody."

Understanding dawned on Sree. "You needed her status as an assassin."

"Yes. And her family name. Even your Mother and Father fought with the Liberators against our government. Your family is known to fight for the truth."

Sree hadn't been old enough at nine standard years to understand his Mother's and Father's involvement in the

Liberator group, and after the Aleet Army disbanded, no one really talked about it anymore. But if some citizens still remembered that and knew Faan searched for the truth as well...

He finally understood Wiin's alternative choice. "That's why you chose me. You rigged it so that I would be your assassin after Faan Passed On because she and I are kin. I'm still her family, still a Kaano."

Wiin nodded. "When I heard she died, I created an artificial loop in the system to keep my name as her Target. Then all I needed to do was to wait until you applied for your First Assignment and change her name to yours."

"You could have done that indefinitely. Been safe from ever being a Target again."

"Yes. But if I'd done that no one would know what I've discovered. No, I stayed in the shadows long enough. This," he said, his tone soft but weighted as he waved an arm to incorporate the contents of his apartment, "is more important."

Sree's head spun at the massive undertaking this man had gone through. This should've been for Faan to deal with. Wiin chose him because of the Kaano name, but Sree couldn't do anything like this. He would never measure up to his sister.

Wiin continued spraying their surroundings, then stopped as if he finally noticed Sree's silence. Placing his hands on the young man's shoulders, he said, "I know this is a lot. Too much to ask of you. But it *has* to be you. You know that once you've completed your First Assignment, you will be taken to Central Processing and interviewed about my elimination. You'll use the answers we've gone over to pass the lie detector test. Then, you'll attend the Crossing Over ceremony. After its completion, you can use the elevator to access room 174-45 with the code I've given you. The only door you'll see will lead to the Stasis Room. Once inside, the door at the back end of the room leads to the Archive Room. I believe in there you'll find the final pieces to our puzzle."

Sree swallowed. "Okay. Once I've taken what I can from the Archive Room, we can meet up somewhere. Where should we meet?"

Wiin let go of Sree's shoulders and held his gaze. "Still trying not to kill me? Don't you see? The only way you can get access to the elevator is after you attend the Crossing Over ceremony, which you can't do until you pass the interview at Central Processing, after you've *completed* your First Assignment. That's why I told you, you'll have to eliminate me."

Sree's eyes almost doubled in size. "I can't. *I can't!* I told you that when I first got here."

Wiin picked up the container and finished spraying the remaining fluid on his shelves. "If you don't, they will know. You *must* be able to pass that lie detector exam. You must be able to say truthfully that you killed me. If I die by any other means or kill myself, they will know. You *must* do this!" Wiin handed him the stack of evidence to hold with one arm while he placed the twisted glass bulb container that had the flame inside it into his free hand. "Throw it against the stacks of books. They will ignite quickly and I will be consumed in a matter of minutes."

Sree's face twisted into a look of horror. "You want me to burn you *alive*?"

"I have taken a nerve-numbing serum that will deaden my nerves as soon as my external body temperature increases by five degrees. I will feel no pain."

Recalling the small vial of liquid Wiin had consumed earlier, Sree trembled, the light from the flame flickering as his hand shook. "I can't," he whispered. How could he kill this man? Wiin hadn't done anything wrong. He only searched for the truth, a truth that should've been told to begin with.

"You can and you must. My work here is done. I have taken many lives as an assassin. I have seen the Makers, at least what remains of them. I have passed on my knowledge to you and I know my death will allow you to continue on. You *must* do this so that you can find any remaining evidence you need to convince others. And to possibly save yourself."

Sree's anxiety threatened to consume him. He couldn't kill this man! But even worse than that, he began to sense he would. "What if there is no other evidence in the Archive Room that will help?" he asked in one last-ditch effort to change Wiin's mind. "What if you've done all this for nothing?"

A serene look crossed Wiin's face and he spoke, as if reciting a speech he'd already prepared. "I believe that death is a part of life, but not our purpose. I believe we were created to preserve life, not to destroy it. Even though I must die now, I Pass On with the knowledge that I have truly lived. And I believe that you will find the answers needed to give that knowledge to our planet."

Shaking his head, Sree took a step back.

Wiin pointed to the flame-lit light. "Do it, Sree. Show the world that we are more than what they've made us believe. And do not be afraid to grieve."

Closing his eyes for a moment, Sree took in a shuddering breath. Letting out a guttural howl, he opened his eyes and threw the lamp.

Within moments, Wiin's smile became lit up by raging flames. "Thank you, Sree Kaano."

Sree ran from the apartment, crushing the books and evidence against his chest, tears blurring his vision.

Chapter 19

"Did you hear?" Vuun asked her friend over her audiolink connection. Claiming she still needed to dress for the day to save face with her friend, who remained unaware of Vuun's financial changes, she wore her best clothes. Hopefully Sree would bring home some income soon. Not that she really wanted Sree to move out—Vuun hadn't expected having to live alone—but it seemed that the brighter the stars burned in her family, the faster they fell. And after such an intense story about his First Assignment, who knew what sort of publicity they might have before long.

She'd never quite felt like she'd fit in with her kin, from her own Male Mate's success in designing and creating weapons to her Daughter's and *her* Male Mate's political endeavors, to her Daughter's Daughter, Faan's, extraordinary genetic mutations and assassin capabilities. Vuun had been an average assassin, an average-looking woman, and other than making it to retirement, lived an average life. She never stood out in a crowd, never stepped out of line, never did anything adventurous. She felt she embodied what a Re'Ris represented without all the fanfare and fame of the rest of the Kaano family.

And now her Daughter's Son, who'd had a seemingly rough life—both orphaned and then losing his only sibling—had just prospered through one of the most incredible First Assignment stories ever told.

"I couldn't believe it either," Vuun continued. "I was right! Sree *had* been taken hostage by his Target. I guess his Target was a little more prepared than Sree expected. He'd arrived on his final day and had been held against his will for almost twenty-four standard hours! He finally managed to overpower his Target and then eliminated him by setting fire to the Target's unit. Can you imagine having a live-flame apparatus in your home? Unbelievable." She shivered at the thought of how dangerous it would be to have one of those in her home.

Vuun paused as her friend added a passive aggressive comment. "Well, I *know* a hostage situation is unorthodox," she replied, "but you can't account for all the insane mindsets out there. I'm not sure what that Target planned to accomplish, but I assume it would have ended in some sort of blackmail. Our family's name and faces are too well known. The assailant probably recognized Sree and changed his tactics. Blessing in disguise, I say, since my Daughter's Son could've been killed instead. How embarrassing would that have been?'

Another pause as her friend asked a question.

"No, I don't think it matters that he was over his time limit, considering the circumstances. Besides, no matter the details, the fact is he completed his First Assignment by eliminating his Target, and they are still going to let him Cross Over...yes, he reports to Central Processing tomorrow to attend his Crossing Over ceremony. Ah, it seems like only yesterday that was me..."

Chapter 20

Knock. Knock. Knock.

Sree ignored the noise.

A voice, muffled by the thick door to his bedroom, called out, "Sree, dear? It's almost time for us to head over to Central Processing. You don't want to be late, do you?"

Closing his eyes, he rubbed his head. "I'll be out soon," he answered his Mother's Mother. He listened to her footsteps diminish as they padded away from the door.

Lowering his hand, he returned his gaze to the ceiling. He'd been fixated on the same spot for the last several hours. No sleep. No food. He'd barely moved. Nothing since he'd returned home the previous day from Wiin's and finished his interview with Central Processing.

Just lying in bed and staring.

How could he possibly do anything else when his mind constantly flitted between the image of Wiin's grinning face enveloped by flames, and the knowledge that he would soon be breaking into Central Processing to search for hidden evidence of a possible conspiracy while the only one who could help him was dead.

A man he'd killed.

Sree never thought he'd *actually* eliminate someone. He'd been positive that somehow he'd find a loophole. And when Wiin first told him about his theories, Sree convinced himself they would provide his way out.

But in the end, it changed nothing. He still ended up killing someone.

When he first returned home, he snuck to the rear of the house and hid the contents Wiin gave him behind a few landscaped bushes. The last thing he needed would be to explain any of it to his Mother's Mother.

Once inside, exhausted and smelling of smoke, his Mother's Mother rushed over to him, rambling on about something Sree hadn't been able to register. She'd cleaned up his sooty face and oily hands, and then asked where he'd been, what happened, and if he were all right.

Sree only muttered a few sentences, based on what he and Wiin had discussed should be his story, each part based on some sort of truth. It needed to be at least partly true in order to pass the lie detector test the following day in Central Processing.

A delay in his attack.

A chance for Sree to lose his advantage.

Then, instead of killing Sree, his Target kidnapped him.

In the end, Sree had been able to light the place on fire, killing the Target by doing so.

Even though the statements were technically true, everything left unsaid coated Sree's mouth like an unsavory film.

Vuun listened to every word, drinking in Sree's story. Then, she told him to eat something, though Sree's stomach couldn't stand the idea of food, before she called Central Processing to report that Sree completed his Assignment.

Keeping his mouth closed, Sree slowly came to realize that over the audiolink, Vuun told them the story of what happened; how he'd been captured, how he'd escaped, and finally how he'd set the Target on fire. When she disconnected the call, she came over to him, repeating the story several times as if in both disbelief and relief before their house's indicator light turned on, signaling that someone waited outside their front door.

Several Re'Ris in baggy sage green Central Processing uniforms came in and made their way toward Sree. They carried some sort of equipment with them. Behind them stood a couple of other individuals wearing tightly fitting yellow uniforms.

Central Authority officers.

Terror clenched his heart. He thought he wouldn't have to deal with any of this until tomorrow when he went to Central Processing, but they were testing him, *now,* to corroborate his story.

And they'd brought officers along...

What would they do if they caught him lying? Eliminate him on the spot?

They hooked up multiple devices to his fingers and the edges of his face then watched their monitor screens closely while they asked a series of questions. Exhaling slowly, he'd answered them with his hands clenched on his lap, telling them the story he'd just recited to his Mother's Mother. At the very end, the interrogator closest to him leaned forward, her face hardly a hand span away.

"Did you kill Wiin Niino?"

Sree's hands went limp and he looked straight into her eyes. He pictured the man's sad smile as he'd thrown the flamed lamp towards the flammable room. It would not be a lie.

"Yes. I killed Wiin Niino."

After a few more questions, they seemed satisfied with Sree's responses. The entire group packed up their belongings, handed a datapad to Vuun, and left. She skimmed it and told him he needed to report to Central Processing the next day for his Cross Over Ceremony, a grin blooming across her wrinkled face.

Sree just sat there, staring at the door through which the group had exited.

Vuun then led him upstairs to his room, took off his shoes and jacket, and tucked him under the covers.

"You just need some rest. You're in shock. Try to sleep," she told him. "I will come and get you in the morning. We'll go to your ceremony together and make a day of it." She brushed the hair from his eyes. "I'm so proud of you. Your Mother and Father are proud of you. Faan is proud of you. You've succeeded in continuing the family's legacy. Good job, Sree. You are family, we are one." She left, closing the door behind her.

He hadn't moved since that moment. Even the smell of the old food he'd shoved under his bed when he thought he wasn't going to return didn't stir him. And now that morning shone through his windows like an uninvited guest, somehow he had to get out of the bed, clean himself up, leave the house, and head over to Central Processing like nothing was wrong.

Like he wasn't about to commit treason.

CHAPTER 21

"Unfortunately not," Vuun told an acquaintance. Multiple calls from random associates over the past few hours occurred as news of Sree's hostage situation went public. She glanced at her Daughter's Son's closed door. He really needed to get up soon or he'd be late to his own Crossing Over ceremony. Perhaps the events had exhausted him more than she could understand. She wondered about the last time someone had actually been abducted by a Target. As far as she knew, not during her lifetime, at least.

She wondered how often news actually circulated around these types of situations. She knew the only reason Sree's First Assignment became a headline at all was because one of her close associates found out and called the media to report it. Vuun saw the woman's face on her vidlink broadcast all morning, giving her "insider's" perspective on the family and the situation. Vuun prickled at the idea of talking to that woman again. Hadn't the Kaano's been through enough already? She supposed fame brought out a different side of some people, whether it be the fame of her family's achievements, or this woman wanting her own brief time in the spotlight for personal reasons.

Bringing her attention once again to the woman on the line, she continued, "Sree's Crossing Over ceremony is this afternoon, so I won't be able to make it to lunch. I want to prepare a celebratory dinner for him when he returns home."

Vuun paused while the acquaintance—someone she'd attended Lessons with as a child and currently wondered if they'd even spoken since then—asked another question. So many people she barely knew suddenly reached out to her via audio calls, vidlinks, even in person, like moscats drawn to the sticky-sweet kuat fruits. Individuals she hadn't spoken to in years, claiming sympathy and empathy, but really just wanting to hear the scandalous story.

Vuun replied to one of these individuals now, lying through her teeth. "He was a little shaken up, but otherwise fine. He's sleeping in a bit. I thought it best for him." The last thing she wanted would be for more gossip to emerge about him having trouble adjusting to society again after his ordeal. "It would have been quite a trying event even for a seasoned assassin. The fact that it was his First Assignment just shows how strong and capable he is."

She waited, listening.

"True," she answered, ready for this conversation to be over, "but it's no surprise someone would want him as a hostage with his family lineage. Perhaps the Makers wanted to challenge him from the beginning—wanted to determine his potential.

"Regardless," Vuun continued, talking over whatever other issue the woman tried to bring up, "he made it through. And with that thought, I need to go. I think I hear him getting up," she lied again. "I'll pass on your congratulations to him!"

Vuun disconnected the audiolink line and sat down hard at her kitchen table. The relief since Sree had walked in the previous day ebbed and she squashed down her feelings of fear. She didn't know all the details about what happened to her Daughter's Son, but whatever they were, they'd been bad. He'd looked...haunted when he entered the house. Abducted? Vuun didn't know how to talk to him about that kind of experience. Should he speak with a counselor? Or would that look like weakness, taint their family name?

In these sorts of moments, she felt truly alone. She hadn't expected to be taking care of a sixteen-year-old by herself at this point in her life. Missing a departed loved one wasn't encouraged, but right now, having even *one* other member of her family alive would help her so much with support and decision-making.

Nevertheless, she wouldn't abandon him—no matter the cost.

He was all she had left.

They were family, they were one.

The rest of the morning passed in the usual way for her. Or so it would appear from an outsider's perspective. She called her dearest friend and spoke about the incident, then worked on her Puzzler Pictures, ignoring multiple calls from reporters and other "random acquaintances," went out for a short walk, even made Sree breakfast in the hope he might be hungry. Unfortunately, he didn't leave his room, even to eat.

Uneasiness settled over her. Though her family always remained in the public eye, this felt different. The idea of someone watching her seemed preposterous, but once again, this situation had become anything but normal. The fact that Central Authority members showed up last night with the processing Laborers instead of waiting for today to question Sree spoke volumes to this effect.

Vuun began to prep lunch when her vidlink connection beeped, indicating she had another incoming call. Wanting to ignore it, she saw it came from Central Processing. Opening the connection, Vuun's eyebrows rose at the sight of the Re'Ris on the other end. A young woman with dark greenish-gray skin and wearing a faded green jumpsuit, the uniform of a Central Processing Laborer, smiled at her.

"Good afternoon, Retired Kaano. My name is Laborer 61-622. If you have a moment, I'd like to speak with you."

Vuun fought the urge to frown. A Laborer calling? Why? Most of the time any calls from Central Processing were done by a member of Central Authority, or at least a Superior. "Of course. What can I do for you?"

"Well, we normally don't do this, but seeing as how your family name is so highly regarded, Central Processing decided to extend to you the courtesy of this call."

Vuun paled slightly. *What now?* "I appreciate the courtesy."

The young woman smiled wider. "Of course, Retired Kaano. The reason for this call is to let you know that there were inconsistencies with your Daughter's Son's account of his first Target's death. Because of your family's status, we are allowing Sree to come down to Central Processing to clarify the situation. If he does not do so within the next standard hour, he will be retrieved from your home by Central Authority."

Vuun swallowed. Inconsistencies? She wondered what that meant. "I can see why this has been an extended courtesy. It's appreciated."

Laborer 61-622 nodded. "Yes. It is highly irregular that we would inform anyone beforehand, much less allow them to rectify the situation. However, as I stated before, your surname is legendary and frankly I don't think anyone wants to be assigned to, um, 'retrieve' a member of the Kaano family. We would simply prefer that the situation gets remedied as soon as possible. I'm sure it's nothing and will be cleared up in short order."

"Not a problem. Sree will be heading to Central Processing soon for his Crossing Over ceremony anyway. I'll make sure we arrive there sooner—"

"You won't be allowed in the room during the process," she

cut in, her voice cheerily bright. Vuun wondered, since she appeared so young and still seemed to have quite a bit of life left in her, if she hadn't been a Laborer for very long yet. "Once he arrives, he can meet me at the front desk and I will escort him to an interrogation room. He won't need to check in, I'll be waiting for him. I'm sure it's not really a big deal. It's just such an unusual situation."

Though still concerned, Vuun forced a grin. "Of course."

"Central Processing thanks you for your cooperation and will gladly pay for this vidlink call. May your life be guided by the Makers."

"And may you do their will." Vuun disconnected the call after replying with the standard farewell phrase. She sat down again on her kitchen chair, this time more slowly, the worn cushion barely providing enough padding for her bony flesh.

What could possibly be the inconsistency? she thought. With a glance towards the staircase, she wondered, *What really happened to you, Sree?* She shook her head to clear her thoughts as she heard Sree's footsteps coming down the stairs.

"Please don't let me lose him, too," she whispered into the silence before her Daughter's Son entered the kitchen.

Chapter 22

Eight individuals, all between the ages of 15 and 16, sat in a gray and blue windowless room inside Central Processing, listening aptly to the Superior who stood before them. Superiors were well known to all—they were the Re'Ris who determined and taught the Lessons to children about the Rules—but outside of a classroom, such as now, they somehow seemed...more imposing.

This would be a monumental day for them, as they had all completed their First Assignments and were receiving the final words before they Crossed Over into adulthood, including all the benefits such an achievement entailed.

The Superior smiled—her grayish-green skin pale and iridescent. Her bright green eyes round and soft as she scanned the room, stopping briefly on each soon-to-be adult, as if speaking for a moment only to them.

"This is the beginning," she stated, her voice low and smooth. "What you have been through, what you have accomplished, are the moments which define who you are in our world.

Many have come before you and many will follow, but right now, at this precise point in time, you have fulfilled your purpose as a Re'Ris.

"The number of completed First Assignments grows fewer each year. This is because we as a species are becoming more and more refined in our abilities as assassins, as per the Makers' desire. You are the elite, because the First Assignments you have completed were more difficult than any from the past.

"Be proud of who you are. Be proud of what you have accomplished. You are not a title, like Laborer, or even Superior. You are assassins and so you keep your true name. You are the future. You are *our* future. You are the future the Makers planned for us so many years ago.

"Let this be your final Lesson. Do not feel sorry for those who could not make the cut—your friends or family members who will never attain the status level you are about to receive—for they will serve their purpose as you must serve yours. You are now icons for the rest of civilization. You must hold your heads high, for you are responsible for maintaining the balance determined by the Makers—for weeding out the weak so that the strong may thrive.

"May your life be guided by the Makers and may you do their will."

The Superior bowed and left the room, which then filled almost immediately by collective sighs of awe from the graduated students.

This was the beginning of their lives.

The beginning of everything for them.

They had Crossed Over.

Panaan smiled at the others' innocence as they began to stand, ready to head out into a new life. Their lives were forever changed now that they'd completed their first kill, but they were the same as everyone else who'd done the identical thing across the planet. At this moment they knew nothing about the harsh realities the world held, only the satisfaction of completing their premiere elimination.

Envy at their naivety surged through her. She wished she could feel the same way, proud in this moment and looking forward to a life she'd wanted for so long. But the joy wouldn't come while memories of her Mother falling to the ground filled her mind.

The smile melted from her face as if a flame had been lit beneath it. Chastising herself, she tried once again to push aside her grief, to release the feeling of vengeance.

Perhaps if she let go of the thought concerning the young man who'd killed her Mother she could find peace. Bring pride to her family name.

But then her eyes narrowed and her breath caught in her throat at the sight of the figure who'd just walked past the open doorway.

It was *him.*

Chapter 23

Sree walked past an open door to a room inside Central Processing and noted out of the corner of his eye the ten or so teenagers, some of them beginning to rise from their seats.

A Crossing Over ceremony, he assumed. He recently learned they scheduled one during both the morning and afternoon each standard week. This must have been the morning session, since his had been scheduled for later in the day.

Those inside just completed their First Assignments. Most likely heard some speech congratulating them on their success.

All their faces were flushed with joy and pride.

It made Sree sick, disgusted with the fact that all these Re'Ris, still basically children, were excited to become adults and continue killing for the rest of their lives. Especially since they had no idea that what they were killing for could all be a lie.

A Superior, who'd just left the room, strode down the corridor in front of him. Sree would be in one of those rooms soon enough himself, hearing the same speech. But first, his Mother's

Mother told him he'd been summoned to meet with a Laborer at Central Processing. Vuun had been quiet about the reason why, simply telling him he'd received a special courtesy call to come in. He wondered about the reason—maybe some sort of extra "congrats to the remaining Faano family member" type of garbage.

Originally, apparently, someone planned to meet him at the front desk, but the guard at the entrance to the building intercepted him, told him there'd been a change, and to simply head to the designated room.

Either way, Sree didn't want to deal with any of it. While he walked, he concentrated instead on recalling the details of the plan Wiin had set out for him.

"You'll have to go to the Stasis Room first," Wiin had told him the evening before his death. "Room 174-45. Use the access code I gave you to enter it."

"That's where you saw the Makers' bodies?" Sree had asked, the words still feeling blasphemous in his mouth.

"Yes. Once inside, there's a door at the far end which leads to the Archive Room. That's where you need to go. To find... whatever else is needed to prove everything I'm saying is true."

Currently, as Sree made his way to meet with whoever'd called him in, all he wanted was to find a way to access the Stasis or Archive room, grab whatever he needed, and get the stars out of this place. But he needed to handle whatever this "courtesy" call happened to be first.

Letting out a sigh, he took a turn away from the direction of the Superior in front of him, per the guard's instructions, and headed down a corridor similar to the one where he'd walked when he'd gotten his First Assignment.

Had that only been a little over a standard week ago? It felt like months...years even.

Like a different lifetime.

Straightening his shoulders, he found the correct room he'd

been told to look for and knocked on the edge of the open door.

A middle-aged woman, with heavy bags under her eyes and deeply dark gray skin, even darker than Sree's, gave a weak smile.

"Yes?" she asked, her voice hoarse.

"I'm Sree Kaano. I was told to report here."

She blinked, slowly. "Of course." With a wave, she gestured for him to sit, which he did.

"I'm supposed to ask you a few questions. Shouldn't take too long." The Laborer stifled a yawn.

"Questions?" he asked. "Uh, yeah, sure." *What was this all about?* He wished his Mother's Mother had told him more before he'd left home that morning.

With a cursory glance at the datapad in front of her, the Laborer began. "Do you swear that the testimony you are about to give reflects the full truth of the Assignment and that any falsehood given can be pursued to the full extent of the law?"

Sree swallowed. "Testimony?" He nervously twisted one of his wrades. At first he'd taken them off the previous night, wanting to shed anything that evoked the feeling of being an assassin, but when he finally emerged to head over to Central Processing that morning, his Mother's Mother pouted about him not wearing them to his Crossing Over ceremony, so he'd run upstairs and slid them on. Part of him hated how comfortable, almost natural, they felt on his wrists.

Another wave of her hand. "'Testimony' is just a fancy word for your answers. It's standard terminology. Don't worry. They just say it like that to make it sound scary. You'll be fine, I'm sure."

He gave a curt nod. "Okay."

With a few quick motions, the Laborer strapped the lie detector equipment to his head and fingers, just like it had been the previous day. "All right. Question one: "Did you know Wiin Niino before you received him as a Target?"

"No." A sense of relief washed over him. These were just questions about what happened. For some reason he feared they'd figured out his intent to infiltrate the Stasis and Archive Rooms. But he shouldn't have been surprised at a follow-up—not after something as odd as an abduction. He'd heard his Mother's Mother repeatedly talking about the rarity of the situation.

With a forceful exhale, he released his dread. He could answer these. Wiin had rehearsed with him for quite a while to prepare him.

The Laborer tapped on the datapad. "Great. Question two: What do you think he wanted to accomplish, by holding you hostage?"

Sree thought about all the books Wiin had kept, all the theories he'd postulated, all the insane ideas that just couldn't be true… and yet…

A direct answer wouldn't be necessary. His response needed to be based on the truth, even if it got twisted along the way, to pass the test. "Honestly? I think he wanted recognition. And what better way than focusing on me, with my family's reputation."

"Excellent. Next question: Did he mention anything about your Mother's and Father's Passing On or the death of your sister, Faan Kaano?"

"He did. He said he grieved for them," Sree answered.

A *tsk* noise issued from her before she muttered, "Pathetic."

Sree ground his teeth.

"Final question. There seems to be a discrepancy as to how Wiin Niino became your Target. Did he give you any insights as to how that happened?"

Sree's stomach clenched. Preparation failed him. He and Wiin hadn't thought of being asked this question.

And he couldn't lie. They would know.

"Yes," he answered.

A hesitation. "What did he say?"

Frantically searching for a way out, Sree couldn't find anything else to say except the truth. "That he'd changed the system to make himself my Target."

An eyebrow raised. "Did you believe him?"

Focusing all his energy, Sree remembered the moment when Wiin told him that, and his complete disbelief that it could be possible. "No. I didn't believe him."

A small nod from her. *Tap. Tap. Tap.* "Thank you, Sree. You'll be just in time for your Crossing Over ceremony." She paused. "I'm glad no harm came to you. We need assassins of your caliber."

A lump lodged in his throat. "Uh...thanks," he managed. Plucking the devices from his fingers, he paused while reaching up to remove the headpiece as she spoke again.

"For my own curiosity," the Laborer asked, "after he kept you for as long as he did, do you believe him now, about how he made himself your Target?"

Sree froze, his fingertips gripping the edges of the headset still on his temples. His heart raced in his chest.

They knew. They had to know. And they would still be able to tell if he were lying with this contraption hooked up to him. He needed to put her off her game, so she wouldn't notice when he removed the rest of the equipment in order to lie. So he needed to start with a truth.

With every ounce of will power he could muster, Sree drew on all the anger and frustration he'd had the past few weeks, all the pride and arrogance of his family's status, and spoke the harshest honesty he could.

"You're *curious*? You think you can just ask me anything you want about an Assignment? Those *above* you wrote the questions. It's not your place to fulfill your own wants." He yanked off the device and dropped it on the table. With it off his head, he could now lie. "However, to satisfy *your* curiosity, of course not. The Makers assigned him. It's not my problem *you* messed up. I did my job correctly, which is why I'm an assassin and not a Central Processing Laborer, like you." With a scoff he added, "The next time someone wants to question me, make sure it's someone who's earned the right to speak with a Kaano."

The Laborer's eyes widened and her lip quivered. Sree didn't wait for a response before he stormed from the room, disgusted at himself for what he'd just said.

Chapter 24

Laborer 61-622 peeked into a large, open room at Central Processing, filled with tables and chairs meticulously arranged on a gray tiled floor. Wisps of hair fluttered around her face as the recirculated air vent above her blew softly against the top of her head. She automatically brushed them away from her eyes as she let out an exasperated exhale.

Where did Sree go? she thought, after realizing he hadn't been in that room with the morning Crossing Over group. *Why didn't he show up at the front desk as planned?* As soon as she'd ended the call with Retired Vuun Kaano, she immediately staked out the reception area, waiting for Sree to arrive, so she could escort him to a room for "questioning." But he never showed.

After the allotted timeframe of a standard hour came and went, panic hit her. Perhaps the message to his Mother's Mother got garbled in the transmission? Perhaps he thought he needed to meet *after* his Crossing Over ceremony ended?

She then made her way to where the ceremonies were held

and currently checked inside, noticing the young individuals spending time with their families, their faces alight with pride, but she didn't see Sree anywhere.

Staring at the young, happy faces, a few moments of nostalgia took over, shifting her focus from the task at hand, as she heard words of encouragement and congratulations from family members float around the room.

They must have just heard the speech from the Superior that they've Crossed Over, she thought with a sigh. She remembered the day she'd finished her First Assignment, nearly 3 years ago. Her name had been Biin Sool then, when she'd been an assassin and worthy of a name, not just a Laborer number. Excitement at the time overwhelmed her so much she'd nearly fallen off the edge of her chair during her Crossing Over ceremony when the Superior entered the room. It had been such an achievement, especially since her older brother and sister failed their First Assignments, making her the last child in their family with a chance to become an assassin.

Pride glowed on the faces of her Mother and Father at that moment. They'd beamed, jeweled points of light in the corners of their eyes from their tears of joy. Worry over her success had created tension in their household, as their concern grew that none of their children would excel and become assassins like themselves. Her brother's failure resulted in his death, killed on his First Assignment, because his Target set a trap for him when he'd arrived. Her sister's story somehow seemed worse, since she actually accomplished killing her Target, but on a technicality. Her Target had slipped and fallen on her sister's weapon and her sister lied about what actually happened to claim the credit, which resulted in her downgrade to Laborer after she failed the lie detector test. Central Processing sent a Labor team to their family's house the next day to collect her sister and add her to their ranks.

To this day, Biin always believed her Mother and Father felt worse about her sister's lie and demotion than her brother's death. Once Biin became an assassin, she knew she'd never have to see that shame in their eyes again.

Until she herself became a Laborer as well.

About six months after she'd finished her First Assignment, she received a new Target. Eagerness filled her; she'd been practicing her weapon of choice—a poison dart gun—for months. She'd become an excellent shot, exceeding even her own Father's accuracy.

Biin wasted no time tracking down her Target—she didn't want to give him a head start to evade her. Located in an apartment building on the outskirts of Cand, she walked there, stationed herself outside the building, and waited for a clear shot of him through the window—which never came.

The unit, dark and without movement, remained that way for three days.

Frustrated, she proceeded to track him down, following the "How to find a Target on the Run" article she researched previously and memorized word for word. After several weeks, success finally struck. He'd apparently bounced from relative to relative until, unfortunately for him, one of them called Central Processing to report his whereabouts. This led her to his new hiding place in the city of Hund.

Biin had been furious, both at the lost time and at the several individuals who *hadn't* reported her Target's whereabouts. Why wouldn't they follow the law and immediately inform the authorities of any known fugitive? Whether they were family or not was irrelevant. The Makers had determined that he no longer maintained a useful place in society, so instead of being a drain on natural resources like food, shelter, clothing, and any other necessities that the government provided for worthy individuals, he needed to be eliminated. As far as her own beliefs, such citizens were failures at being Re'Bis and so deserved their fate as a Target.

But she also didn't understand why some individuals ran when they found out they had been targeted. It struck her as such a cowardly act. If you were a Target, it meant you weren't useful anymore. Period. Why would you *want* to be a drain on society? And the Makers, in their infinite wisdom, even gave them a second chance. They gave you the opportunity to find out if you are a Target, and in doing so, the chance to reclaim your honor and become useful again by killing your assassin first.

Biin shook her head as she arrived at the border of Hund. Regardless, her job did not entail getting inside the heads of those who didn't follow the Rules, only removing them from society so they could no longer threaten the balance.

She located her Target, entered the living unit where he resided, and found him asleep in his bed. Curtained windows kept the place dark, except for a single light hanging above her Target's head. A gentle breeze circulated through the room, even though the windows remained closed. Ignoring the tickling sense of unease at the odd situation, she held up her loaded gun, her Target perfectly lined up. Just before she pulled the trigger everything went black.

Later, Biin woke up tied to a chair in what appeared to be a basement. The scent of soil and moisture reached her nose and she fought the urge to sneeze. Her Target stood over her, swabbing her face with a cool, damp cloth.

She struggled uselessly against the restraints as her Target, who called himself Jaan and not by his Laborer number, urged her to listen to him. He reassured her by telling her that if he wanted her dead, she would be already.

"This wasn't easy," he'd told her, "to get you to be my assassin and lure you here. I had to report myself to help you figure out my whereabouts. You stayed in Cand longer than I would've liked. But no matter. I'll work with the time we have left." Jaan had then proceeded to tell her about a conspiracy concerning the Makers and Central Processing. He spouted facts and showed her items that proved he spoke the truth.

Biin resisted his theories at first, recoiling from the blasphemy that poured from her Target's lips. He must have been a heretic. And she would bet pretty good odds that this determined why he'd been targeted.

But too many things he told her made her think. Too many points of interest made her question what she believed. By the end of the day, after she'd been released from her restraints, she found herself not wanting to leave, but instead wanting to know more.

Jaan asked her to join him, join his cause, become part of a group looking to shine a light on inconsistencies in their government. They called themselves the Crypt, because they originally met at one of the underground mausoleums used as a place to bury bodies before the creation of Disposal Teams, who employed more efficient incineration methods.

Terrified, but unable to hide from the truth about the corruption of their government, she'd defected with him. And went on the run.

Since she didn't complete her Assignment in the allotted timeframe, she, of course, became a Target. She lasted three weeks until her own assassin caught up with her.

Having just returned to her most recent lodgings from a meeting with Jaan and several other Re'Ris who believed in his cause, she'd pulled her sweaty hair off her neck, plopped down at her table, and began looking over the datapad information from that day. They'd planned to collect information from other cities, hoping to expand the Crypt movement without drawing too much attention to themselves and putting Laborers' lives at risk by having them become Targets. She'd just started reading through the newest content on the datapad when her assassin sprung out of her cabinets and wrapped his hands around her neck, strangling her.

She'd gotten one kick in, which released his grip enough for her to suck in a snatch of air.

"Kill me," she said, her voice hoarse from the strangulation, "but others will discover Central Processing's lies!"

Her attacker retightened his grip at the last word and the world swam before her eyes. A vague notion that she couldn't feel her legs lodged in her mind and then...blackness.

When she awoke, no one hovered over her. Ragged breaths, raw throat, her neck tender to the touch. She lived. Her assassin hadn't killed her. Had that been on purpose? Or had he thought she died?

She never had the chance to find out. Only a few moments after she regained consciousness, her front door burst open and several individuals in the tight, yellow jumpsuits of Central Authority restrained her and brought her in for questioning.

Shortly after their questions began, she realized her near-death experience had caused some sort of memory issues—she remembered being attacked and blacking out, but she couldn't remember anything before that—her whole life felt enshrouded in a blurry wet blanket. As time went on, snippets of her childhood wove in and out of her dreams, but after several interrogations with Central Authority over the following days, even they had to conclude that she simply didn't remember most of her past anymore.

So, they left her alone, giving her a Laborer position.

The situation never hit the media and as far as she was concerned, her previous life meant nothing anymore.

Months passed. She knew herself to be Laborer 61-622—a dedicated individual helping to create a perfect society as dictated by the Makers.

Over the following year, however, flashes of her past began to creep into her thoughts during her waking moments. She began to recall her parents, her family, her life before becoming a Laborer. Details from her Assignments, what happened on them, being taken prisoner by Jaan, and how she'd decided to not follow the Rules.

With these new memories, she didn't know what to do. The ideas spoken to her by Jaan grew in her mind, leading her to believe once again that something had gone wrong in their society. Tentatively, she'd reached out and reconnected with a member of the Crypt organization. It seemed Jaan disappeared, whether on the run or targeted she never found out, and without their leader, the group withdrew in their efforts to create more changes, most too afraid to gamble their lives.

Frustrated by their dispersal but still brimming with her new sense of determination, Biin couldn't restrain herself any longer, and continued the pursuit to create change in the government. She reached out and recruited anyone else in the Crypt who still wanted to take the risk. She realized more and more how much Jaan sacrificed. The Crypt movement may have existed for decades, but hardly any action on their part took place during that time. Jaan's "kidnapping" of her began to alter that. Appreciating all he'd done for her, Biin wanted to push forward into more deeds effecting change, even though she didn't know how.

Then she'd met Sree Kaano. Biin had been the one to originally interview the young man at his house the evening of his finished First Assignment. Held hostage, like her, though he'd eliminated his Target, Wiin Niino. The tests showed he told the truth. Even though he'd killed his Target—he hadn't been lying about that—some of his story didn't seem to make sense to her. He'd been distracted, listless almost.

When she reviewed the facts the next morning, they didn't seem quite right to her. They reminded her of her own abduction with Jaan. Intrigued, she chose not to report these irregularities to the Superior in charge. Instead, she wanted to talk to Sree first, ask him about Wiin, find out what really happened. That morning, she called Sree's home, spoke with his Mother's Mother, and said he needed to come in for further questioning.

After the call, she'd seen a news bulletin, which broadcasted the details about the sensational hostage story. A picture emerged shortly thereafter of Sree's Target.

Nearly spitting out her drink, Biin stared at the displayed picture. She recognized Sree's Target! He'd been the same man who'd been her assassin, who'd attempted to strangle her to death, and left her alive.

More than ever, she needed to ask Sree questions.

Shaking her head to dispel these memories, Biin strode away from the morning Crossing Over room. The space for the afternoon group hadn't opened yet.

So where was he? Why hadn't he gone to the front desk? Had he not shown up? Or had he been diverted from meeting her?

Suspicion tweaked up her spine.

Something had gone wrong.

Chapter 25

"Yes, this is Sree's Mother's Mother, Vuun." Vuun nervously stared at the code where the vidlink call came from: Central Authority's main office. She paced across the kitchen, her attention no longer on the dish bubbling on the stovetop and absentmindedly fixed her hair. "Is there a problem?"

"There's been a breach in the system," the officer replied. His face, almost as aged as her own, peered at her with dark eyes, a sharp contrast to his pale gray skin. She recognized him to be one of the officers who'd stayed at their home while Sree was being interviewed yesterday.

Vuun's eyebrows furrowed. "What does that mean?"

"You were contacted this morning by a Laborer. Number 61-622."

"Um...I was contacted, yes. But to be fair, I don't remember their number."

"Of course. It was a statement, not a question."

Vuun grimaced at the harsh tone. She'd never been the

biggest fan of Central Authority. Their only real responsibility revolved around collecting individuals who deviated from the Rules. She felt as though they thought of themselves on par with assassins, even though they were just another branch of Laborer.

"What can I help you with?" she asked, as politely as she could muster.

"A situation has occurred that now needs our attention. It was determined because we have been recording your vidlink and audiolink calls."

"You..you've what?" She thought about all the vidlink and audiolink calls she'd received the past day. Gossiping with friends, lying to some acquaintances because she didn't want to tell them the whole truth. Had Central Authority discovered how poorly Sree's recovery went and that Vuun had been trying to cover it up?

The officer continued. "Yesterday, when we interviewed Sree, we tapped into your system. Within our rights, of course, due to the unorthodox nature of his First Assignment. That Laborer who contacted you made an unauthorized call about your Daughter's Son, requesting his presence. We believe she'd planned an attack on him and tried to lure him to Central Processing through you."

Vuun's eyes widened. "Oh Makers, is Sree all right?"

"Yes. We sent a guard to intercept him at the main entrance before she could contact him. A different Laborer questioned Sree instead this afternoon, so as not to arouse suspicion, but Laborer 61-622 did not approach the front desk where she instructed you to tell Sree to meet her, nor did she return to her post, and is currently a suspect in a treason investigation."

Vuun inhaled sharply at the shocking news. "Is Sree still in danger? Am I?"

"We aren't sure of her final intentions, but we are taking steps to ensure your safety. If she contacts you again, in any way," he prompted, "alert us immediately. We will continue to monitor your links as well as station a Central Authority tixa outside your house until further notice."

"I understand," she said, relief washing over her, although she couldn't help sneaking a quick peek towards the window, wondering if someone currently watched her. Even though officers were there monitoring her for her safety, she had the sudden urge to close the kitchen curtains.

"Please inform your Daughter's Son when he arrives home of the situation. And...on a personal note...I was proud to have met you and Sree, members of the Kaano family, yesterday. Um...may your life be guided by the Makers." The call ended abruptly, even before she could reply in the traditional ending, as if he'd been embarrassed by his declaration about her family.

Vuun's cheeks color-fluctuated in humility as she hurriedly returned to the stove to try and save the food she'd been cooking.

Maybe Central Authority wasn't as bad as she'd thought.

Chapter 26

Laborer 71-882 let out a huff as she watched the young Kaano exit her office after he'd just insulted her. Children these days. No respect.

She didn't even know what the interview had been about. She'd been minding her own business on her lunch break when her boss yanked her from a chair, muttering about a brief change in schedule, high priority, blah blah blah.

He'd plopped her down in her office, handed her the lie detector equipment, and gave her a set of questions to ask.

"You MUST follow these EXACTLY," he emphasized. And this last question HAS to be asked when he is about to leave, BEFORE he takes the headpiece off. You're my best Laborer. I know you won't fail me."

Laborer 71-882 had straightened with pride at his final comments and followed the script precisely with Sree Kaano. But she hadn't expected such an attitude from someone so young.

She'd never understood the animosity between assassins

and Laborers. Sure, Re'Ris were designed to be assassins, but that had been centuries ago. The world revolved differently now. Laborers made up the bulk of the population. Because they'd been streamlined and honed and tailored over the years, less assassins were needed, as usefulness within the populace sky-rocketed. She'd even heard of Laborers being transferred to other departments if they weren't faring well in their current positions, switching things around for variety if Laborers seemed less enthused about their jobs. She assumed in earlier times they would have been eliminated.

Laborer 71-882 felt perfectly content in her role. She did her job well, got along with her coworkers, had a nice place to live, plenty of food every day, and transportation. The life of an assassin, though more glamorous and wealthy, sounded like a lot of unnecessary work. Having to do all that research about your Assignment? Hoping you're skilled enough to eliminate them within the timeframe? Not to mention the process of killing them all together. Sounded messy.

Even the status level of those considered Laborers often felt higher than assassins. Superiors, Central Authority officers. And especially Head Superiors. They may "only" be Laborers, but they wielded power over assassins, shaping them through education, keeping them in check with the law, and creating boundaries for them to follow.

No, Laborer 71-882, though originally ashamed when she'd failed her First Assignment, later felt secretly glad she did. She liked her life.

While contemplating her status in society, a figure suddenly shimmered into view, having been camouflaged in the corner of the office during the meeting.

Laborer 71-882 shrieked. "What...?! What are you doing in here? Color-changing isn't allowed inside Central Processing!" She reached over to depress the button to call security.

The Re'Ris who appeared narrowed her eyes. With two

fingertips, she tapped the edge of her collar.

Laborer 71-882 gulped and pulled her hand away from the button. The collar, rimmed in black and gold, with three pips, signified this individual to be a Head Superior, the highest level of Laborer that could be obtained. Only 5 existed on the entire planet. They roamed throughout the cities, randomly keeping watch and tabs on suspicious individuals and unfavorable situations, and then met three times in a standard year in Cand to review their efforts, making any changes to the current system as deemed necessary. Odds remained high against seeing one at a distance, much less inside a small, cramped office.

"I-I'm sorry," Laborer 71-882 whispered.

The Head Superior dismissed the Laborer's apology with a flick of her fingers. "You were unaware." She moved towards the desk, using those same two fingers to first shut the door. "I need you to show me the results from the interview you just obtained from Sree Kaano."

Gulping again, the Laborer showed the data accrued.

"Interesting..." the Head Superior muttered. She then stared at the Laborer, as if calculating, before saying, "Will you come with me, please? I would like to submit you for reexamination of your status, based on your excellent conduct today."

Laborer 71-882's cheeks fluctuated with different colors. "Really?" she asked in a breathy voice. She'd always felt she'd been penalized unfairly when she became a Laborer. They found her in school, before she'd even turned 15 and could apply for her First Assignment, and stated that medical records indicated she would be unable to fulfill any assassin duties. She'd never even had the chance to try, but since then, she always felt undervalued. She had so much more to offer as a Laborer. "Th-thank you," she stammered.

With light steps, Laborer 71-882 followed the Head Superior up the elevator into a section she'd never seen before. The doors opened and she entered, with the Head Superior following behind.

The room appeared empty, except for an oblong table on wheels, about the size of a Re'Ris body, and a door located at the far end. The space seemed out of place, because Central Processing's rooms were normally painted in grays and blues, and this location had white walls, ceiling, and floor. It reminded her a bit of the white domed rooms at school, except without the desks, and much smaller. Only about ten people could fit in this space comfortably.

The Head Superior spoke, her voice higher than it had been in the office. "The information you acquired concerning Sree Kaano was highly sensitive. As a Head Superior, my duty is to protect this planet from any possible threats. The knowledge you now contain is a possible threat. There is only one way to ensure that knowledge can never be used." A clearing of the Head Superior's throat. "This is the first time I've ever been sorry."

Laborer 71-882 wondered briefly why a Head Superior would ever apologize to someone as lowly as herself.

Then the brief sting of a syringe in the Laborer's neck and the blackness that overtook her terminated any ability to question anything ever again.

Chapter 27

Sree dragged his feet as he headed up the walking path to his home, the scent of freshly rained-upon flowers tickling his nose. He'd never felt so defeated in his life. After leaving the room where he finished the follow-up questions, he spent the rest of the day in the main CrossLattice terminal section of Central Processing, waiting for an opportunity to find the Stasis Room, but the chance never arose.

First of all, two guards safeguarded the door to the area with the elevator. Wiin had forgotten to mention that little fact. Sree supposed that since Wiin worked there, he didn't think about the difference in accessibility between the two of them, how he'd be able to enter rooms easily, unlike Sree. Rooms such as those where the Crossing Over ceremonies were located and the central hub which contained the CrossLattice terminals, found on the first floor of the massive building, could be accessed by anyone. But personal offices and other restricted areas kept only for staff, including the elevator, lay behind the guarded door.

Secondly, staff members or escorted individuals came and went through the guarded door at random intervals, although fairly often, leaving Sree no time to sneak through without being detected. Wiin told him that door led to other areas of the building, but Sree had no idea how many employees had access to the area containing the Stasis Room. It made him even more doubtful that the room could exist as such a secret if so many others walked past it every day and didn't know about its contents.

And yet, he reasoned to himself as he skirted the lotha tree in his front yard, that's how buildings were. After all, he'd attended the same school for years, strolling past doors to places like the Superior's Lounge and janitorial closets, without once thinking about entering them. He always assumed their innards would be what the sign on the door stated, so he had no interest.

The Stasis Room didn't have that title plastered on its door, enticing passersby to wonder about what lay behind it. No, according to Wiin, it simply had a number, room 174-45, like every other office in the back area. If you didn't need to go into that office, why would you ever wonder about it and explore?

It could hide in plain sight.

Just like a color-changed assassin.

After hours of waiting, there'd been no safe way through the guarded door to even *get* to the elevator, much less reach the Stasis Room. So, following feelings of deepening failure and frustration mounted over time, Sree slunk home once Central Processing closed to the public for the day, feeling like a waste.

He wasn't sure why he thought it'd be easy. Wiin made it seem so simple. But he had *no* clue how to get into that area. And he knew of no one else to help him figure any of this out.

Reaching the front door, Sree squared his shoulders and put on a "happy" facial expression.

"I'm home," he called out as he entered, wiping his shoes first on the mat.

A rush of arms encircled him in a hug.

"Oh, I'm SO glad you're all right!" Vuun gushed as she squeezed tighter.

"Was I not supposed to be?" he asked after he could intake some air.

Vuun pulled away and searched his face, as if looking for signs of injury. Sree hadn't noticed before how deep the bags were under her eyes. She looked...old.

"I got a call from Central Authority after you left," she said, directing him to take a seat at the kitchen table.

Sree froze. Did they know his plan? Had he been foolish, watching the same door all day, causing someone to report his loitering as suspicious activity?

Vuun continued. "They said a false Laborer wanted to question you, that it had been some sort of setup—the videolink call I'd gotten this morning. The officer told me they would be watching the house and that they'd keep an eye on our ingoing and outgoing calls, in case she tried to contact us again."

Sree's initial panic subsided to be replaced with bewilderment. "A false Laborer? What does that even mean?"

"Apparently, she's under investigation for treason and wanted to meet up with you under the pretense of 'follow-up' questions. They had someone else question you, to keep you in the dark, in case she approached you after the questioning. They aren't sure of the fake Laborer's true intent, but it makes me wonder...Do you think maybe she's in league with the Target who held you hostage?"

Sree's mind raced. Could this Laborer have been working with Wiin? Or was this still just a setup to see if Sree knew more than what he'd let on?

"I don't know," he answered, truthfully, more questions than answers circling through his head.

Sree lay in bed that night, once again staring at his ceiling.

This time, however, instead of picturing nothing but Wiin's face at the moment Sree had thrown the lit flame into the apartment, he wondered about the situation he'd somehow managed to get into.

At this particular moment, he felt certain about three facts:

Fact #1: He hated being a part of this family. If he hadn't been a Kaano, then Wiin would have never reached out to him in the first place. He'd targeted Sree because of his parents involvement against the previous invading Aleet Army—so the citizens knew his family would do anything to protect their fellow Re'Ris—as well as because of his sister, who'd not only been the most famous assassin on their planet, but she'd also proven their parents had been murdered, *not* assassinated, which meant the system had somehow been corrupted and was not infallible, as was universally believed. Because of his family, Sree had clout, and Wiin wanted to use that to influence others when the truth he claimed about the Re'Ris and the Makers came to light. So yes, at this moment, being a Kaano remained far down on his list of prideful self-identifiers.

Fact #2: He hated Wiin Niino. Without his involvement, Sree wouldn't be mixed up in this at all. Why couldn't that man have left things alone? So what if their government hadn't been telling the whole truth? Their current system worked. Mostly. Those with skills and usefulness stayed alive, the others were killed. Except...Wiin suggested that this wasn't *exactly* the case. And if one lie, how many others? Who did the choosing of Targets if the Makers were extinct? And *how*? But more importantly, Wiin opted for it to be Sree's problem. So yes, at this moment, Wiin came in low on the list of Re'Ris he liked.

Fact #3: He hated Central Processing. Why? Because even though he'd managed to kill Wiin, pass the lie detector test, and attend his Crossing Over ceremony without revealing his revulsion, they'd already sent him his next Target.

Sree's gaze shifted from the ceiling to the datapad next to him. It had been delivered a few standard hours earlier, while he and his Mother's Mother had been eating dinner. The Laborer from Central Processing seemed anxious—most likely from delivering an Assignment to the Kaano residence—and had nearly dropped the datapad at his feet.

"S-sorry," the Laborer stammered.

"It's fine," Sree replied with a dead voice.

"You're *really* Sree Kaano?" she reiterated, even after he'd confirmed it when she first arrived. Her eyes widened, as if she just realized the audaciousness of her question.

"Yep." He'd shut the door in her face. "Lucky me," he muttered.

Currently, he had no desire to look at the datapad. How could they have already given him another Assignment? His Mother's Mother had been overjoyed, spouting something about life returning to normal and how competent they must think he is for assigning him another Target so soon, how most Assignments weren't that close together.

But Sree simply stared at the darkened screen with unease and exhaustion. He'd spent the previous week doing everything possible to avoid killing his Target, only to be kidnapped, let in on a conspiracy theory, seen proof of that theory, offered to help get more proof, and then *still* had to kill Wiin. That type of situation would not happen again with his next Target. Wiin didn't exist anymore to "fix" the targeting process. That meant whoever he'd been assigned to, he wouldn't have an out.

Which left him right back where he'd started.

And now that Sree knew something remained amiss in the government when it came to Assignments, who knew what helpless citizen had been chosen next, and why? Perhaps they were useful but had learned something they weren't supposed to know. Perhaps they'd spoken against a Superior and that was now grounds for elimination. Or perhaps they'd merely been in the wrong place at the wrong time and "needed" to be removed.

Whatever the reason, Sree couldn't trust anymore that his Target actually deserved to die.

Not that he'd kill them anyway.

Which of course led him full circle back to his first problem—he still didn't want to kill. *And* he knew he wouldn't be able to simply enter the Labor Force. If he didn't complete this new Assignment, he'd become a Target himself.

Moments trickled by, mocking him, reminding him he lived on borrowed time. He only had until the timeframe given to him to eliminate his next Target. It could be days, weeks, even months, but regardless, it gave him a deadline: either prove Wiin's theory and expose the whole planet's wrongdoings or go on the run and eventually get caught.

Because this time, he wouldn't kill anyone, no matter what.

Wishing more than anything in that instant that his sister would magically appear, he knew Faan would tell him what to do. Even though she'd been a stickler for the Rules, she'd risked everything when she thought something seemed wrong with what happened to their Mother and Father, and succeeded in proving so.

Show off, he thought with a smile.

The notion somehow calmed him down and he inhaled deeply.

But then he remembered that she'd died for that knowledge.

One step at a time, he told himself. *Just because she was the best assassin on the planet and* still *died, doesn't mean that's what will happen to you.*

The words of comfort felt hollow, even to him, although he still believed that's what she'd tell him. That every situation, moment, and experience could have a different outcome because every circumstance allowed for a variation in the scenario.

So, on a long exhale, he finally picked up the datapad and turned it on to find out how much time he had left to determine his fate.

CHAPTER 28

Panaan stared at the unconscious, not yet dead, body at her feet. Being an assassin proved easier than she'd thought it would be. She'd gotten her new Assignment the very next day after her Crossing Over ceremony. The timeline gave her three weeks to complete this present objective. It took her merely a day to find her Target and subdue them.

And that had been the point—subdue, not eliminate.

She wanted to use the rest of the remaining three weeks to find the young man who she'd seen at her Crossing Over ceremony in the hallway, who she'd tracked that day. The one who'd killed her Mother ...

What is he doing? Panaan had wondered to herself after following him from the ceremony room. She'd rushed out of the Crossing Over ceremony, sure that she wouldn't ever find the young man who'd she'd just seen walk past the doorway of the room she'd been in, but she needn't have worried.

Reaching the main hub of Central Processing, where citizens could utilize the computer systems for free, she peered around, searching among the groups of Re'Ris using the terminals, but couldn't find him. Most of them used this service for everyday issues—paying their bills, checking on their Laborer job status and schedules, replying to their children's Teacher's orders, etc, but some of them used it to see if they had become Targets, like her own Mother. Individual datapads were common for most citizens to use, but only consoles were connected to the CrossLattice system through Central Processing, so a specialized unit had to be installed in someone's household in order for them to have access to anything outside of personal use, such as the notice for being a Target. Her Mother could not afford that specialty item on her Laborer's salary, which is why the two of them made the trip to Central Processing every day to check.

She found him. The young man had stationed himself at one of the public consoles.

Panaan took a seat across the room, pretending to be waiting to meet with someone. She absentmindedly flipped her personal datapad around in her hands, which now contained a copy of her Crossing Over certificate, but she hardly looked at the screen. Without access to the CrossLattice system, it wouldn't be able to tell her any public details she could use to learn more about the young man. However...

...she *could* use it to digitally capture and store his image for future reference.

But how to do that without drawing attention? No one could use their individual datapad inside Central Processing for anything other than audio or vidlink communication or accessing personal messages and files. If anyone found out she'd used hers to acquire his image, her own name would become a Target faster than she could quote the first Rule.

Unsure of how much time he would remain in her sights, Panaan felt panic begin to creep up her body. She didn't want to lose him, but who knew when he'd finish his business at the console and leave.

Yet, as each moment moved forward, Panaan's anxiety ebbed. The young man didn't seem to be going anywhere. In fact, he didn't even seem to be paying attention to the console.

What is he doing? she wondered for a second time. She watched for quite a while longer and noticed his eyes darting towards a short hallway that led to a door, where staff members occasionally entered and exited. Two bored-looking guards stood on either side of the doorway, allowing staff members to pass in and out.

Curious, she watched for a while as well, trying to determine his goal. Could he be waiting for someone? She studied his face. No glimmers of hope crossed his eyes, like he'd perhaps identified the citizen he waited for, no sign of a letdown when the individual he searched for didn't appear. No, his facial expression showed furrowed brows and a clenched jaw—the signs of frustration, not disappointment.

Panaan switched her attention to the door once again. There didn't seem to be anything special about it. Or, for that matter, the employees who went in and out. Perhaps the guards interested him. Could his next Target be someone who worked here and he was watching to do recon on how to eliminate them while at their job?

That didn't make sense either. Color-changing inside Central Processing was against the law. Also eliminations. Unless he planned to wait for his Target to leave and kill them right outside the building? At one time, many assassins were bold like that, almost flaunting their skills and making a show of their prowess by doing so in public. However nowadays, a lot of Re-Ris found it distasteful, so it fell out of favor in the past several decades. Could this young man belong to a group that fetishized kills?

The longer Panaan watched him, the more those types of notions filtered through her mind, and the more she disliked him.

Finally, after several hours, when the main lobby would be closing for the evening, the young man slunk away, shoulders stooped.

Defeated, she surmised from his posture and movements. Whatever he'd hoped to accomplish hadn't panned out.

A decision had to be made, and quickly. The young man flowed with the crowd towards the exit. Did she dare attempt to follow him? Would he notice? Would he recognize her?

Shaky breaths lasted only a few moments before Panaan abruptly made the choice to see where he headed.

Keeping a bit of distance, she saw him walking away from the building, heading to the right. A sigh of relief escaped her lips. He moved towards a busier district. She could easily follow him through there and not seem suspicious.

Her sense of relief ended abruptly.

With a quick turn to the left, he headed to an area with three holes in the ground and called for a transportation orb.

A single.

No, no, no! she thought. She couldn't lose him, not now.

Desperate she screamed out, "What's that?!" The crowd turned to look at her and she pointed to her right. As one, the crowd turned their heads and the young man in front of her did the same.

She held up her datapad and snapped a shot, hoping against hope that it caught his profile.

While the crowd stared in confusion, she lowered her head and quickly slid among them, moving in the opposite direction from where she'd pointed, and from the young man, clutching her datapad as if it meant the difference between life and death.

If his picture is usable and I can identify him, it will *be the difference between life and death.*

His.

The last word resonated like a ricocheting echo inside her head.

Dragging her thoughts from her memories of the day before to her current situation, she stared down at her subdued Target. Now, she needed to figure out what to do with him—how to keep him alive and out of sight for the next three weeks, while making it seem as though he was both alive and present.

Assassins had the freedom to go where they pleased while on Assignment. Unlike Laborers, they didn't have to report their whereabouts each day to Central Processing. A perk of success for the higher, more esteemed level of assassin.

However, if this Laborer didn't report to work each day, someone at Central Authority may notice his absence and ask questions. But Panaan needed this extra three weeks to find the young man. So...how to keep her Target alive long enough to complete her real mission, without raising suspicion about his non-attendance at work?

With a deep exhale, Panaan began to form a plan...

Chapter 29

Strolling down the street, Sree passed multiple storefronts as he meandered aimlessly. Their brightly colored flags and multi-toned window displays contrasted against the whites, grays, blues, and silvers of the main city and Central Processing. A sense of comfort washed over him in the midst of the vivid color schemes while his mind struggled with his new reality.

Three standard weeks.

That represented the timeframe given for his next Assignment. All the time he had before he needed to either kill his Target or infiltrate Central Processing, get to the Stasis Room, enter the Archive Room, find the evidence he needed to prove a corrupt system—assuming it even existed, and...

...and what?

Tell his Mother's Mother? What could she possibly do except admonish him for his foolishness and hide the evidence so they wouldn't get caught?

Take it to the authorities? What could they do? Arrest

someone? But who?

Talk to a Head Superior? Assuming he could even get a meeting with one, what it *they* were in on the conspiracy? And even if they weren't, they'd never consent to listen to a citizen about something so preposterous. Maybe if he had his sister's assassin standings he'd have a chance... but a lowly first-time assassin? He'd never get approved. He doubted even the name Kaano carried enough influence for that sort of acceptance.

Reveal his findings to the media? Would they even dare to report something so blasphemous? It had taken Sree an entire day to believe Wiin's theories, and only because he desperately *wanted* to believe. Did Sree really imagine he'd survive that long once he said anything to anyone?

Anxiety threatened to engulf him once more. He again wished Wiin never sought him out in the first place. Or at least had some other more tangible plan to help Sree make choices moving forward.

Regardless, he needed to make some sort of decision: either go forward and try to get to the Stasis Room or not.

If he did, he ran the risk of being caught and becoming a Target.

If he didn't, he'd have to kill someone or become a Target.

Not exactly stellar selections.

Still, the best option would be to make the attempt to find proof. It held the only possibility to change the status quo, *possibly* stay alive, and even better, not kill anyone else.

Sree's thoughts were interrupted when something small smacked him against the side of his head.

"Ow!" he cried out, placing a hand against his temple. He whirled around, trying to locate what could have possibly hit him. A stray bird? A rock kicked up by a nearby tixa?

No movement around him.

Rubbing the painful spot, Sree continued to walk, a frown on his lips.

Thwack!

This time, something hit him on the shoulder.

"What is going on?" he cried out, spinning in a circle.

There. Behind him to the left. A shadow slipped into the doorway of a store.

Sree stood, frozen. Why on Re'Ris was someone pelting him with stuff? And why do it twice just to run? Did they know him? His family? Or could it just be some kid thinking they were funny?

Anger overtook fear. Sree recklessly strode toward the doorway. *Why can't everyone just leave me alone? I have enough stupid problems to deal with that I don't need some punk...*

Sree's rant trailed off as he forcibly shoved the store's door the rest of the way open and peered inside.

The tiny shop looked well maintained and clean. Shelves housed cases and decorative items for people's personal datapads and communication devices: bright spots of color, mixtures of patterns, and even some plain and monotone to please any type of buyer. The place smelled clean but also carried the scent of something like cookies. Possibly to entice buyers? Sree wasn't sure. He hadn't spent much time in shops, preferring to order on the CrossLattice system and have whatever he wanted delivered.

In the center of the store stood what he assumed to be an employee of some sort, who looked like she could be his Mother's age, helping a customer. Two other patrons, possibly assassins out to shop or their Laborers doing the shopping for them, wore toned down attires of grays and steely blues, reminding him of Central Processing. None of them seemed to register his abrupt entrance.

The customer being helped looked...familiar. She appeared to be close to Sree's age, perhaps a couple years older, with flyaway hairs dancing around her face. Flushed cheeks in tones of dark pink highlighted her grey skin and she moved her hands in an almost comical sense of animated whimsy. But her sage green colored uniform caught Sree's eye the most.

Frowning, he thought, *A Central Processing Laborer in a shop at this time of day?* Perhaps she'd gotten the day off, but then why wear the uniform? He then realized he didn't really know much about the world of Laborers. He'd spent most of his time at home or in classes. Somehow, he supposed, he imagined they just...*lived* in Central Processing? He snickered at the notion, understanding in that moment the ridiculousness of such an idea. Of course they must have lives outside of work. He'd just never thought of them as anything more than necessary bolts in a machine.

Then, he remembered where he knew her from. She'd been the Laborer who'd interviewed him two nights ago after his encounter with Wiin.

The woman he'd taken for the employee turned to look at him. "Well?" she asked. "In or out of my store? I'm not made of heated money, you know."

Guilt at causing a scene in front of the store's owner made him lower his head, and he quickly muttered an apology before stepping fully into the store and closing the door behind him.

In that moment, a gated set of metallic bars slid down over the door. The windows tinted darker and the bright signage stating "ACCESS" quickly shifted to the duller tones of "SEALED." The two patrons on either side stopped browsing through the items and stood with their hands clasped in front of them, staring at him.

Sree's guilt instantly snapped over to fear.

"Don't be scared," the Laborer in the sage green uniform said, turning towards him. Her face, though roundish from youth, had the look of someone with the weight of the planet on her shoulders.

The store owner, however, tilted her head, as if sizing him up.

"What's going on?" Sree demanded, happy that his voice sounded steady.

"Do you remember me?" the Laborer asked. "I met you the other night after you returned home from your First Assignment."

Sree swallowed, hard, then nodded. He took a step backwards towards the door.

The Laborer put up her hands to show she meant no harm. "I have two questions and then you're free to go. Please."

Sree paused in his movements to leave. "What?" he asked.

"Did your Target, Wiin Niino, talk to you about his time as an assassin, before he became a Laborer?"

What? How could she possibly know something like that? Without thinking, Sree simply nodded again.

A greedy glint of desperation shone in her eyes. "Did he tell you about the Target he couldn't kill?"

Silent, Sree stood there, caught completely off guard by the question. And then he remembered—the story about the woman Wiin had left for dead, but began to breathe, and he'd run, not finishing the kill.

"Yes," he whispered.

The Laborer's body visibly slumped, as if all the tension left her after hearing that one word. "That was me. I was his Target."

It couldn't be possible. "You?"

She bobbed her head a few times to confirm her statement, then lowered her hands to her sides. "Honestly, it was a hunch, about him being my assassin. I didn't know if he even remembered me, much less might talk about me. But after your interview about being held hostage...things just didn't sit right. And then I saw his image on the news bulletin the next morning and I recognized him as the man who'd let me live. Plus, the circumstances around your 'kidnapping' situation were too close to what I went through myself."

Sree moved his hand fully away from the door, his thoughts of leaving having vanished at her words. "You were kidnapped, too?"

"Yes. By a Re'Ris named Jaan." With a slow movement, she

gestured for him to have a seat at one of the small tables near him.

This could be a trick, he told himself. *A way for Central Authority to catch you.*

She spoke a little more, as if noticing his hesitation. "When I realized the similarities between your case and mine, and when I saw it was Wiin who detained you, I tried to set up an interview with you through Central Processing, to reveal my side of things and find out the truth about yours, but I'm pretty sure Central Processing figured out my plan."

It could still be a trick... but the voice in his head seemed less sure. This Laborer knew that Wiin had let someone live. And hadn't his Mother's Mother said someone from Central Processing had tried to interview Sree under false pretenses?

This whole thing, now, may still be a setup to get him to confess, but if they really doubted him this much to create such an elaborate ruse, why not just target him for assassination and be done with it? Unless they wanted information about Wiin's plan...

Still a bit dubious, Sree took a seat, deciding to let this young woman talk more until he could determine her intentions.

An exhale released from the Laborer's lips. "Thank you for talking to me."

"I'll listen. That's all."

Slightly stiffened shoulders showed the only indication that the Laborer must have realized Sree hadn't sided with her yet.

"I understand," she said slowly. "I have more reason to believe in you than you in me. So, I'll start with the basics. You met me as Laborer 61-622. But my *name* is Biin Sool."

A feeling of unease blossomed inside him. This woman was a Laborer. And yet she openly used her name instead. Though he knew all Re'Ris *had* names, the idea of one of them claiming it when they weren't an assassin felt...wrong.

And yet I don't want to kill. Am I less "wrong" than she is?

Biin continued. "I'm eighteen standard years old. When I

was fifteen, I became an assassin. I completed my First Assignment, Crossed Over, and made my Mother and Father...very proud." Her voice hitched a little when she mentioned her Mother and Father, but she continued as if that hadn't occurred.

"About six months later, I received my next Assignment. But once I found him, like you, I was captured instead. The man who took me, Jaan, spoke to me about a conspiracy surrounding the Makers—how they weren't who we all thought they were—and how others, like him, wanted to prove it." She smiled, as if recollecting the moment. "I thought he was insane."

Sree forced himself not to nod in agreement. He remembered that feeling all too well with Wiin, but didn't want to show any type of emotion until he knew for sure he could trust her.

"Anyway, when I realized he *wasn't* spouting nonsense, I panicked. I couldn't kill anymore, not after what I'd learned, so I went on the run."

Interest piqued, Sree listened more closely. Could this be an option for him? Could he go on the run, too?

"Even with help, it only took my assassin three months to catch up to me."

Well, there goes that *idea.*

"I should say, that's when Wiin caught up to me."

Sree rolled his tongue around in his mouth before asking the question he knew would prove to him if she were a spy or not. "What did you say to him?"

She blinked, as if not expecting him to have spoken. "What?"

"Right before he tried to kill you, what did you say to him?"

Without missing a beat, she said, "I told him to kill me, but that others would discover Central Processing's lies."

That had been what Wiin had confided in him that she'd said. No one could have known that outside of Wiin and the Target he tried to kill.

The young woman in front of him.

She was real, not some undercover agent. The conspiracy was *real.*

A shudder rippled through Biin, unaware of Sree's bombshell of a realization, causing her skin to color-fluctuate momentarily. "I'll never forget those words again. I couldn't remember my past, not for a long time—trauma response the doctors told me. But when I did get my memory back, I thought it was the stupidest thing in the world to have said at the time. I was *convinced* that because he'd been sent to kill me, he must have known the truth, must have been in on the conspiracy. So, I thought I was rebelling somehow, letting him know even if I died, he, and Central Processing, wouldn't win." She paused. "But he hadn't any idea who I was or why I'd been targeted, did he?"

"No," Sree answered. *This would be the moment. If she were against me, this would be all the proof she'd need, me confirming that I'd spoken with Wiin and* not *merely been held hostage, and she'll kill me.*

But nothing happened except she continued to speak.

"Then *why*?" she asked, a note of pleading in her tone. "Why didn't he complete the Assignment? The status report would've shown I hadn't died. His orders would have been to resume his task and finish the job. So why didn't he? And how did he survive for over two years without getting targeted himself? Until you became his assassin, that is."

Sree took a breath. The time had come for him to be open as well. Either he planned to be fully in this or not. And since he'd felt so alone this whole time, here and now could be the opportunity to collaborate with others.

He may not have to deal with this whole "find more proof by stealing it from Central Processing secret rooms" by himself.

"Wiin said he didn't know why he didn't finish the job with you," Sree answered. "He said killing just didn't make sense anymore. And as for how he survived, he told me he changed the system and demoted himself to Laborer. He hid in plain sight."

A different voice, rougher and sharper, chimed in. "He was a Binder?" the store owner said to Biin, who had leaned against the counter. She scoffed. "Figures."

Sree turned his head to look at the new speaker. He assessed her a little more closely, noticing the heavyset bags under her eyes, the greenish color of her deep grey skin. This woman seemed to have been a Laborer for quite some time, based on how tired she appeared.

Sree frowned, unfamiliar with the term. "Binder?" he asked.

Biin explained. "When the codes were created so our computers and the CrossLattice system could connect, they were designed by, bits of...oh how do I put this...? Bits of Maker genetic material were entwined into the computer codes. This created a bind between themselves and the system, so that only they can access and change anything internally.

"This 'binding,'" she went on, "means only someone with Maker genetic material can create changes to the system, such as assigning Targets or demotions. They are the only ones who can unweave the computer bonds to make these changes."

Sree frowned. "But if only they can do it, how could Wiin have changed something in the system to demote himself to Laborer?"

The owner crossed her arms and spoke up. "There have been rumors that some Re'Ris actually have Makers genetic material inside their own cellular structure. It's never been proven, but..." she swore, then looked at Biin. "If only we would've known about Wiin beforehand! Think of what we could have accomplished!"

Sree sat stunned, though neither woman noticed. Wiin had shown Sree proof that the man's genetic structure presented itself as almost *identical* to The Makers. But Wiin thought that meant *all* Re'Ris were nearly identical. Not just that he himself exhibited it as a unique trait.

Biin finished explaining to Sree by saying, "If Wiin was one of those individuals, a Binder, and it sounds like he'd have to be to do what he did, then we could've used his genetic material to splice into the computer system and...effectively do anything we wanted."

The owner sneered. "We could've brought the whole system down. Or revealed highly sensitive information to the public. I bet he didn't even have any idea of how powerful he was."

Biin waved the owner's comments away. "It's too late now. He's gone. We can't use him anymore." She turned once again to Sree and said, "After my near-death experience with Wiin, I lost all memories of what had happened to me for years. And I think..." she hesitated, looking over at the owner, who gave a tiny nod for her to continue, "I think Central Processing suspected about Jaan, the man who'd kept me hostage. But I was an unusable witness. I passed all the lie detector tests when Wiin tried to kill me because I actually *had* forgotten my encounter with Jaan. But I believe the Head Superiors kept me around in case my memories came back—so they could gather information about the Crypt movement. When months passed and I showed no signs of remembering, I think they just...forgot about me. Then my memories did come back, and after I reached out to your house yesterday so we could meet at Central Processing, I'm sure they now know I remember again."

Sree's head spun. So much new information at once. "The *what* movement?" Sree asked, forehead furrowed.

The owner threw up her hands and let out a grunt. "He doesn't even know what we're *called*? What under the skies did Wiin talk to you about?"

"Wiin wasn't one of us, remember?" Biin stated in defense. "He learned everything on his own and still came to the same conclusions as us." She waited a moment. "Well, to be sure, we should compare notes. I don't know exactly what Wiin told you."

Sree opened his mouth to speak when the owner abruptly

said, "Not now. The store has been sealed long enough. People will report me if I'm not accessible for too long."

Biin nodded. "All right, you're right." She glanced at Sree, her eyes soft. "I'm sorry you got involved in all of this. I don't really know why Wiin went to such trouble to include someone as young as you."

Finally feeling like he had an answer, he blurted out, "He wanted me for my family name. And I may be young, but don't forget, Jaan did the same thing to you when you were my age." Sree couldn't help the defensive tone in his words at the idea that she saw him as a child when she wasn't more than a couple years older than him.

She grinned, a genuine smile that lit her whole face, and she looked like her actual age. "You're right. Sometimes I feel like that was lifetimes ago and that I'm Muura's age." She nodded toward the owner.

Muura grunted again.

Once more, Sree felt that same unease at hearing a name instead of a number. Did all Laborers secretly use their own names? Or did this group do it as some sort of protest against the system?

"Unfortunately, we don't have enough time right now to go over everything we need to. You have to leave," Biin said to Sree. "But I'll contact you when we can meet up again."

"Central Authority is watching my place," he warned. "And both the audio and vidlink lines are tapped."

"I know. That's why I didn't reach out to you at your home." She nodded towards his head. "Sorry about the pebbles."

Sree laughed. He'd completely forgotten the reason he'd stormed into the store in the first place. "Well, it worked. It got me in here. But maybe next time you can call out my name or something instead?"

"Deal. We'll meet up again, soon. Don't worry. In the meantime, just do everything you'd normally do."

Sree turned towards the door, but just before he left, he asked one more question. "I know Wiin wanted me for my family's name, even though I'm so young. But why did Jaan recruit *you?*"

"He believed I had Maker genetic material, that I was a Binder."

A blossom of hope opened inside Sree's chest at the idea but quickly closed in on itself as the smile on her face faltered while she spoke four more words.

"Unfortunately, he was wrong."

Chapter 30

Sree couldn't help himself. He'd begun to panic.

A week slipped by since he'd met Biin and the store owner, Muura, but neither of them contacted him. Only two more standard weeks left until he needed to kill his own Target. Twelve days left to learn what they believed about the discrepancies in the government, tell them about Wiin's Stasis/Archive Rooms theory, and hope they'd want to help him infiltrate Central Processing, find proof of Central Processing's lies, and expose those falsehoods.

A scoff emerged from Sree's mouth without his consent. The absurdity of the situation wasn't lost on him. Even if they figured out a plan *and* found the evidence they needed, how could they share it with the citizens of the planet? And even if they found a way, why on Re'Ris would anyone believe them?

On the other hand, Sree felt so relieved to learn about Biin and the Crypt movement. It meant he didn't have to face this mission alone. He hadn't realized the amount of stress building within him at having to carry out Wiin's wishes by himself. He felt lighter, his mind more at ease that somehow he wouldn't really need to do anything anymore—just pass on the information and the few items Wiin bestowed on him and let the rest of the group figure it out.

Once the conspiracy miraculously became revealed to the public, Sree felt sure he wouldn't have to kill anyone.

At least, that's what he told himself for the first few nights.

But a dull ache settled into his stomach on the fourth night after no one communicated with him. The ache grew into a solid lump on the fifth night. And yesterday it made him feel absolutely sick to his stomach.

Today, he dragged his feet to the kitchen table, sat, and stared with no appetite at the breakfast in front of him.

"You feeling okay?" his Mother's Mother asked. She pressed her fingers against the skin on his arm and removed them, observing how his skin tone responded to her firm touch. "Hm, no unusual color fluctuations, so you aren't sick."

Rubbing his arm, he said, "I'm fine. Just...tired, I guess."

"How's your Target coming along?"

Sree knew the words were meant to be casual, but he could hear the worried tone woven through each syllable. Sree had felt Vuun's eyes on him since he'd returned from his "kidnapping" escapade, watching him nonstop. Not to mention the Central Authority warning that they were now being spied on.

It felt as though she were waiting for him to fall apart or explode or get killed at any second.

Sree paused at those thoughts and let out a sigh. Truthfully, she had every reason to believe those things. What he'd gone through had been nearly unprecedented and she most likely wondered if he'd bounce back from it.

With a false sense of wellbeing, Sree took a huge mouthful of the warm mashed food and replied, "It's coming along great, Mother's Mother. I've already identified their location and am in the stages of preparing my mode of attack." Assignments weren't allowed to be discussed beyond generalities, so he knew she couldn't ask more than that.

A small smile touched her lips. "Wonderful. I'm happy to see you are settling into the lifestyle of our family. They would be...no, they *are* very proud of you."

The ache of anxiety in his gut spiked and sent a shiver of fear throughout his system. Swallowing, he stood, feeling the need to escape the room as fast as possible. He didn't want any uncontrolled skin-shifts to show her his unease. "I should get going, then. Strategies need to be figured out. You know."

A nod. "Of course! Will you be home for dinner?"

Sree hesitated. "I'm not sure. Once I figure out my course of action, I'll have to travel for quite a bit. I may not see you for...a while." A new feeling, a lump of sadness, caught in his throat. He realized he had no idea what would happen if everything *did* work out. Would the citizens rejoice in the streets to learn the truth, finally allowing him to roam around freely, no longer having to kill? Would he be eliminated on sight by the authorities? Would he have to flee the planet, only to be chased for the rest of his life?

I don't want to do any of this, he thought, overwhelmed at his possible futures, the words desperate inside his head. Now, more than ever, he needed Biin to contact him. He wanted out of *any* responsibility. Let her or someone in the Crypt group break into the Stasis Room and find the proof needed in the Archive Room. Let them deal with the consequences. He never asked for this. And he didn't want to be a part of it.

But you don't want to kill anyone, either. You can't have it both ways.

Sree frowned at his own intrusive thoughts. He hated his own logic. He didn't want to abide by the regulations of the system, yet he didn't want to be a part of causing possible change.

I just want to be left alone...

A laugh emerged from his mouth. Just a short while ago, after learning of his sister's Passing On, he hated the idea of being so alone. And then again, after Wiin died, he couldn't stand the feeling of being on his own.

Like I said, his mind reminded him, *you can't have it both ways. It's time to make a choice: Either be an assassin and ignore the conspiracy or take the risk and do something about it.*

So...what are you going to do?

Chapter 31

Any pride Panaan felt after figuring out that to cover her Target's missing days at work she could call him in as being ill subsided as she realized she wouldn't need to use that excuse anymore.

Because he lay dead at her feet.

Cursing under her breath, Panaan glared at the body. She hadn't *wanted* to kill her Target within the first standard week of her three-week Assignment, but she'd miscalculated the binds on his wrists and he'd nearly gotten away, so she'd had no choice. On top of that, the punch he'd managed to drive into her face wouldn't stop stinging. Luckily for her, he'd tripped as he headed towards the door of the abandoned store where she'd decided to hide him, and her head cleared enough from the blow in time to catch him and finish the job.

Once again, she'd felt nothing about killing her Target. He'd pleaded with her for the final few moments he'd been alive, but she didn't care. Her thoughts centered only on the fact that he'd foiled her plans to have extra time to catch the young man who'd killed her Mother. Luck had evaded her with the young man's captured digital image, and she hadn't been able to identify him based solely on the partial picture. Since the last time she'd seen him, she'd gone each day to Central Processing, but he hadn't returned, so she felt like any progress she'd made in determining his identity had vanished. Having to start over in trying to find him, she needed the extra two weeks. But now, she'd be off Assignment and wouldn't be allowed to deviate very much from her day-to-day schedule.

Panaan thought about that. She'd never questioned the life of an assassin—she'd only strived to be one to help her Mother's situation. But an assassin's life always seemed so...prestigious. They could stay home all day or go on a trip, attend artistic shows or travel off-planet. Not that Laborers *couldn't* do those things, but they lacked the funds necessary to do them on a regular basis. The only restriction for assassins stated that when they *weren't* on Assignment, those movements could be tracked, such as what events they attended or where they went on vacation. However, when on Assignment, Central Processing only cared that the job ended up completed within the timeframe, finalized by passing the lie detector test after you eliminated your Target. They didn't track anything else you did during the actual Assignment time. So, Panaan needed that freedom of being on Assignment to search for the young man and kill him, because Central Processing wouldn't ask her about that pursuit, just her own Target's demise.

Now, she'd have to report her dead Target and her Assignment would end. A Disposal Team always checked a body for time of death, to verify the truth of an assassin's story, so she had to report him right away. But that meant she'd lost her freedom to find the young man, track him, and kill him.

And though she knew she could wait until her next Assignment and start this process all over again, it remained uncertain as to how long it might take before she'd be given her next Target. A standard week? A month? A year? The darkness within that drove her to avenge her Mother wouldn't be sated until she'd made that young man pay. She could barely stand each moment—the thought of day after day, week after week of this unrelenting pressure overwhelmed her. Her skin color-shifted at the mere unease of this blackness living inside her for one moment longer.

Forcing breath in and out, she made herself focus and occupied her mind with the next action. Right now, she needed to report that she'd finished her Assignment. With measured steps, she first hit the nearest Disposal Team button to alert them. Because she needn't stay at the scene, since the interview would take place at Central Processing, she left before they arrived, and headed to the main hub to submit her statement.

Once there, she methodically went through all the steps, confirming that yes, she'd killed her Target in that abandoned store after tracking him. She didn't have to lie—they didn't ask her anything strange like if she'd held him hostage first—so the process moved along quickly and within an hour after starting the interview, she left the main building.

Strolling without purpose while doing her best to keep her emotions at bay until she decided what to do next, Panaan found herself in the courtyard of the Assassins' Accolades, where over the centuries the Re'Ris elite had been acknowledged for their outstanding contributions to the title of assassin.

Blue and silver flowers dotted the teal blades of turf around the pathways, while curved flowerbeds housed more luxurious plants, including potted crawling vines and kuat bushes. Archways arced above the four main entry points and benches sat at various junctures around the central sculptures area.

The outskirts of the courtyard, surrounded by walls, had the names of many noteworthy Re'Ris assassins carved into it. Progressing towards the middle, there were plaques and small statues for more distinguished assassins, but at the center stood five statues—the most revered Re'Ris in history. The statues stood upright in the courtyard: each erected over 50 years ago except for the newest one which sat in the epicenter—Faan Kaano.

Panaan glanced up at this newest statue. She'd always seen it from afar, but she and her Mother never ventured too far into the courtyard, because they usually had other places to be, since their free time was never actually free. Now, Panaan could go anywhere she wanted, and as she didn't have another Assignment yet, she found she couldn't think of a single place she truly desired to go. Somehow her feet had brought her here, perhaps hoping for inspiration from other assassins before her.

Peering more closely at the statue, with its detailed carvings, she could sense the awe it inspired, even within herself. Faan Kaano represented the peak of Re'Ris abilities, and she'd only been an assassin for seven years before she died off-world at the young age of 23. The statue had been designed, carved, and revealed before she'd even Passed On—the first time in Re'Ris history a statue became constructed while its subject still lived.

Decoratively woven vine and leaf patterns curled around the bottom edges of the statue, etched with intricate detail and precision. At the base, two plaques were placed into the stone, one for her Mother and one for her Father, both of whom had stood up and fought against the Aleet Army's attempt to infiltrate the capital city. Everyone knew they'd died defending their world.

There had been rumors, of course, that their transportation orb accident hadn't been an accident at all—that in reality, Re'Ris members who'd aligned with the Aleet Army at the time had taken it upon themselves to commit murder.

Panaan dismissed the rumor immediately when she'd heard it. No one would do that. No Re'Ris would ever murder someone to forward their own plans. If the murders were true, members of the Aleet Army themselves, "off-worlders," must have done it.

And yet, she paused, uncomfortable. Wasn't *she* doing the

same thing right now? Deciding to kill the young man without being assigned to do so? Could she be no better than a murderer?

Unease crept through her innards like a snake loosed in the turf. Doubt gnawed at her, and she began to wonder if she were doing the right thing, if she should give up this pursuit that clashed with what Re'Ris represented, what Faan Kaano represented.

Then, she noticed that between the two plaques of Faan's Mother and Father sat a stone partition containing a digital picture.

A family picture.

Six individuals. Panaan immediately recognized three of them: Faan and her Mother and Father. But to Faan's left stood a young man.

The young man.

There could be no mistake. He may be a couple years younger in the picture, but it was him.

He was related to Faan Kaano?

Incredulity swept over her. From the looks of it, he appeared to be...a younger brother?

Creeping closer, Panaan read the inscription softly out loud: "The Kaano family: from above left to lower right: Twaan Kaano, Vuun Kaano, Yeela Kaano, Giili Kaano, Faan Kaano, and Sree Kaano."

Sree Kaano.

He now had a name.

She could find him.

Determination consumed her once again and almost all the apprehension about murder vanished. He would pay for what he'd taken away from her.

But one feeling, like the beginning of an itch, still tickled the edges of her mind: doubt.

She suppressed it, allowing her anger to consume her once again, fueling her forward to her prey.

Chapter 32

Sree wished he could wait for Biin or Muura to contact him, but because they didn't know his timetable for killing his next Target, he had no clue if they'd show up before it ended. The decision to move ahead without them hit him, hard, but he couldn't keep hoping some other miracle would help.

Once he'd made the decision to continue on the path Wiin had set him upon, an eerie sense of calm resolve took over. Especially because he knew the reasons behind any targeting process could be corrupt.

The difficulty for him ran high enough already in envisioning the eliminating of someone no longer useful to society, but he could never live with himself knowing he may kill an innocent person.

This way, at least he could go down trying to make things change. If in no other manner, maybe he could live up to his family's name in that sense.

So, the morning following his decision, he returned once

more to Central Processing. He *knew* there had to be a way to get through that door. He just couldn't see it. Yet.

As he entered the familiar environment, with its computer alcoves and charging stations, he looked at it with new eyes. Everything appeared to be designed for a citizen's comfort, and yet...he felt twice as uncomfortable as before. The place seemed stifling to him. The lack of windows made the space feel more like a contained prison than a welcoming vestibule. Muted grays and blues gave off a synthetically cold vibe, a far cry from the luscious plant life and warmth of the extra heat lamps outside. Even their red sun cast a warming glow across the city—unlike the harsh artificial lights inside this lobby area.

Sree wondered why they'd designed the place this way. It seemed a shame to waste the natural beauty of the city by dulling it down and closing off access to it by not having windows.

And yet, he felt like maybe he could now understand it. This represented a place of business but also...a place of safety.

The world outside, however beautiful, contained assassins. Though the Re'Ris were taught not to fear death and to revere those who followed The Makers' wishes, the air constantly held the tension of every hunter searching for their prey. Those who couldn't defend themselves could find refuge, at least during business hours, at Central Processing. Eliminations were not allowed to happen inside the building, nor was skin-shifting. A person could spend all day here, away from the unknown lurkers outside, and be safe.

The muted colors, the closed-in feeling—they could be seen as a relief from that tension found outside.

Sree never had that worry because no children under the Age of Progression could be targeted. Even the Makers must have thought it unseemly to eliminate those underage. Because of this, he never wondered about the anxiety associated with knowing you *could* be a Target. Also, even though the Rules didn't state it specifically, he assumed assassins would never *be* Targets. Unless they failed at their Assignment, they were productive members of society, so Sree figured only Laborers would be deemed unworthy and become a pursuit.

Now that he knew there could be corruption in the Rules and that some of them were disregarded completely...

A chill iced his spine. What if children *were* sometimes Targets? What if assassins who displeased the government became Targets as well? What if...?

Sree shook away the catastrophizing thoughts. That spiraling hole of questions would do him no good right now.

No. Right now the only mental energy he should be using must revolve around how to get to the Stasis Room.

Sree took the same position inside the terminal hub as last time, in an alcove where he could see the door to the staff area but not appear to be watching it.

After a couple hours, Sree let out a frustrated sigh. This wouldn't work. The intermittent entering and exiting of staff through that door, not to mention the guards still stationed there, allowed for no undetected access.

What else could he do? He didn't have any breaking and entering skills, so showing up after hours wouldn't do him any good. Could he somehow approach a staff member and ask to be let through? He snorted a laugh at the idea of simply questioning the information desk.

A flash of his sister's face flooded his mind. *She'd* know how to get in.

She'd just walk right in, he thought to himself. *No one would question her because of her status. She could go anywhere on the planet and no one would blink an eye.*

A different thought edged its way into his mind.

Status.

The beginnings of a possible plan began to form...

Chapter 33

The next morning, after finalizing the idea for what he planned, Sree found himself following a Central Processing employee through the guarded door. As they stepped through, he wiped his sweaty palms on his pants.

He couldn't believe it. His stupid idea might actually work.

"This way," the Laborer said. Sree had already forgotten the man's number. The Laborer spoke very little. An older gentleman, he had the hollowed-out look in his eyes that Sree always associated with Laborers who'd been working for multiple years.

More like automatons, going through the motions of life on programing instead of choice.

A shudder of color rippled across Sree's skin at the thought. Out of habit, he thought about how he himself could become a Laborer if he didn't complete his Assignment, but then he remembered Wiin had told him that assassins, if they didn't complete their Assignments, simply became Targets themselves.

He couldn't join the Labor Force now even if he wanted to.

Focus, he told himself. *Pay attention.* Sree returned his concentration to the current moment and studied his surroundings. Once through the guarded doors, the space opened up into three corridors: one to the left, one to the right, and one straight ahead.

They headed to the right. Sree took a note of the numbers on the offices as they walked past.

272-45, 273-45, 274-45...

They seemed to be a floor above where he needed to go, since the room he searched for, 174-45, began with a lower set of numbers.

Needing more information, Sree decided to take a risk. "This place is huge," he said to the Laborer.

No reply.

Sree switched tactics. "How long have you worked here?"

No answer...but then...

"Since I was sixteen."

Repressing another shudder, Sree said, "That's a lot of years. You must have been everywhere in this building by now."

The Laborer slowed his pace, as if allowing Sree to walk next to him instead of behind him. Sree took the offer. He noticed the Laborer's face seemed a little less taut, his eyes a touch less glassy as he answered.

"Not everywhere, there are a lot of restricted areas, but I've seen quite a bit. You know there are seventeen floors? I always wondered if that were on purpose, you know, cuz of the seventeen Rules. Of course, there are two annexes as well, each with five floors, so maybe it's just coincidence. I used to work in the eastern annex before I was promoted." A tinge of pride touched his words.

"That's quite an accomplishment," Sree said, having no idea of the truth behind that statement, but feeling like inflating this man's ego may keep him talking. "I noticed the door numbers on this level are in the two hundreds, but we're on the ground floor," he said, trying to keep his voice steady. "Does that mean there is another floor below us?"

The Laborer shook his head. "No. There's nothing below us. The ground didn't support digging during construction, so they solidified it and built only on its surface." He cricked his neck to the side before they entered the elevator, peering at the doors as if for the first time. "That's strange. I wonder why they numbered the doors that way."

With a lick of his lips, Sree said, "Does that mean the one hundreds are in the annexes?"

Frown lines creased the man's forehead. "No. Those rooms use letters first, but the first floor does start with 'A'..."

Sree didn't want to put too much attention on why he asked these questions, so he changed the subject as they entered the elevator. "Well, who knows how things get designed. I'm always noticing stupid things like that. Tell me more about your work, now that you got promoted and aren't in the annex anymore."

The Laborer spoke animatedly at length for the next couple minutes while they ascended, particularly about datapads and research and conducting polls for this department or that. Sree didn't really understand *exactly* what the man's job entailed, only that it sounded like something Sree would never be able to follow. He'd never been great at facts and figures and his memory proved to be less than stellar as well. In fact, he'd been very thankful that Wiin had slipped in a datapad—not connected to the Cross-Lattice, of course—with a summary of all the details they'd talked about, including the Stasis Room number, because Sree had completely forgotten most of the information by the time he'd set the fire and run.

"Oh," the Laborer said, suddenly, interrupting his own monologue. "We're here." The elevator doors opened to reveal a small alcove with a single door in front of them. The metallic sheen on it looked like it had been polished recently. A beautifully carved number 3 sat in the upper center, with tiny etched swirls trailing off its edges. A Laborer standing next to the door smiled at the two of them.

"Welcome!" she said. "You're right on time."

"Of course," the older Laborer said,. Sree watched as the man's shoulders slumped and his eyes darkened once more. "Have a pleasant day," he said to the two of them in a monotone voice. He abruptly turned and trudged away.

The new Laborer, her eyes bright, shook her head. "Poor man. He's been here so long, but not very useful anymore." She shrugged and pressed a panel next to the door. "Head on in. She's ready for you."

The door opened.

"Enter," a voice called from inside.

The space dwarfed him. It seemed to be a large chunk of the entire top floor. The entrance, wide and curved, came to a point at the rear of the room, like the wedge of a pie. Soft swirls of pastel pinks and yellows floated across the walls, accenting the deep golden carpeting. Several comfy chairs and a small couch in deep pinks and corals dotted one side, while the other sported a long table with six upright chairs surrounding it. Datapads and personal effects were scattered across the room, on the furniture, tables, even the floor. Several works of art lined the walls, their digital images changing every minute or so. Except the one furthest away, which hung in front of the corner behind a wide, off-white desk. That piece appeared to have etchings of flowers and vines engraved onto a fused multi-colored metal background.

Behind the desk itself sat a Head Superior, whom Sree assumed must be Three, based on the number etched into the door he entered. One of the five that existed on the entire planet. She looked every bit the part of someone who must be more important than others, from her fitted black-and-gold collared shirt to the air of authority in her upright posture.

"It is a pleasure to meet you, Lone Kaano," she said, gesturing for him to sit across from her.

Sree cleared his throat. "Th-thank you," he stammered. The traditional title of "Lone" for anyone orphaned while under the Age of Progression caught Sree off guard. An antiquated practice, no one else had ever called him that since his Mother's and Father's Passing On, except one of his Mother's Mother's friends once, but he felt he shouldn't be surprised that a Head Superior would use the term, knowing how strictly they adhered to tradition.

A tiny nod from her. "It is rare indeed to acquire a meeting with a Head Superior, but your family's name holds a high standing amongst us."

She even spoke differently, more intelligently. Sree found himself hoping he didn't sound dumb. He spoke the words he'd rehearsed the night before. Just in case, he'd doublechecked that every word he said contained the truth. He didn't think anyone would be monitoring him, but in all honesty, Head Superiors were shrouded in mystery.

And now that Sree had learned that things behind the scenes were anything but law abiding, who knew *what* those in charge would do to keep their secrets covered.

"I've come to realize just that—how important my family has been to the Re'Ris. To the Rules. I know morale has never fully recovered since the Aleet Army infiltration nine years ago and, to be honest, since my sister recently Passed On. We all know it's an event that isn't something to mourn, but somehow, she became a symbol of hope, and that symbol was lost with her death. I thought a ceremony for the public to celebrate my family, those who other Re'Ris idolize, would lift their spirits."

The Head Superior gave a soft smile. "You are not wrong. Hope is very powerful. Which is why I granted you this meeting. For you see, Lone Kaano, *you* are valuable as well."

Sree frowned, caught off guard. "Me?"

"You are the last remaining active member of your family. The abduction you went through, and your successful elimination of your Target as a First Assignment, was global news. You represent your entire family line and the Re'Ris have elevated you to be their new symbol of hope."

No words emerged from Sree's mouth at these statements. The pressure of living up to his family's name, which he'd so diligently worked on reducing, came back full force.

Head Superior Three continued. "We, as keepers of the Rules, should have foreseen this. Your First Assignment should have been monitored more closely. We should have anticipated the upheaval in our citizens, which may have filtered down to your Target. We failed you."

This stance from a Head Superior surprised Sree and he didn't know what to do with the thoughts tumbling through his mind. *She* was admitting their errors to *him*?

He decided to take a risk. Perhaps she would be more forthcoming. Wiin told Sree that The Makers were all dead, contrary to what the Rules say. Would she tell him the truth? "Don't the Makers assign Targets? Weren't they aware of who was assigned to me?"

The Head Superior interlaced her fingers and placed her hands on the desk. "Though it may be difficult to believe, the Head Superiors are not infallible. I understand that statement almost has a tinge of blasphemy, but it is the truth. We, as Head Superiors, have done everything we can to preserve what The Makers set out for us, following their designs and their choices, as our Creators. But we have also been tasked with understanding *why* they choose who they choose. It helps us learn and grow as a species.

"What happened with you," she went on, "was a test, as most Assignments are. A test we failed. And we almost lost you because of it. The Makers needed us to see that we as a species are no longer as one. Our loyalties have become divided. Ever since the Aleet Army invaded our world, the Re'Ris have questioned their place in this universe. As well they should."

Sree raised his eyebrows.

"Oh yes. We encourage questions and doubts. We want the citizens of our world to feel right and good about what they do. To understand that there are others on alternate planets who deal with situations in their own ways, but that the way we were created lends us a purpose that many others don't have. Without that purpose, it can lead to confusion and chaos, and the building of armies like the Aleet Army."

She gestured behind him and he gasped. On either side of the door sat long windows, letting in the sunlight. Sree automatically took a few steps closer, admiring the stunning view. He felt higher up than only the 17 floors of the building, but he didn't know the height of each level. The lobby itself took up about three floors just on its own and this office's ceiling reached higher than twice his height. He could even see the distant statues in the Assassins' Accolades memorial and knew one of them portrayed his sister. Shame flushed through him as he realized he'd never even gone to see it.

"Do you know that we've not had a single war in our history since The Makers created us?" Head Superior Three said. "Not a single uprising. Not one in thousands of years. That's because of purpose. Without it, an individual is lost, confused, and hopeless. They struggle. We do not. We thrive. Because we follow The Makers' plan."

Sree returned his line of sight to the Head Superior.

"This is why *you* are so important," she concluded. "Your family members were not only the most talented assassins this world has seen in a long time, but you all pushed the boundaries toward protecting this planet. Your Mother and Father stood up to the Aleet Army. And your sister was instrumental in its final takedown. They've shown their commitment to pursue difficult routes because they loved who they were and where they came from. And *you* carry that legacy. The Makers knew this. So, they assigned you to an individual who wanted to remove the remaining symbol of your family name. Who wanted to laugh in the faces of The Makers."

Sree couldn't help himself. He blurted out, "But why? If everyone is so happy with how our society works, why would Wiin have done that?"

A frown touched her brow. "The Aleet Army changed everything. Minds were altered, thoughts transformed. Literally. And the consequences of that trickled through to anyone who would listen. Your Mother and Father could see these changes. They devoted their lives to end the infiltration. But after nine years, the Re'Ris still haven't recovered. Even you have seen this. The balance of our world has worked for so long...it saddens me and the other Head Superiors to know that there is discord among the citizens."

Sree contemplated her words. He'd only been seven standard years old when his parents had Passed On. Most of the Aleet Army infiltration at that time had been completely off his radar. All his knowledge centered around that one moment he and his Mother and Father were traveling in an orb and the next moment he felt pain and neither his Mother nor his Father answered his cries for help. And then, they were just gone.

Faan had tried to explain things when he'd been older, how she had her theories that the Aleet Army actually planned their deaths, and that it had been on purpose, unlike what their world believed. But Sree didn't understand. If that were the case, why had Central Authority deemed their deaths an accident? Why not just admit the truth?

Sree stared at the Head Superior in front of him. The voice in his head told him to leave it alone, that it may jeopardize his mission, but he didn't care. He wanted answers.

"Why were my Mother's and Father's Passing On reported as an accident if that wasn't the case?" He instantly regretted the words as they left his mouth, but a part of him held his ground. He needed to know.

The slight rise of an eyebrow by the Head Superior didn't go unnoticed by Sree.

"How do you know that?" she asked.

Sree recognized the same power-dynamic he'd faced with Wiin. These individuals saw Sree as something they could use, control. Knowing he'd probably be dead in less than a couple weeks anyway for not finishing his current Assignment, Sree threw caution to the wind. Raising his chin, he said, "You answer me and I'll answer you."

A tiny sliver of a grin touched the edge of her mouth. "Very well. You've shown yourself worthy, between your family name and your deeds to honor them. It is true, the transportation orb incident you were in which caused them to Pass On was not an accident. A member of the Aleet Army was hired to eliminate them because of their resistance to the army's infiltration."

Sree couldn't believe she just admitted to the lie.

"We kept it a secret," she went on, "well, the Head Superiors at the time kept it a secret—I wasn't in my position yet. I was given my post of Head Superior Three a year after that event. When I learned about the demise of your Mother and Father, I was...conflicted by the secret. I had no desire to hide the truth from anyone, but..." she let out a sigh.

"You were young," she continued, "and you cannot imagine the chaos that ensued from the Aleet Army's destabilization of our world. With their leader's ability to change thoughts, members of our government began contradicting themselves. They tried to change the Rules. They tried to murder other Head Superiors. And they influenced members of Central Authority to create factions which would rise up against the government. No one knew who to trust. No one knew who to believe anymore. It was...terrifying...and beyond our Head Superiors' control."

She placed her hands flat on the desk and lowered her eyes. Sree never thought of the idea of a Head Superior being nervous, but she appeared this way to him right now, as evidenced by the color in her hands rippling slightly.

"Your Mother and Father joined a multi-world group called The Liberators, determined to stop the Aleet Army. The Aleet Army were determined to remove any obstacles in their path, and any members of the Liberators were highest priority for removal. That's what made them pursue your Mother and Father. After they Passed On, the Head Superiors didn't want to induce panic. The fact that members of the army could take out such accomplished assassins as your Mother and Father...it was unthinkable. And it would have only caused the citizens to fear each other even more. Because..." She said the following words carefully, "the Head Superiors never discovered if it *was* a member of the army, or if their leader had corrupted a Re'Ris to murder them. Can you imagine if the public knew about this, that a friend or family member could have been corrupted by the army's leaders' powers? They would have suspected anyone and everyone who did anything remotely out of the ordinary."

She tilted back in her chair, her voice softer after speaking for so long. "The Head Superiors at the time had no idea the army's leader would Pass On the following year, making that fear of other Re'Ris moot, because when he died, his mental hold on those he controlled disappeared. But the secret about your Mother and Father had already been created. How could we say we'd lied? How could we know that *all* the influence from the army's leader was gone? And even if *we* were sure, would the public believe it? Or would they still question the actions of everyone they loved? The Head Superior at the time, who made the decision, retired after the Aleet Army left our world and I took his place. Though it left a sour taste in my mouth, I knew the secret about your Mother's and Father's Passings On had to be kept. But it has pained me every day, especially knowing you, your Mother's Mother, and your sister never knew the full truth about your own family."

Unexpected anger surged through Sree. Faan's search had

been for nothing. "My sister was killed because she knew something was wrong. She left to prove that *you* all lied. She didn't Pass On from following the Rules. She died because you never told our family the truth."

"That is the other reason I granted you this meeting." The sadness in her voice did not go unnoticed by Sree. "The Head Superiors had never been faced with an issue like the Army before. They did what they thought was best, but...they were not always correct in their decisions. Faan Kaano proved this. And an excellent assassin perished well before her time because of it. Creating a day to honor her, and your family, should be the highest priority. No matter if they've Passed On, they can remain a symbol of hope for thousands of years to come."

"A day to honor them is fine," he challenged, "but the truth. It's time to tell the truth, too. To the public. It's the only way they'll understand what my family truly did for this world."

Head Superior Three squared her shoulders. Moments trickled by. Sree held her gaze.

Finally, she let out a deep exhale. "Agreed. It is time."

Chapter 34

Sree left Head Superior Three's office a short while after she'd finally agreed to tell the entire truth on what would be known as Celebration Day. After reassuring the Laborer outside her door that he could find his own way out of the building, Sree reflected on the details of the upcoming event. The Head Superior assured him she'd appoint appropriate speakers and make the announcement herself about the truth of what happened to his Mother, Father, and Faan. If he thought of anything else he wanted to add to the ceremony, he only need contact Central Processing and ask for her directly. She gave him a code that would prioritize his request.

With a head full of swimming thoughts, Sree entered the elevator. He'd gone to that building with such a different purpose, but now...so much of what Wiin had spoken of didn't quite make sense anymore. Could Wiin have been one of those confused individuals who wanted to follow the Army? Or had he simply made the information he'd found to fit his own theories?

Wiin had told him the Makers were extinct because he saw a few of their bodies. But the Head Superior spoke of them as though they were still alive.

Wiin said his Mother's and Father's group, the Liberators, was created to overthrow the government. But the Head Superior said it was created to overthrow the Aleet Army. And if the Army's leader had powers to corrupt minds, the government at the time may have been corrupted as well. So...his Mother and Father *could* have technically done both: fought against the government officials who were also in league *with* the Aleet Army.

Who was right? Or were they somehow both right?

And what about Biin and Muura? Were they on Wiin's side or their own? Sree didn't actually know any of their plans, just that they wanted Sree on their team. He felt like one of the balls in play on a nah-tsu court, smacked back and forth between the players.

The determination he'd felt the night before, his plan to infiltrate the Stasis and Archive Rooms, all seemed to melt and swirl inside his brain. How could he decipher the truth?

All these questions happened within mere moments of stepping into the elevator. He hadn't even gone down more than a few floors while these thoughts folded over themselves. As he stared absentmindedly at the elevator buttons on the panel in front of him, his eyes focused on something unusual. He noticed the floor he'd chosen, the ground floor, had two smaller, curved buttons below it. They didn't look like the other buttons. Curious, Sree ran his fingers over them.

Nothing happened.

But the curved marking felt odd to his touch. Almost...warm. He slid a finger over the upper button. Then the lower. Impulsively, he pressed them both at the same time.

A panel of numbers lit up beneath them.

Sree recalled the "tour guide" who'd led him upstairs in the first place. How he'd claimed there were no floors below the ground level. But Sree remembered about the numbered doors on the main floor: in the 200's. If the Stasis Room was 174-45...

Sree stopped, mid-thought.

The code Wiin gave me isn't to get into *the Stasis Room. It's to get* to *the Stasis Room.*

Licking his lips, Sree entered the code sequence into the lit panel.

The two buttons glowed orange.

But at that same moment, the doors opened. Sree had reached the ground floor.

Snatching his hand away, he nodded at the Laborer who entered, then Sree exited. Travelling down the hallway by retracing his steps from his "tour guide," Sree's mind raced faster than it ever had before.

He would bet anything that if he pressed the curved buttons after he entered the code, the elevator would lead him to the lower level.

But the question remained, did he still want to pursue that route?

Did he trust Wiin or the Head Superior?

Dull throbbing filled the inside of his skull. He felt tired of not knowing what to do, who to believe, or how to move forward. He'd accomplished some sense of direction this morning and now his path seemed more convoluted than ever.

Making his way home in a thought-filled blur, he entered, and vibrant flavors of spice and meat hit him as they wafted through the air.

"Oh, hello, dear!" Vuun called out, shuffling towards him. "You're home earlier than I expected. Have you finished your Assignment already?" She tapped against his wrades, as if wondering if he'd used them.

Sree internally swore at himself. He'd completely forgotten he planned to stay in a hotel during the three weeks until he "finished" his Assignment, in case Biin or Muura wanted to contact him away from the prying eyes of his home. Of course, they didn't *know* he'd be at a hotel, but he still thought it safer than getting his Mother's Mother mixed up in anything. Without thinking, or perhaps because he'd been thinking too much, he'd gone home on autopilot instead of returning to the hotel.

"Uh, no..." he said, struggling to find an excuse without revealing more than necessary. "I need some more clothes."

"Ah," she said, a knowing look on her face. "A long-term Target. I've been there. Just pace yourself and you'll be fine. Rushing in never works."

Sree gave half a nod and headed to his room to fulfill his bluff and get extra clothes, but before he got to the stairs, he paused.

"What's going on here?" he asked, just noticing the massive amounts of food being cooked and the several sets of plates on the kitchen counter.

"Oh, Sree, it's just been wonderful," Vuun gushed. "The outpouring of support and care has been more than I ever could have imagined."

Confusion stole over his face. "Support for what?"

"Well, for *you,* my dear."

The confusion deepened. "For *me*? Why do I need support?"

Vuun continued stirring something in a pot to prevent it from boiling over. "I received a vidlink call a few days ago from my friend. She said she was contacted by someone who wanted to show support to you, well, and to me, for the hostage situation you'd been through. And also, the Passing On of your sister. Not that they weren't glad for her to have Passed On, only that the removal of a family member is still felt. And everyone knows it's just the two of us left."

He frowned. "So...you're throwing a party?"

She *tsked.* "A gathering. Of the leaders of the group. They want to come here and speak with me about exactly what we may need, how to best show the support they want to give. Naturally, I'm not going to leave them hungry."

Sree rolled his eyes. If the point of this gathering revolved around getting help and support, then why go to the effort of preparing a *huge* meal, feeding everyone, and then cleaning up afterward? Sree hoped the group would just hire someone to help his Mother's Mother with her housework. That would be the most helpful offer, in his opinion.

Curious as to why he cared about the housework, he realized it was because he knew he wouldn't be around in the near future. He'd picked up most of the slack, cleaning and doing chores around the house, after Faan had died. How much she'd actually done hadn't been apparent until she didn't exist to do those things anymore. And for some reason, even though he knew they employed Laborers to take care of the groundskeeping and deliveries, he vaguely remembered his Mother and Father at some point talking about Laborers and how the two of them didn't want to use hired help anymore.

Sree wondered about that. He'd been so young at the time, perhaps five or six standard years old when they'd had their discussion, and hadn't really thought anything of it at the time. But now, it seemed a strange thing to do. His family had the funds, and didn't such work give Laborers meaning?

Except...except now he *knew* some Laborers. They weren't automatons. They weren't useless and only good for fulfilling the requirements of their position, like he'd always thought.

Words trickled through his mind. The Liberators. Wiin had said his Mother and Father had been part of that group. The Head Superior had told him the same thing. The former said they were displeased with the government. The latter said they were displeased with the Aleet Army.

But if his Mother and Father had only been in a political group against the Aleet Army, why care about their Laborer staff?

Sree thought harder, forcing himself to recall his Mother's and Father's exact words.

They didn't want to use Laborers anymore.

They didn't want to *use* Laborers anymore.

Instead of firing them, his Mother and Father meant it as not to *use* them, that Laborers were worth more than to simply be used.

They meant they believed the government was *using* the Laborers.

That's what they'd fought against. The treatment of the Laborers, not whether or not to keep them employed.

His Mother and Father fought against the government's viewpoint of Laborers.

The chime to their door rang. Though a pleasant sound that almost jingled throughout the house, it startled Sree from his insights.

Vuun cried out, "Oh! Someone is here early. Go on, Sree, get upstairs. And don't let them see you when you leave."

"Why not?" he asked, as she gently steered him to the staircase.

"My friend, Raali, has been asking a TON of questions about you, ever since your First Assignment. How you are, if you're mentally stable, if you can handle your next Assignment..." Vuun rolled her eyes, a movement Sree had never seen before, especially when speaking of her closest friend. "If she sees you, she's going to bother you. And if you haven't finished your current Assignment but you've returned home, I'll never hear the end of it!"

Sree scoffed as he put a foot on the first stair. "Why are you even friends with her if you hate the way she talks about me?"

"Because other than her jealousy of our family fame, she's quite lovely!"

A snicker escaped him as he climbed the rest of the staircase, two steps at a time. He never understood that type of friendship.

But, he supposed, he didn't really have any close friends to have to deal with in the first place.

Sree wondered about that as he haphazardly packed a few sets of clothes into a bag. He'd never really connected with others, since they focused mostly on school or Assignments, and he didn't care much about either. In fact, he never really had a plan for his life. With most everything provided for him, he never worried about money or buying things. But now, during this time of crisis, he realized a friend would make a *huge* difference. Imagine confiding in someone about his concerns, about his plans. Having someone help him make decisions or...just be there when everything fell apart.

He realized maybe he'd put up with some odd quirks, too, if it meant someone supported him.

Sounds of voices downstairs pulled him from his reverie and he slung his bag over his shoulder. Heading towards the stairs, he descended quietly, peeking out to check on everyone's focus. Three other women were seated in the living room: one he recognized as his Mother's Mother's friend, the second appeared to be in their same age range, and the third one looked...well, about the same age as Sree.

Sree paused for a moment before sneaking out the back door, taking one last look at the young woman. He wondered why she'd be in such a group. He assumed it would have been composed of individuals around his Mother's Mother's age, retired assassins with money and time to burn. So why the addition of someone who appeared so young? She hardly even looked old enough to have completed her First Assignment.

Having waited a moment too long, the young woman turned in his direction and locked eyes with him. The briefest look of recognition danced in her gaze before she returned her attention to his Mother's Mother and the rest of the group.

Sree let out the breath he'd been holding. He would never hear the end of it from his Mother's Mother if that girl made a scene upon seeing him.

Slipping the rest of the way out of the house, he headed to the hotel, choosing to walk to clear his head. A light breeze ruffled his hair, and he let himself use this time to give his mind a rest from the bombardment of thoughts. Heated lamps popped on in the twilight, giving off a reddish hue that bathed the streets. He inhaled deeply, the scent of recent rain filling him, and let himself relax for the first time in weeks.

About a block away from his destination, someone grabbed him and yanked him into an alley. Before he could so much as yell out, pressure constricted his throat and he couldn't breathe. Lashing out blindly behind himself, he hoped to hit his attacker, but the lack of breath incapacitated him, and he felt himself slip down within his attacker's grip. During one last moment of clarity, Sree unleashed the wrades on his wrist and struck out behind himself, hitting something solid.

Then, blackness overtook him.

CHAPTER 35

"Well, maybe not the neatest kill, but that hardly matters when the end result is the same, right?" Vuun told her friend, having a difficult time keeping the defensiveness from her tone. Irritation grew at the recent snide remarks about her Daughter's Son.

No, it hadn't been the cleanest elimination. Sree's own Target had gotten the jump on him in an alleyway the previous evening. *And* rendered the poor boy unconscious.

But Sree prevailed. Using his wrades to finish his Assignment.

So what if the Disposal Team needed to wake Sree up from unconsciousness? He'd still been the victor.

"The point is," Vuun said loudly, talking over her friend, "Sree completed his Assignment. No one should care how."

In the middle of her meeting with the "support" group the night before, which she felt had been going rather well, she'd gotten a vidlink call about Sree being in the hospital. Apparently, there had been some damage to his neck and throat from an attempted strangulation and the doctors wanted permission to proceed with any tests needed. As his next of kin, Vuun needed to confirm the liability waiver of any surgery required while he'd been unconscious. She'd hesitated at first, wanting to go down there and check on him herself, but she didn't want to bring attention to the situation in front of her group. He'd already had one strange encounter. She didn't need more gossip about another.

Vuun agreed to the terms, then returned to the support group. They'd been delighted to learn about Sree's idea for the upcoming Celebration Day for the Kaano family, the official announcement occurring over multiple news broadcasts before the group convened. Vuun couldn't be sure after their discussion went on for a while, though, if they really wanted to support her and Sree or if they simply wanted to ride the wave of fame from her family name.

Only the youngest of the group, who appeared to be Sree's age, seemed genuinely interested in helping. She spoke of being on her own, after her Mother had been Targeted, but had successfully accomplished her first two missions. She'd found herself gravitating towards Vuun's family as a kindred spirit and thought she could benefit from Vuun's wisdom; in exchange, she would help around the house.

Vuun had been genuinely touched. Most assassins avoided engaging in any household activities normally reserved for Laborers. But, as Vuun herself enjoyed cooking, she could understand the tradeoff in learning about eliminations while doing something beneficial for the family between Assignments.

Besides, if this young woman's Mother had been a Laborer, she most likely knew how to do household tasks anyway.

As the meeting came to a close, Vuun asked the young woman—Panaan was her name—to stay and help clean up, if she'd like, and they could finish their conversation.

"I'd love to!" Panaan agreed with a smile.

While they applied the final finishing touches to a now clean kitchen table and countertops, Sree entered the house.

* * *

"Hey," Sree said to his Mother's Mother as he strode through the door. His throat, still a little raw from his encounter, made the words sound scratchy. "I'm home."

"I'm glad you're all right," Vuun said, rushing over and eyeing him up and down. Her gaze lingered on his neck and he wondered if there were marks left from his assailant's fingers.

Sree gave a weak smile as thoughts flittered through his mind. He couldn't believe what had happened. His own Target ambushed him. The man he'd been trying to avoid because he didn't want to assassinate him. And in Sree's own desperation and instinct, he still killed the man.

Two Assignments completed.

Two deaths not of his choosing.

When he first awakened in the hospital, he'd been stunned. Everyone stood over him, doling out their congratulations.

Except he'd had no idea what they were talking about.

Then he learned that in his desperate attempt to survive, he killed his attacker. They'd even cleaned the blood off his wrades and replaced them on his wrists.

Mixed feelings had raced through him. Revulsion. Panic. And...

...relief.

That feeling sickened him. How could he feel relieved that another death occurred?

And yet, it bought him more time. More time to expose the corruption in the system because it meant his Assignment had been completed. More time for him to *not* have to kill anyone else. He could hardly be at fault since his Target attacked him first. It was self-defense. He would've let the man live otherwise!

Still, the relief made him feel sick to his stomach. As soon as he could, he slipped away from the hospital, from the gleamingly proud looks showing on each doctor's and nurse's faces.

Now he only wanted to hide in his room and sleep for as long as possible. But first, something to eat before some real rest.

"Hi."

A voice Sree didn't recognize sounded from behind his Mother's Mother. Craning his neck, he peered around his kin's body to see the young woman he'd noticed from the meeting earlier that evening.

"Uh... hi?"

Vuun tutted, as if scolding herself. "My apologies, Panaan. This is my Daughter's Son, Sree. Sree, this lovely young lady is Panaan."

Something sharp lingered for a moment in Panaan's eyes at the sight of him before it disappeared and she cleared her throat. "Pleasure. Your Mother's Mother has been telling me all about your family line. It's impressive what happened tonight, that you managed to defend yourself against your attacker. Although, with someone of your genetic background and family upbringing, I don't' know why your Target bothered even trying."

Quick words on a breathy voice made Sree wonder if she were nervous about speaking to him. Not that he hadn't encountered this before—he'd met several people who'd been in awe of him simply because of his family name. But something else caught his interest...something he couldn't place about her...

Eagerness?

Sree focused instead on her remarks. He wanted to tell her he'd hated every second of it and that his Target hadn't deserved to die, but instead he thought about keeping up appearances for his Mother's Mother's sake and he crafted the most well-spoken answer he could muster.

"Every Target has the opportunity to defend themselves. It's what makes our system work."

A shadow passed briefly over her face. "True. Though most Targets wouldn't stand a chance against someone like you." Her face brightened. "But that's why you and your family are so incredible at what you do."

Vuun cut in. "Panaan is going to be here every so often to help around the house. In return, she'll learn from me about my experiences, and of course those of our family."

Sree did his best to hide his disbelief. Wanting to know more about killing, how to be better at it, learn at the feet of "masters..." His sense of revulsion increased. He didn't belong on this planet. He didn't belong to this family. He was a mistake.

"That's great," he muttered. Suddenly, his appetite vanished. "Sorry, but, after what happened tonight, I'm pretty tired. I'm going to go to bed."

They both said their goodnights but he had already turned away. On the way to his room, he heard two more comments from them to each other before he'd made it all the way upstairs.

"He seems...sad..."

"I'm sure he's just tired, my dear. Now, let's get back to what we were discussing..."

Chapter 36

Another one. Another Target.

Sree's mouth and throat felt like they were coated with ash.

He'd barely awakened before a knock sounded on his door. Cheerful, his Mother's Mother entered, dropping another packaged datapad on his lap.

"They must think extremely highly of you!" she exclaimed. "The turnaround time on your Targets is faster than I've ever seen!" She ruffled his hair, told him breakfast would be ready soon, and left the room.

Sree sat in his bed, stunned. How could this be possible? Even his sister hadn't gotten this many Assignments in a row and at this speed. What were they trying to do, kill him?

The thought struck him, hard.

Could that be a possibility? That the Makers, or whoever remained in charge, wanted him dead?

But why not just make him a Target, send an assassin after him, and be done with it?

However...if they wanted it to appear as though they were following the Rules, why would *he* be a Target at all? It wouldn't make sense to the public. His family was famous. *He* was famous. Nothing about him warranted the status of "useless." So, no one would accept the idea of him being a Target.

But the more he thought about it, the more he continued to wonder if the notion held truth. Because one thing hadn't made sense from when he'd been ambushed the previous night: his Target had known his whereabouts.

Targets were allowed to know they would *be* a Target, but not by whom. And since Sree hadn't planned on killing the man, he hadn't approached the Target's place of residence or work or anything to tip his hand.

But his Target had been waiting in that alleyway to the hotel. How could he have known Sree would be there?

Someone must have told him.

The notion pierced his mind, and a chill scurried up his spine.

And only a Maker—or someone who could manipulate Targets—would do such a thing.

Sree's thoughts hovered on the image of the Head Superior he'd spoken with. She'd seemed genuine in her support of him and his family. Could it have all been an act?

It also meant he needed to stay on alert with this next Target. Who knew if they would be informed of Sree's whereabouts as well, intentionally positioned for another surprise attack? Any possibility of a reprieve giving him more time to get into Central Processing disappeared from his hopes.

He'd have to break into the Stasis Room as soon as possible.

Expecting a pit of dread in his guts like before, he realized he only felt a mild fear. Perhaps because, in a way, the choice had been made for him. If they'd left him alone, he may have taken his time, still waiting for Biin or Muura to contact him in the coming weeks or months about what to do. But the higher ups showed their hand.

And that hand wanted him dead.

Opening the packet, Sree noted the name and location of his new Target.

Shock coursed through him and he swore under his breath.

Biin Sool
TVH Building
Cand

This couldn't be possible.

His Target could *not* be Biin.

Theories raced through his brain.

Could this be a setup by Biin, similar to what Wiin had done, to meet with him?

No, unlike Wiin, she didn't have Maker genetic material, so she didn't have the ability to change his Target's name to her own.

Could this be a ploy by someone who knew what Sree planned? Did they know he'd been contacted by Biin? Was this a way to expose them both somehow? Or have them both die?

But why make her his Target at all? Only one of them would be killed. It wouldn't expose anything. And they could have any assassin go after her if they just wanted her dead. They could've assigned him any Target if they just wanted *him* dead.

Connections clicked together in his mind. If someone believed the two of them were working together, they knew he and Biin wouldn't kill the other. *That* would be all the exposure, all the proof needed.

But, of course, neither of them *would* kill the other.

Right?

Glancing at the timetable on the datapad, Sree gasped.

Two days.

They'd given him two days to eliminate her.

Not enough time to plan anything. Not enough time to

prepare to go on the run. Not enough time to let her know.

And on top of all that, tomorrow would be the ceremony to celebrate his family, which required his attendance. He wouldn't even have time to visit Muura's shop and give some semblance of a forewarning before his deadline expired.

With a tightening in his chest, Sree struggled to find a way out of any of this.

What was he going to do?

Chapter 37

Panaan felt oddly calm, even though her hands shook, as she knocked on the door in front of her. She'd made a decision the previous night.

The young man who killed her Mother, Sree Kaano, would die today.

She worried when she created the plan to start a "support" group for the Kaano family that it would be immediately dismissed by Retired Vuun Kaano. Or even worse, seen through as the ploy it represented: a way for her to get close enough to Sree to kill him.

But no. A few others had shown up with her at the house the previous night—over a hundred more joined the group system she'd created over the CrossLattice since the Celebration Day announcement had been made the evening before.

She hadn't expected to see him the previous evening when she noticed him sneaking out of his own house. And even more of a surprise, when he showed up after the meeting that evening, looking worse for wear. Vuun filled her in later on about what had happened—his Target defended himself by attacking Sree, but her Daughter's Son prevailed.

At first, Panaan felt a bloodthirsty fury because someone else almost robbed her of the joy of killing him. But the anger subsided when she learned he'd be all right, which meant she'd still get her chance.

The door in front of her opened and Panaan forced a smile onto her face. She'd managed to get herself invited over for breakfast at the Kaano's. She figured the best way to catch a killer like Sree off guard would be in his own house, early in the morning, when he wouldn't be prepared for an attack.

"Good morning, my dear," the older woman said.

"Good morning, Retired Kaano." Panaan opted to choose the more formal greeting as a show of respect.

"Please," Vuun said, opening the door wider so Panaan could enter. "Call me Vuun."

Panaan nodded to show she would. "Thank you again for this opportunity," she gushed. "I know I can learn a lot from you." She glanced around, hoping to catch a glimpse of Sree inside. Patience didn't sit well with her so she boldly asked, "Will anyone else be joining us this morning? Your Daughter's Son, perhaps? Although I imagine he's busy preparing for Celebration Day tomorrow."

"I'm sure he'll be down shortly," Vuun assured her. "After his ordeal yesterday, I thought it best if he slept in."

Panaan paused at Vuun's choice of words. "Ordeal? I thought he was fine."

Vuun entered the kitchen and began to prepare food for breakfast. "Oh, he is, he is. Minor bruising around the neck and a few scrapes from the encounter. But I tell you, a surprise attack is not something you can shake off that easily. Especially since this is the second Assignment he's had where the tables had been turned on him—first his kidnapping and now an ambush on his way to his hotel." She hustled around the table for a moment, arranging three place settings.

"In fact," she continued, pausing for a moment while putting a serving plate down, "during all my years of service, in all my Assignments, I only had one Target fight back. And that had been my fault. I'd come out of camouflage too early and she'd seen me. She managed to land a few decent blows—rattled my head a bit with one good jab—but she really was no match for me. But Sree has just had the strangest luck so far." She shrugged. "No matter. He prevailed. That's a true Kaano for you."

Panaan had gone very quiet during Vuun's babbling. A word stuck out.

Ambush.

Sree had been *ambushed* on his way to his hotel.

How could that be possible? Targets could know they were a Target, but not *who* came for them. They'd have no way of knowing Sree had been the assassin assigned to them and therefore have no idea to lie in wait for him on the way to his hotel.

Unless Sree somehow tipped his hand, like Vuun just said—coming out of skin-shifting too early—and the Target realized Sree's identity, followed him, found out about his hotel, and then waited in an alley and what... *hoped* Sree would go that way to get to the hotel that night? But that didn't add up either.

Panaan frowned.

"Is something wrong, dear?" Vuun asked.

"What? Oh, no. Sorry." Panaan replaced the frown with a smile. "Just thinking about something else."

Vuun paused. "If you're certain..."

With a nod, Panaan said, "It's not a problem." But she felt less sure about that. The intrusive thoughts remained for the next several minutes while Vuun continued to speak. No matter which way she twisted the events in her mind, Sree's attack made no sense. There would be no way a Target would have known to be in that alley at that time to attack Sree.

The only way would be if the Target had been purposefully told to wait there.

That's absurd, she thought, taking a seat at the table as Vuun plated a generous helping of steamed pleen in front of her. *No one has the ability to tell a Target something like that. No one knows about the Assignments except the Makers when they create the Assignment. And a Maker would never send a Target after their assassin.*

Panaan's conclusions shifted to her own Mother's words from a few days before her death. She had spoken about Panaan's Father being a Target, how he claimed it happened because someone perceived him as a threat. And then her Mother, saying she and her coworkers had "seen too much," that she'd been viewed as a threat as well... though the knowledge of *who* thought this wasn't revealed to her. Whatever she'd "seen" hadn't been told to Panaan either.

Perhaps her Mother wanted to keep Panaan from becoming a Target as well?

But that's silly, she thought. *I wouldn't become a Target just because I knew something.*

Except now this strangeness with Sree. A kidnapping on his First Assignment, her Mother on his second one, and now an ambush that shouldn't be possible on his third?

Panaan froze. Except...Vuun said he'd only had *two* Assignments.

"Wait..." she said out loud.

Vuun stopped mid-sentence at the interruption.

Panaan glanced over at the older woman. "Did you just say this ambush was Sree's *second* Assignment?"

"Yes, dear."

"He's only had two, the hostage situation and now this one?"

Placing a plate on the table, Vuun asked, "Why are you making me repeat myself?"

Panaan gripped the edge of the table. "It's very important.

Please answer me."

"Yes. Only two."

"He couldn't have gotten another one without your knowledge?"

Vuun frowned. "I was here when both data packets arrived and handed each of them to him myself. Although...it really isn't proper etiquette for you to ask about it." She turned towards the stairs. "He's coming down right now. I suggest you keep your curiosities to yourself."

Panaan's stomach lurched at the sound of footsteps moving down the staircase. Footsteps belonging to the young man who'd eliminated her Mother.

But...if he'd only had two Assignments and since her Mother's death had nothing to do with a kidnapping or an ambush...

Sweat pinpricked her brow as Sree stepped into the kitchen.

"Morn..." He trailed off when he saw Panaan at the table. His face darkened with a flush. "I didn't know she'd be here."

"Don't be rude," Vuun scolded. "She arrived this morning and is going to spend the next several hours with me. You won't be here, since you already have a new Assignment. And you'll have to prepare for Celebration Day tomorrow as well."

"I know," he told her. Panaan smiled despite herself. She recognized in him the annoyance she used to feel when her Mother would nag her.

The memory of her Mother hit her, hard. She'd give anything to hear her voice again, regardless of the tone.

And yet here Panaan sat, staring at the young man she believed had killed her Mother. Wanting to eliminate him like he'd done to her Mother.

Her hands shook. What if she were wrong?

You're not, she thought, trying to convince herself.

Still...she needed to be sure. All these feelings, this rage towards him, if she were wrong...

"I've had two Assignments already," she blurted out, trying to make it sound like a brag. "How about you?"

"Pannan..." Vuun said, a warning in her voice.

A startled look crossed Sree's face, but he still answered. "Uh...same? Well, I got my third one this morning, but I haven't started it yet."

Breath came in and out of her lungs more quickly. "You're the same as me? You've only done two so far?"

"Yeah." His expression shifted to one of...she couldn't quite tell. Discomfort?

"I told you," Vuun said to Panaan as she gently guided Sree to take a seat. "And they were both headline news. Not a bad introduction to Celebration Day." She paused, a misty look in her eyes. "I'm so proud of you for suggesting that," she said to Sree. *And*," she continued, shifting her eyeline to Panaan, "he got to meet with a Head Superior!"

"It isn't that big of a deal," Sree said through a mouthful of food.

"Of course it is!" Vuun continued to gush as she took her own seat at the table. "Why, no one in our family has ever met a Head Superior. Not even your sister."

"Yeah, but this meeting was about Faan, and Mother and Father. The family. Not me. That's why it happened."

"You're a part of this family and *you* made it happen." She daintily ate a bite of the steaming breakfast.

"Only because everyone else in our family is dead," he spat.

A flutter of fingers to dismiss his statement. "Yes, our family members have Passed On, but that's hardly—"

Sree cut her off. "Passed On! Are you joking? Faan was murdered off-world not by a Re'Ris, so no one looked into how she died. Before that, Mother and Father were killed because of their beliefs. Not an accident, like we were told. And the Head Superiors covered it up!"

Vuun coughed on a morsel of food in her mouth. "What...

what are you talking about? That's nonsense!"

Sree pushed away from the table and stood. "No, it's the truth. Head Superior Three told me that her predecessors chose to keep that knowledge a secret from the public. But she's going to announce it tomorrow at Celebration Day."

Palpable silence descended upon the room.

Panaan, who'd basically been forgotten during the exchange, didn't know how to feel. She'd been so certain that when she finally met Sree he'd be cold, callous, and rigorous about the Rules. If he were in league with a conspiracy, he'd be proud to fulfill his Assignments and celebrate the Passing On of his family members. But he sounded...bitter. Upset. And at a loss.

Like herself.

Confusion twisted inside her mind, causing her skin to shimmer with emotion. She couldn't stand not knowing the truth, not for one more moment.

Throwing all caution to the wind, Panaan exclaimed to Sree, "Did you kill a woman in an alleyway by the Cand hotel? Was that one of your Assignments?"

"Panaan!" Vuun cried out. "How dare you ask that!"

"I need to know. It's important. Please!" All sense of purpose rested on this one answer. Her insides felt like eels slithering around, her guts twisting. She'd never felt so scared, angry, and muddled at the same time.

Sree stared at her, his eyes tired. "The only Targets I killed were men. There were two of them."

"You're lying," she accused.

"I wish. I remember every second of each one."

The empty look in his eyes confused her. She'd felt nothing when she killed her two Targets. But his expression...he seemed genuinely ill at ease about it.

"Panaan," Vuun said near her, her voice quiet. "Put the knife down."

"What?" Panaan looked down at her hand. She hadn't even

realized she'd picked the utensil up.

"I..." she started, trailing off. The weapon loosened in her grip, which had been held so tightly her hand felt slightly cramped.

Vuun stood, slowly. "It's all right, dear. You can let it go."

The words soothed her, and she managed to release the knife fully. It balanced on the edge of the table for a moment before clattering to the floor.

In a flash, Vuun grabbed her own knife and held it up to Panaan's throat.

"No!" Sree cried out, standing up.

"She wants revenge," Vuun said, the previous dulcet tones now cold and full of malice. "I've seen it before. Pathetic, whiny fools who cannot accept the truth of the gloriousness of our system."

Shame welled up inside Panaan. Vuun was right. She'd taken matters into her own hands, had even screwed up the facts. If she'd killed Sree, she would've been a murderer, pure and simple. Something detested and disgusting to anyone on their planet.

"I'm so sorry..." she whispered, tears running down her cheeks.

"Mother's Mother, stop it!" Sree moved around the table and took a step between them.

"Get out of the way, child. She is disturbed. She needs to be taken by Central Authority."

Panaan just sat there, waiting for them to determine her fate. She felt all drive and semblance of care slip away from her, with only guilt and embarrassment filling the void.

Vuun continued. "You don't understand, Sree. She used us. She used me to get to you. I can't—"

"Stop." The one word spoken by Sree held the weight of a thousand years.

To Panaan's amazement, Vuun lowered the knife at her

Daughter's Son's command.

Sree turned toward Panaan. She wanted to shrivel up and die.

"Did you come here to kill me because you thought I'd eliminated your Mother?"

She couldn't speak. Only a dejected nod spasmed from her.

To her astonishment, he placed a hand on her shoulder. She peered up at him.

"I didn't," he told her.

A lump formed in her throat. "I know that now."

"Why did you think I did?"

"I...I saw you. For a couple of days. At the restaurant across the street from the Cand Hotel. And on the day she...was gone... you weren't there anymore. I thought you were watching us, following us. And I..." She shook her head, trying to dislodge the horrible thoughts. "I don't know what happened. I know the Rules. I follow the Rules. I wanted us to defend ourselves from our attacker. Go up the ranks. But something inside me...it was all black and sickly when I saw her on the ground, not moving. I couldn't think of anything but you. Your face. I couldn't get it out of my head. The next day I turned fifteen and immediately applied for my First Assignment. I needed the freedom...to find you."

The words came, as if she needed to keep going or she'd never survive this. "But now, talking to you...it's not what I thought. My Mother spoke of a conspiracy. I thought she was being dramatic. But my Father...he also said something similar before he was targeted. I didn't believe...but then when she was killed, something felt...wrong. It didn't make sense. She excelled at her Laborer job. There was no reason to remove her from society. And I believed if you were the one to kill her then you must have been in on the conspiracy."

She let out a hollow laugh and sank further into the chair. "Actually, when I think about it, that doesn't even make any sense! You don't *choose* who your Target is. Why would you have any idea if there was a conspiracy or not?"

"I'm not a part of it, but I don't think you're wrong."

Panaan's eyes widened at his statement.

He *agreed* with her? That something in the system was amiss?

At that moment, loud banging on the front door made everyone jump. Vuun made a move to investigate when the door burst open and several individuals barged in.

Panaan jumped up. Vuun shrieked, clutching her chest. Sree yelled out some sort of profanity.

Then they noticed the apparel. Bright yellow jumpsuits.

Central Authority.

Chapter 38

Sree's head swam. He tried to ignore the throb of a headache beginning to form at the base of his skull, but found it difficult to concentrate.

He'd just spent the past three hours at the hospital.

Waiting.

Waiting for someone to tell him his Morther's Mother was going to be okay.

Not very many individuals sat in the waiting area with him. One, a man whose eyes kept darting towards the surgery door, his gray skin almost as pale as the light gray tiles on the floor, and the other, an elderly woman who'd nodded off to sleep some time ago, snoring lightly, her skin's grayish-green color fluctuating rhythmically with the vibrations.

But then the surgeon emerged from the *Staff Only* area heading straight for Sree and he knew the results of his Mother's Mother's fate from the man's face before he even said a word.

The surgeon's expression looked exactly the same as the one

on the officer from Central Authority who told him about his Mother's and Father's demise.

It also matched the expression his Mother's Mother had when telling him about Faan's death.

Sree knew his Mother's Mother hadn't survived the heart attack caused by Central Authority bursting into their home.

She'd Passed On.

Sree heard the surgeon speak, but he couldn't register anything past, "We did everything we could, but..."

Slumping down on the plastic bench he sat on, Sree nodded occasionally, having no clue what he agreed to. But eventually, the surgeon moved away, leaving Sree alone with his thoughts.

What happened?

The morning had started off so strangely already, what with that girl—Panaan—being there for breakfast. Then she'd asked questions about his Targets. Shortly after she admitted she wanted to kill him. And his Mother's Mother threatened her, and Sree stood between them, and Panaan began to rant about her own family's deaths and then...

...then Central Authority had stormed in.

Chaos ensued. His Mother's Mother clutched her heart and fell to her knees. Panaan began to shriek. Sree cursed and prepared to run, certain they were coming for him, certain they knew about his lies and his plans to find the Stasis Room.

But they hadn't advanced on him—no more so than to push him out of the way and keep him to the side.

They went for Panaan.

They placed a stasis bracket around her upper body, constricting her arms to her sides, and briskly marched her outside.

Then, still without a word, they left.

And his Mother's Mother, lying on the floor, gasped his name.

The next several minutes went by in a haze as he waited for

Emergency Rescue Facilities to arrive. His Mother's Mother, his only remaining living relative, lay in his arms, barely breathing.

"I'm so proud of you," she whispered.

Grinding his teeth, he said, "Don't. You're not leaving me."

"I tried my best, but you are your Mother's Son. Do not be satisfied with the world if you think it isn't right. Do not be like me and ignore your heart." She took a shuddering breath and no amount of hushing her made any difference. "I was a good assassin, but I was nothing compared to the rest of the family. And I was blessed to have been included, though I never really belonged. Because they...they were the epitome of what the Makers wanted. Why couldn't they leave things be? Why couldn't they fall in line? Because they were more than assassins. They were for the people. Sree, be for the people. I'm sorry I tried to make you not be like them."

At that moment, she'd stopped speaking. ERF arrived shortly after, and they all traveled together to the nearest hospital. Three standard hours after their arrival, the surgeon emerged, his face sympathetic with the tint of failure.

And now Sree sat, alone.

Truly alone.

Chapter 39

Panaan could not wrap her head around the past few hours.

Everything had been a blur after Central Authority restrained her at the Kaano household and removed her from the premises.

She'd been guided to a large tixa, placed inside, and someone with a blood-testing kit proceeded to take a sample from her. Protesting made no difference as she couldn't move her arms to stop the procedure. After that, the technician nodded at the results but wouldn't tell her anything about what he'd been checking for.

Several roads and turns later, they arrived at Central Processing, rather than to a Central Authority location where she assumed they would go, and they escorted her inside. They brought her to a small room, removed her restraints, and told her to wait. Windowless, with only a chair on the opposite side of the table from where she sat, the small space felt cramped and unused. The slight scent of mold reminded her of dark corners never looked at.

Nobody processed her. Nobody asked for any identification. She sat alone, mortified at her predicament.

Being arrested symbolized the ultimate shame. It was one thing if you were no longer a viable member of society and had to become a Target. It was another that whatever you'd done brought so much disgrace that you needed to be made an example of and be kept alive for the duration of that humiliation.

Cand's population contained very few arrests. But those who became prisoners were often displayed on vidlink channels as "examples" to the rest of society.

Most people would prefer to be targeted or demoted to Laborer than be arrested. In fact, many prisoners took their own lives while incarcerated.

Wondering about her current predicament, she thought about the whole process. She'd always assumed there would be more to being taken into custody, such as checking identification or asking her questions, but since she'd never known anyone who had been arrested, perhaps this followed the normal procedure? Perhaps a blood test in the tixa by some silent tech was how they identified you?

Panaan scoffed. That sounded ludicrous even to her. She could determine no reason for them to take a blood sample inside a vehicle as opposed to a clinic or lab. It seemed very rushed and unprofessional, since no one said one word to her about what they were doing.

Fear crept through her. Even if they were arresting her because she'd kept her last Target hidden for a few days before killing him, that didn't mean she couldn't know what they planned for her, did it?

Or did her transgression warrant that they could do whatever they wanted?

When the door to the room opened Panaan lowered her head and averted her gaze for a few moments.

"I know why I'm here," she said, barely above a whisper. She raised her eyes. "I know I..." The words died on her lips. She registered the four pips on a black and gold collared jacket.

A Head Superior.

Here.

In the room.

Taking a seat across from her.

Panaan's mouth went completely dry.

"Salutations, Lone Luura," he said, addressing her by her surname and extending a hand, turned sideways, across the table.

The title of "Lone" grated against her, reminding her of her orphaned status. Hesitating, Panaan reached out and placed the back of her hand against the back of his, a very traditional greeting that she'd never actually done before. Luckily, she'd seen her Mother do it and knew the technique.

"I apologize for your treatment," he continued, pulling his hand away, "but it was necessary for your safety."

"My...?" Panaan couldn't even finish the statement. *What is going on?*

"We've been waiting for you to reach the Age of Progression and Cross Over, but also wanted to make sure you were worthy of the title we wished to bestow upon you, so you were given two quite difficult Assignments, which you carried out beautifully."

Panaan just sat there, silent. She had *no* idea what he spoke of. They'd been waiting for her? Title? Difficult Assignments?

The Head Superior leaned forward in the chair, a touch of a smile on the edge of his mouth. "You have been chosen. To be a Head Superior."

Panaan would've been less surprised if he'd killed her on the spot than what he'd just said. The words rumbled around in her mind for a few moments before they finally made sense.

"Me?" she squeaked out.

"Indeed."

She laughed. She couldn't help it. Of all the ridiculous

things she'd ever heard in her life...

The Head Superior merely waited for her to regain her composure. When she finally did, he spoke again. "I suppose you have questions."

"More than I know what to do with," she replied.

"Well, to reassure any doubts, yes, Lone Luura, you will be the next Head Superior."

"I'm...I'm too young!" The words sounded shrill, but she couldn't help it. This was ludicrous.

"Perhaps. But regardless, you've been chosen, no matter your age."

"But there are only five Head Superiors that are allowed to exist at one time. And we have five right now."

"At the moment, that is true."

An eeriness hung on his words.

He continued. "The offer is valid and has been approved by the other Head Superiors and the Makers."

A shudder ran through her that had nothing to do with fear, but reverence. The Makers knew about her? And approved her?

She couldn't help her next question. "Why me?"

"You have qualities we look for in Head Superiors."

Though he didn't exactly specify she couldn't ask more, she recognized the tone from when her Mother used to let her know the subject was closed.

"When do I need to decide by?"

"Tomorrow morning."

"To—tomorrow?" she stuttered.

"If you accept, you'll begin your new appointment immediately."

Panaan's head swum. After her Father's death, she'd always felt embarrassment at the fact that he'd been targeted. Then, when the same fate befell her Mother, she wanted her family to gain status by having her Mother defend herself and rise up in the ranks of assassins. When *that* didn't happen, Panaan's view on life changed. She didn't care about status anymore, just vengeance.

And then she realized her focus centered around the wrong assassin the entire time. She made a mistake, a huge one, about Sree.

She didn't deserve this post. Whatever they'd seen in her held no merit. She'd only killed her first Target to get him out of the way to pursue Sree. She'd kidnapped her second, which completely went against the Rules, again, to pursue Sree.

The Makers and Head Superiors were wrong about her.

The Head Superior spoke again, perhaps misinterpreting her silence as surprise instead of doubt. "I will contact you tomorrow morning and you may tell me your decision. It is not a task to be entered into lightly, but it is an honor. You will be helping all Re'Ris, not just the citizens of Cand, with your inclusion into our group. But it is a very different life than one may conceive. Lonely, isolating, difficult, and challenging, but also rewarding in ways you couldn't imagine." He held his hand out again and she absentmindedly placed the back of hers against his once more.

He stood to leave.

Panaan asked one more question. "Can I tell anyone about this?"

"Not until after you've made your decision. It must be yours, and yours alone." He gave her a brisk nod. "I am hoping we can work together for the future of our planet. I believe you would make an excellent addition to the Head Superiors. And if you do, you'll be privy to the inner workings of who we are and what we do. But the decision lies solely with you. I will speak with you in twelve standard hours. Good day and good thinking, Lone Luura."

Chapter 40

When Sree entered his home that night after returning from the hospital, he found Head Superior Three, the one he'd recently met with about Celebration Day, sitting at his kitchen table.

By herself.

The shock of someone in the house faded quickly, though he'd unleashed his wrades for a moment without thinking. Sree couldn't seem to be that surprised by anything anymore, especially since they were still monitoring his house. And since he'd just heard the news about his Mother's Mother Passing On, he didn't even remember how he'd made it home in the first place.

The journey home had gone by in a haze. Every step felt like someone else's movement. He'd finally turned off his communications device as never-ending calls from reporters wanting to speak to him kept the line constantly ringing.

He just wanted to crawl into bed and pretend this day hadn't happened.

Instead, he paused in the entranceway to his home, staring

at the uninvited guest.

The Head Superior raised her chin when he continued to enter.

"No," he told her, rewrapping the weapons around his wrists. They were the last connection he had to his Mother's Mother and he couldn't stand the thought of removing them anymore. "I'm going to bed."

Without looking behind him, Sree headed towards the staircase.

"It's about tomorrow," she called out after him.

He paused at the bottom step. "The only thing you need to know about Celebration Day for my family is that there is one more name to add to your list: Vuun Kaano."

"I heard what happened. She is now reunited with the those who have Passed On before her."

A sigh. "I know I shouldn't be sad, but she didn't die as a Target. She didn't die on an Assignment. And she didn't die of natural causes. Central Authority bursting into our home for no reason killed her. We would've opened the door!" Fists clenched, he screwed his eyes closed to restrain his grief.

A pause. "Will you still be there tomorrow?" A note of longing tinged her words.

Anger shook him for a few more moments before he forced an answer. "I will be there tomorrow, because the truth about my family needs to be known and they deserve to be celebrated. But for tonight, get out of my house." Sree continued up the stairs, half wondering if he'd broken some sort of law by speaking to a Head Superior that way, but not really caring. Nothing could hurt him more than the pain he felt right now.

Curling up into a ball on his bed, Sree closed his eyes as tightly as possible and wished for this to all be a bad dream.

"I'll open my eyes and everyone will be okay. Mother, Father, Faan, Mother's Mother...they will all be here and I won't be alone..."

Chapter 41

"Wake up."

Sree snorted awake at the quiet yet urgent words. Aches infiltrated every part of his body, having been curled up in a tightly-wound fetal position for hours. He assumed it hadn't been the whole night, however, as darkness still invaded his room from the curtainless windows. It took him a few moments to get his bearings—and to realize someone sat on his bed.

Adrenaline spiked through him and he sat up.

"Who are you?" he demanded.

"It's me. Biin."

Several sleep-encrusted blinks later, Sree finally registered her words. "Biin? What are you doing here?" He thought about the officers monitoring the house. "It's not safe for you to be here."

"Am I your next Target?"

Fear flooded him. Did she plan to kill him? To defend herself? But if that were the case, why would she ask? And yet...how could she know she *was* his Assignment?

Licking his lips, he answered softly. "You are. But obviously I'm not going to eliminate you." Frowning, he asked, "How did you get in here? My place is being monitored by Central Authority."

"Everything is wrong," she said, her voice still neutral. She used a handheld device to illuminate the area around her, though he noticed she shielded the bulk of the light with her palm. It cast strange shadows across her face and the bedspread around her.

"What do you mean?" Scooting himself up into a sitting position, he ignored the strain of his tight muscles. Leaning against the wall behind him, he pulled his knees up to his chest.

Her sentences came out clipped. "I was tipped off. That I am your Target. I was told where you live." She snorted. "Ironic. I already *know* where you live."

Silence ticked by until Sree understood the gravity of her statement. "Someone *told* you about me?"

She nodded, the light flickering across her face. "I received an authorized message on my personal communications device. When I opened it, it let me know the situation, that I was your Target, but also that I could defend myself. It gave me your information, name and address. Then, it deleted itself. I couldn't find out who'd sent it."

"Seriously?" he muttered.

Biin peered around his room, as if taking in his décor in the dim lighting, before continuing. "Yep. The message was very brief. It said it supported the Laborers. That we didn't deserve to die at the hands of assassins anymore. That we deserve to climb the ranks ourselves."

"That's it?"

"That's it."

"And you believed it? That they are trying to help Laborers?"

She brought her gaze to him again, her eyes narrowed. "Of

course not. But that's not the point. The point is someone who has access to private information sent it to me. To warn me about you. How could they do that?"

Thoughts flickered through his head, all coming to a different question. "Not how... *why*."

"That matters more than how?"

Sree nodded. "Yeah. Because my last Target was warned about me, too."

The light fell to the floor, spinning for a moment.

"Stars," she cursed, fumbling for the device. "Sorry, sorry." After picking it up, she placed it on the bed, so it shone up to the ceiling, casting light upwards and illuminating their faces from below. "Really? A different Target went after you?"

"Yes."

"I mean, I saw on the news that you defended yourself when your second Assignment attacked you. You're pretty popular, if you didn't know, after what happened with Wiin, so reporters are all over you and your life, especially with Celebration Day coming up tomorrow. The news bulletins said you prevailed."

"They left out the part where the Target knew the route to my hotel and ambushed me."

She frowned. "I mean, so he followed you? Why is that so strange?"

"Because I never approached him. I had no intention of killing him, so I never went to find him. He couldn't have had any idea I was his assassin. Someone had to have told him *and* knew the route I'd take to my hotel, which means *I* was the one being watched."

He shuddered at the thought, then paused, wondering about the surveillance on him at this moment. Could Central Authority be involved in this, too? If they were, wouldn't they already be in here by now, having seen Biin enter? Or did they want Biin to kill him?

Curious, Sree moved from the bed and peeked outside.

Emptiness greeted him in the space where the tixa normally sat stationed outside his house. "The guards watching me are gone. They are supposed to be there all night."

"So? Maybe they went on break?"

"Maybe, but the Head Superior made it seem like I was pretty high priority. Maybe whoever sent you here wants to catch *you,*" he said. "Not as my Target, necessarily, but could someone have found out you were the Laborer who contacted me illegally?" A pause as he put the pieces together, not even giving her time to answer. "On the other hand, if they wanted you caught, why did the tixa leave exactly at the time you arrived?" He shook his head. "You're right," he said. "Something is *definitely* wrong."

Biin stood. "I need to get you out of here, head to a safe location. We'll have to go on the run. It's too dangerous for both of us, now that we're both being manipulated. Especially because we don't know by who or what their true intentions are."

Still staring out the window, Sree rubbed his eyes, about to agree with her, when he saw the Central Authority tixa pull up and park once again. He cursed. "I can't come with you."

"But—"

"Biin, you don't understand." He gestured towards the street. "Central Authority is back. If we leave, they'll see us. They either want you dead or caught, or whoever messaged you wants you dead or caught. Or me. If I'm seen leaving with you, then they will make us both Targets. Going on the run won't make any difference. You've tried it, Wiin tried it. It's only a matter of time before someone catches us."

"You don't know that."

Sree could hear the pleading edge to her voice. "Yeah, I do. And you know it, too. Hiding won't help us. Not in the long run."

Taking a seat once again on the bed, Biin asked, "Then what do we do?"

"There's stuff Wiin told me, stuff I didn't have the chance to tell you at the store." He quickly explained Wiin's plan for him, about finding new evidence at Central Processing.

"Oh, that's all you have to do?" she said, sarcasm tainting her words.

"It's the only way to get proof."

"Well, even if that *does* work, it doesn't help us right now. How do we get out of this?"

Sree didn't like what he planned to propose, but he told her anyway. "You'll have to hit me. Hard. A few times, for good measure."

She paused, then dragged out the following word. "Whyyy...?"

"Because the only way you can leave here is if you escape. I won't be able to lie. I'll have to say we fought, that you hit me, that I fell. And you ran. It'll buy us both some time. Not much, but..."

"Why not?"

Sree squinted, seeing the first glimmers of red sunlight poking in through his window. "It's already today, technically. It's Celebration Day. I'll be busy all day. And I'm supposed to kill you by the end of tomorrow."

Biin's grey skin mottled with fear. "That soon?"

"You were right when you said something was wrong. There are too many inconsistencies. I'm not sure we are only dealing with one individual trying to pull our strings. I think someone made you my Target, but someone else tipped you off. Or someone hired Central Authority to watch for you, but someone else doesn't want you caught? I don't know, exactly, all I know is this doesn't add up anymore."

"But why? Why would the Makers do that?"

Sree paused. "I didn't really want to drop this on you, but Wiin told me he believes the Makers are gone. Extinct."

The mottling of her skin stopped and big flashes of dark coloring bloomed briefly on her face. "That's...that's..."

"Blasphemy, insanity, whatever. I know. Trust me, I know how you're feeling right now. I felt the same way when he told me. He said he's seen their bodies in a room inside Central Processing. And because he could access all the files, he found census records of the Makers that abruptly ended after reporting massive deaths. But honestly, the more I think about the possibility, the more it makes sense. Especially now that I know about Binders."

Biin frowned. "Re'Ris with Maker genetic material? What about them?"

"You said they can adjust the computer systems because they can access and change the files, since Maker genetic material is needed to do that." He hesitated, still not sure of his own theory. "What if... what if the Head Superiors are using Binders?" Sree watched a myriad of colors cross her face. He smiled. She was not adept at hiding how she felt. Hiding one's emotions had been one of the first things his sister taught him.

She spoke slowly, her forehead furrowed. "We, the Crypt movement, that is, always believed something was off about the Makers. We thought...maybe they'd changed their minds about us, or were experimenting in different ways, like splicing in their own genetic material, but we never had a reason why. But if they don't exist anymore...the only ones left in power and can change the system are..."

"Binders. Or...the Head Superiors using them," he finished for her.

"Why would the Head Superiors do this? Lie about it?"

"What would you do if your entire society was based on beings that don't exist anymore? But *you* have the power to create change and keep up the illusion that the Makers are still around?"

With a furrowed brow, she answered, "I guess...I guess I'd keep the system running, if it works. Otherwise, there'd be mass panic and uprisings and possibly..."

"War."

She shuddered. "There's never been a war on our planet. And the vidlink images and reels I've seen from other worlds, the devastation and murder and destruction..."

A few moments of silence passed, and Sree knew she contemplated the same horrendous idea of their planet under siege.

Finally, Sree began again. "But it would mean lying to the citizens. And those lies would keep getting compounded anytime something came up that contradicted what you were trying to hide. Even to the point of fixing things, changing the system...or eliminating anyone who may be on to you."

"Supposedly using their power to protect, but in reality causing more chaos from within." Biin shook her head. "We can't let them do this."

"Hence Wiin's plan. Without proof, there aren't enough of us to create a change. The Head Superiors can negate anything we say, or wipe us all out. But if I can find that proof..."

"Everything will be exposed." She said, finishing his thought. She paused before continuing. "Our world will change, you know. Who we are. What we are meant to be. How we live."

He still didn't feel safe enough expressing his desire for that change to occur. "That's why you need to stay alive. You and the Crypt movement can help deal with the backlash once the proof is revealed. You need to organize yourselves, and fast, for the changes that are coming up."

Biin quieted, as if calculating what would need to be done.

Sree looked at her, only a couple of standard years older than himself. Here they were, barely past the Age of Progression, and were planning a coup on their own government.

What if they were wrong? What if no other proof existed? What if...

He shook his head. It didn't matter. If there wasn't any proof, then there wasn't. He had to continue on in case it existed, otherwise he'd always wonder. More than that, he'd always feel like a coward for not even trying.

Light crept further into the room. The guards would most likely check on him that morning, since it was Celebration Day. They were supposed to make sure he made it to the ceremony.

He and Biin were out of time. "We need to get you out of here," he said softly.

"I know." Biin explained briefly where he could meet up with her the following day, at a remote location in Bria. Then, she squirmed. "I don't want to hit you."

Sree thought about how Wiin sacrificed himself. How Faan had gone off-world to prove their Mother's and Father's deaths weren't right. How his own parents pushed society's boundaries, even at the risk of their own lives. And his Mother's Mother's dying words:

"Be for the people."

What the Head Superiors were doing was wrong. They were changing things based on their own agendas. No matter the outcome, no matter the conflict afterwards, the people had a right to know.

He would do what it took to show that. He would make his family proud.

Taking a deep breath, Sree steeled himself for the pain coming his way.

"Do it."

Chapter 42

Panaan hadn't slept a wink.

How could she? She'd been offered the highest position on the planet: to be a Head Superior.

At 15 standard years old, she would be one of the five individuals who would help orchestrate the Makers' will, would travel the planet, make sure other cities were running smoothly, and report back to help determine if any improvements could be made.

And yet, she barely thought about any of this during the night.

All she could think about were Sree and Vuun.

Because the first thing she'd done when she got home had been to try to contact him. No response. She didn't really know what she planned to say, but the way the situation at their home unfolded left a heaviness in her gut. Now that she knew Sree didn't have any part in her Mother's death, guilt over using Vuun to get to him ate at her.

But she felt more than guilt. Sree's words from that night dug into her, even during her meeting with the Head Superior. Her mind kept turning all the information he'd revealed over and over again, mixing it with everything she'd learned from her own Mother's and Father's circumstances.

Her Father had claimed he'd been targeted on purpose.

So had her Mother.

Sree said his Mother and Father were also killed, and the Head Superior he spoke with admitted the real reason behind it had been hidden from the public.

Sree also believed in a conspiracy.

She wanted...no, she *needed* to talk to him about that. Before she made any decision about her new position, she needed to know what he meant, what he believed.

Because nothing felt right anymore.

But no one on his end answered her call. She wondered for a while if he wanted to avoid her, but she couldn't recall feeling any animosity from him, even though she'd been prepared to kill him. The idea to visit him at his home instead of calling seemed... too intrusive. Besides, Vuun may arrest her on sight if she showed her face again. So, she kept trying to contact him through her vid-link.

Then, while she ate dinner alone, the shadow of her Mother in the chair next to her, she'd seen a news bulletin aired over the nationwide emergency broadcast and had dropped her utensil in shock.

Vuun Kaano was dead.

Increasing the volume, Panaan devoured every word.

"A momentous Passing On has occurred as Vuun Kaano, member of the famous Kaano family, died of natural causes tonight. The Mother's Mother of Sree Kaano, last remaining member of the Kaano family, Passed On peacefully at Cand Central Hospital. To be such an acclaimed retired assassin and Pass On in such a natural way is the highest honor in death someone can receive. Though we will feel the loss of her presence, it couldn't have come at a more joyous time, as tomorrow is Celebration Day! I hope you'll join us on this channel as we broadcast the event. Both Sree Kaano and a Head Superior, that's right!, will be there tomorrow in the courtyard at Assassins' Accolades in Cand. Speeches will be made at the Kaano memorial statue starting at 10 morning hours and festivities will continue on after daytime Laborer hours have ended so that everyone can participate. We hope you can come and join the event!"

At this point Panaan muted the alert; she didn't care about the list of festivities they were planning.

Vuun was dead.

And *not* due to natural causes.

Panaan remembered all too clearly the elderly woman clutching her chest when Central Authority burst into her home.

The media was covering up what really happened.

Again.

"What is going on?" she muttered to herself.

The bulletin said Sree would be attending the celebration tomorrow. Perhaps she could speak to him there, although she had to make her decision about becoming Head Superior that morning before Celebration Day even began. She really wished she could talk to him first...

Her audiolink pinged, interrupting her thoughts.

Sitting up, thinking maybe Sree was returning her call, Panaan answered without looking at the caller's identity.

"New day," she said, giving the standard morning greeting.

"New day, Lone Luura. This is Head Superior Four, who you met with yesterday."

Panaan sat stock still in her bed.

Morning had crept up without her noticing it. She'd run out of time.

"Uh...hello."

"I hope you slept well and have come to a well-thought-out decision regarding joining the ranks with myself and my fellow colleagues."

Panaan felt relieved it wasn't a vidlink call as she knew her sleep-deprived eyes and grimace would've given her away. "I have thought about it, yes," she said, uncomfortable with lying to a Head Superior about not sleeping well, but she felt the statement to be more or less true. She *technically* had thought about the position.

"Excellent. Then I know the choice you're going to make is the correct one. What did you decide?"

Panaan took a few moments to circulate everything in her brain that she'd wondered about over the past several hours. All she knew was that something wasn't right. The system wasn't right. How could she become one of those who kept things corrupt?

But if she turned down this offer, she didn't trust what they would do in response. Would they let her return to her life as an assassin? Or silence her?

If they killed her, how could she explain to Sree what had happened? And what about the blood sample they'd taken? And if this were merely a job offer, why "arrest" her first? If they could abuse their power that way, what would stop them from "arresting" her again if she turned down the offer?

Too many questions and not enough time to answer them.

At least, not without more information. And only one thing could get her more information: access.

With a resoluteness that made her stomach clench, she said, "I've decided to accept your offer."

CHAPTER 43

Sree winced at the poking and prodding of an EMF member, while the Central Authority officer who'd been in the tixa below his window stood to the left of the medical technician.

"It doesn't appear that anything is broken," the technician said. She tilted his face and handed him a de-puffer packet. "But you'll have some bruising. You're lucky."

Sree watched her glance around the room, noting the dresser standing askew and scattered personal items. The room looked a mess, which had been the point. Biin had to actually push him into the dresser, so Sree could claim it when interviewed about the attack. He grimaced at the taste of dried blood in his mouth. She'd definitely hit him hard at one point.

"Yeah," he replied, placing the packet against the side of his jaw. "Lucky."

"Someone from Central Processing will be here shortly to take your statement." She paused. "This shouldn't prevent you from attending Celebration Day and we are all *very* much looking forward to seeing you there, representing your family. You're the last hero we have." Her face color-fluctuated, as if embarrassed, but Sree had gotten quite used to these kinds of statements—even at the hospital while waiting for news about his Mother's Mother, citizens couldn't help but approach him and gush their praises and hopes.

"I'll be there," he assured her. Her color returned to normal, and she smiled. He thought about how the Head Superior's admission about his family may cause a bit of an uproar with this woman and other individuals. It may not be the Celebration Day they'd hoped for, but the truth needed to come out.

Central Processing arrived and, as far as Sree could tell, everything had gone smoothly during the interview, since Biin technically was his Target. He recounted how she caught him asleep, startling him awake. They fought and she punched him, then pushed him, hard, into the dresser. Then, she bolted. When questioned why he believed she fled instead of killing him, he'd shrugged.

"I think maybe she wanted to use the element of surprise, but that failed." He quickly flicked open his wrades and then sheathed them again as a scare tactic. "I mean, she's just a Laborer, not an assassin. She didn't really stand a chance against a member of the Kaano family."

The Central Processor's eyes widened at the movement of his wrist-weapons and nodded in agreement with his statement before finishing up with some cursory words about how to take care of his injuries during the next couple days. Sree's status as assassin and Biin as his Target had not changed and he could continue with his Assignment. He knew Biin planned to head out of town, since the deadline for him to eliminate her expired tomorrow. If anything happened to him before then, they'd send a different assassin after her at that point, so she needed to be as safe as possible.

Once everyone left, Sree cleaned up and allowed himself to complain out loud to no one for a few minutes about how much he *actually* hurt. He'd never been in a fight before—well not anything more than training exercises with Faan—so the hits he'd received from Biin had been more than adequate to pass off as real when interrogated.

Either way, he had a big day ahead of him.

Heading down the staircase, the silence of the house struck him, hard. He'd never realized how the sounds of cooking or vidlink calls or even saying good morning to him from his Mother's Mother had been almost soothing background noise. A part of his life he'd taken for granted because he'd never had to think about what it would be like without it.

Even after his Mother's and Father's deaths, he'd still had family. Even after Faan dying, he'd still had family.

He had no one now.

A brief flicker of thought entered his mind—what would happen to the house? He couldn't afford it on his own. And yet, he wondered if they'd let him stay here anyway, seeing as how it had been in his family for generations.

The notion, though fleeting, caught him and he hesitated, his hand on the doorknob, ready to leave the house.

How could he come back here after what he planned to do?

If he even survived.

Sree swallowed against the lump in his throat. One step at a time. His only goal right now revolved around getting through Celebration Day.

But tomorrow...

Shaking his head, he dispelled the fear-laden plans of infiltrating Central Processing and focused on the task ahead. He needed to be there for the people today, when the Head Superior informed them of the truth about his family, to help them to the first step of belief that not everything in their government happened above board.

Then if, no...*when*, he corrected himself, he found proof about the Makers and the corruptness of the system, the citizens would be primed and ready to listen with more open minds.

At least, that's what he hoped.

In the meantime, Biin would spread seeds of the truth throughout the Crypt, who would start rumors of their own. He would then meet up with her and Muura tomorrow to give them the evidence he found, and they'd do what needed to be done with it while he went on the run.

The plan felt so stupid in his head. How could they possibly expect to pull all this off and stay alive?

And yet, he'd managed somehow so far.

Only because you killed those you were supposed to.

Ignoring the morbid thought, Sree took a deep breath and left the house...

...where beeping scanning devices and a barrage of questions assaulted him.

Holding up a hand to stave off the influx of reporters, Sree registered that they must have all arrived for the beginning of Celebration Day. Central Authority, who was still monitoring him, apparently sent more officers, most of whom were holding the reporters at bay, but just barely. At the end of the walkway sat a large, personalized orb, designed to navigate the streets outside of the underground tracks, with two Central Authority figures hovering around it. When Sree emerged from his door, they pushed their way towards him, hooked an arm around each of his, and half carried him to the transport.

Once inside, the smile of the Head Superior from their previous meeting, who'd also been in his home the night before, greeted him.

Is she in on everything? he wondered. *Does she know what Biin and I have planned?*

"Pleasant Celebration Day, Lone Kaano," Head Superior Three said, a smile on her lips.

"Uh, yeah, you too," he mumbled, his gaze still on the slew of reporters outside the vehicle, knocking on the windows, trying to capture images on their devices. A few moments of silence passed as they pulled away and Sree finally returned his attention to the Head Superior.

She appeared to be waiting for this and began to speak again. "I trust you are doing well, even though you had an eventful evening last night with your Target?"

A few beats. "Oh, uh, yeah," he said, wishing his vocabulary consisted of more than those few syllables. Then he frowned. "How do you know about that?"

"The Central Authority member stationed outside your house sent me his report this morning."

"Oh." He paused again as the vehicle slid into a tunnel slot reserved for group orbs which would take them through the underground to Central Processing. "Wait, how do you know about him?"

"I placed the agent there. To protect you."

"Hold on...*you* did?"

She nodded. "When I learned that a Laborer reached out to you through illegitimate channels, I worried about your safety, especially after you were kidnapped during your First Assignment. I am well aware of your notoriety, simply through your family. I feared that some citizens wanted to create a name for themselves, and what better way than to eliminate a member of the Kaano family and claim your status as their own. As the youngest and least experienced, I am sure several individuals believe you to be an easy choice to pursue."

The Head Superior *appeared* to be on his side, at least, from her viewpoint. But he couldn't be sure if she might simply be lying to get him to trust her.

Well, trust ran both ways. If she really told the truth about his Mother's and Father's deaths today, then he knew he could believe her. Or, at least, it meant she didn't have an alliance with anyone trying to manipulate the system for their own gain.

But there was still one question he wondered if she'd answer. "The Central Authority guard you stationed at my house...does he only monitor me during the day?"

"There is one for the day shift and one who covers overnight. As mentioned to Retired Kaano, you were given highest priority status."

Sree cocked his head. "Then...why wasn't he there all night last night?"

A wrinkle formed between her eyebrows. "I do not understand."

He had to tread carefully. "When I told Central Processing during my interview about what happened with my Target attacking me last night, I wondered later why the guard hadn't seen her enter my home. I checked the official report and..." he said, stressing this point, "his report said they saw someone leaving the premises, but didn't chase after them. He didn't come up at that time to check on me. And he didn't call EMF. In fact, I did, and he didn't come upstairs to see how I was until EMF arrived."

"Are you positive about this timeline?" The Head Superior's gray skin had turned a strange silvery white. She may be good at covering her color-fluctuating, but she couldn't hide her body's natural response to fear.

"Absolutely. I just thought maybe the guard switched over during the night."

He watched her closely and could tell by her face that this news disturbed her. Crossing her hands in her lap, she spoke slowly at first, then with more confidence. "You are the crux, Lone Kaano, of a long-standing family whose reputation has been a beacon to us all. But your family has also spoken up about injustice and not everyone has...supported their determined nature. I placed those Central Authority members to monitor you of my own accord. None of them were supposed to leave their station. They were ordered to report any suspicious activity immediately to me. If they left..."

He took a chance. "Head Superior Three, what's going on?"

With a shake of her head, she unclasped her hands. "Lone Kaano, things are not all they appear to be on our world."

Sree held his breath. Could she be about to admit something to him?

A voice sounded throughout the car. The driver spoke through the speakers. "We have arrived, Head Superior Three."

Clearing her throat, the Head Superior smiled at him. "No matter. Right now, we celebrate your family. And reveal their truths."

With one more daring question, he asked, "I know something's not right, either. Will you tell me more about what's going on, after the ceremony?"

She paused as the door to the orb opened from the outside. Peering at him, as if seeing him for the first time, she replied, "I will."

Chapter 44

A specialized orb picked Panaan up at her home, then whisked her through the underground tunnels until it arrived at Central Processing. After accepting the Head Superior position, anxiety mingled with excitement even before she entered the facility. A Laborer led her past the common areas through a doorway reserved for staff. Heading up to the highest floor, the elevator opened to reveal a door in front of her with the number "4" engraved on it. With a nod from her guide to the Laborer standing in the small alcove, the door opened for her to enter, and she saw the Head Superior she'd met the other day sitting behind a black and chrome desk.

Stark silvers, blacks, and whites covered the room, with a few deep red accents sprinkled throughout the tiled floor. No artwork hung on the walls, but the bottom half being black and the top half being silver kept the space from looking bare. A large vidlink screen filled a quarter of one of the walls, which met together at the back forming a point behind the desk at the far end, turning the room into a triangle.

"Greetings, Lone Luura," Head Superior Four said. "Or, should I say, soon-to-be Head Superior."

Panaan shivered at the title. She could hardly believe it. In her best dreams, she hoped to be an assassin. In her wildest ones, her Mother would have become one, too. But this...Head Superior...

Focusing on the task at hand, Panaan smiled. "Thank you, Head Superior. It is an honor I can scarcely put into words. I promise, I will do everything within my power to respect this title." *Which you don't,* she added to herself about the individual sitting in front of her.

"I know you will live up to your full potential. Officially, you will be sworn in this afternoon. Until then, there are some things you must acknowledge and agree to with your Oath of Name. Then, once confirmed and sworn in, I will begin your training."

She hesitated, but thought it would be strange if she didn't ask anything. "I still don't quite understand. Why me? I know I am past the Age of Progression, but that just recently happened. Surely there are older and more experienced Re'Ris who would be better suited candidates." She held up her hands in defense. "Not that I'm saying I'm changing my mind, I just don't quite understand why."

He angled his head, as if studying an animal. "You will learn, soon, what makes you so special. What makes you the perfect candidate for Head Superior. It is a rare thing, rare indeed, and age does not matter. Only state of mind. You have performed your first two Assignments in splendid form and your attachment to the Kaano family, while unfortunately short-lived, was inspiring. You gravitate towards greatness, and this is another one of the reasons why you will be an excellent Head Superior."

Panaan noticed that his answer, though seemingly specific, still held a vagueness. Also, he appeared to be unaware of her personal interactions with her Targets. However, he believed she'd completed both Assignments without any issues, so he clearly didn't know about keeping one of them hostage.

As if sensing concern, he tapped the datapad. "I will reveal everything once you've signed each document with your Oath of Name. I advise you to read through all the materials carefully. Once authorized, you will be entitled to all the privileges of a Head Superior, but also all the restrictions."

"I get it." She cleared her throat and tried to speak more eloquently. "Sorry. I mean, I understand."

He gave a slight smile. "Excellent. I will leave you to this. There will be a Laborer outside my office, should you need anything to eat or drink. If you have any questions about what you are reading, skip that particular document and ask me about it once I return." He paused. "I almost forgot. I'll need your personal communications device."

Confused, she pulled the device from her pocket. "This?"

"Yes. Since what you are about to pledge to is sensitive material, we do not allow anything that could transmit the information on these documents. It will be returned to you once you've completed everything."

After she handed it over, the Head Superior nodded, then exited.

Panaan let out a long breath. The whole situation seemed surreal. She still didn't understand why she'd been chosen, but she knew she didn't have all the information needed yet.

She shivered at the immensity of her situation.

And then, she felt the room rumble beneath her, as if it moved.

Nervous, she made her way to the door and opened it. Outside stood a Laborer, just as the Head Superior had mentioned would be stationed there, but the elevator door was gone. A blank wall greeted her on the other side of the small alcove.

"What just happened?" she asked.

The Laborer gave a smile. "It scared the life out of me the first time it happened, too." She pointed to the floor. "The floor rotates. This level consists of five offices, one for each Head Superior. Of course, only one or two are usually in use by a Head Superior at the same time, since they travel so often. It's incredible that all five Head Superiors are in Cand today!"

Panaan asked, "All five are here today?"

"Of course!" She paused. "Didn't Head Superior Four tell you that?"

Not wanting to make this Laborer feel like she'd given away too much information, and hoping to maybe glean a little more from her, Panaan added, "He was in a hurry and said he would fill me in on more details later. I'm sure he just didn't think to tell me, what with everything going on today."

The look of slight concern on the Laborer's face melted away. "Of course. That makes sense. Celebration Day is going to be a pretty big deal."

She'd completely forgotten about Celebration Day. "Are you excited about the festivities?" Panaan asked.

"I am, though I'm working through the whole thing." Her shoulders drooped for a moment. "But because I've been here, I'm probably one of the only citizens on the whole planet who has seen every Head Superior! It'll be a great story to tell my children, even if I do miss out on the festivities."

"That's incredible that all five are in town."

"Head Superior Three is leading the festivities. Head Superior Four is here to oversee your induction into their group. Although..." the Laborer paused, scratching her chin. "That was surprising to me."

"Why's that?"

"Why do they need a new Head Superior when all five are still active?"

Panaan had wondered about this as well. "Maybe one of them plans to retire?"

The Laborer shook her head. "There have been no orders issued. And I see everything that comes across Head Superior Four's desk." The pride at being a privileged member of the Labor force came through in her voice. Panaan could hardly blame her. She couldn't imagine the type of screening process used to promote someone to such a delicate position. And, though she never thought much about it, the Laborers must have some sort of hierarchy amongst themselves.

She realized how little she knew about her own homeworld.

Well, soon I'll have access to all the information I could ever want, she thought.

Not wanting to delay things any longer, Panaan reached out her hand and turned it sideways. "It was nice to meet you..." Panaan trailed off.

"Laborer 51-322." The Laborer flushed with a brief color-change before extending her own hand, placing the back of it against Panaan's.

Panaan nodded and pulled her hand away. "Nice to meet you, 51-322."

The Laborer smiled. "You, too. I look forward to working with you, soon-to-be Head Superior...hm, I wonder what number you'll get eventually?"

Panaan gave a weak smile and reentered the office. She wondered that, too. Perhaps they planned to keep her in training until one of them retired? She needn't be active right away, she supposed. Shrugging off the thoughts, she glanced at the vidlink monitor set into the wall as she took a seat at the table with the datapads. Thoughts of Sree filled her mind. Had they begun the festivities yet?

She made a decision. "Wouldn't hurt to take a peek at what's happening." Turning on the device, she found most stations were broadcasting the event, so she chose one at random and left it on as background noise, waiting until the speeches began. She then picked up the first datapad from the stack. It seemed like fairly standard stuff: where she would live, the location of her office, her obligations on assigned cities, her required time commitments to meetings with other Head Superiors. The second document provided a non-disclosure agreement, stating she couldn't discuss any Head Superior matters outside the group, unless all five members agreed.

She'd gotten about halfway through the third, which reviewed the procedure for the swearing in of new Head Superiors, and found the content fascinating, making her completely forget to keep an eye on the speeches.

A piercing set of noises, emitted through the vidlink screen, broke through her focus.

The sound of screams.

CHAPTER 45

Screams filled the Assassins' Accolades area.

Confused, Sree searched around, trying to find the reason why. And then he saw it.

Someone had attacked Head Superior Three.

Celebration Day had started off so wonderfully. Even with his grief at the loss of his Mother's Mother, even with his anger at the corrupt government, and even with his fear about his plans to find the Stasis and Archive Rooms the following day, Sree still couldn't help but feel the outpouring of love and support towards him and his family from all the people present.

Apparently, the gathering brought in so many citizens from all over the planet that Central Authority needed to turn thousands of them away because of the lack of room in the square. As he and the Head Superior left the orb to make their way to the platform set up near the statue of his sister and the memorial to his family, the cheers and applause deafened him.

Even though he'd originally created this day as a ruse to

scope out the inside of Central Processing, it turned into a moment in history. It became a beacon of hope to millions who he hadn't even realized needed it. It shifted into a symbol of respect for their world, a way to reunite them after the hardship they'd endured under the Aleet Army, and it helped renew their sense of purpose.

And to see a living member of the Kaano family in attendance overwhelmed many in the crowd who chanted his name as he followed the Head Superior to the platform.

Once the roar died down, an introduction of Head Superior Three silenced any remaining murmurs.

With a smile, she began her speech.

"It is a glorious day. It is Celebration Day!"

Another roar.

After a few moments, they settled once again.

"This day is a day of celebration, yes, but also a day of remembrance, a day of unity, and a day of prosperity. The Kaano family," she said, nodding to Sree, "has served with dignity, respect, and loyalty. They represent the best of the Re'Ris, what many of you strive to become, and they have provided a light when darkness swayed you.

"It is on this day that we uphold those values the Kaano family represent, and we will renew those values in ourselves each yearly cycle in which this day is celebrated. Our citizens faced a dangerous adversary when the Aleet Army emerged to corrupt us. But we held firm."

A cheer.

"Our citizens banded together to fight for our way of life, to show that we are *meant* to exist the way the Makers designed us to."

Another cheer.

"And yet it is our duty to never forget that we must also strive to be better every day, beyond the mere basics of our design, to help ourselves and each other. The Kaano family also upheld this vision." At this comment, the Head Superior turned towards Sree and nodded. "And because of this, the truth about them must be revealed."

Sree held his breath. This was it. The moment where everything would begin. Where his whole life would change because the planet would know the truth about his family's deaths.

"The Passing On of Yeela and Giili Kaano was not what you know to be true."

Absolute silence smothered the crowd.

"Their deaths were—"

The Head Superior gasped, mid-sentence.

Before Sree could understand why she'd stopped speaking, several individuals screamed.

Chaos erupted. The crowd tried to scatter, but their massive numbers prevented them from moving, so they began crawling and climbing over each other. More screams and yells erupted from those being trampled upon.

Sree, on the other hand, caught movement from the corner of his eye, and leapt over to catch the falling Head Superior, noting the throwing knife sticking out of her chest. He glanced around wildly, trying to find the source of the attack, as he laid Head Superior Three down onto the platform. Central Authority figures quickly blocked his view, forming a tight perimeter circle around the two of them. Sree then shifted his focus onto the woman next to him.

Her mouth moved, but no words emerged.

"I'm sorry," he said lamely.

Head Superior Three shook her head, placed a hand on the side of his face, and smiled.

He knew in that moment she understood this had been a possibility. That exposing the truth about his family could make her a liability. Could somehow make her a Target.

A lump formed in his throat as her eyes closed and her hand fell away.

Chapter 46

A Head Superior had been attacked! In front of a public crowd!

Panaan could hardly believe it. She'd heard the screams while reading through the most recent datapad about her new job position and her focus shifted towards the vidlink screen.

The Head Superior, clutching her chest.

Sree, catching her as she fell.

Central Authority surrounding them.

And then the broadcast ended.

At that point, after waiting for a short while and checking other stations—which also covered the attack—Panaan tried to leave the floor to find out more information. Turning off the screen, she walked from the office to the alcove, but the elevator door and Laborer 51-322 weren't there.

She couldn't leave.

Backtracking, she searched the office, convinced there must be a mechanism to rotate the floor so she could exit, but she had no idea what it looked like. Or, for all she knew, it could be something portable or only accessed wirelessly through a datapad.

Frustrated that she couldn't even communicate with anyone outside this room because Head Superior Four had taken her personal device, she paced, thinking someone must show up soon. Then, realizing that with all the chaos outside, the Head Superiors may be dealing with quite a bit of commotion and probably wouldn't return for some time. She sighed and forced herself to sit down and continue reading the datapad confirmation documents.

Her mind, completely unfocused, could barely process the information on the forms, and she knew she hadn't read all of them in their entirety before confirming them with her Oath of Name.

No matter, she thought, rushing through the datapads. *I'll figure everything out later. I just want to get this finished before he comes back.*

As if reading her thoughts, the floor rumbled. Anxious to hear about what happened during the attack, Panaan hastily added her Oath of Name to the final document—which mentioned something about genetic material and access to files—and turned towards the door.

It opened and Head Superior Four strode inside.

Smiling.

Confused by his expression, Panaan paused in her question about what happened to the other Head Superior, to Sree, to the crowd. He seemed...happy. Could he have not heard about the situation?

"I'm sorry for the delay. There were some matters I needed to attend to. How are things progressing in here, Lone Luura?" he asked.

"I just finished," she answered automatically.

"Excellent!" He collected the datapads and checked through them. "Everything looks in order. Did you have any questions about any of the material in the documents?"

She shook her head as a reply but remained confused. Did he really plan to keep the day's events from her? Or could he somehow *not* know what happened? Had he been occupied with other matters and the news hadn't reached him? Not knowing if she should ask or not, she remained quiet.

Head Superior Four continued, taking her silence to mean she did not have any questions. "Wonderful! We'll get you sworn in soon. I assumed you would be hungry and we have time before the other Head Superiors gather to confirm your position, so I thought we could eat first." Without waiting for a response, he headed towards the door and opened it, placing an order with the Laborer who stood once again outside the room.

She hesitated, changing her mind concerning asking about the attack, to assess the situation. "I was surprised to hear all the Head Superiors are in Cand?"

"Of course. Swearing in a new Head Superior requires the presence of all of us." He frowned, then nodded in understanding. "Ah, yes. That's part of your training documents, so you don't know all those details yet." The Laborer had already returned, slightly out of breath, and handed over two saucer-like containers.

Panaan continued with her questions. "But that's why they are here today? To swear me in?"

"Yes." This time Head Superior Four paused, holding the containers of food just above his desk. "Why?"

"I thought..." she began, worried about her next words. "I thought they might be here for Celebration Day?"

"They are. But they are mainly here for you." His smile widened and he finished placing the food down on the desk.

Panaan didn't consider herself overly intelligent. She'd never excelled in school. In fact, the only thing she seemed to have a knack for was being an assassin, but even that had been out of necessity to get to Sree, not merely because she wanted to be good at it.

However, even she discerned the error in the Head Superior's words.

She remembered the datapad she'd just read through that said, "Head Superiors will not be replaced except if death or illness prevents them from fulfilling their obligations, if they retire, or if they are unanimously voted out."

This Head Superior currently implied that all the other Head Superiors had returned from their appointments elsewhere on the planet to swear in a new Head Superior.

In advance. To swear *her* in.

But before this morning's death, all five Head Superiors had been alive. And Head Superior Four's Laborer said there hadn't been any documents about a change in position, except for Panaan joining them. No one retired. No one had been voted out.

But there could only be five Head Superiors at one time.

So...why would Head Superior Four call in the other Head Superiors to swear in a new one if all the positions were filled?

The only reason would be that he knew one of the current Head Superiors wouldn't be in their position any longer, starting today.

And the only way to know *that* is if he knew the Head Superior would no longer be able to fulfill their duties after today. Therefore, by day's end, this position would be vacant.

Head Superior Four already knew a Head Superior would be killed today.

More than ever, Panaan now realized the dangerousness of this man. And possibly the other Head Superiors as well. They'd known about their fellow Head Superior's death beforehand. Which meant they must have orchestrated it.

And she'd just used her Oath of Name to include herself in this group.

Would she be privy to all the conspiracies created and upheld by this man and the others? Learn that a Head Superior could be disposed of on purpose?

Or were all her conspiracy theories moot because in the end, the Makers were responsible for organizing this. Had the Head Superior at Celebration Day been pre-destined to die as a Target?

But no, the document said Head Superiors cannot be Targets. They only die or retire or are voted out unanimously by the other Head Superiors.

That could only mean... The Head Superiors were doing whatever they wanted to with no repercussions. And it sounded like Sree already believed these issues existed in their government.

Panaan set her jaw. She wouldn't be wrong this time. She'd learn the truth about any corruption amongst the Head Superiors. Refocusing herself from her realizations to her original plan, she would discover whatever she could to prove these notions, now that she had access to files in her new position.

Raising her chin slightly, she told him, "I'm looking forward to meeting all of my fellow Head Superiors."

"Excellent."

With a forced smile, she made herself take a bite of the food in front of her.

Chapter 47

Four hours after he'd heard the first screams during Celebration Day, Sree found himself in a small room inside Central Processing. The door had been locked from the outside and he'd been told nothing, except to wait there for his safety. The grey walls and windowless room gave him nothing to focus on. Dried blood from Head Superior Three caked the front of his shirt.

The only thing to occupy him had been cleaning himself the best he could with the moistened towel they'd brought him a couple hours ago and to eat the meal set before him.

And to think.

The scenes from earlier that day replayed in his head over and over again.

The screams.

And the look on Head Superior Three's face.

She knew. Somehow, she knew this could be her fate.

He fell into a state of apathy as the magnitude of the situation engulfed him.

None of it mattered anymore.

How could he, a 16-year-old with no family left, on his own, with his only possible allies in a different town, have a chance at succeeding when a Head Superior couldn't even stay alive because of *one* truth she chose to expose. Whoever attacked her decided to kill someone in the public eye, someone globally considered off-limits for assassination.

Any possibility his plan would work seemed insanely ridiculous now.

After a while, his indifference slipped into despair. He quit. They'd won.

When the door finally opened, it took him several moments to even raise his gaze to meet the new visitor.

A Head Superior stood just inside the doorway. Sree noted the four pips on the black and gold collar, but he didn't care about anything that may happen next.

"I want to go home," Sree said. The words were hollow inside his mouth, but he couldn't muster anything else to say.

"Lone Kaano," the Head Superior began. "I need to speak with you about—"

"I want to go home," Sree repeated, cutting him off.

A touch of a frown crossed the Head Superior's mouth. He fully entered the room and the door closed behind him with a hard snap. "Lone Kaano, I understand today has been an ordeal, but a member of my order has been killed. In full view of everyone. And you were standing right next to her. I need to speak with you about the incident."

Sree let out a sigh and looked down at the table. "I don't know anything. One minute she was speaking, the next she stopped, and then there were screams. I tried to see where the attack came from and couldn't see anything out of the ordinary. Central Authority surrounded us, and then they put me and her in separate transports. They checked me out at the hospital, cleared me of any injuries, and then I was brought here. I got some food for lunch and then...that's it."

A few moments of silence. "She was speaking about your family when the attack happened. Do you know what she was going to say?"

Sree caught a tone in the Head Superior's voice. When he raised his gaze, the man's face showed an expression solely of interest. If Sree hadn't been looking down, he may have missed it. But he heard it.

The touch of a threat.

Sree had heard that tone a hundred times with his sister. She always knew how to say words that seemed innocuous, but in reality were a warning to him.

This Head Superior represented one of the ones he wanted to fight against. He most likely knew the truth about Sree's family's deaths, had possibly even been part of the cover ups.

Had this Head Superior been the one alerting Sree's Targets about his whereabouts to have him killed?

Sree couldn't be certain of the right answer in this moment. He only knew he didn't want to be here anymore, didn't want to play this game. But something inside him resisted giving this man the satisfaction of the truth. He didn't deserve it.

"All Head Superior Three told me was she wanted to say something about my family. And then someone murdered her before she could."

The Head Superior flinched at the word. No one on his planet used that term. Killing, eliminating, assassinating—those were all acceptable. But taboo surrounded the notion of murder.

Sree felt a twinge of satisfaction at Head Superior Four's reaction. It may not be much, but for some reason it dispelled a portion of the hopelessness which had settled over him. This smug official had destroyed not only another Re'Ris' life, but caused Celebration Day to die before it even started. No one would want to celebrate his family under the perpetual shadow of a Head Superior's assassination. And even more so, his family name would now be tainted by unwarranted bloodshed. Citizens would keep their whispers to themselves until no one spoke about the incident, or his family, anymore.

The Head Superior cleared his throat and straightened his shoulders. "I understand your frustration. I promise you, I will take care of this situation."

The smile lingered on the face of Head Superior Four, but Sree heard the tone once more.

A threat.

Sree stared him squarely in the eyes. "I'm sure you'll try." The words hung in the air. Sree didn't bother to cover the insult that tinged them. "Can I go home now?"

"Of course. If I'm not mistaken, you still have an Assignment to finish. I wouldn't want to keep you from a task you need to fulfill."

Sree thought instead about the Stasis Room. "Yeah. Yeah, I do."

CHAPTER 48

Panaan would now be known as Head Superior Three.

Her confirmation "ceremony" came across a bit lackluster, compared to any of the other day's events.

After she and Head Superior Four finished lunch, in which she remained as faux pleasant as possible, they'd headed out of the office, down one level in the elevator, and entered a large meeting room, which looked like it could hold about fifty individuals.

Panaan stood in the middle, while one by one the other remaining Head Superiors, beginning with Head Superior One, pledged an oath to follow the Makers' will by having five Head Superiors to watch over the Re'Ris, guide them, and maintain their connections to self, world, and Makers. After each one repeated this oath, Panaan was instructed to reply with, "As will I."

Once the ceremony ended, they handed her a jacket with a gold and black rimmed collar with three pips.

It fit her perfectly.

The fact that they had this jacket ready, in her size, confirmed her theory: they knew beforehand that she would be replacing the Head Superior who Passed On that day.

Before they all exited the room, Head Superior Four told Panaan she could return home, gather whatever personal belongings she wanted, and make a list of anything else she needed for her new lodgings, which would be transported there by a pair of Laborers later tomorrow. She would be allowed to sleep in her home tonight, but afterwards she would be moved to her new location.

After the other three Head Superiors left, only Head Superior Four remained.

"Tomorrow begins the first day of the rest of your life, Head Superior Three," he said, returning her personal communications device. "Once you've settled into your new place, we'll have a tixa sent for you, and you'll return here to claim your office. When you exit the elevator into the small alcove, there is a panel located on the right. Place your hand on it and the floor will rotate to bring you to office number three. Without prior permission, such as if when you are away and one of the Head Superiors wants to access your office, the panel will only respond to you. Arrange things within however you'd like, as you'll most likely spend quite a bit of time here at Central Processing for training before you begin any traveling, and I'll meet you for lunch tomorrow to go over your first duties. Any questions?"

"Too many," she said with a forced grin, tucking her communications device into her pocket. "But for now, when I went to leave your office earlier, the elevator was gone. How do I access it when it's not there?"

He gestured to the doorframe of the meeting room. "Unlike this room, our offices have an access panel on the right, inside the doorway, just like on the outside when you exit the elevator. If a different office faces the elevator, you just place your hand on the panel and wait for it to rotate the floor so you can leave through the elevator."

"How did the Laborer leave the alcove, then?"

He frowned. "She left?"

Fearing she'd get the poor woman in trouble, she said, "I'm sure she just had to use the bathroom or something."

The creases on his forehead lessened. "Of course. They have their own entrance and exit points, which allow them to move between the alcove areas, so they can use the elevator when the office they are guarding doesn't face it. But don't worry," he said, misinterpreting her concern, "they can't get into your office unless you let them in."

"Got it," she replied.

"If there are no other questions...?"

Panaan could read his impatience since he edged towards the exit. "Just one more, for now. I'm sure I'll have many more as the days go on."

He paused in his movement. "Of course. It's not surprising. This is all very new to you. I promise I'll answer more tomorrow, but I have time for one more before my next meeting."

"Why did someone take my blood in the tixa when I was brought here by Central Authority?" She watched his reaction closely.

A slight narrowing of his eyes. "Yes. That. You have been sworn in and so, of course, you'll know everything. But I'm afraid it will raise more questions than I have time for right now."

She knew she needed some kind of response. For some reason, this felt important to her. No one had answered her with anything besides vague words. That led her to believe there must be importance attached to her questions. She could only think of one trick to make him give her some kind of answer right now: feign fear. She often used this ploy to get information her Mother hadn't wanted to give. She decided to see if it would work with this Head Superior as well. So, she pretended to be worried about her own health.

"You said there's something special about me. Is it in my blood? Is there something wrong with it?"

"No, of course not," he replied, reassuring her.

"So, there *isn't* something special about me? Or it's not in my blood?" she asked, purposefully misreading his negative answer.

He took his hand off the door panel. "What? Oh, no. I see where you might have been confused. There is nothing wrong with your blood. Quite the opposite. It *is* what makes you special. Very unique. You have the genetic material of the Makers inside you."

Panaan felt genuinely confused at that statement. "We all do. The Makers made us."

He shook his head, as if dealing with a small child. "They made us, yes, but we are not *of* them. We are our own species. However, a very small few on our world, a smaller percentage than I can even quote to you, have Maker's genetic material mixed with their own. You are one of these individuals. Which is one of the main reasons you are now a Head Superior." Something in his pocket beeped. "Apologies, but I must be off. If you need assistance, your own Laborer will help you." With that, he opened the door. Outside stood the Laborer Panaan had spoken with that morning, the one who worked for Head Superior Four, and a new one next to her.

"Thank you," Panaan remembered to say as the doors to the elevator closed with the Head Superior and his own Laborer inside.

The new one gave her a slight smile. "Congratulations, Head Superior Three," he said, the timbre of his voice higher than she'd imagined for such a broad-chested man. "I am Laborer 60-555."

"Nice to meet you," she said, awkwardly. She didn't really know what to do with a Laborer assistant. Did he just stand out there all day, waiting for her?

As if anticipating her question, he said, "I am the day-shift Laborer, so you'll see me most of the time. The night-shift Laborer only works if you stay late or overnight. They are on call for that." He gestured to her as the elevator door reopened and she entered. He followed her in and they went up one floor. "I know you are scheduled to return to your original home this evening and two other Laborers will help you move any personal belongings to your new lodgings tomorrow, but I wanted to show you your office first. If you have anything you know you'll want to change immediately, I can begin that process for you while you're handling your other responsibilities. That way, when you arrive for work tomorrow morning, changes for your office will already be underway."

His words, though quick, showed pride in his efficiency. She could tell he liked his job, but even more so, wanted her to see that.

"That's a great idea," she praised him. She caught the brief smile on his face out of the corner of her eye at her flattery.

They arrived on the top floor and when the doors opened, a door with the number 3 engraved on it stood in front of them. As instructed by the Laborer, she placed her palm on the panel next to it to scan her handprint, which lit up with two curved crescent shaped lights, and the door opened. Inside, the pastel pinks, yellows, and corals assaulted her sense of style. However, unlike Head Superior Four's office with personal items and datapads stacked on his desk, this room appeared nearly spotless, without a trace that anyone had ever been here, except for the furniture and wall adornments.

"The Head Superior before me must've been intense about cleaning."

"On the contrary," he said, speaking to her as she gazed around the room. "She often had datapads strewn all over her office. She liked to spread out, usually working on the small couch or at the table instead of her desk. Said the change in perspective in the room often gave her a change in perspective toward whatever she was working on."

"So where are all her datapads now?"

"When I was assigned yesterday, I was instructed to clean everything up early this morning, and to place the datapads and any other belongings in a storage container. The other Head Superiors will look through them, I'm sure, and then get you caught up on any projects they might want you to take over."

Panaan paused while gazing at the only artwork in the room she liked, which hung behind the desk. Eventually she turned towards him. "You cleaned up...this *morning*?"

"Yes. I was given instructions last night to make it my priority this morning as soon as I arrived."

Last night? He'd been given instructions to clean up her office before *she died?*

Not wanting to give away the knowledge she'd just gleaned, Panaan said, "Well, you did a great job. It's really clean."

"Thank you, Head Superior Three." He cleared his throat. "Is there anything you've decided on that you'd like for me to begin to change here?"

Peering around the room, she realized the décor didn't really suit her. Except for the artwork with the flowers and vines...

An hour later Panaan reached her home, with two Laborers in tow to help transfer any items she wanted to take with her. The timing of becoming Head Superior and moving to a new location didn't go unrecognized in comparison to the other changes in her life. Her current home had been her Mother's house. At her age, Panaan couldn't hope it would be transferred to her, even at an assassin level, since she'd just started out and her Mother's Laborer status had accumulated over the years. She'd already received a notice letting her know the overdue standing of the next payment on the house and that she'd need to vacate the premises soon.

Strange how the universe worked sometimes.

The one-bedroom standard Laborer home may have been small for her and her Mother, but Panaan hadn't cared. Sleeping on the pull-out couch had been worth it for the time spent with her Mother. Now, she scanned her "room" and wondered what she wanted to take to her new place or leave to be discarded, when the gravity of the situation hit her.

She would never come to this home again because she was currently a Head Superior.

Her.

This should be the most thrilling moment of her life. No one could attain a higher status than this on her planet outside of an overachieving assassin, like Faan Kaano, or a retired assassin, like Vuun, and yet she didn't feel excited at all. She felt absolutely sick to her stomach.

Because she couldn't deny what she knew. The other Head Superiors assassinated one of their own at the celebration this morning to make room for herself to join them.

Nothing in her life was as it seemed. And with this new knowledge, she now understood the true power behind the Head Superiors—they could choose their own kills.

But if that turned out to be the case, then how did the Makers not know about this? If they were the only ones with the power to assign and eliminate Targets, how could this be allowed? According to all the literature she'd read that morning, Head Superiors were untouchable. They'd earned the right to retire or step down, just like assassins who filled their quotas.

So why kill the previous Head Superior Three this morning? Why not simply vote her out?

Panaan realized she hadn't packed anything. She'd just been standing, staring at this soon-to-be-evacuated space, lost in thought.

Rubbing her fingertips on her temples, Panaan felt truly alone in the world. She may now be part of an elite group, who knew more than anyone on the planet, but she couldn't discuss any of this with them because...

...because she couldn't trust them.

She wished her Mother were here.

Anyone, at this point.

She needed someone to talk to.

An image of a face popped into her mind.

Sree.

He seemed to be the only one left to have some sort of understanding of the system not being what it appeared.

Turning towards the Laborers, she lied and told them she wanted to go to dinner, and instructed them to take everything from the current room, except for the furniture. Pointing to the kitchen, she wanted to keep the knickknacks, but leave the utensils, cookware, and appliances, as all of these things would be provided in her new place. As for her Mother's bedroom, she planned to use it that night, so she gave them instructions about what to take when they returned the following morning. They both nodded vigorously, obviously eager to prove their worth to a new Head Superior.

On that note, she left the house, not thinking about dinner at all.

Chapter 49

The evening of Celebration Day, Sree believed he'd gathered everything he needed to enter both the Stasis and Archive Rooms that night and packed the items into a small backpack on his bed in front of him, along with a larger empty bag he rolled up to carry out any items he found.

His plan changed. He couldn't wait for tomorrow anymore. Tonight would be his only shot. Head Superior Three's death changed everything.

Earlier that morning, each step had been painstakingly outlined in his mind:

1) Go to Central Processing the day after Celebration Day, a hero, respected, and ask to see Head Superior Three to talk about what would happen after her revelation to the public.

2) Then, on his way out at the end of the day shift, he'd color-change, and wait for the majority of employees to go home.

3) Next, heading down the elevator, he would find and enter the Stasis and Archive Rooms, collect the evidence he'd

need, then slip out.

4) Finally, the meetup with Biin in Bria, give her everything he'd found, and finally hide out until the Crypt found a way to make that evidence useful.

But the death of Head Superior Three changed his ability to follow these steps. Seeing her would now be an impossibility. The news reported that Central Processing had been mostly shut down, except for essential employees, for the entire day, out of respect for the Head Superior's Passing On.

No one even mentioned Celebration Day or Sree's family on the news bulletins. The emergency broadcast which went out to everyone's devices spoke only of the attack on the Head Superior. No one cared about Sree anymore. He no longer possessed the clout he needed to stroll into Central Processing. Even those guarding his home dispersed, since Head Superior Three had been the one who'd assigned them.

And since he still had been tasked to kill his Target—Biin—by tomorrow, he couldn't wait any longer to find the Stasis Room.

Because he now truly believed everything Wiin told him.

Which meant that if he didn't find the Stasis Room today, there wouldn't be another opportunity. The day after tomorrow he himself would become a Target for not finishing his Assignment. And heading into Central Processing as a Target would be tantamount to suicide. He remembered when his Mother's Mother suggested he wait outside Central Processing to see if his Target went in to check their status or if they'd worked there, because it employed many Laborers. Some newer assassins did this, since most Laborers wouldn't know about this little trick. Because this concept seemed to be fairly well-known among assassins, Sree couldn't take the risk the one assigned to him wouldn't try the same thing.

Not to mention this nasty habit recently of his Targets being *told* where to find him. Safety now eluded him everywhere.

He prayed to the stars that these rooms he planned to investigate would have whatever proof he needed to change things once and for all. Because the only thing left for him to truly be afraid of would be if all these risks were for nothing. With no proof, he'd be on the run until they found and killed him.

Sree snorted a laugh to himself. That's how everything started, with his revulsion to eliminate anyone in the first place.

Any amusement at irony died in his throat at the sound of the house chimes ringing.

Probably another reporter, he thought. *Even though they don't care about me or Celebration Day anymore.* Interviews had consisted of the reporters wanting him to repeat the gory details of the Head Superior's Passing On. As sensational news, even if he could live a normal life as an assassin, he'd be forever haunted as the "witness to the atrocity" and not as a member of the Kaano family.

In one fell swoop whoever had orchestrated Head Superior Three's death ruined Sree's credibility, murdered the only person with prestige before she could reveal the truth about his family, and would soon remove Sree as well, making him just another "failed" assassin.

He had to admit the brilliance of the plan. The only thing the culprit hadn't counted on was Sree's encounter with Wiin and the knowledge about the Stasis and Archive Rooms.

The chimes to his home rang again.

With a sigh, Sree made his way downstairs. Only threatening the reporters with a call to Central Authority if they didn't leave made them scatter. He'd thought they'd all gotten the message, but apparently one reporter must have been late to the scene.

Flinging the front door open, Sree opened his mouth to speak his threat, when he stopped, his jaw hanging open mid-breath.

In front of him stood the young woman he'd seen yesterday

afternoon, the one in his kitchen who'd been arrested. The one who'd tried to attack him.

Panaan.

"You!" he exclaimed.

Panaan held up her hands, empty. "I can explain. Things have changed, Sree. And you are right, everything is wrong."

The similarity of her words to Biin's struck him and any fear she meant him harm vanished. In that same moment he noticed the gold and black rimmed collar on her jacket. With three pips. It took a few moments for him to register their meaning.

It couldn't be.

"You...you're a Head Superior?"

She nodded, then slowly lowered her hands. "Can I come in so we can talk?"

Hesitating for a moment, he then held the door open wider and she slid past him. She took a seat at the kitchen table while Sree remained standing next to the door which he'd just closed. The curtains on the windows fluttered with the breeze that swirled through the room. The scent of rain lingered in the air as the sun hung low in the sky.

"How...?" Sree began. Anger flooded him as he thought about the last time he'd seen her. "You...you were arrested. They broke into my house and arrested you. My Mother's Mother *died* and you're a Head Superior?!"

In the same calm voice, she said, "I can explain."

He glanced over at the timereader on the counter and rubbed his hand across his forehead. He couldn't wait much longer or getting into Central Processing after the day shift ended would be impossible. He needed to leave, soon, so he could make it inside, skin-shift, and remain until closing. But as he stared at her, he wanted to know how someone like her, who'd plotted revenge against him and tried to kill him *and* got arrested, could became a Head Superior?

The same anger that bubbled up inside him moments ago

transformed into curiosity when he peered at her face. She looked...scared. And young. So young. A year younger than him but she'd become a Head Superior.

"Talk fast. I have to leave soon." Striding across the room, he sat across from her, the chair legs scraping against the tiled floor as he pulled himself up to the table. "I'm listening."

After taking a deep breath, she spoke, explaining what happened after she'd been arrested, her becoming Head Superior, and the realization that the one who'd recruited her had orchestrated the death of Head Superior Three on the platform. Only about ten standard minutes passed from when she began her story, but Sree felt like he'd learned a lifetime of knowledge. Just like when he'd met Wiin and his whole world changed in a matter of hours.

"That's...insane," he said when she finished.

She gave a weak smile. "You think I don't know that?"

A laugh of incredulity escaped him. "So...why did you come here?"

"The last time I was here, you told Vuun the Head Superiors had covered up the truth about your Mother's and Father's deaths and when I said my own Mother and Father previously spoke about a conspiracy surrounding their own Passings On, you said you weren't a part of it, but you didn't believe I was wrong." She took a deep breath and he noticed the shaking of her hands as she clasped them together.

She seemed terrified.

"I'm here," she continued, "because you're right. There is something going on with the Head Superiors. And it's corruption at its core."

"Why should I believe you? Last time you were here, it was to kill me." He motioned to her collar. "And now you've come back *as* a Head Superior. Maybe this is to falsely lure me into—"

She scoffed and cut him off. "They just killed a Head Superior in broad daylight. When they want you dead, you'll be dead. They don't need to send me. They just need to place you at a certain spot at a certain time and poof, someone will end your life."

Sree remembered how his Target had been told what alley to wait in, how Biin had been given his address.

"Then why did you join them?" he countered.

"They'd just arrested me. Brought me to a secure location. Offered me the job. They told me I was free to turn it down." She rolled her eyes. "After everything I'd put together, I realized if I said no, they'd just lock me up. Otherwise, why 'arrest' me in the first place? If I were a real candidate for Head Superior with the freedom to turn down the job, why not just approach me at my home or summon me to Central Processing? So, I figured it was smarter to accept, and I could figure the rest out later."

Sree processed this new information. Her view contained merit. Why stage the arrest if she were being offered a prestigious job, unless they needed a contingency to fall back on?

Leaning against the kitchen table, he countered, "Okay, I can see why you took the position, but it still doesn't answer why you came here."

"The Head Superior that hired me, number Four, orchestrated the death of Head Superior Three in public. I was brought in to replace her *before* she died. They already knew they'd need to fill her position. Which means they are making their own choices, against the Makers' wishes. I know, because the Rules for the Head Superiors say a Head Superior can only be removed from office if retired, ill, unanimously voted out, or dead. *But* they are not allowed to be Targets. I just don't understand why the Makers are allowing this."

Steeling himself, he decided to take a chance. This young woman had already gone through so much, even risking her life to tell him what she'd learned. Besides, maybe she could be a way in for him if she could now access places inside Central Processing...possibly like the Stasis and Archive Rooms?

It was now or never.

"This is going to come as a shock, but you should know what I learned. The Makers don't exist anymore." Sree's words hung in the air. He watched Panaan anxiously look around her, as if convinced they'd be attacked where they sat.

"What?" she whispered, her eyes locking onto his.

Sree divulged everything about his experience with Wiin: about the abduction, Wiin's belief that the Makers were extinct and that the Head Superiors ran everything, how Wiin had seen the Makers' bodies in an area called the Stasis Room and had instructed Sree to get inside the Archive Room and find more definitive proof.

Studying her face closely, she seemed surprised at first by his words, but as he continued, she began to nod.

When he finished, however, she shook her head. "There's no way Wiin could have known this, accessed all that information and those areas of Central Processing. Not as a Laborer."

"Apparently, he's a Binder, so, he could get into the system and find out information, like codes and stuff, without anyone detecting him. It's how he made himself my Target."

A frown. "A Binder? What's that?"

"Oh, yeah, sorry. It means he has Makers' genetic material mixed with his own. And since the Makers used that to program the systems, only someone with their genetic material can use and change the system." He paused. "I wondered before if the Head Superiors know about this and have been keeping or using Binders to change the system the way they see fit. It makes sense, right?"

Panaan's face color-changed rapidly, punctuated by swirls of light and dark grey.

"What?" Sree asked, alarmed. "What is it?"

"They aren't using Binders. They *are* Binders."

"The Head Superiors?"

She nodded, then gripped her hands together more tightly.

"It's why I'm a Head Superior."

A moment passed before Sree realized the implication. "You? You have Maker genetic material?"

"That's what they told me. I...I didn't really understand what it meant. I mean, you make it seem really important."

Sree's mind whirled with thoughts. This changed everything. He could just have Panaan go in any day, multiple days even, and collect all the evidence and then give it all to Biin and no one would be hurt or targeted or...

The glass to his kitchen window shattered.

Both of them jumped to their feet as shards splattered across the room. One of them grazed Sree's face and he reached up and winced at the shallow cut on his cheek. The item which broke the window puffed smoke on the tiled floor.

"What the...?" Panaan said.

"MOVE!" Sree yelled, grabbing her by the hand, and yanking her towards the rear exit. He flung open the door and they managed to make it to the first row of pristinely trimmed bushes in the back yard when a terrible burst of heat pushed against his back and flung him forward. He lost Panaan's hand, tumbling head over feet. Luckily, he landed on the soft turf next to a row of decorative metal blocks. He felt his back burning. With quick movements, he rolled around on the dewy backyard surface until he felt cooler. Throbbing in his right ankle concerned him, but when he stood, it held his weight.

Searching around, frantic, Sree spotted Panaan several meters away, lying face-up.

"Panaan!" he called out, rushing over to her.

She let out a moan, and rolled over onto her stomach, pushing herself up onto her hands and knees. "I'm okay," she said, coughing. The edges of her shirt still smoldered. "What happened?"

"Incendiary device," he said through gritted teeth. He remembered his Mother's Mother telling him they were considered "cowardly" types of assassination devices because they were hard to control and ran the risk of hurting others nearby, causing property damage, and were obnoxiously noticeable. They were usually used, according to her, by those afraid to be "real" assassins.

Sree quickly assessed the situation. Half the house had been blown to pieces. Chunks of debris still hung precariously from the barely attached roof. The two of them couldn't return inside safely and neighbors would soon come to check on the commotion. Plus, if the assassin was still nearby, they may come to finish him off.

Without thinking, Sree camouflaged himself.

"Sree?" Panaan whispered.

"Hurry," he said. "Follow my lead."

But she hadn't been looking at him. Instead, she pointed to the ground near the house. A young woman's body lay there, unmoving. Sree could tell from here, from the frozen look in her wide-open eyes, that no life remained in her. She'd gotten caught in her own blast. The sight halted him in place.

A flash of lightning ripped across the sky, attracting Sree's attention. He tore his gaze away from the woman who'd probably been sent to kill him. If he thought too hard about it, it would paralyze him right now.

Forcing himself to focus, he barked out commands. "Panaan. Shift. Now." He took her hand so he wouldn't lose her once they became invisible.

Panaan slowly blinked twice, then followed the order, disappearing in front of his eyes. She appeared to be skilled enough, he noted, though she seemed to have some issues with light reflection. It would have to do for the time being.

"Let's head to the left," he said, arbitrarily picking a direction. Right now, it didn't matter where they went.

They just needed to disappear.

CHAPTER 50

About a standard hour later, after many twists and turns, they reached the courtyard near the main entrance to Central Processing. Sree had never felt quite so eclipsed by the hugeness of the complex currently towering over him.

Rain splattered the ground in great dollops, splashing them just as hard from above as from the drops hitting the ground. Tree limbs whipped around in the wind, creaking and moaning in the otherwise vacant night. While they stood there, he only saw one Laborer leave the building, her hair swirling violently around her head as she bent low against the storm. Now that they'd stopped moving, the chill soaked him thoroughly through his meager clothes.

It had been strange to navigate the streets while invisible. No one really did that. Camouflaging oneself took an enormous amount of energy, so assassins only used it when stalking or approaching their Target. It didn't make sense, either, in crowded areas, because Re'Ris would continually bump into each other if invisible. So, for he and Panaan to move around that way, they needed to be careful.

Taking the time to catch his breath, Sree placed a hand on a nearby lotha tree, while he heard Panaan plop down on an adjacent bench. He watched her color-changing ability flitter and then finally falter.

"I can't anymore," she gasped.

He didn't feel surprised. She'd become visible multiple times on their journey, being drained of too much energy to keep the skin-shifting skill intact. He himself depended on the constant practices with his sister to have been able to maintain his camouflage for so long, but even he'd flickered several times in the past quarter of an hour.

Coming into full view, he took a seat next to her. "I know. I can't anymore, either. We can rest for a while here."

"Sree...someone blew up your house to eliminate you. And got themselves killed."

"Yeah." He paused, still shocked because he realized another horrible notion. "The really scary thing is...I'm still on Assignment." According to the Rules, Re'Ris couldn't be targeted while on Assignment.

"So that had to have been your Target, coming after you first. But...how did they know where you lived?"

"It's worse than you think." He glanced at her, knowing his Target had been Biin and the woman who laid on the ground next to his demolished house had not been. "That wasn't my Target. It's someone else. They sent someone else after me, even though I'm on Assignment."

"That's...that's impossible!"

He laughed, weakly. "After all the stuff you've talked about tonight? Like the idea of a Head Superior killing one of their own. The fact that *you* were made one of them. And your theory that your own Mother and Father were probably targeted by the Head Superiors for their own personal reasons. Are you still surprised that they can do whatever they want?"

"But...the Rules..."

"They don't follow the Rules. They haven't for years. Without the Makers, they don't have to."

Several moments of silence hung in the air around them.

"I can't believe the Makers really don't exist anymore," Panaan finally said quietly. "But they can't. They would never allow all these things to happen." She fidgeted on the bench. "I wish I didn't know any of this. Because what's the point of knowing? I'm still going to go back to being a Head Superior tomorrow and will have to look them in the eye and, what? Do nothing. And you..." she trailed off.

"At some point, they'll catch me. They have no problem sending both Targets and assassins after me, whenever they want. They won't stop until I'm dead."

"It's hopeless." She slumped further onto the bench, her head hung in defeat.

Sree glanced towards Central Processing, now looking menacing in front of them. "I didn't get to finish telling you this, because as you noticed, my kitchen exploded, but there is an underground movement called the Crypt, where other Re'Ris also believe something is wrong in the system. When Wiin kidnapped me, he did so on his own. He didn't know about the movement. But he'd figured out more things than they even knew, because he was a Binder.

"Now," he continued, transferring his gaze to her, "there are Re'Ris waiting for me in Bria to report to them after I get more proof of these conspiracies. Proof from the Archive Room."

"Aren't I enough proof? What they did to me? What I realized they'd covered up about Head Superior Three?"

Sree thought about it. "Unfortunately, it's not really proof, just your word. They made you a Head Superior at a young age. You don't have anything real to show they ordered the kill. Or that they are doing anything outside the Rules. And if you say anything to the contrary, why would anyone believe you?"

She licked her lips. "But could I get proof? I mean, be like...like a spy? On the inside?"

Sree respected her courage. "I thought about that. Maybe. But you can't guarantee they will let you in on their processes. Or give you access to these restricted areas. They may keep you in the dark. And if you try to speak out...well, you saw what happened to your predecessor."

"Urgh!" she said, letting out a grunt and stomping the ground. "This is so stupid! We can't do anything."

"That's not necessarily true..." Sree nodded to the building. "There is still the Archive Room. Wiin told me it's where he got most of his information. Books of all different types and materials. Artifacts made by the Makers' own hands. He showed me some of these items, I got to touch them and hold them, and there were documents about all sorts of things. I took some home, kept them hidden..." he trailed off. "I buried them near my house. Oh, Makers. They're gone. All the evidence is gone!" The realization of all that information being destroyed hit him. Sree pressed his hands onto his face.

"But the room," Panaan said slowly, not seeming to understand how devastating that realization had been for Sree. "The room where he found all of that stuff. It's inside Central Processing?"

Sree nodded, shaking himself from his anguish as best he could. "I found out how to access the floor where I think the Stasis and Archive Rooms are, but that's as far as I've gotten. I couldn't make the elevator go down to that floor. There are these curved button-like things that I can't make work. I think it must be some sort of access I don't have. Wiin did, but he didn't tell me what I needed to do. He must have missed a step in his explanation."

Panaan stared for several moments at her hands before she said, "You said Wiin is a Binder, because he has Maker genetic material?"

"Yeah."

She held out one of her hands. "What if...what if those curved lights aren't just buttons, but they read genetic material?"

Sree frowned, confused. "How do you mean?"

Panaan continued. "The offices on the top floor, they are kept locked by what you're describing. Curved carvings that light up. I was told to put my hand on them. The Laborer said it was a handprint ID scanner. But it's not shaped like a hand. It's just these curved, glowing buttons."

A glimmer of hope stole into his chest, but he didn't want to embrace it. Not yet. He'd never pictured anyone else joining him when he broke in. He'd planned to do this himself. And yet here she sat, able to get him further than he could on his own. But...he didn't want to be responsible if something happened to her. She could still have a life, one as a Head Superior. That could open a lot of doors for her in the future. All the doors, actually.

"I can't ask you to go in there."

She stood, a glint in her eyes. "You don't have to. I'm going. What else can we do? By morning they'll find out you didn't die in your home. If I simply go back to work, they'll most likely not tell me anything anyway, like you said. And without proof, nothing will change. They'll find a way to finally kill you and I'll be stuck, a puppet, until I either do what they do or they eliminate me as well."

Her determination became contagious, but Sree felt his sister's mindset tempering him, reminding him to check his emotions and think things through logically. "I don't have bags to carry stuff out. Or it could all be for nothing. And if we get caught..."

"Then we get caught," she finished. "The alternative isn't any better. At least this way, we have a chance to at least find out what we're up against. We have a chance to have a different fate."

Once again, thoughts of his family circled inside his mind. His Mother's and Father's struggles to make things right. His sister's proof that their Passings On were a cover up. And even Head Superior Three's decision to tell the truth about his family to the public.

Of course, each of those individuals who'd tried to make a difference were now dead.

But perhaps his family's legacy involved something other than to be incredible assassins.

Perhaps they were meant to change things.

No matter the cost.

Noticing that same employee, hair still relentlessly whipping around her head in the wind, Sree let the hope fully bloom inside his chest. Giving a nod to Panaan, he color-changed and grabbed her hand. Without another word she followed suit.

As the wind gusted around them and the clouds rumbled in the sky, he told her, "Let's go change fate," before they sprinted towards the doors, following the Laborer inside as she reentered the building.

Chapter 51

Sree's breath clung to the inside of his throat. He and Panaan, both invisible, were pressed against the wall of the corridor inside Central Processing which led to the elevator. A lone guard, looking extremely bored, hummed while he strode down the hallway towards them.

Nervous thoughts filled Sree's mind.

If the guard's arm swung a little bit closer to the wall...

If he paused to stretch and heard them having to take in a new breath...

But the guard did neither, continuing past them.

Once again, this validated to Sree how ingrained the Rules were in the Re'Ris that they'd never think anyone would be invisible inside of Central Processing.

After the guard passed them, Sree gave Panaan's hand a squeeze, to indicate they could keep moving. Feeling like he breathed too loudly and that every step echoed like a drum throughout the space surrounding them kept the anxiety inside him teetering at the surface.

Cautiously, they made it to the elevator and Sree allowed himself to breathe normally, instead of stealing and holding darts of air as he'd done over the past several minutes. His brain thanked him by allowing him to feel less dizzy.

"What now?" he heard Panaan whisper.

He squeezed her hand again and they entered the elevator.

The doors sliding open sounded extremely loud in the silent hallway—a noise most likely not noticed during the normal hustle of a workday.

Sree's head craned around towards the guard.

Who had stopped.

And began to turn around.

Sree pulled Panaan into the small space and the door closed behind them, but he could hear the guard's footsteps heading their way.

Materializing, Sree pointed at the space below the ground floor button. He entered the code from Wiin and the two curved lights appeared again, like last time. Panaan's eyes widened, no longer camouflaged either.

Sree grinned and pressed the curved lights.

Nothing happened.

Fear shot through him like shards of hot glass.

She pushed him aside and he remembered, feeling like an idiot, that *she* had to be the one to press the buttons. They required her genetic Maker material.

Panaan reached over, but before she could place her fingers on the curved lights, the elevator opened.

The guard stood there, apparently expecting to see a malfunctioning elevator, and *not* two young Re'Ris holding hands.

A quizzical look crossed the guard's face.

Panaan's hand, still holding Sree's, flashed out. Sree felt a force connect with his wrist and a warm liquid splash over his skin.

Yanking his fist away, he realized what Panaan had done. She'd initiated the wrade he wore and used the weapon on the guard's throat. Sick to his stomach, Sree forcefully untangled his hand from hers and turned away from the guard's falling body. The door closed and they were alone again.

Panaan reached over to depress the buttons, but they weren't lit up anymore. "Put the code in again," she said, her voice calm.

Sree spun around towards her, disgust creeping through his guts. "What is *wrong* with you? Why did you do that?" he asked, pointing towards the guard.

A touch of a frown graced her mouth. "What do you mean? He would've reported us."

Sree didn't understand how she could be so calm. She'd just murdered someone, and used his hand to do it.

"You...you just..." he couldn't even form the words.

Suddenly, the look on her face changed, to one of confusion. "Why does this bother you? You've had two Assignments already. You know what it means to kill."

He violently shook his head. "No. I don't want to. It's not who I am."

"But...but your Assignments?"

"Wiin set things up for me to kill him, but it was basically suicide. And the second one was by accident. He attacked me and, while trying to get him off me, my wrades killed him."

She let out a small laugh, not a mean one, but one of sympathy. "Imagine. A Kaano not wanting to kill? You were *definitely* born into the wrong house."

"You don't know how many times I've thought that over the years." Forcing an exhale, he refocused, though he still refused to look at the body. "Well, we can't change this now. His death will be reported as soon as the day shift starts. We better get going." He entered the code, the curved lights lit up, and Panaan pressed her hand against them. Before they moved, he warned her, "No more killing, though."

She hesitated for a moment, then nodded.

The elevator shifted, moving downwards. During the descent, part of Sree felt terrified there would be nothing; that the Stasis and Archive Rooms and everything else didn't exist, or even worse, had been moved or destroyed.

The other part of him felt just as scared the room *would* be there. It meant he could no longer hide from the truth, whatever that turned out to be. He still didn't know for sure if he could do this, and even if he managed to, would anyone believe him?

The door opened, revealing a corridor similar to the ones above them, though this one appeared dimly lit with what seemed to be emergency lights. When they exited the elevator, the hallway lit up fully. It only ran in one direction: to the left. At the end stood one door.

"I guess that's it," Panaan whispered. Sree noticed the perspiration on her brow.

They'd come this far...

He took the lead, heading forward.

In front of the door, two curved lights lit up next to it on the wall.

"Here goes," he said, nodding to her hand.

She pressed the lights and the door hissed open.

Both panic and relief washed over him as he walked into the exact room Wiin described—sterile metal walls with dozens, perhaps hundreds of handles connected to pull-out chambers. Were the dead bodies of the Makers really in those compartments?

Sree moved toward a wall, reaching for one of the handles. The two sides of him fought: one repulsed by what he planned to do, and the other filled with a morbid curiosity to see the Makers for himself.

What if they were really in there? Did Sree actually want

Wiin's conspiracies to be true? What if they *weren't* in there? Would he continue on anyway?

I have to know now. I have to know if this has all been the ravings of a lunatic or if my creators are really lying cold and dead inside these chambers.

I have to know.

Sree wrapped his hand around a handle. The metal felt cool against his flesh and his grip slipped due to sweaty palms.

Holding his breath, Sree began to pull...

...when he stopped dead at Panaan's hand on his shoulder.

"Look," she said, motioning to the wall. An orange light, though silent, flashed.

Suddenly, the rest of the lights went out, except for the flashing one.

Hardly daring to breathe, a few moments passed and the emergency lights flickered on again, accompanied by a sound that sent a skin-crawling current across his flesh.

The sound of the door unlocking.

Someone must be coming into the room!

Frantic, Sree spun around in search of an alternate exit. His gaze fell on a door toward the rear of the room. It must be the Archive Room, but he didn't know if that led to another exit either.

At this point, they didn't have much of a choice.

Grabbing Panaan's hand, they vanished from view again and moved quickly as the front door began to open. The line of sight to the Archive Room door wasn't impeded, so Sree waited, not opening their only escape yet. Sree realized whoever entered would know where they had gone because if it were a dead end, they'd be caught for sure.

Hope rose once more as the door opened but no one entered.

A faulty mechanism? An automatic unlock when the emergency lights came on?

Either way, he didn't want to lose their chance. He reached

up to the door handle and tugged.

It didn't budge.

Sree swore under his breath. He crouched down, pulling Panaan down next to him, and pressed his back against the wall.

"It's locked," he whispered. "Stay shifted."

Focusing as hard as he could, Sree concentrated on keeping up his color-changing ability, but the ups and down of adrenaline made it extremely difficult. He peered over and saw Panaan struggling even more, parts of her appearing and disappearing at random.

He pulled her behind a column which held up a table so she'd be as hidden as possible, just before she became fully visible, panting. She held her hand over her mouth to minimize the sound, but her widened eyes spoke volumes of her terror.

Sree could hear low murmured voices now, too far away to understand. Any possibility of a malfunctioning door vanished when two individuals entered the room. He concentrated fully on keeping up his camouflage and peeked out at the new additions.

Both wore jackets with gold and black collars.

Two Head Superiors.

Here. Now.

He didn't recognize either of them as the one he'd spoken with previously, number Four. But why? Why were they here?

Sree retreated, and tugged on Panaan's own black and gold collar, trying to make her realize who they were dealing with. He held up his hand in front of her and materialized two fingers, then tugged on her collar again.

He didn't think her eyes could have widened any larger, but he would've lost that bet.

We're going to get caught, he thought, terror-stricken.

Panaan pointed at him, then the Archive Room door. Then, she pointed at herself, and towards the nearing voices.

He took her hand to indicate they were *not* splitting up.

She pulled her hand away, then made the same pointing motions again.

Uncertainty hit him. He couldn't let her take on two Head Superiors. She'd get herself killed.

Reaching forward, she held out her hand, face up. He took it, and felt her unlock his wrade. With a swift movement, she slid it between her fingers, slicing the inside of her pinky.

Shocked, he became visible. "What—?" he began.

She signaled for him to be quiet. Taking her bloodied finger, she wiped it onto his open palm, then pointed at the panel above him, next to the unopened door.

Understanding hit him. She wanted him to escape through the door while she dealt with the Head Superiors. The only way for him to enter involved the use of the genetic makeup in her blood to open the door, and then possibly access whatever lay inside.

He saw her let out a deep breath and close her eyes, preparing herself.

Without thinking, he removed one of his wrades and placed it on her wrist. With his non-blood covered hand he squeezed her shoulder. "Do you what you have to," he said, negating his previous request that she not kill anyone. She looked at him and he nodded.

Panaan stood.

Sree, still invisible, peeked out to follow her movements. He watched the Head Superiors react upon seeing her.

"What are you doing here?" one of them asked with a husky yet soft voice.

"You're the new Head Superior!" the other one exclaimed at the same time, the voice brighter and more lyrical than the first.

"I was told to come down here," Panaan said. Sree admired her bluff. She strode away from Sree and moved towards the other two. "Head Superior Four told me to meet him by the elevator after hours. He said he wanted to show me something.

But when I got inside Central Processing, the emergency lights were on. I made my way to the elevator and I found a guard, dead."

"We saw him, too," said the husky voice. "But how did you get down *here*?"

She moved closer to them, and Sree could see her circle a bit to the side, to get them to turn towards her, and away from Sree, so they wouldn't see him open the door.

"I was worried about Head Superior Four, that he'd already shown up but had been attacked. I checked inside the elevator and didn't find anyone, but I slid on some blood on the floor and my hand hit these...I don't know, little lights under a keypad? Next thing I knew, the doors closed and I showed up in this hallway. I called out, but no one answered, so I came in here to check. But no one was in here. Then I heard you two outside and I hid—I didn't know who you were."

"After hours would be a better time to show her all of this," the brighter voice said.

"But so soon after pledging her in?"

"The timetable has quickened. Perhaps Four didn't think he had the luxury of waiting."

While they were speaking to each other, Sree knew he needed to take this opportunity to open the door behind him. His camouflage wouldn't last much longer. But it was one thing to know it and quite another thing to actually make his body move.

If either of them turned just a little bit...if they saw the door open out of a corner of their eyes...

Come on, he coaxed himself. *Come on! MOVE! She can't hold them off forever.*

Sree's paralysis broke and he reached up behind him, keeping his eyes on the Head Superiors at all times, and slid his hand with Panaan's blood down over the curved lights next to the handle. It opened, silently. As soon as the gap became large enough for him to fit, he edged through backwards.

Shutting the door as quietly as he could, Sree sat down on the floor with his back against the door, taking in a few deep breaths and wiping away the sweat on his brow with his other hand.

He then blinked in the dim lighting.

Sree's jaw dropped open.

The contents of the room, the *vastness* of the room, made what he'd pictured from Wiin's description vanish in an instant. Cavernous, the space stretched further than he could see. He guessed it took up the space of the entire breadth of the Central Processing building. As Sree walked down the center aisle, he noted medical journals, books, pictures, urns, weapons, pottery, clothing, and strange technological gadgets. The plethora of items lined the walls and filled the space, each one mounted on stands and bathed in soft lights.

He had no clue where to start to look for proof of...well, anything.

Several objects appeared to be missing near the entrance area of the room, which aligned with Wiin's comments about taking them. But as he progressed further along, he wondered which of these journals held the key to revealing the truth about a conspiracy? Which of these books or artifacts would prove to the other Re'Ris about the system's corruptness?

Time slipped away as a frantic panic built inside him. He'd need hours to sort through everything, to determine which items would help his cause.

He didn't have hours. If he were lucky, he had moments. Because looking at these cases, he had a feeling that if he disturbed any one of them, another alarm would sound, and anything Panaan currently did to detain the two other Head Superiors wouldn't be enough to combat the full force of Central Authority.

Dashing around, he needed to do something. To have come all this way and not get any proof? And he knew he'd never be able to return since the alarm alerted others of their presence. He only had this one shot.

His gaze locked onto a stand holding a transparent cube in the center of the space, set apart from everything else. A soft golden light emanated from above, showcasing not only the cube but several other aisles spreading out from each side. He walked toward it and peered through the case's display. It revealed a single sheet of tree material, stretched thinly across a marble background. The edges of it were frayed and yellowed and they curled around the ends of the stand.

Sree held his breath as he leaned over to read the scroll.

It looked like some sort of list, but in a language he didn't understand. The markings were strange, yet somehow familiar, as if he'd seen them before. Wracking his brain, he remembered. It seemed to be the same writing that lined the painting in the Great Hall, the one depicting the Makers.

Sree willed himself to take in a slow deep breath to keep from passing out. He was actually looking at something created by the Makers. He couldn't believe it! He...

Someone entering the room interrupted Sree's amazement.

Time was up.

Without thinking about any further consequences, he tipped over the display case. The covering smashed when it hit the floor, scattering glass everywhere.

With a quick grab, he took the parchment, rolled it up, and tucked it inside his shirt. His theory about a different alarm had been correct. A horrifying screeching wail sounded throughout the room.

"Stop!" The husky-voiced Head Superior's words echoed against the walls.

Sree dove behind one of the artifacts just as a sharpened blade whizzed past his head, nicking his left ear.

I'm going to die, he thought, his heart pounding in his chest. *I'm in a room full of Maker relics and am being attacked by a*

Head Superior.

I'm going to die.

In that moment Sree realized he could no longer see his attacker, who must have skin-shifted to match his surroundings.

Oh Makers, I'm dead.

All sense left him. He couldn't fight an invisible foe. Forcing his own camouflage to take effect, Sree bolted for the door. He had just reached the door handle when he felt his invisibility flicker.

"Got you!" the husky voice called out.

The Head Superior tackled him and slammed him into the nearest podium, holding up some sort of gadget he didn't recognize. The podium teetered but didn't fully fall over. Survival instinct kicked in and Sree lashed out. He made contact, but not enough to loosen the tight grip. His arm became wrenched up behind him and pain lanced through him at its unnatural angle.

Desperate, Sree strained, pressing the side of his wrist against the edge of the nearly toppled podium. He heard the wrade mechanism unlock. The piece of metal extended over the back of his hand in one fluid motion.

Sree awkwardly punched over his shoulder as the sharp metal from the wrade hit something solid.

A scream of agony roared from his attacker, whose pain apparently caused him to lose his focus and therefore his camouflage. Sree's assault tore a chuck of flesh away from below the tackler's right eye.

Scrambling, Sree retreated as the wounded man came at him again. Even though his hand slipped on the floor in his own blood, he managed to grab Sree's foot.

"You will never escape me, thief! I'm going to KILL you!"

Terrified, Sree stabbed at the hand which held him, hitting it right above the knuckles which released its grip. Once he freed his foot, he kicked the attacker's bleeding face and ran.

He tore through the Stasis Room, desperately scanning for

Panaan.

Nothing.

Scraping sounds from the Archive Room indicated his attacker was rising from the ground in pursuit.

After taking one last look around and shouting Panaan's name, to which he heard no answer, he exited the Stasis Room and headed down the corridor to the elevator. He called it and it rumbled down from the floor above him.

The doors parted.

A body lay on the floor.

"No!" he cried out, dropping to his knees next to it. But even before he flipped it over, he could tell from the size it didn't match Panaan's frame. It was the other Head Superior. Panaan must have gotten the upper hand.

But if that were the case, where was she?

A gurgle sounded farther down the hallway. Sree peeked and saw hands grab the edge of the Stasis Room doorframe.

Sree didn't wait any longer. Standing, he hit the button for the main floor, and the elevator door closed. Taking every last mote of energy he could muster he forced himself to color-change, and as soon as the door opened, he bolted from the elevator and the dead body, jumping over the guard laying in his path.

Unable to locate the one individual he hoped for, he once again yelled out Panaan's name, wondering if she'd skin-shifted

Silence.

He could hear the sound of sirens outside, heading towards Central Processing.

Praying that Panaan had somehow made it out, Sree fled through a side exit.

Chapter 52

Water streamed down from the sky. Sree couldn't even see two meters in front of him. The rain came in sheets, soaking him to the bone.

Sree knew he had to get off the street. It being the middle of the night, drenched from the rain, and moving hunched over, while doing his best to cover the stolen Maker parchment from getting ruined by the water, he felt exceedingly conspicuous; skin-shifting was out of the question in this type of atmosphere.

"You will never escape me, thief! I'm going to KILL you!" The words of his attacker rolled through his mind.

What under the stars do I do? I can't go home. I'll never make it to Biin's location all the way in Bria right now. And Panaan is...who knows where.

Guilt ate at him as he pictured her body lying somewhere underneath Central Processing, having sacrificed herself so he could get into the Archive Room. Or, if she were still alive, in custody.

Mopping the water from his eyes once more, he focused on the present. He needed a place to hide. Now.

On his left, an abandoned warehouse up for demolition caught his eye. Without another thought, he ducked through the boarded-up entrance.

Once inside, Sree shook himself out of his wet shoes, socks, and jacket and sat on the floor. Luckily, many jackets he owned were waterproof, since it rained often in Cand, so his back and chest were still mostly dry, even with his dripping hair and pants. He barely even noticed the coat of grime and grit his feet and legs picked up from the floor. Dust tickled the inside of his nose.

Lifting his arm to rub his face caused Sree to feel the document shift inside his waistband. Then he froze.

Was it okay? After all this, had it survived unscathed?

Gently, he removed the parchment. Luck seemed to be with him when he noted the transparent protective coating covering the document. Even though its edges appeared yellowed and curled, it wouldn't get damaged from being handled. Rain would've bounced off it as well. The irony hit him, and he let out a snort.

Then the immensity of the situation suddenly set in.

I can't believe I just stole a Maker's document from Central Processing!

Sree began to laugh, quietly at first, but soon it bubbled over into hysterics. Tears streamed down his moist face as he desperately tried to breathe.

I won't even need an assassin to kill me! I'm going to laugh myself to death!

Sobered by the thought, Sree's laughter slowly died down, and his breathing returned to normal. He glanced at the parchment, which now lay on the floor next to him.

"Guess I might as well look at what I'm going to get killed for."

Sree stared. A title on top. Lines underneath, short in length, were separated by spaces.

It didn't matter what it said. He still couldn't read it.

It's just some list that's in a language I don't understand and...

Sree yanked his hands away, as if burned.

A list.

He currently stared at a list of...he counted quickly... seventeen separate sections.

"No," he muttered out loud. "It can't be." But all the pieces seemed to fit. The document had been kept in the heart of the Archive Room. Written in the language of the Makers.

And a *list.*

"By the Makers, I think these are the original Rules of Assignment!" Sree cried out. His head began to pound. Not only had he stolen a valuable artifact, but he'd stolen *the most* valuable artifact. The document from which a Re'Ris's life got its purpose and meaning.

As soon as they found him, he'd be *worse* than dead.

And they know I have it. Head Superior Four will realize immediately what's been taken.

His mind suddenly switched gears. Did this document actually prove anything? It wouldn't show a conspiracy within the Head Superiors. It didn't provide evidence of the Makers' extinction or of their genetic code existing inside some citizens or of the Head Superiors doling out Assignments of their own accord. He'd risked his life, and lost Panaan, and for what?

A list that simply said Re'Ris were designed to be assassins.

The exact opposite of what he needed.

Sree's despair didn't have a chance to settle before it twisted into terror.

The door to the warehouse opened. In the doorway, sopping wet, the gash on his face still fresh, stood the Head Superior who'd attacked him in the Archive Room. He grinned like a man possessed and held up some sort of device, an orange light flashing.

Sree blinked, then saw it. Out of the corner of his eye, in the pile of clothing he'd removed after ducking into the warehouse. One of his shoes flashed orange as well.

A tracking device.

The man charged, screaming. Sree awkwardly slid across the floor on his butt until he hit a wall, his hands and feet slipping on the grimy floor. The Head Superior lunged at him and Sree instinctively put his hands out to protect himself. The man's weight crushed against him and Sree felt his attacker's breath being expelled from the impact. With his remaining strength, he heaved the man off himself and scrambled to his feet, prepared to fight.

To Sree's surprise, his assailant didn't move.

Carefully, Sree crept toward the body and gingerly nudged it with his foot.

Still nothing.

It could be a trick. He could just have the wind knocked out of him. I mean, all I did was punch him in the chest...

Sree took this moment to look down at his left fist—it dripped with blood.

He'd never retracted the blade on his wrade.

"Oh no..." Sree flipped over the body and closed his eyes for a moment at the sight. There was a puncture wound in the man's chest. The assassin's face looked pale, but he still breathed.

Sree knelt by the man. "Can you hear me? I'll...I'll call for help."

The Head Superior reached up and grabbed Sree's hand. Although his breaths came in spotty hiccups, he managed to speak. "When I realized...that it was you, a Kaano in that room...I was foolish...and thought I would win. It's been...an honor... having death...at your hands. You...have earned...all that I am..." The hand slackened its grip as the man slipped into death.

"No!" Sree yelled. He began to shake. He'd only wanted to

find a way *out* of killing and now he'd murdered *another* someone, again. It didn't matter that the first man wanted to die or that the other two men would have killed him and it had been self-defense—he'd still done it.

Not able to deal with the guilt, Sree's feelings turned into rage. 'This is all YOUR fault!" he screamed into the air at an imaginary Wiin. "You dragged me into this because you were too *cowardly* to do it yourself!"

"I've never been called a coward before," a voice said from the doorway.

Sree peered over his shoulder and saw Panaan, leaning heavily against the doorframe of the entrance. Blood trickled from her right temple, but the smile on her face showed him she wasn't too badly injured.

With an overwhelming sense of relief, Sree stood and rushed towards her, pulling her into a tight hug.

"Easy," she said. "My ribs."

Pulling away, he noticed her grimace. "Sorry. You okay?"

"You should see the other Head Superior."

"I did," he said, recalling the body in the elevator while he fled. He then gave a shaky laugh as they moved further inside the building.

Panaan frowned. "I didn't try to kill her."

"It's okay, he told her. "You did what you had to." He wondered if he said the words for her reassurance or his own as they moved past the dead Head Superior on the floor. Leading her to a broken table with some barely functional chairs, he pulled out a seat and she sat. "How did you know I'd be here?"

"I didn't. I was following him," she said, pointing at the deceased Head Superior.

"But...how? What happened to you?"

Panaan leaned back a bit, wincing. "It didn't take long for the Head Superiors in the Stasis Room to stop believing my story, because after a few questions they realized I didn't have the code to the elevator, so I couldn't have gotten downstairs on my own. We fought," she continued, wringing water from her long locks, "and I left the room, trying to draw them away from you, so you could get out. Only one of them followed me, but I didn't realize that until we got into the elevator. It was," she said, pressing a hand against her ribs, "a tight space. She knocked me, hard, against the wall," she said, indicating her bleeding temple, "but I got the final blow, and she went down."

"I saw her body in there. I thought...for a second I thought it was you."

"It almost was."

He paused, unsure of what to say next. She'd just eliminated another Re'Ris. Not only that, a Head Superior. "I'm glad you're okay, but I'm sorry about what happened to her."

Panaan shrugged. "I didn't want to let you down, but I'm not sad she's gone. She gave me the creeps at my pledging ceremony. Kept looking at me like...like someone's pet. Probably what they thought of me. Young, inexperienced, and usable." She shook her head, as if shaking away the memory. "Anyway," she continued with her story, "by this point I'd made it up to the ground floor. I was going to come back down, but..."

"But you didn't know the numeric code to get the curved lights to turn on again."

"Exactly. I planned to wait for you to come up the elevator, or deal with anyone else who may not be you, but with all the flashing lights, I remembered what my Mother told me about protocol for Central Processing–in an emergency, exits are sealed. Well, except if it's a fire, of course."

"We wouldn't have been able to leave?"

"Nope. So, I ran to the nearest access point and requested emergency response for a fire. It superseded whatever other alarm we'd set off in the Stasis and Archive Rooms. When I tested the main doors, they opened. But then, I...I don't know, I sort of blacked out I guess?" She touched her temple, which still bled a bit, and grimaced. "When I woke up, I found myself laying on the ground just outside the building. Did you come out while I was unconscious?"

"I didn't go out the main entrance," he said. "Otherwise I would've seen you on the ground."

"Ah. That makes sense. But I *did* see the other Head Superior leave, so I followed him. How'd he find you?"

"A tracker," Sree said, supplying the information. He pointed to his pile of clothes. "I think he tagged my shoe during our fight."

"I almost lost him, in the rain, and my skin-shifting was awful, but in that weather, I wasn't too worried. I saw him pop into this building. And...here I am."

"Here you are. I'm so glad you're okay." He paused and nodded to her head. "You *sure* you're okay?"

"Yeah. I haven't had any issues since the door. And I'm happy you're okay, too. Honestly, I wasn't sure..." She let the word hang there.

"You didn't think I'd make it out."

She gave a weak smile. "Sorry."

"Nah. You aren't wrong to think that. I almost didn't."

Motioning to the body on the ground, Panaan said, "Well, you did okay in here."

"Accidentally."

"Still...he's taken care of."

Sree glanced over at the body and a new surrealness hit him. They'd just killed two Head Superiors. Out of five. Which meant only two others remained besides Panaan.

They'd changed their whole government structure in a couple of standard hours.

Panaan, who'd apparently been thinking about something else, asked what he'd found in the room he'd entered.

Still fazed by the gravity of the situation, Sree retold his experience in the Archive Room, the items he'd seen, and the encounter with the Head Superior before escaping.

"Can I see what you took?" Panaan asked.

"I think it's the Rules, the original ones, by the Makers," Sree said, handing it over.

"Well, of course they are the Rules," she said, holding the document in front of her. "But why do you think they are the original ones?"

With a furrowed brow, he said, "Because it's in the Makers' language."

"No, it's not."

Sree took the parchment again. The letters were still indecipherable to him, just like the ones around the artwork of the Makers he'd seen with Wiin. "Uh, yeah, it is."

Panaan scoffed. "What, do you need eye enhancers? See, right here at the top, it states, um, 'Below are the seventeen tenets a Re'Ris must know to exist.' It's right there."

Shock coursed through him. "You...you can read this?"

"Of course I can," she said. His confusion mirrored hers. "You can't?"

He looked at her squarely in the eyes. "Panaan, I'm telling you. This is not in our language."

"B-but..." she stammered, "then how can I read it?"

Sree wracked his brain and it hit him. "You are part Maker. Your genetic material. It must be programmed into you. I never thought about it when Wiin told me what was written over the picture of the Maker artwork from the Great Hall, which is *in* Maker language. I guess...at the time I just thought he knew the translation somehow. But he must have actually *read* the words. Just like you're doing now!"

With shaky hands, Panaan returned the parchment to him. "This is making my skin crawl."

He shoved it back into her hands. "You have to read this. You're the only one who can."

"Okay." While the words spilled from her trembling lips,

Sree's eyes widened more and more in astonishment.

Wiin had been right.

The Rules as the world knew them were a lie.

Chapter 53

Sleep eluded Panaan. Instead, she sat at her kitchen table, still wearing her bloodied and mostly dried clothing from the previous evening, while the sky's red sun lit up the horizon with crimson streaks. Shortly, Laborers would come to pick up the rest of her items, but she couldn't focus on that. Instead, she wished time would stand still. Ironic, seeing as how she usually lacked patience in almost every other way.

She and Sree had parted ways hours earlier, he on his path, she on hers. Sree planned to meet up with the Crypt or whatever they were called. But Panaan couldn't imagine succeeding with the plan they'd decided for her: remaining among the Head Superiors, attempting to gain restricted information, and possibly returning to the Archives to take more items for evidence.

The original Rules document currently lay on the table at her fingertips. It had not only disturbed her to be able to read the words, but much more so what the words actually said, very different from what she'd believed her entire life. Because of her distress, she'd flipped the page over face down and left it that way all night.

But she couldn't escape time. Or the start of the new day. Moments would continue to go by no matter how much she wanted to delay them.

The guard and Head Superiors' bodies would have been found by now. And possibly the one in the deserted warehouse as well.

But what will happen next?

Both she and Sree determined the remaining Head Superiors, by her count Four and One, would have to keep things quiet. The population couldn't know that two of their elite group were dead. There were *always* five. The "loss" of the one who'd been killed on the platform during Celebration Day had already been a shock to the citizens' systems. Head Superior Four, when he'd recruited Panaan, told her they were going to announce her new position publicly, which would reassure everyone that five Head Superiors were still intact.

But now? The remaining Head Superiors didn't have any new recruits. Because they hadn't prepared for these other two to die.

Panaan must now play dutiful Head Superior until the dust settled. She needed to wait until they had more proof before announcing the contents of the document they'd found. Besides, she now knew the code for the elevator to get to the Stasis and Archive Rooms and could go there at her leisure, collecting any other evidence they'd need to prove the Head Superiors' corruption.

Her problem revolved around the fact that she couldn't make herself get up out of the chair to do that. She didn't know how she could face the remaining Head Superiors anymore. It had been one thing to know they'd killed a Head Superior to keep her quiet, but to know they were part of a conspiracy that changed the Rules altogether? Or had they just gone along with the alterations? Or did these changes happen so long ago that even the current Head Superiors didn't know about the original ones?

No, Sree said Wiin told him he'd gotten into the Head Superior files. All five of them knew the truth. And all five chose to cover it up.

As a new member of their group, when would the remaining Head Superiors tell her the truth and expect her to keep it secret as well?

She knew these thoughts and questions were just her way of stalling. She wouldn't be able to get any answers without actually going to the office. *Her* office.

With a deep inhale and exhale, Panaan pushed herself away from the table to get dressed. This morning would be the last time she'd be in her home. Glancing around, she took in the deep russets and golds, the ivory accents and flecks of burgundy. Her Mother had redone the entire kitchen after her Father Passed On, as it had been his favorite room in the house, and she knew her Mother experienced much heartache over his absence. Panaan didn't even remember how the space used to look before those changes. Would she eventually forget this renovation as well?

Not wanting grief to grab hold and overwhelm her, she headed to the washroom to splash away the remaining sleepiness from her eyes, when she stopped at the sound of the chimes for her front door. She let out a sigh. *The Laborers must be early.*

Turning, she went to the door and opened it.

Red light from the end of some sort of weapon shone in her face.

Panaan shifted her head to the left just as a wave of heat swept past the place her face had been. The edges of the beam from the weapon caught the side of her jaw and she screamed at the pain from what felt like fire torching that spot.

Activating Sree's wrade on her wrist, she quickly took care of the assailant, and his body crumpled to the ground on her front step.

Panting, Panaan's gaze darted around the area, but most of her neighbors' houses were still dark. A couple of lights popped on, however, most likely because of her scream. Grabbing an arm, she dragged the body inside and bolted the door behind her.

Why would someone be after *her*?

She wanted to communicate with Sree, tell him about this new development, but they'd been scared his personal communications device would be monitored, so he'd gotten rid of it. She didn't have any other way to contact him.

Just then, her own device beeped, indicating an emergency broadcast. Automatically, she opened it up to view the announcement while she grabbed a rag and doused it with cold water to press against her burned cheek.

Two pictures floated above her communications device in mini-holographic form.

The first one, Sree's face.

The second one, her own.

The headline read: TWO MURDERERS SEEN AT CENTRAL PROCESSING. *THEIR STATUS GIVEN TO ANYONE WHO ELIMINATES THEM.*

It then showed video of the two of them killing the guard outside the elevator from a surveillance system in the hallway.

Panaan couldn't *believe* their stupidity. She and Sree were relying on the fact that the murders would be hushed up. But of course there had been security footage! And Central Authority would've seen it immediately, because they'd arrived in response to the fire alarm. Head Superiors Four and One wouldn't have had a chance to keep things quiet because Central Authority would have moved on the case immediately.

She and Sree had been shown as murderers. To the entire capital city. And most likely the broadcast would be picked up and delivered to citizens around the globe.

They wouldn't be safe anywhere. She couldn't return to her life as a Head Superior now, not as a wanted criminal.

Everything had changed.

Panaan didn't think. She grabbed the Rules document, shoved it into a backpack from a packed box in her Mother's room, along with a change of clothes, and added some food and drinks from the kitchen. She took the few monetary credits she owned and stuffed them into her pocket before taking one last look around. With a final desperate grab, she seized a holo-image of herself and her Mother and Father from her Mother's nightstand and added that to the bag.

The final check she made let her know she still had a certain small device in the other pocket of her gold and black collared jacket.

Chapter 54

Head Superior Four sat in his office, long fingers steepled in front of him, chiseled chin resting upon them. Dark silvery eyes, rare for a Re'Ris, flitted back and forth, calculating his next move.

He didn't know by now how many times he'd watched surveillance videos of the same elevator, only that the current time indicated the afternoon, and he'd done little else since arriving at Central Processing before sunrise. Having run out of power during the night for his personal communications device, he'd been unaware of the events of the previous evening until he showed up for work.

The scene had been chaos. Dozens of officers. Hundreds of spectators.

Everyone quieted when Head Superior Four exited the personal orb near the entrance to the building and walked up to the main doors. Luckily, he'd planned to come into the office early, in order to deal with the official documents pertaining to the Passing On of Head Superior Three and the installment of

Panaan...or the new Head Superior Three as she'd be known going forward. He hadn't expected crowds or sirens.

The bystanders parted before him, their raucous voices now hushed murmurs.

*First, some order...*he thought. He glanced over at the leader of the Central Authority group. He blinked, then tilted his head towards the crowd. The leader nodded, then signaled to his team. They held the crowds at bay, telling them to return home, that Central Processing would be closed for the day. In a very short time, barricades and signs indicating closure were placed around the perimeter.

Shortly thereafter, the leader of the Central Authority team onsite filled him in—a fire had been signaled. But when services arrived, they found two bodies inside and no fire. Emergency Response Facilities were already onsite because of the fire alarm, but an officer also called the Disposal Teams for the bodies. Those two groups were currently arguing about jurisdiction for removing the bodies. Head Superior Four approached and stood in front of them until they noticed him and stopped their heated discussion. He told them to wait until he investigated, and he'd let them know who could take the remains.

Returning his focus to the leader of Central Authority, Head Superior Four ordered him to station a minimal group of officers at the entrance to keep everyone out of the building, but not to do anything else until given further instructions.

Four then entered, alone, noticed the dead guard in the hallway, and moved into the elevator shaft, where he found the corpse of Head Superior Two. Seeing her lying there hit him, hard, and questions bounced around inside his mind. Why had she been here after hours? Catching up on work, perhaps? But for some reason killed inside the elevator by the guard? Why?

A sense of trepidation pulled at his insides as he examined the elevator. Staring at the buttons, he noticed blood smeared beneath the numerical code section, and he had a stray thought he didn't like. Had Head Superior Two been heading downstairs for some reason? If so, why? The only reason he could think of would be if she'd been responding to the silent alarm...

Anxiety peaked inside him. Heading once again outside the building, he demanded a portable charging unit for his communications device from one of the officers. Once it had enough power, he initiated it and received the notification of both the fire and the silent alarm in the Morgue.

Oh Makers, he thought, *no, no, no."*

The underground Morgue and Vault hadn't been accessed in...he didn't know how long. He, himself, hadn't been down there in years. Relics from the past meant nothing to him. He'd always prided himself on looking ahead to new solutions. And he thought it idiotic to keep those rooms at all. As far as he was concerned, everything should just be melted down into a scrap heap.

But who'd been in there? And, why?

He knew the emptiness of the building would prevent him being followed, so Head Superior Four headed inside, made his way to the elevator, entered the code, pressed the glowing curled lights, and waited within until the doors opened one floor down. Striding through the hallway, he entered the Morgue. Everything appeared to be in order, except for the signs of a fight. Had Head Superior Two fought with the guard all the way down here? But why would a guard be down here in the first place?

Then he looked across the room and saw blood on the lock to the Vault.

Crossing quickly, his breath in his throat, he accessed the room.

Multiple books, tomes, datapads, and journals were absent, from the area near the doorway.

Head Superior Four clenched his hands at his sides. Had Head Superior Two been stealing? Had she hired the guard and they'd double-crossed each other?

Moving through the space, he noted multiple stands with empty slots. However, though empty, their cases were intact. Someone had taken their contents, but replaced the protective coverings without breaking them. This definitely pointed to a Head Superior, since only Maker genetic material could open the locks on the cases.

After about a tenth of the way into the large space, the rest of the items were intact. Only those towards the front had been removed.

Four kept walking, still mostly in shock, until he noticed one thing which stood out in the center of the room: crystalline glass shards carpeting the floor.

"No..." he muttered. With quick steps he cleared the distance.

The display case had been smashed.

The Rules, *the* Rules, were gone.

Bile fought its way up his throat.

Focus, he thought, swallowing it down. *You can handle this. One step at a time.*

Heading back upstairs, he assigned the bodies to the Disposal Team, but he'd removed Head Superior Two's jacket first to conceal her identity. He told the team both bodies had been identified already and could simply be processed for ash-piling. He didn't want to cause a panic by having *another* Head Superior's death become public knowledge.

Once the crowds dissipated and most of Central Authority departed, except for the few remaining officers to secure the perimeter, Head Superior Four headed upstairs to his office, and immediately checked surveillance.

Which is where he currently sat, still dumbfounded, since all his theories about the guard and Head Superior Two fighting each other went out the window. He watched Sree Kaano and Head Superior Panaan kill the guard when he reached the elevator. Only later did Head Superiors Two and Five show up.

A short while after they'd exited the elevator on the floor below the main level, he watched Panaan kill Head Superior Two inside the elevator, saw her head towards the main entrance, noted when the elevators opened and closed, which he assumed happened when Sree Kaano left while shifted, and then saw a worse-for-wear Head Superior Five come up the elevator as well.

Reclining, Head Superior Four's mind raced.

The two of them, Kaano and Luura, had made their way to the floor underneath the building. They'd gone to the Morgue and Vault.

They'd stolen items.

Astonished, Head Superior Four didn't have any idea what to think. He'd planned things so carefully. The death of Head Superior Three on Celebration Day. The induction of the new young Head Superior, over whom he'd have complete control after targeting her Mother and Father. He believed he'd executed the perfect plan.

The newest head Superior had been on their radar ever since they'd learned her Father had Maker genetic material. But he'd been resistant to their ideas, tried to thwart the Head Superiors on his own, so they'd eliminated him. And then her Mother's group of employees witnessed a Head Superior, Two, he believed, kill someone, which Head Superiors weren't supposed to do. So, each of her coworkers besides herself had to be targeted and eliminated. That had taken many resources and much time, but he knew the Mother wouldn't have told her daughter, since that would've put Panaan in harm's way.

As a candidate, Panaan seemed perfect. She'd excelled at her first two Assignments, beating almost every record recorded as far as time it took to complete her first one, with the exception of Faan Kaano and his own.

So, why had she been in Central Processing? Stolen items? Killed a guard and another Head Superior? And been teamed up with Sree Kaano, of all Re'Ris?

The fury inside Head Superior Four at Sree Kaano surprised him. He'd never have thought the young man would be any trouble. And yet, he was a Kaano. The most revered and proficient assassins on the planet had done nothing but interfere, veer off course, and follow their own theories. Head Superior Four shouldn't have been surprised.

When he'd made the decision seven years ago to eliminate Sree's Mother and Father, it took a bit of convincing for the other Head Superiors to agree, but in the midst of confusion around the Aleet Army infiltration, cooler heads eventually prevailed.

The sister's Passing On had upset him personally. Faan shone like a beacon of hope to make every Re'Ris fall in line. But she'd played her role well, biding her time after her Mother's and Father's deaths until she could go off-planet and prove what had truly happened to them. Fortunately, she only showed they were murdered by Aleet Army agents, and the Head Superiors hadn't been suspected.

So, why hadn't Sree fallen in line? The young man suggested Celebration Day, which seemed like something to help promote the assassin side of his family. But then Head Superior Three decided to reveal the truth about his Mother's and Father's murders, one of the Head Superiors' most guarded secrets.

Frowning, Head Superior Four shook his head about Head Superior Three. She'd often clashed when voting on a new change or brought up ideas that didn't fit with the others' agendas. So, he'd planted a surveillance device in her office and hadn't noticed anything too amiss, until her meeting with Sree Kaano about Celebration Day. But that hadn't revealed anything about the Morgue or Vault, only that she'd planned on revealing the truth about his Mother's and Father's eliminations, which could not be allowed to happen.

Upon learning of her intentions, he'd been grateful he'd already put into play the plan to eliminate her because of her rebelliousness, and Celebration Day gave him the perfect opportunity to execute it. He then recruited Panaan, who had just Crossed Over, to take Head Superior Three's place. Everything had been coordinated so perfectly!

As for Sree's involvement, Head Superior Four thought he'd have to eliminate such a disappointment. He'd been upset to have to give Sree's Assignment the coordinates to the alley where Sree would be. It gave him no pleasure to remove a Kaano from their society. But the young man had thwarted his plan and prevailed!

So, Head Superior Four tried again. The next Target, Biin, had been a low-level Laborer who no one would've missed. But she'd also failed to kill Sree. This time, she'd gotten away, so the Head Superior placed her name on a "watch" list, while removing her as Sree's Target. He couldn't have her blabbing that someone tipped her off about her assassin and give her the upper hand. With a public bulletin out about her, only a matter of time would pass before someone identified her and eliminated her.

His final choice of assassin blew up Sree's home, but also herself in the process.

He knew it had been risky to send Targets after Sree, though he knew a smart Target wouldn't skip an opportunity to not only save their own lives, but also to claim the status of someone as well-known as a Kaano. Unfortunately, the young nuisance managed to avoid those three attempts on his life as well.

No matter. Sree would be dealt with soon enough. His face and name were broadcast everywhere now via the emergency signals.

Head Superior Four would have chosen an alternative option to the one now in play—he hadn't expected Central Authority to check the surveillance footage in the elevator before he'd gotten there. Taking off Head Superior Two's gold and black collared jacket became a moot point since the footage showed her wearing it. Then, without consulting him, they'd put out a planet-wide alert announcing the death of the guard and that another Head Superior had been murdered, showing both

Sree's and Panaan's faces—at least Sree wouldn't be a problem much longer.

Neither would Panaan, for that matter.

Which returned him full circle to his current predicament: When had she teamed up with Sree Kaano and how did they know about the Morgue and Vault? Not only that, but they'd known how to access it. They'd entered the code in the elevator. They'd figured out about Panaan needing to press the curved lights.

But how?

If the slain Head Superior Three hadn't told them, had one of the other Head Superiors betrayed him? Is that why Head Superior Two now lay dead? Or had the former Head Superior Three told Sree much more about the entire situation at some point outside of her office before her death on Celebration Day?

To what end?

While Head Superior Four mulled over his thoughts, new information penetrated his mind. He recalled how in the Vault only one case had been smashed—the one with the Rules. The number of missing items towards the front of the room didn't match up with surveillance. Sree and Panaan hadn't taken all those objects that evening, because footage showed their hands to be empty when they left.

And why smash one case when all the others were meticulously opened and returned to their appropriate places?

The Vault must have been accessed previously, perhaps multiple times, to remove all those items so carefully and without anyone noticing. Except, access to the Archives hadn't happened for years. The government hadn't found any new historical items to add. The place itself felt more like a museum, or an unused shrine, designed to prove to new Head Superiors the current truth, and to remind themselves how far they've evolved from Maker influence.

Except no notification of break-ins ever crossed his path

since the other cases weren't damaged. Only the smashed glass on the center display set off the alarm in the Vault. So, who'd been removing items this whole time? It *must* have been a Head Superior, right?

Determined to find the culprit, Head Superior Four spent the last several hours of the day poring over surveillance videos. He searched for all instances showing when a Head Superior used the elevator. Weeks, then months' worth of time swam before his tired eyes.

Finally, he realized the mistake made in his search. He just needed to look up the occurrences when someone entered the code.

There. Multiple access moments, starting from about two years ago. Head Superior Four pulled up the oldest timestamp. Continuing to watch the footage from that time forward, someone in a sage green Central Processing Laborer uniform, *not* a Head Superior, entered the code, pressed the curved buttons, and accessed the level below ground floor.

Head Superior Four zoomed in as best he could on the image and used facial recognition to construct a more solid picture.

He stared at the face as it ran through the system. Before the results came in, he could swear he recognized it from somewhere. But where...?

Many minutes later, the program completed its search. The identity of a Laborer appeared.

Wiin Niino.

Greedily reading the file, he noticed at the bottom that the man recently Passed On. A special note had been added underneath it.

Eliminated by Sree Kaano. Outside of time frame. Due to hostage situation. Case dismissed after lie detector confirmed the truth from the assassin.

Hostage.

That situation had only happened one other time in the past

fifty years, though he couldn't recall who was involved.

And it now just happened with Sree Kaano.

Pieces were starting to fit together.

Head Superior Four pulled up the file on Wiin Niino, plus made a search for the file from the previous hostage situation, then called for his Laborer to bring him some stimulant drink.

He had a long afternoon ahead of him.

CHAPTER 55

After Panaan left the warehouse to return home, Sree remained overnight in the soon-to-be demolished building, since he had no home to return to and the two of them decided it wouldn't be safe for him to go to hers.

He slept in fitful bits—having the Head Superior's body nearby didn't help—until the red rays of sunrise slid through the slitted sides of the dilapidated building and woke him. He snuck out, skin-shifted, and made his way through the city streets as cautiously as possible until he reached a less populated area. There, he became visible and bought food from an on-the-street vendor with the monetary credits he had, ate briefly, and packed the rest into a small shoulder bag he purchased for the day-and-night travel to Bria. He couldn't get anything to drink, since the small vendor had very few offerings, and he didn't dare go further into the city, so he'd just have to manage.

As he traveled, deep trenches to help redirect rainfall for farms and small rolling hills met his gaze. Re'Ris as a planet didn't have a particularly mountainous topography, so most of the view ahead remained unobstructed. Silvery blue wildflowers dotted the yellow and brown stones and pebbly first half of the trek. The second half of the journey brought about a walk around Lake Sula at the border of Bria, with its reddish algae giving a hint of depth and murkiness to the otherwise clear water.

It felt freeing to not see other Re'Ris around him as well as not having his personal communications device on him. He felt like he could breathe for the first time in weeks, free of anything and everything.

Early that morning, after sleeping in an open field and trying his best to ignore the wingless moscat insects—in their pre-winged state they found him to be a tasty meal—he arrived at Bria and color-changed once more until he found the location where he planned to join Biin and Muura.

Crumbled concrete and debris were all that remained of their meeting place.

Sree couldn't believe it. He'd made it all this way, and their headquarters had been destroyed. Falling to his knees, he became visible, unable to hold up his focus during his despair.

"She never lost faith that you would come," a voice said from behind him.

Spinning his head around, he saw Muura standing in the doorway of a nearby shed, the only intact structure in the area.

"What happened?" he croaked, his throat dry from not having drunk anything since the previous morning. As if she knew this may be the case, she handed him a container of liquid, from which he drank greedily.

"I destroyed the place, just in case. Not really useful anymore. Biin thought she could get away with something. She was wrong." Muura's words were flat and emotionless, until in her following words Sree could hear the notes of pain. "Someone caught up to her and killed her right outside the building. I hid, invisible, until a Disposal Team took her body away. I couldn't do anything. There was no point. She was already dead. So, I destroyed any traces of this place that could tie it to the Crypt. She would have wanted that."

A shock almost as bad as when he'd heard the news about his sister's death hit him. Biin was dead? "But...why would she risk anything when we had a plan?"

"She knew you couldn't stay. *Here.*"

"I knew that, too. I was only meeting up with you two to go over what I discovered at Central Processing. I planned to stay on the run as long as possible until you could show everyone the proof needed and change things. But—"

She cut him off. "You don't understand. I don't mean here, like our headquarters. I mean *here*, there, anywhere. On the planet. Things have changed. Your face is everywhere."

Confusion overtook him. "What?"

"Didn't you see the emergency broadcast?"

"I-I got rid of my comm device. Just in case."

"They showed you and some girl dressed as a Head Superior killing a guard. Inside Central Processing. You aren't a 'capture,' anymore. You are a 'status claim' through elimination. And with your family name, everyone will want to kill you." She paused and Sree held his breath, wondering if that price enticed her enough to turn on him.

She continued, "You can't show your face anymore. Anywhere."

Sree let out his breath but then the revelation struck. He and Panaan figured the government would cover everything up. Lie about the guard's death, find new Head Superiors, not let the public know a thing. But instead the absolute opposite happened.

"I didn't know," he said lamely. "I've been traveling."

"Well, Biin figured that might be the case. So, she acquired something for you. The item is safe, but who she procured it from reported her to Central Processing. Because she was a renegade Target. *Your* Target. Until yesterday, when your time to kill her expired. Normally, that would make her safe. Only the assassin gets penalized if they don't fulfil their elimination within the allotted amount of time. But, you forget, someone manipulated the system to get *her* to kill *you*. They apparently wanted her dead instead, probably to cover their tracks. So, her picture popped up before I could warn her, and when she left the store with your supplies, someone reported her."

"That's what she got for me? Supplies?"

"Don't you understand?" Muura asked, her words cutting through the air. "She. Died. Because of YOU."

"I-I'm sorry. I don't...I don't know what to say. I never thought—"

Muura's face contorted in anger and grief. "No, you didn't! Whatever your plan was, you didn't think about the possible consequences. And all she could think about was helping you." She flung a sack and a datapad towards him. They slid across the ground and skidded to a stop at his feet. "These are the last things the Crypt will do for you. We were doing *just fine* until you showed up. All you've done is create a chaotic mess and got Biin and several others killed. So, take what she got for you and leave. If I ever see your face again, I'll call the authorities on you myself." She turned away.

Desperate, he sputtered, "B-but...don't you want to know what we found?"

Speaking over her shoulder she said, "Anything you found is tainted. No one will listen to thieves and murderers."

Without another look, even though he tried to get her to stay by yelling out to her about the Rules being untrue, Murra strode away.

Sree could barely process what had happened. Everything took place so quickly. More dead. Because of him. Once again, he only wanted to *not* kill anyone. Instead he had more bodies to his name than weeks he'd been legally able to eliminate Targets.

With unsteady hands he checked the bag first, finding a full change of clothes and food and drink for a day or two. Next, he picked up the datapad, wondering what could've been so important for Biin to obtain for Sree which couldn't wait.

The item on the screen made his eyebrows raise.

Chapter 56

"That's her! Stop her!"

Panaan hurriedly wove across the mass transportation underground platform towards the exit, dodging passengers, her hand pressed firmly into her side, trying to stem the pain from a stitch there. She bumped into citizens and tripped over their bags and luggage, wondering why she thought taking the public transportation orb while invisible made any sense in her head. She'd bumped into the crowds as soon as they moved into the vehicle's compartments and as she got knocked over, her camouflage flickered away. Not to mention the Re'Ris she'd collided into felt her presence and immediately yelled out about someone being skin-shifted.

At that moment, some of the individuals screamed and moved away, terrified the invisible Re'Ris may be an assassin come for them. But after being revealed, it didn't take long for someone to recognize her.

"She's that murderer from the news bulletin! Grab her! Get

her status!"

Terrified, she'd engaged Sree's wrade, and a few slashes at outstretched hands scared most of the Laborers, causing them to retreat. Then, she ran until she cleared the masses, dodging one outstretched foot meant to trip her, and barreled through those who methodically exited the area. Her still painful ribs from her previous encounter with Head Superior Two screamed at her as she took an elbow to her sternum, but adrenaline forced her to continue.

Still drawing attention to herself, she ran through the streets until she couldn't breathe anymore, and eventually collapsed against the side of a building in an alleyway. A couple of concerned citizens, who didn't seem to recognize her, asked if she was all right. Without looking at them, she waved them away, and thanked the stars when they moved on.

Curling up next to a dumpster, she lay in the fetal position until her breath returned, although the pain from several bumps and scrapes made themselves known as the adrenaline finally drained from her system. Completely exhausted, sleep overtook her.

A few hours later, Panaan awoke. Panic hit her until she remembered her location. Something sticky coated the side of her face. Sitting up, she pulled the backpack she wore onto her lap and checked the contents while rubbing away the gunk she'd laid in with her other hand. Everything was still there. She allowed herself a few minutes to drink and eat then changed her shirt, which had gotten ripped during her escape. She still didn't want to wear the Head Superior jacket, because she thought it would actually draw more attention than less, and re-tucked it securely into the bag.

After checking the Rules document for any damage and finding none, she pulled out a small device, which glowed a faint purple.

She knew it had been selfish. She knew she should've discussed it with Sree first. But the thought of dealing with the Head Superiors and Central Authority and her personal Laborer on her own for the next weeks or months to come had been too much for her to bear. Of course, this thought process revolved around their original plan of her returning to work, before she'd been displayed with Sree as elimination Targets one and two.

But the previous night at the warehouse, when she and Sree moved the Passed On Head Superior's body to a less conspicuous part of the room, she'd taken the tracking device he'd used on Sree and pocketed it. In all the excitement, Sree forgot to remove the small mechanism from his own shoe, and now Panaan could track his location.

She never planned to actually use the device. She wanted it more for reassurance—a way for her to feel connected to him no matter where he'd gone to hide—but now, since she also needed to go on the run, she didn't know what else to do except to find him.

Steeling herself against whatever came next, she rose from her spot against the dumpster, color-changed for long enough to escape the most populated areas of the city, and followed the light on the tracking device as it switched from purple to red, indicating she was currently headed in the right direction. Eventually it would reach orange, which meant she'd be closer in range to Sree. But for now, she just felt happy to know the distance between them lessened.

As long as he didn't leave the planet or anything crazy like that, she'd find him.

Chapter 57

Invisible, Sree crept up to a gated fence, uncertain how he could obtain the item Biin acquired for him. She'd done so under her own name, most likely assuming that she would not have been hunted herself but be with him to retrieve it.

And also alive.

Guilt over her death chewed on the edges of his mind, but he pushed it aside as best he could. There had been no way for him to know events would have transpired this way. Logic may be on his side, but his emotions didn't care.

Shaking away the negative thoughts, Sree wondered instead how he could access what she'd gotten for him without her here. All information needed to acquire it lay in the datapad she left him, but he needed her in person to actually get the item released.

He'd have to steal it.

Chewing on his lower lip, he circled around the outer edges of the scrapyard, searching for a location that seemed better suited for entering than the main gate, but though the fence appeared easy to climb over, he could hear the buzzing of an electrical current. Shifted or not, he couldn't handle being electrocuted.

Besides, even if he found a way over it, who knew what kind of security measures would be safeguarding the item inside.

There could be no other recourse. He could either figure out a way to turn off the current, which he didn't know how to do, then find the item amongst the thousands in front of him, which would be impossible, and disarm any defenses so he could use it, which, again, he didn't know how to do.

He had to face reality.

It didn't matter that Biin procured him a ship to fly off-world—he'd never get to it.

And since this planet had a worldwide bulletin out to eliminate him on sight, without said ship, he wouldn't last more than a few days before being killed. If *that* long.

Sree sat down, tired from holding his invisibility, but not quite ready to leave the area. While he sat, he watched individuals coming in and out of the scrapyard, being buzzed in through the gate.

Even with everything against him, Sree hoped against hope. If he could make it inside...maybe...

Mustering up the courage he didn't feel, he crept, hunched over, towards the main entrance and waited. The traffic in and out appeared too busy for him to get the opportunity he wanted.

But then...

Now!

A lone woman, hooded against the harsh wind kicking up dirt and dust, approached the entrance by herself. She spoke at the gate, held up her ID, and the door buzzed open.

Sree edged up behind her, as close as possible without touching, and followed her in. As the gate closed it caught him on the edge of his shoe, and the gateway froze.

"What's goin' on?" a Laborer called out.

The woman turned around, looking right over Sree at the ajar gate. He inched his way to the left, away from where she and the Laborer stared.

"I'm not sure," she said.

The Laborer approached, spitting on the ground when he got to the gate, flecks of it hitting the top of Sree's head.

Glaring at the doorway, he gave the gate a kick. "Piece o' junk. Malfunctionin' again, I reckon. Last time it caught hold a someone's jacket and the electricity weren't off. Mess that day. The smell, too."

"Sounds like a hassle for you," the woman said, sounding cold and indifferent to someone having been burned, or possibly killed, from a malfunctioning gate.

The Laborer sniffed and turned away, motioning for the woman to move towards a small building with a hand gesture. "You don't know the half of it." They continued to converse, but the wind blew towards them, so Sree couldn't hear any more of what they said.

No matter. He'd made it inside.

Now, to find the ship based on the datapad information and...

...and what? Hope it can fly? He didn't have too much worry about being *able* to fly it—the picture looked similar to his sister's ship, and she'd taught him the basics. But he had no idea its condition, its fuel level, its range. Would it even get off the ground or had Biin planned to haul it away and fix it up first?

One crisis at a time. You're in. Just...get to the ship and see what the deal is.

Creeping along, Sree checked row after row and realized by the identification numbers on the datapad that his ship would be somewhere towards the rear end of the lot.

Hundreds of ships' lengths away.

Even the thought of that much distance to cover made his camouflage flicker. He couldn't keep his invisibility going much longer. He'd have to rest.

Sneaking behind a rather large engine turbine, he crouched and took a breather, dropping his skin-shift. While he sat, he heard the faint hum of a smaller engine running nearby. He shifted for a moment to peek out.

A different Laborer and a heavyset Re'Ris, who took up two seats, glided by on a lifter. Seats with no arms rose from the floor of the vehicle, and a cris-crossing of bars and belts kept the riders from falling off during the tilted turns and quick changes in speed.

Of course. There were lifters to take buyers to their ships. No one would be expected to walk the whole way.

Could he get on one somehow? They weren't moving particularly quickly, but there seemed to only be room for about four people at a time. And he'd have to stay shifted as well. His energy levels felt iffy at best. But he knew he couldn't hold up his invisibility for the few standard hours it would take him to walk through the aisles to reach his destination, either.

Risking a second peek, he noticed another lifter coming along with two individuals on it. Though still a bit of a ways off, the passengers looked like the Laborer who'd spit at the gate escorting the hooded woman.

Pulling his head from sight, he un-shifted for a few moments, gathering as much energy and focus as he could. Then, he camouflaged and crept out from behind the turbine. The lifter moved closer...closer...

This won't work!

And yet, he flung himself onto it anyway.

Shrieks from both driver and passenger reached his ears as the lifter swayed from Sree's additional weight.

He also smacked right into the woman's leg.

"What was that?" she exclaimed, as the lifter corrected its pitch.

"Probably a muffskuk," the Laborer said, his attention

focused behind the lifter's back end, as if looking for something. "Vermin. They feed on the power coils sometimes. Ain't too bright. Sometimes run out right into our lifters."

The woman, who'd felt Sree's body hit her, tilted her hooded head straight down at the lifter, not away, like the Laborer. Shadows hid her face under its covering.

Sree's skin-shift flickered and he became visible for a moment.

She brought her hand up to her mouth, as if in shock, knocking the hood askew.

Jump off! he told himself.

Except...

He froze, now invisible once more, staring up at her.

It was Muura.

She said if she ever saw you again she'd turn you in. JUMP OFF!

But his body wouldn't move. He watched her facial expression slowly return to normal and she returned her gaze to the Laborer. "There better not be any of these vermin on my ship or it'll come out of the cost."

Sree breathed a sigh of relief as the Laborer reassured her that the creatures never got into ships themselves, just sometimes gnawed on the power supply to the fence, and that her merchandise would be everything she expected it to be.

They continued to move along. Sree remained awkwardly huddled halfway onboard the mechanism, gripping its metallic edges. His fingertips ached and his camouflage threatened at any moment to reveal him.

Then, a swift turn, and Sree's faltering strength betrayed him. He went tumbling off.

The two on the lifter continued on. Sree finished rolling, the scrapes and bumps causing his shifting to end. Catching his breath for just a moment, he then scrambled off the main pathway and hid behind a few barrels of who-knew-what.

The trip on the lifter, though short, had taken him almost to his destination: the ship. He only then realized Muura and the Laborer were headed in the same direction he planned to go.

Did Muura plan to take the ship for herself? Was she so angry with Sree that she wanted to sabotage his ability to get away?

No. If that were the case, she could've easily exposed him when she saw him on the lifter.

More tired than he ever thought possible and bleeding from several scratches and scrapes, Sree inhaled deeply, forced himself to color-change, and sprinted the rest of the way towards the ship. With his lungs about to burst and a twinge in his ankle he hadn't noticed until he started running, he finally cleared the distance and saw the lifter parked at the side of the ship which matched the image on the datapad from Biin.

Moving a little ways off to the side of the stationary vehicle, Sree hunkered down behind a giant engine block, his camouflage gone. Based on how little energy he had, he feared it wouldn't return for quite some time. He could barely focus on the exchange in front of him, much less conjure the energy needed to maintain a shift.

A sound made him freeze.

The sound of an electro-volt weapon, near his ear, being loaded with electricity.

Then a nasally sounding voice said, "Got you, Sree Kaano."

Chapter 58

Head Superior Four hadn't slept. Neither had the remaining Head Superior, One, or the dozen Laborers Head Superior Four called to aid in his research earlier that day.

The morning he'd arrived at Central Processing and discovered the murders, and after spending hours poring over the records of Wiin Niino, Head Superior Four uncovered an uneasy realization: the man possessed Maker genetic material.

Previously an assassin, and a talented one at that, during an Assignment Wiin let a seemingly random Target live.

But...somehow...he never became a Target. He became...a *Laborer.*

That surprised Head Superior Four. Even though the Rules stated that a failed assassin would become a Laborer, the Head Superiors had abolished that practice long ago. Previous Head Superiors learned that unsuccessful assassins weren't the same as those who simply weren't cut out to be assassins. The ones who failed at their Assignments were generally targeted within the first six standard months of becoming Laborers. They just... couldn't adjust to that lifestyle.

So, the Head Superiors internally changed the Rule. Not officially, of course. Couldn't have assassins worried about being targeted if they failed.

But Wiin Niino, a failed assassin, somehow ended up a Laborer.

For three years.

Off anyone's radar.

The Head Superior began to look for the clues needed, the orders made, the job tasks for Wiin and from these details, discerned that the man could manipulate the system.

Another individual with Maker genetic material. This time right under Four's nose.

Into the early hours of the evening, he analyzed every move Wiin had made and eventually found evidence of multiple entries into both the Archive and Stasis rooms over the past several years.

This one man somehow stole dozens of artifacts, ledgers, and items written by the Makers themselves and no one detected it.

Before the very middle of the night, Head Superior Four uncovered Wiin's plan and how he'd created a scenario for Sree to Target him.

He set that whole thing up from the beginning, he thought, astonished.

But Sree passed the lie detector test. He *had* killed Wiin.

Digging deeper, Four unearthed a second interrogation of Sree, ordered by a false Laborer. This arrangement was thwarted by Head Superior Three who used an alternate Laborer to ask the follow-up questions. But that alternate Laborer died...though her file didn't specify how. Another anomaly.

Probably did it herself, he thought, accusing Head Superior Three in his head. *Perhaps the line of questioning from the Laborer revealed something about Sree. Could that be why she offered to meet with him and create Celebration Day? Because she felt compelled to expose even more truths she no longer wanted to hide?*

Pre-dawn hours brought his attention to the original Laborer who'd created the false interrogation in the first place. It took some time, but he found out her identification: Laborer 61-622: Biin Sool.

He'd laughed, slightly hysterical at the irony. He'd chosen a random, low-level Laborer as Sree's Target, with a strange past as an assassin herself, to go after Sree. But she ended up being the same Laborer who contacted Sree to learn more about his "hostage" situation with Wiin, since her own file spoke of a hostage situation as well!

Head Superior Four then put the final pieces together. The "escape" Biin made from Sree's home after not killing him hadn't been because she'd been scared and run away. It gave her the exact opportunity she'd wanted: to speak to him. Sree released her freely from his home.

But again, Sree passed the lie detector test, claiming he'd fought her and she'd fled. He'd figured out a way to not tell the whole truth but not really lie to pass those examinations.

Reddish light seeped its way through his slatted office windows as the sun began to rise.

Head Superior Four continued with his illuminating notion, finalizing the situation.

Biin had been identified yesterday at a ship dealer in Bria, after Head Superior Four put her name and picture out as a "find and eliminate," since he couldn't leave her alive with the knowledge someone previously tipped her off about her assassin. She'd been killed after authorities tracked her down.

But she'd been procuring a ship.

A way to leave the planet.

She bought the ship *before* she'd been put on bulletin to make her a "find and eliminate" Target connected to Sree.

But she'd already been buying a ship.

She'd fled, not to her home, but to a seemingly abandoned building.

She'd already been in hiding and possibly thinking about leaving the planet.

Clenching his fists in angered shock he thought, *Because she and Sree already* were *in league with each other!*

Head Superior Four truly believed he'd merely invented the scenario of the two of them working together when he'd sent out the bulletin to eliminate her. But in actuality it had been the truth all along.

The understanding sent flashes of wrath surging through him. These insignificant, unsuccessful, barely even past the Age of Progression *nothings* were foiling him.

Sree was on the run.

Panaan was nowhere to be found.

And Biin was now dead.

A glimmer of greedy hope stirred inside his chest.

But......Biin had bought a ship.

From a shipyard in Bria...

Chapter 59

Pain jolted through Sree's side. Coughing, he held a hand up to protect against another kick from his attacker.

The Laborer spoke. "I've called Bria Keepers, you filth. They are on their way, so don't try anything."

Sree peered upwards and stared straight into the barrel of the electro-volt weapon he'd heard earlier—usually used to keep livestock in line. A brief image of the muffskuks that roam around the vicinity entered Sree's mind. Would he die like a lowly animal?

Putting both hands up in a defensive manner, he stayed seated. His side, where this Laborer had kicked him, ached a bit less, but any thoughts of escaping quickly slipped away as he could do nothing except rest anyway. That and the knowledge of the Bria Keepers, this city's authorities, being on their way.

He'd honestly made it further than he thought he would.

His only bit of luck revolved around the fact that this Laborer obviously missed the "eliminate on sight" mandate to collect Sree's status, or he wouldn't have called the Bria Keepers, but instead finished Sree off himself. So, at least he still lived.

For now.

Sree let out a laugh. The whole situation suddenly hit him as extremely ridiculous.

"Something funny?" the Laborer asked, his eyes narrowing.

"No. Sorry. Just...it's been a long day. A long few days. I didn't expect to end up like this."

"What's that supposed to mean?"

He snickered, attempting to control his amusement. "My friend. Bought me a ship. I didn't even know." He hiccupped another laugh. The words kept coming, though he didn't know why, but he couldn't stop them. "She's dead now. Cuz of me. I didn't ask for this. None of it. I just didn't want to kill anyone. But nobody cared. They all wanted something from me: to help them with this or find that or reveal these other things. And even if I did, so what? Not even sure it'll make a difference to help me not kill others. I just...stalled for time I guess."

The Laborer cocked his head to the side. "Are you all right? Do you need a doctor?"

Sree let out one last laugh mixed with a sigh. "No. Although, maybe. I don't know why I feel this way. I just...I don't want to kill anyone. But that's the point of me, isn't it? All of us? Except, if it's what we are designed to do..." he looked up at the Laborer, "then why are so many of us Laborers? Why do so many Re'Ris fail at our kills?"

The man stood there for several more moments, then, unsure to Sree as to why, lowered his weapon a few centimeters.

"I believed something was wrong with me," the Laborer said, "for years. Why couldn't I complete my First Assignment if this was what I was created for?"

Could it be? Could this Laborer feel the same way as Sree, just hiding it all this time? Keeping an eye on the weapon still pointed in his direction, Sree took the biggest chance of his life. "I actually think I know why. The Makers didn't create us to be killers."

"Oh, sure."

"I have proof." Breath held, Sree waited. The smell of engine oil and rust wafted on a nearby breeze, tinged with the traces of rain that may or may not come. Everything seemed so much more real, more alive in these few moments to Sree, moments that may be his last.

The Laborer lowered the electro-volt weapon the rest of the way. "I'd like to see your proof."

A shadow sild up behind the Laborer.

"No!" Sree screamed out. "Wait!"

The Laborer raised his weapon again, his eyes wide, his finger on the trigger.

"Muura, STOP!"

Muura, still hooded, halted in her tracks, mere meters away from the Laborer, a pipe in her hand, poised and ready to strike.

The Laborer turned and fired. Blue arcs of electricity sparked and hit Muura, striking her arm. She dropped the pipe and cried out, grasping her now limp appendage.

The Laborer swung his weapon wildly between the two of them. "What under the stars is going on!"

Sree, leaning onto his hands to support his tired, aching body, let out a shaky breath. "I know her. She's just trying to protect me. She didn't know you weren't going to shoot me."

"I still might," he said, but his hand holding the electro-volt weapon shook.

"Muura," he said, nodding over to her, "is on my side. She knows that things aren't right, either, that we aren't supposed to be killers." He looked over at Muura, who'd been eyeing the pipe on the ground.

"It's okay," he said to her, slumping against the engine block. It felt good to rest. She returned her gaze to him. "He wants to learn," he reassured her, indicating the Laborer.

Muura stepped away from the pipe and headed over to Sree. The Laborer still had his weapon trained on them, but Sree could see the look of curiosity on his face.

"Are you okay?" Muura asked Sree.

Sree nodded. "Been having to shift a lot. I can barely keep my eyes open, but I'm all right." He nodded at her arm. "You?"

The Laborer answered for her. "It'll wear off in a about a standard hour. I only planned to use it to subdue you before the Keepers showed up, not to do any permanent damage." He paused. "They are still on their way." He shook his head and muttered to himself. "What am I doing?"

"You can still turn me in," Sree said, trying to reassure the man. He felt the need to convince the man, not trick him. "It's your choice."

A long pause. "You *really* have proof?"

Sree nodded. "I got ahold of the original Rules, written by the Makers," he said. He noticed Muura perk up. "That's what I was trying to tell you," he said to her, "while you were leaving."

"I was so angry, I didn't want to care," she said. "But what you yelled, it...stuck in my head. I needed to know what you'd found. I hoped you'd try to come here, eventually. I came to see if the ship was still here. If it was, I'd wait for you to show up. If not, well...I had to try." She smiled. "When you landed on our lifter though, I nearly lost it!"

He grinned back. "I'm just glad you're here."

By this point, the Laborer had fully lowered the electro-volt weapon. "You bought a ship here?"

Sree nodded. "A friend of...ours...got it for me yesterday." He handed over the datapad with the ship information to the Laborer. "It's still there?" he asked Muura.

This time she nodded. "Yes. The other Laborer dropped me off at the ship and said he'd recently sold it, but he'd try and find the buyer for me to see if she'd be willing to sell it. He just left to head back to the office. But I don't really want to buy the ship, so it doesn't matter that he can't contact her," she said, referring to Biin no longer being alive.

The Laborer chewed his lower lip, staring at the datapad with the ship's identification on it. "*This* ship? That's not good."

"Why not?"

"This ship was tagged this morning. It said the buyer was killed, but we were supposed to report immediately to Central Authority in Cand if anyone came asking about it. Laborer 63-111, the one who just left you, is lying. He'll probably reach out to them as soon as he gets to the main office."

"Oh, Makers," Muura muttered under her breath. "So, what now?"

Flashing orange lights in the distance drew everyone's attention.

"That'll be the Bria Keepers who I contacted earlier," the Laborer said, his eyes wide. "I have no idea what to do."

"Can you stall them?" Sree asked. "We can then get to the ship, wait for you to come back, and take off."

"I won't be able to. There won't be time." The Laborer paused. "I-I shouldn't be helping you. You haven't shown me any kind of proof."

Sree locked eyes with him, putting every sense of trust and convincing into his words. "You know, somewhere deep down, that this isn't the way things are supposed to be. We are going to try to change that. Proof or not, you have to make a choice about it. Right now."

A gulp and then a nod. "I'll try to keep them occupied."

"Thank you," Sree said.

The Laborer got on his lifter and headed towards the main gate.

"We gotta go, now," Muura said, helping Sree to his feet. Between the kick to his ribs, the bruises and bleeding scrapes from his fall off the lifter, and his energy still not fully restored, he leaned onto Muura much more than he thought he'd need to as they ambled in the direction of the ship.

They could hear shouts from behind them and they both peered around.

A second set of light-flashing tixas, this time with yellow lights, approached the gate.

"Those are Central Authority lights," Muura said, her eyes wide.

Baffled, Sree said, "They are here, already? How? It'd take them at least a couple standard hours from when that other Laborer reached the office and called them."

"I don't know how. But that's definitely them. And...a LOT of them."

They picked up the pace, making progress as fast as they could.

"The datapad," Muura said when they were only a few meters away. "Yours, I mean. We need it."

Sree slung his bag from his shoulders and opened it, clawed through his old clothes and foodstuffs and finally pulled out the tablet. Handing it over to Muura, he accidentally dropped the bag, and when he reached down to retrieve it, he noticed something on his shoe.

A tiny, blinking, orange light.

Chapter 60

"Oh, Makers," Sree exclaimed. "They are still tracking me!"

Muura, who'd taken the datapad to call up the details about the ship, asked over her shoulder, "What?" She entered the keycode needed from Biin's information and the ship's rampway unlocked. It began to lower with a rusty squeal, but the air inside didn't smell too stale to Sree.

Panic tinted his next words. "One of the Head Superiors who'd followed me from Central Processing. He put a tracker on my shoe. After I killed him in the warehouse...I forgot to take off the tracker, but someone, maybe whoever discovered the body, must have found it! That's why they are here so soon. They tracked me!"

Muura stopped halfway up the ramp, turning to him. "Wait...wait...you killed *another* Head Superior?"

Shame slithered up his spine. "Yes, but he was trying to kill me. I didn't kill the other one, though," he said in a rush, as if to alleviate any other guilt.

Muura stared at him, wide-eyed, as Sree scrambled up the ramp. She followed him, muttering something about being in *way* over their heads.

Sree took in a cursory glance of the space. The ship itself appeared very similar to the one his sister had owned. Meant to be a small, personal transport, its max capacity held 10 individuals. But as Sree made his way to the cockpit, he noticed several internal dissimilarities to Faan's shuttle. The differences made him nervous. Could he still fly this ship?

When he reached the cockpit, however, Sree stared, at a loss. Here, any similarities between this ship and his sister's ended. "I don't...I don't know how to fly this. The image on the datapad looks like the one my sister piloted a few times, when she went off-world. She showed me the basics, so I figured I could fly this one, but this system is different. It looks...upside down. And...I don't even *know* what those levers are for. Plus, where are the fuel and proximity alert gauges?"

"What?" Muura sputtered. "You're supposed to be able to escape the planet on this thing!"

"I'm not the one who got it, *remember*? Biin got this! Maybe she planned to come with me because I am not actually a pilot!"

A growl emanated from Muura. "I can't believe this. I cannot under the stars believe this! She didn't tell me."

"Tell you what?"

A begrudging anger coated her words. "I don't think she planned to go with you. She can't pilot a ship either. I think she planned for *me* to go with you."

Sree blinked, dumbfounded. "Wait, *you* can fly this?"

"Yes."

Amazement stole through him. He could escape. After everything he'd been through, he could leave.

With a sigh of relief he said, "Well, whether you want to or not, with all those authority officers out there, do we have much of a choice right now?"

Grumbling, Muura inspected the flight area and determined the ship contained full fuel and seemed to be in working order. Strapping himself in, he nodded to her once she finished to indicate his readiness for them to depart. As she began the liftoff sequence and tried to pull away, a horrific squealing sound issued from either side of the ship.

"What...?" Sree asked, peering around.

"I can't lift off," Muura said, peering at the controls. "We're grounded. Something is holding us down."

A sense of anguish washed over him. So close. They'd gotten so close.

Staring out the front viewscreen, Sree could see that the flashing lights of the authorities, both from Bria and Cand, had reached the main gate.

"We have to run for it," he told her, releasing the safety straps while knowing the futility of the statement. And yet, what else could they do? They couldn't hide on the ship. It would be searched. And they couldn't take off.

Muura shook her head, but followed him to the ramp anyway.

Running down the slope, Sree peered ahead, noting the multiple number of flashing orange and yellow lights parked near the gate. He could see lifters on their way, each carrying four individuals. One lifter which led the pack, however, only carried a single occupant. As it drew nearer, Sree recognized the Laborer as the one who'd gone to try to stall the authorities, driving by himself, and he pulled up to the ship as they descended the ramp.

"There is a Head Superior here!" the Laborer yelled out. "Leading Central Authority!"

A weapon in the distance discharged and hit the rear end of the Laborer's lifter.

The Laborer shrieked and jumped off the sparking vehicle, sprinting towards Sree and Muura. The three of them hid behind the landing ramp, calculating their thinning odds of escape.

"Muura," Sree said, "you and the Laborer...uh, sorry, I didn't catch your number...but you two aren't implicated in anything yet. You can surrender. I'll shift and try to sneak away while they take you in."

Muura violently shook her head. "As soon as they question us, they'll know we are lying, and we'll be labeled as traitors." She looked over at the Laborer. "I'm sorry we got you mixed up in all this."

The Laborer shrugged. "It was my choice. I always felt like something was wrong with this life. I can't go back to thinking the other way now."

"I think it's best if we all shift and split up," Muura said quickly, taking over the situation. "Multiple focal points will make things more difficult for them. And it'll give each of us a better chance to escape."

Sree concentrated, ready to skin-shift again. How long he could actually hold it after his recent excursions would be a different matter. But for right now, he would make the invisibility last as long as possible.

"I am a terrible shifter!" the Laborer cried out.

Muura had already become invisible, and from the nothingness they could no longer see she said, "Do your best. I'll try to distract them." Sree watched her footprints in the dust at the bottom of the ramp move to their right before he couldn't track her anymore.

Sree shifted, feeling awful for the man who flickered and twisted in front of him, panicking as the Laborer only changed somewhat to match his surroundings. But he couldn't do anything to help.

The lifters moved in close enough that Sree could see the glimmer of the gold and black lined collar on the Head Superior's jacket. She must be the other remaining Head Superior, number One, since she hadn't been one of them he'd spoken to recently.

A throng of clanging to the right made Sree turn his head,

and he saw a stack of empty fuel cells fall over and roll around in the open space. *It must be Muura's distraction,* he thought.

Sure enough, the lifters altered their course towards the disturbance.

As soon as they swerved, Sree took off to the left, using her diversion to the best of his ability, when he heard the first scream.

Terrified, he glanced around at the overturned parts.

But the yell hadn't come from Muura's direction.

One of the lifters near the rear of the group had swerved into the side of one of the parked ships, the vehicle crashing and burning as the occupants went flying.

"Ambush!" a Keeper cried out.

Ambush? Sree wondered? *From who?*

Another lifter near the back veered off course, as if hit by a chunk of debris. It slammed into a different lifter and the two exploded on contact.

Even with these casualties, over a handful of lifters remained. Each with four members of trained authority figures.

And one Head Superior.

Head Superior One, her eyes narrowed and her mouth taught, skin-shifted, and the vehicle she rode on came to a stop. The other officers on the lifters followed suit, and each of them blinked out of existence, one by one. But technically Central Authority and Keepers were still Laborers. They weren't assassins. This was confirmed by the fact that some of them weren't very good at camouflaging themselves.

Whoever had destroyed the three lifters must have realized this, too. One by one the color-changers who couldn't quite turn fully invisible were spotted, and yelled out in pain before they reappeared, dead.

More banging from Muura's direction. A body went down near her.

Sree stayed still, watching the footprints in the dust around him more than the shimmers in the air. He couldn't decipher any real pattern. The soldiers weren't trained for this.

Two of them bumped into each other, cursing as they became visible again. They were immediately taken out by an electro-volt weapon.

Was it the Laborer on their side? Or a Keeper shooting accidentally?

Too much happened too quickly to stay on any theory for long.

A pair of footprints headed straight towards him. Before he could dodge fully out of the way, someone ran into him. Slammed backwards, his camouflage disappeared instantly, as the air inside him was forcefully expelled. With a gasp, he tried to push himself off the ground, but an officer became visible and struck him squarely in the face. Pain exploded across his jaw. He tasted blood.

Kicking out, he caught someone else's foot and they tripped, falling backwards onto a pile of scrap. They became visible and didn't get up, whether unconscious or dead, Sree had no time to wonder. He rolled out from underneath the officer and shifted again. The officer imitated him.

But Sree had the advantage. He'd learned tricks from his sister about what to focus on in a fight. Footprints. Breathing. Patches of background that couldn't be copied as well.

Keeping perfectly still, Sree could follow the man's movements.

He heard the rapid breaths, saw the footprints turning this way and that.

Sree chose his moment and swung, making contact. The officer shifted into view, but before Sree could strike again, his attacker fell over, smoke wafting from his uniform.

The Laborer who'd joined their side shimmered into view, gave Sree a nod, then turned his electric weapon towards the scattering Keepers and Central Authority members.

Between Muura picking them off to the right and whatever

helpers were taking them out from behind, it appeared that most of the Keepers had run away. Central Authority still fought, but Sree noticed the reflection of gold coming off the collar of one of the bodies.

"The Head Superior is dead!" Sree yelled out, still invisible.

Several Central Authority officers flickered into visibility at this statement, and they all turned to look at the body. They then seemed to realize half their support, in the form of the Keepers, were fleeing the scene.

"Everyone, on *both* sides," Sree shouted in a gruff voice, "stand down!"

No more yells. No more scuffles.

"You can't win," he continued to the officers, bluffing. "As you can see, we were prepared for your forces. If you unshift now, you can leave. We have no problem with you. If any of you stay hidden, we will find you and hunt you down. I am Sree Kaano, of the Kaano family. You know what we can do."

Several moments passed. Then, one of the officers glimmered into view. Others followed suit, revealing themselves to be scattered here and there. Several appeared shocked when they noted how close or far apart they were from their comrades in all the scuffle.

"We are supposed to bring you in," the first officer called out, taking command. "By order of the Head Superiors."

About 10 meters in front of the officer, between him and Sree, a different figure shifted into view. Her gold and black rimmed collar glistened in the setting sunlight.

"You have new orders."

It was Panaan.

CHAPTER 61

The relief Sree felt at seeing Panaan almost hurt with its intensity as it rushed through him. Questions about how she'd found him in a random scrapyard in Bria would have to wait till later since their current predicament kept him from asking her.

Besides, she kept talking.

Words emerged from her mouth towards the remaining officers, holding them in place, and Sree also couldn't help but listen in awe at the power emanating from them.

"Changes are happening to our government," Panaan called out, arresting the attention of everyone and sounding years older than her youthful face showed. Her stance amidst the strewn bodies of several Bria and Cand officers while smoke wafted across the area from the wreckage of the damaged lifters increased the impact of her statements. "Only two Head Superiors remain. I am one of them, Head Superior Three. The other is Head Superior Four. The rest are dead."

She nodded to the body on the ground of Head Superior

One and waited a couple of beats as the murmurs of her statement passed among the remaining officers. "I am newly assigned to their order, but found myself shocked by what I discovered. I now have proof that shows the other Head Superiors hid the truth about ourselves from us all. It states that we are *not* meant to be assassins. This proof will be made public."

At this, Sree could hear the audible gasps and stunned comments from the crowd.

Panaan waited a few moments and then continued. "As the days and weeks progress, you will have to choose: to follow what the Head Superiors have lied to you about, what they have changed in the Rules themselves, or to follow the true meaning of the Makers as originally set forth by them, a truth that will radically change our world.

"Go," she continued, "and tell others what you witnessed here today. A breaking of our government. And a change to the Rules, to our lives, a change many of us have felt in our hearts—that none of us need be mindless killers or mindless drones—but, instead, something we dared never dream could be real: we can be ourselves."

A few of them shuffled back and forth on their feet, unsure of what to do.

Panaan's voice softened. "Go," she said again. "And remember your oath: 'I pledge to uphold the Rules of Assignment as were handed down by the Makers.' Remember these words when you learn the truth about the Rules."

Most of the remaining individuals scattered to the wind, some on the remaining lifters, some jogging away. A few stood, bowing their heads briefly to Panaan, asking to hear more, but left when she assured them they'd learn more soon.

Panaan turned to face their small group and for the first time, Sree understood why she'd been chosen to be a Head Superior. Not because of her genetic Maker makeup, but because she radiated leadership.

"That was quite a speech."

She broke into a smile and suddenly Sree could see the fifteen-year-old in her once more. "I had time on my way here to practice it. Figured I might need to use my 'Head Superior' status. You okay?" she asked.

The aches and pains in his body let him know he definitely needed to recover from his wounds, but at that moment, he couldn't care about any of it. "I'm good. You?" He noticed a fresh burn mark on the side of her face and wondered what happened to her.

"I'll live."

"I can't believe you're here. How are you *here*?"

She held up a flashing orange device.

He glanced down at his shoe and laughed. "You! I thought the Keepers or Central Authority had somehow gotten it."

"No," she said, moving closer. "I stole it from the Head Superior you took out. I...I was scared to be alone." Her gaze dropped.

He smiled. "I'm glad you took it."

After looking him in the eyes again, she gestured to the junkyard. "I tracked you here, but didn't expect this kind of 'welcome.' You drew quite a crowd."

"I thought they arrived when they did because *they* were tracking me. We're just as surprised as you are that they're here. Well, we know the Bria Keepers were called, but we aren't sure how Central Authority found us."

Panaan theorized, "It must have been Head Superior Four, right?

Muura shimmered out of her camouflage and said, "I have a thought."

Startled, Panaan, struck a defensive pose.

"Sorry!" Sree said, holding a hand up to stave off any fighting. "I forgot." He briefly introduced the two to each other, giving a little background on what he knew about each of them, and then thanked the Laborer for his assistance, before asking Murra what she'd planned to say.

"I think...Head Superior Four you said?...tracked us down through the connection to Biin, and her purchase of the ship. That's why Central Authority got here so soon. I would guess he most likely sent them here before the other Laborer even reported my presence and alerted the Bria officers."

"At least now we can take off on the ship," Sree said. "Panaan's talk sent all the officers packing."

The Laborer hobbled closer, favoring his left leg. With a shake of his head, he said about his coworker, "I think there's another problem. Laborer 63-111, the one who reported you, has always been a stickler for the Rules. I doubt he'll release your ship and let you leave if he can help it. He'll know who you both are by now from the news bulletins," he continued, gesturing towards Sree and Panaan.

"Well, then, I guess we wait until the officers leave and then make him release the ship, right?" Sree continued.

Muura frowned. "This young woman's words were striking and powerful, but once they step away, I don't think her speech will be enough to hold the officers at bay over their orders."

The Laborer added, "I agree. Bria is a very small city. We're all trained not to resist Central Authority. Everyone on the planet is. If even one of those officers who walked away tells Laborer 63-111 to lock down your transport, he'll do it, gladly. Not only that, but he's not going to miss the opportunity to claim the glory of helping to catch Sree Kaano."

Everyone turned to look at Sree before Muura said, "And even if some of them side with us, they won't let us leave the planet. They'll want proof, or they'll probably switch sides again. The situation is still too unreliable."

Frustrated, Sree asked, "Is there *any* other way to shut off the grounding clamps?"

The Laborer's brow furrowed. "Short of exploding the

whole place? Not really."

Panaan shook her head. "I don't think we have any incendiary device of that magnitude, anyway," she said.

"All of this, for nothing!" Muura cried out, punching the side of the ship.

Sree rocked on his heels, anguish threatening to settle over him. They'd gotten further than he thought they would, to be honest. And at least he knew the truth. He knew what the Makers truly intended for their creations. He knew the original Rules.

Even though he may not survive the night, because he doubted that once arrested and interrogated, they would keep him alive, he at least felt closure for himself.

He'd always felt...wrong...for not wanting to be an assassin.

And now he knew he wasn't.

Everyone had gone silent, perhaps thinking their own thoughts about the situation. Sree peered around, noticing how the red sunset gently bathed their surroundings. In the past it always appeared to him like blood, mocking him on this death-filled planet, but today, it seemed more like the warmth of a soothing fire. The nearby trees swayed in the breeze. Clouds rolled in the distance, indicating the possibility of a light rain to come. The whole planet kept moving, kept breathing, kept surviving. Even the muffskuks began to creep out from their hiding places, in search of electrical wires to chew on, sniffing the bodies to identify them as they wandered around to check for threats. They thought nothing about Sree's plight, nor should they. They only cared about their own survival.

As he stared at their small faces, their rubbery paws, their diamond-shaped tails, a thought entered his mind.

"Hey, uh, what's your name?" he asked of the Laborer.

"Laborer 64-789."

"No, no, what's your *name*?"

The Laborer paused for several moments. Sree wondered if he'd ever said his conceived name since he'd become a Laborer."

"Poora Teem," he replied, his voice low.

"So, Poora," Sree went on. "What happens when the electrical gate shuts down? You know, you said you stop the muffskuks from chewing the wires. But what happens if they actually do that and cause damage?"

"We close down the place until we can replace the wires. Everyone gets rescheduled and we hire a guard crew to keep watch overnight."

"Because thieves could hop the fence?"

"Yeah."

"Could they steal a ship?"

"Well, no, because they don't have the ID number. So even though the ships aren't grounded anymore, they'd still...need...oh, I see what you're saying."

"Exactly." Sree pointed to the ship. "We *have* the ID. We just need to get past the grounding circuit."

Poora rubbed his chin. "We'd have to take out the breakers on both sides of the yard, the east and west ends. It'll cut the circuit. That should work. But, hm, as soon as I cut one, Laborer 63-111 will get notified in the office. He can turn on the backup generator and that'll keep that circuit going temporarily, for a couple of standard hours. Not enough to keep things clear for the whole night, but enough time for reinforcements to arrive. And once one side is down, he can send someone to the other side to protect it faster than I'll be able to get there to finish cutting the other breaker."

"That just means you won't be able to do it on your own. Someone else will have to cut the other side at the same time," Muura said. She straightened. "I'll do it."

"Not a chance," Sree said, not willing to leave anyone behind. After everything he'd been through, each of them deserved a chance. "This plan won't work. The two of you will be stranded here. We won't have time to wait for you, either of you, to get back from the breakers before we take off in the ship."

"You got another idea?" Muura asked.

Searching his mind, he admitted, "Not really, but it doesn't matter. We'll run. We'll figure something out and try another day. If they catch either of you, they won't let Poora live. And Muura, they'll keep you for questioning until you reveal the whereabouts of the rest of the Crypt. You two can't get caught, so let's all run together, protect each other." He could tell by their facial expressions that the absurdity of the plan didn't fool any of them. They'd never survive more than a few weeks, months at most. But he couldn't think of any other plan.

A clearing of a throat. "I'll cut the circuit with Poora," Panaan offered. "And I'll make sure he stays safe."

Sree grunted in dissatisfaction. "That doesn't change the fact that they'll arrest the both of you, if they don't kill you on sight. They won't keep you alive if you get arrested."

Panaan took a deep breath. "Sree, I've been thinking about it. I can't go into hiding or leave the planet. I have to stay. Head Superior Four and I are the only Head Superiors left. He will regain control if there is no one at the same level as him in opposition. When we start revealing the truth about the Rules, the citizens of this world will have to pick a side. They won't follow a Laborer who works in a shipyard," she said, nodding towards Poora. "They won't follow a shop owner who secretly rebels against the government," she said, gesturing to Muura. "And we need you to be an icon, Sree, representing your family. You have to continue on as a symbol and you can't do that if you're arrested. Right now the world sees you as a murderer. But you can show them you're fighting for them by bringing them more proof."

"But you were on that video surveillance, too. Why would they trust you?"

"Because of today. Even though I'm sure all those officers knew what I'd done, no one arrested me. There is still some faith left in Head Superiors. They will have to choose who to follow, me or Four. And with you on my side, safe and away from all this, a movement has less chance of dying with *both* a leader and a representation of hope."

Sree prickled with discomfort at her plan. Once again, he felt useless. Like a coward A stupid figurehead while everyone else sacrificed themselves. Just like Wiin. "I can stay. I can help fight!"

She let out a shaky breath. "You saw what was in that Archive Room. If Head Superior Four hasn't destroyed it yet, he'll do it soon enough. In case he does before I can access the room again, someone needs to find more evidence of the Makers and their wishes. We have the original Rules, but there *must* be more documents or proof. Your sister tracked down evidence of the Aleet Army's involvement with your Mother's and Father's deaths. I *know* there must be more out there about the history of our planet. As part of the Makers, it's in my blood to stay here. As a Kaano, it's in your blood to find what we need."

Sree scoffed. "When under the stars did you get so smart?"

Panaan laughed. "I must have gotten hit in the head too many times." Her face grew serious. "You know I'm right about this."

Sree felt Muura put a hand on his shoulder, giving it a squeeze to let him know she would help him as well.

He glanced behind him at the ship, at the absolute unknown that lay before him. He turned to face the small group in front of him. "We are going to start a civil war," he said softly.

Panaan shrugged. "Sree, it's already started." She gave a weak smile and once again, it struck Sree how young she looked. He probably looked just as young.

They were fools.

Fools or not, everything had changed.

A slight drizzle caused a haze of gray to shimmer across the junkyard. Far off in the distance, Sree saw the lights from Central Authority shining. The officers still hadn't left, and they wouldn't. Soon enough, they'd regain their courage and come back, most likely under orders from Head Superior Four.

Accepting the decision, he promised, "I'll find what we need."

"I know you will," Panaan replied.

He nodded to Panaan's hand, which held the tracking device. "One day, when Muura and I come back, you'll see that flash orange again."

Panaan squeezed the device tightly, a catch in her words. "I better."

Sree took one last look at each one of them directly. The isolation he'd felt his whole life had been a waste. He could've spoken to his family. He could have found like minds in society. But fear kept him from doing so.

And here they all were, just as frightened, just as unsure.

Together.

With one last exhale he spoke his family's motto.

"You are family, we are one," he told them.

He no longer felt alone.

Chapter 62

As Muura pulled the ship through the atmosphere and entered the vacuum of space, Sree couldn't help having the biggest doubt of all enter his mind. His species had based their whole culture on faith in the Rules of Assignment. On the Makers. On assassinations. On the idea of personal worth to society. Did he have the right to throw doubt and suspicion where balance currently existed? Just because their system functioned differently than on other worlds, if it worked, did it matter if parts of it were based on a lie?

Sree recalled the last time he'd seen his sister, Faan. He'd judged her so quickly, thinking that he knew everything about her at the time. He believed she embodied the perfect Re'Ris—the perfect assassin.

But she told him she'd wished things were different. That Re'Ris weren't "meant" to be assassins.

Sree pictured her face and spoke out into the vastness of space. "You weren't meant to be one. You were just really good at it."

"Did you say something?" Muura asked.

"Just thinking out loud," he replied. "Is everything ready?"

"I only need to flip the switch."

Sree nodded at her and she turned on the broadcasting switch, set up by Panaan using her Maker genetic code, to emit an emergency broadcast. It would reach most individuals' personal communication devices on the planet, and those who didn't receive the message directly would likely learn its contents soon enough through news bulletins.

Speaking clearly and with all the hope he could put into his voice, Sree sent out their message to his home planet. Once completed, he and Muura continued with their search for more proof, starting on the world where his sister had found hers about their Mother and Father.

Epilogue

Original Rule #1:
The Re'Ris were created by the Makers to eliminate the illness.

"Hello, dear," Vuun's friend, Raali, spoke through her personal communications device to one of her other friends. It had been a strange week. She knew she shouldn't miss Vuun after she'd Passed On, but she did. They used to speak every day and the void left behind pulled at her. She'd told no one, of course, but the grief made her shy away from many of her normal social activities. As a retired assassin, she didn't draw much attention from city officials, but her inner circle noticed. She knew she should reach out to them again.

"Yes," Raali continued to her friend, "it has been a while since we chatted...No, nothing is wrong, per say, I've just been busy." She paused. "Yes, I heard about Vuun's Daughter's Son, Sree, being wanted for murder. It's...unbelievable, to say the least. I knew them well, that family, and he never struck me as the kind of boy who'd—" Raali waited while her friend interrupted with a question. "Of course I don't know where he went. You think I'd harbor a fugitive?...hold a moment, dear. I just received an audiolink message on my datapad...what's that? You just got one, too? Yes, yes, I'll call you right after—

Her communication got interrupted as a broadcast from the emergency channel came through on her personal communications device. Hoping it wasn't some sort of natural disaster to be receiving multiple messages at the same time, she put down her personal device on the table next to the datapad as they both began to broadcast simultaneously.

Overwhelmed by too much stimulus at once, she asked out loud to no one as she attempted to silence the datapad, "How do I...?" Instead, she simply turned it up, the message stating its high priority status as coming from Central Authority. The two voices, one from the emergency broadcast on her personal device and one from Central Authority on her datapad, clashed against each other as they played at the same time. It took her a moment to adjust, but then Raali's eyes opened wide with disbelief at both announcements.

"Attention fellow Re'Ris citizens..."

"Attention all subjects of the Makers...!"

"You may not know me, but you know my family. I am Sree Kaano, Brother to Faan Kaano, Son to Yoon and Luuv Kaano..."

"This is Head Superior Four using official channels of Central Authority through Central Processing to warn you..."

"I have uncovered evidence that every Re'Ris on the planet should know..."

"There is a traitor in our midst...!"

"It will not be easy for you to hear, since it contradicts centuries of our way of life..."

"He will attempt to fill your head with lies...!"

"But a wise man once told me that the knowledge of the

truth, no matter the consequences, is necessary to live in reality instead of illusion..."

"He has worked with known conspirators...!"

"I have uncovered the Makers' original document, the Rules of Assignment..."

"He has falsified documents to overthrow the government...!"

"The Rules were mistranslated, purposefully, to control us..."

"Do not listen to him. He may try to contact you through your vidlinks or datapads on emergency channels. This is NOT the work of the Head Superiors or Central Authority...!"

"But their true meaning is clear. Every citizen on our planet will receive a copy of these Rules and a way to translate them. Some of you may not *need* a translation. If you can read the words, you are special. You have Maker genetic code in your bodies..."

"Anyone in possession of any propaganda by this individual will be stripped of their title and honors as an assassin or a Laborer and arrested...!"

"The Makers did not create the Re'Ris for death. They created us for LIFE..."

Raali didn't know why, but she turned off the audiolink on her datapad from Head Superior Four as he demanded every citizen's complete cooperation with the government and to terminate any messages received by the traitor. Instead, she picked up her personal communications device and listened as Sree continued on.

"When the Makers created the Re'Ris, they did so to protect themselves. Knowing they would ultimately die off, they created a set of guidelines for the young Re'Ris to follow. These were the Rules of Assignment—written to remind the Re'Ris of where we came from and how to live our lives in harmony.

"Over time, Head Superiors warped and distorted the Rules. Without access to these original files from and about the Makers, the Re'Ris public became ignorant of the truth.

"I offer you all a chance to think for yourselves. You live in a world where death is as natural as breathing. But what if you've been misguided? What if you can grieve for those who have Passed On? What if you don't have to end a life because it's not "useful" anymore, but instead find a use for it?

"I'm not asking you to make any decisions right now. I'm giving you the opportunity to make your own choice about what you learn. Head Superior Three, Panaan Luura, will continue to lead this new path. She knows the truth, has seen the original Rules with her own eyes, and wants to follow the Makers' original will. You will be given a choice, between following her or continuing on under Head Superior Four.

"The Makers spent their dying breaths creating, raising, and providing for us. I, as the last remaining member of the Kaano family, plan to adopt the ideals of that culture by following the Rules they originally made for us, Rules which *embraced* life. I hope you do, too.

"May your life be guided by the Makers."

"And may you do their will," Raali said, automatically replying to the call-and-response phrase.

The audio portion of the message ceased, and a data stream of information poured into Raali's personal device. It contained the original set of Rules with a translation.

Unable to read the Makers language, Raali read through the translation several times. She then turned off her communications device and set it down on the table next to her datapad, which still remained off, unsure what to think about what she'd just learned. Extremely set in her ways, she had a difficult time believing she'd killed other members of her species for the wrong reasons.

But one thing she did know. Whatever happened next, Vuun's family always created change.

And nothing on Re'Ris would ever be the same.

Want to keep following Sree?
Look for: THE BINDERS

Continue on in the trilogy with Book 2, THE BINDERS, slated to be released 2026/2027, which continues the storyline of Sree as he navigates worlds that are not his own in search of more proof.

ABOUT THE AUTHOR

Christa Yelich-Koth is an award-winning author (2016 Novel of Excellence for Science Fiction for ILLUSION from Author's Circle Awards) of the Amazon Bestselling novels, ILLUSION and IDENTITY. Others in the *Eomix Galaxy Novel* collection include COILED VENGEANCE and THE MAKERS.

Christa has also moved into the world of detective fiction with her international bestselling novel, SPIDER'S TRUTH, the first in the *Detective Trann series.*

Looking for something else Young Adult? Try the YA fantasy *Land of Iyah* trilogy, starting with book 1: THE JADE CASTLE.

Aside from her novels, Christa has also authored a graphic novel, HOLLOW, and 6-issue follow-up comic book series HOLLOW'S PRISM from Green-Eyed Unicorn Comics. (with illustrator Conrad Teves.)

Originally from Milwaukee, WI, Christa was exposed to many different things through her education, including an elementary Spanish immersion program, a vocal/opera program in high school, and her eventual B.S. in Biology. Her love of entomology and marine biology helped while writing her science fiction/ fantasy aliens/creatures.

As for why she writes, Christa had this to say: "I write because I have a story that needs to come out. I write because I can't NOT write. I write because I love creating something that pulls me out of my own world and lets me for a little while get lost inside someone or someplace else. And I write because I HAVE to know how the story ends."

You can find more about Christa and her other books at: www.CYKauthor.com

www.ingramcontent.com/pod-product-compliance
Lightning Source LLC
Chambersburg PA
CBHW030340310726
48979CB00001B/125

* 9 7 8 1 9 5 8 1 0 5 1 5 3 *